The Bamboo Shepherd

Kevin Corbett

Peter E. Randall Publisher
Portsmouth New Hampshire
2004

Designed by Peter E. Randall

Peter E. Randall Publisher
Box 4726, Portsmouth, NH 03802
www.perpublisher.com

ISBN: 1-931807-22-1
Library of Congress Control Number: 2004091523

Additional copies available from:

Patricia Corbett
169 Portsmouth Street, Apt. 153
Concord, NH 03301

What is one finger when one gives his life? What is one hand when one sheds his life? What is one arm when one gives his life? What are a thousand thorns when one gives his life? What is a tear but a sign of love? If I must, I will shed my flesh and cover it with my grief. I tell you this, I will shed no tear because of the pain of it, but my heart will ever cry for the Bamboo Shepherd.

—Clastres Bulatao

To my wife Patricia.

To the memory of Father Hugh O'Reilly, a Columban Father, another Bamboo Shepherd who was protected by a band of Filipino guerrillas and brought out of hiding on March 17, 1945 by the U.S. Army 43rd Cavalry Reconnaissance Troop Mechanized.

To my brother Donal and his wife Doris who do all the little things for us.

To the Holy Spirit for guiding my pen across these pages.

ACKNOWLEDGMENTS

I am indepted to the Columban Fathers in St. Columbans, Nebraska, the Philippines, and Australia for taking the time to procure photographs of and information about Father Douglas. Their assistance was a tremendous help in completing this novel.

Thanks to Major C. Douglas Jewell, Training Specialist, New Hampshire Army National Guard, for his expertise in military weaponry.

Thanks to Ned Moore for his assistance in getting the guerrillas across the river.

And to my daughter, Joyce, for her enduring patience and sacrifices made in the editing and preparation of this manuscript.

PREFACE

This is not a love story; it is a story of love. And the process of writing it was a labor of love, a love I will always have for a man I never met. If you were to ask me why I wrote this novel, I would respond that it was to let the world know about a man who laid down his life for his friends and, perhaps by so doing, might have saved one more soul on the road to Laguna de Bay—a road that begins when you take your first step toward a church in Pililia where the shadow of martyrdom flickers amidst the sounds of the swaying bamboo—sounds calling Father Francis Vernon Douglas to sainthood.

There is one more reason: maybe somewhere in Japan there is an old dog soldier who remembers the burial site of Father Douglas, a Columban Father from New Zealand.

NOTES TO THE READER

Although this is a novel, there are certain aspects based on fact. Father Francis Vernon Douglas was a Columban Father from New Zealand assigned to St. Mary Magdalene's in Pililia, on Luzon, Philippines, from 1938 to July 27, 1943. The torture and disappearance of Father Douglas did occur at the hands of the Japanese during World War II; however, I have depicted the torture of this martyr of the church as I imagined it, basing it on information from the Columban Fathers in St. Columbans, Nebraska, and from Father Hugh O'Reilly, who was also a Columban Father

Father O'Reilly, a red-headed priest from Ireland, had been the pastor of St. Jerome's in Morong for ten years, four of which were during Japanese occupation. Father O'Reilly was hiding in the hills beyond Morong under the protection of a band of Filipino guerrillas when the U.S. Army 43rd Cavalry Reconnaissance Troop brought him back to its bivouac on St. Patrick's Day, March 17, 1945. It was a day of great joy for Father O'Reilly, and with this unbounded joy he sang to the angels.

The drama that unfolded in Morong when Father O'Reilly was saying Mass was told to me by Father O'Reilly himself in March 1945.

During the campaign in the Solomon Islands (July 17, 1943) on the island of New Georgia, approximately three hundred Japanese soldiers attacked rear elements of the 43rd Infantry Division on what is known as the Munda Trail. Artillery and scattered ground units eventually defeated this force, but only after the Japanese had butchered to death wounded personnel lying in a field hospital near a crude bridge, thereafter known as "Butcher's Bridge." To this day every man of the 43rd Infantry

Division, now known as the "Winged Victory Division," carries the memory of the Munda Trail.

Mount Morling was captured by the 169th Infantry of the 43rd Division in 1945. The 43rd Cavalry Reconnaissance Troop did take two Japanese prisoners on Mount Morling, but there was no surrender by a Japanese colonel.

The towns around the shores of Laguna de Bay are properly named, but the distances between them are not precise, nor their locations. The locations of the churches and the course of the Laniti River are not exact. Mapalug Mountain is more to the northeast of Pililia (also spelled Pililla and Pillila), and I have placed it closer to Baras than in reality; its height and description are imaginative. The Kalinawan Caves are not in Mapalug Mountain but located more to the northeast of Tanay. I have described these caves more extensively than what they really are.

The homilies of Father Douglas are purely fictional.

With the exception of Father Douglas and Father O'Reilly, all other characters are fictional.

When I opened my eyes I was sitting up in bed. Rain was falling, not heavily but gently, splattering the windowpane when the October wind blew beneath the eaves. Now and then an oak leaf whirled against the glass, and the branches of the oak trees danced a few feet beyond the wall of the building. "A tree can sprout many twigs in a year," I thought, remembering how many times I had neglected trimming them in the past.

I sat wondering what form of intrusion it was this time. I had been getting little sleep of late; many a night I had rolled over wide awake and remained that way for an hour or two. I was getting accustomed to the unwanted habit. However, this was the first time I had awakened to find myself sitting up, both hands propped rigidly against the mattress.

Neither the dripping rain nor the breeze had awakened me. The clock on the night table had not rung an alert, nor would it ever again. I had silenced it with the arrival of retirement, which had been ushered in by a heart attack. The ticking clock drew my attention; it was 2:35 in the morning. A few minutes had elapsed since I had found myself in a sitting position. I was staring at the window. What had deprived me once again of precious rest? There were no apparent sounds to interrupt my sleep, especially for a light sleeper like me.

A dream—could that have been it? Dreams fade quickly and within seconds are past recall but not completely voided. Sometimes what had been encountered in a dream years before is brought to life by circumstances, names, places, interludes in everyday life. A simple thought or a sound almost completely forgotten can arouse the memory of a dream, or at least a fragment of it. For one controlled second my mind reached out to grasp an image. It was black, a shadow of a mountain, the wings of a raven, the depths of night when jungle lizards romp. My mind reached desperately to recapture the entire dream, but I could not retain it, and the memory of it faded.

I seldom try recalling dreams. It is like trying to catch up with a train or jumping a brook and never reaching the other side. They are filled with frustration and anxiety, pleasure and pain, surety and cowardice—all of it, but nothing definite, just pieces that cannot be gathered wholly. I, who once could run like a deer at the instant of a sound, was now cornered by an unfinished dream.

I was alone. My wife had died a year ago, and we never had children. I became a winter hermit in my apartment, handicapped by the snow and choked by the lack of fresh air. Hermits at one time lived in the hills, deserts and valleys and slept in caves. Now we live in houses, apartments and condominiums, barely aware of what exists on the other side of the window shade. Our feet have not touched the soil in years because it is buried beneath the concrete sidewalks and paved streets. Each little world we travel has a key of its own, and one twist locks us in with only our idiosyncrasies for company.

I try not to look beyond any one season, with the exception of winter: being the longest season in New England, winter has a way of becoming burdensome. Nothing hastens winter, not even the sudden appearance of a warm day in February, not even the anticipation of the last hurdle in mid-March.

I now faced the old routine of sitting in the rocking chair, waiting the dawn. There had not been a moon all night, not even a glimmer of it. Now and then the unfinished dream crossed my mind, but I came up with nothing. I thought about my heart attack and how there was no way for me to estimate the results of any undertaking: long or short, laborious or easy. The last time I trekked through the woods on my land in Maine, where silence is broken only by the sound of the brook and night call of the whippoorwill, I felt the strain on my calf muscles and the heaving of my chest. A few years ago I would have ignored these discomforts, but now they were signs. I had finally become beset by limitations. No one had to tell me I was clinging to a branch like an oak leaf, which desperately struggles to maintain contact with its lifeline and fights the wind that tries to tear it away.

Nevertheless, spring, with new buds waiting to push forward, is always an awakening—an ageless recurrence. I can appreciate how the scent of green grass must pound at the senses of the old dobbin as he fills his nostrils. Somewhere in the hills, streams are coming to life with the melting snows. The sun begins its climb through the sky. Windows are opened to let in the newness amidst the final throes of winter. The never-failing winds of March blow away the fumes of the city, and the lilacs of April foretell the return of the migrating geese.

I, too, reached out and began squirming in anticipation of it. As the leaves freed themselves from the frost-bound earth, a sense of freedom surged through me and a growing eagerness rose within.

By May I began to focus on the coming summer in Maine. In preparation for walks on my land I walked the city concrete a little more each day. When June finally arrived I did not hesitate; I turned the car northward, toward the cottage I had built long before the heart attack.

After settling in the cottage I resumed my walking. At first I was exhausted from the uphill and downhill expeditions. My legs stiffened through the night, but with more and more expeditions into the woods I grew less tired. I filled my lungs with clean, fresh air and satisfied my thirst with clear, cool water from the brook. Before long walking became an invigorating pastime.

It was a quiet place, and the still of it belonged to me. The rays of sun streaming through the pines put new zest in my life. I wanted never to retreat from these moments of isolation. The freedom and smell of the woods would be hard to leave. But the summers of Maine are short. Yet it would not be the increasing coolness of the evenings and mornings that would turn me away. There was a moment, waiting to be born, filled with a force that would pull me away from everything I loved and turn me on a course I had once vowed never to repeat.

But not quite yet.

The little town of Limerick was located six miles down the road from my land. There, reaching into the sky and visible for miles from the surroundings hills, rose the steeple of St. Patrick's Church. During the summer months the small, wood-framed church was always filled to capacity. Yet even in these confines no one had to ask others to move in to make room; they always went directly to the center of the pew—there was an understanding about these things here. Seldom was there excessive talking inside the church—these parishioners knew where they were. Although an outsider, I never felt like a stranger at St. Patrick's. Here, in the middle of the hills, I found peace.

The Sunday before Labor Day I headed for St. Patrick's as usual. It was a crisp morning and the sun was bright. I shivered at the thought of the winters hereabouts. The church was on the left halfway up a long hill. Just opposite the entrance to the church parking lot was a gas station, which was closed on Sundays; however, the pickup truck in front of me suddenly turned right into the station. I slowed down as it turned, then flicked on my left signal as I waited for a car coming down the hill. Meanwhile, the pickup truck continued around the pumps, back into the street, and rammed my back bumper, pushing me across the road and into the car coming down the hill. The impact caused me to lurch forward. My head met solidly with the dashboard and I blacked out.

When I opened my eyes, the sun, glaring from behind the wooden cross atop the church, almost blinded me. Someone must have moved me as I was lying on the church lawn; green grass was my pillow. There was a foggy, dark image of a man between the sun and me. A memory flashed—rekindling a flame that would bring life back to some of the old shadows—then it was gone. As the form moved the sun blinded me again, and I was forced to turn my gaze elsewhere. Suddenly I felt my head being raised and someone maneuvering a blanket under my neck. As my vision became clearer, I saw many of the parishioners standing around me, concern etched on their faces. Only seconds had elapsed since I opened my eyes into the fiery orb, but now I was fully alert. Hovering over me was a man clothed in black—the black cassock of a priest. Standing between me, the mounted cross and the sun, he seemed an eclipselike apparition.

"Are you all right?" someone asked.

I turned my head toward the voice—and the glaring sun. "I think so," I replied, as I tried to sit up.

"I think you should remain where you are for a little while longer," the priest cautioned me.

Then he knelt down beside me and said, "I am Father Douglas." The memory flashed again, but even more dimly than before. His hand rested on my aching forehead. "He is giving me last rites!" I thought.

A uniformed man moved through the crowd, approached the priest, and then reached for a pad of paper. Routine questions, which were easily answered from a world of information contained in a single wallet, followed.

"Would you like a ride home?" asked one of the onlookers.

"I would like to attend Mass first," I replied, which elicited some surprise from the crowd.

I sat up. Immediately some of the onlookers began to move to my side, but I assured them I was now capable of standing, although they stayed next to me as I stood up. Now assured I was all right, we went into the church together.

I sat in the last row so I could be near the exit. Someone left the doors open to let in the breeze. It was a standing-room-only Sunday. I focused my attention on Father Douglas standing at the altar. I had an odd feeling that something was eluding me and it had to do with this priest, although I had never seen him before. Sometimes these small parishes borrowed priests from other dioceses to help during the summer; I assumed he was one. Above Father Douglas hung the crucifix, suspended on wires. The eyes of Jesus seemed to be searching my every move, and only by leaving the church would I escape the haunting eyes. I shrugged off the feeling because it was distracting me from the Mass. Father Douglas was a large man, which accounted for the eclipselike apparition I saw when I looked up at him from my prone position on the ground. He gave the final blessing and left the altar. I never saw him again.

The incident at the church haunted me. Uneasiness followed me on my walks to the brook. The peacefulness of the place slid into the background. "What is it about this man of God that has such a grip on me?" I wondered over and over again. If the towering pines, oaks and maples still sang to me as I sat on the rocks, I did not hear them. The brook gurgled just a few feet away, but it, too, became mute to my ears.

That evening as I sat in the rocking chair on the porch, I began to hear the call of the subconscious, that loud voice prodding my mind into action. The voice was demanding a search into the past, and I could not ignore it. It became a pressure without relief, and the annoyance brought concern, so much so that sleep became only a restless repose.

Occasionally we must evaluate what is at hand; occasionally we must retreat in order to progress. Hence I retreated to the spot where I had been stretched out on the ground, where the cycle began—beneath the cross atop St. Patrick's. I sat on the church lawn, feeling the pull toward the heavens and waiting for some kind of signal to erupt out of the subconscious. I hoped for a candle to free me from the darkness.

I watched the sun inch its way up behind the cross until flashing streaks shot out from all sides of its silhouette. Then it passed, leaving me still perplexed. In the emptiness of the moment I closed my eyes, then slowly opened them as I had done when I heard the voice on Sunday morning. In that brief second I suddenly recalled the black object, Father Douglas, hovering above, breaking the beams of the sun and causing them to dance before my eyes. I immediately recalled the fleeting second I had captured in my dream. It was mine again. Fully alert now I hung on to it until I could recall it completely. The black object that had towered above me a few days ago reminded me of the black cassock belonging to another Father Douglas, a priest I had never met but stories of whom I remembered well. Finally, I had recaptured the dream.

But the vision of this black cassock would torment me even more than losing the glimpse I had had of it. Now I would have to reenter my cave of old memories.

In 1945 the United States 43rd Division fought its way along the shores of Laguna de Bay on the island of Luzon in the Philippines. There, southeast of Manila, we drove the Japanese before us. Infantry, artillery and air force as well as Filipino guerrillas combined to rout the enemy in the entire bay area.

Simultaneously in the hills, towns, barrios and villages, existing under the yoke of the Japanese rule, another breed of weary men walked with death. They never knew the hour or day when the yoke would bring their final breath. Their dreams of truth, love and understanding were crushed even before the Bataan Death March had begun. They had visions, though sometimes discouraging, of conquering bigotry, misunderstanding, bitterness and, above all, the evil in the hand holding the sword. Long before any soldier, friend or foe, had passed that way, these men had donned black and white cassocks and crossed the seas as heralds of the Word. They were the Columban Fathers, and they had their own heroes within their ranks.

As the 43rd plunged forward, six of these wearers of black and white—each armed only with a crucifix—defended themselves passively with nothing but the truth and gave their lives for their cause. These unheralded followers of Christ, advocates of the gospels and martyrs of the church died gloriously in the churches and villages. One of the six vanished, his body never found.

He was Father Francis Vernon Douglas.

With little to go on except a few scattered stories, perhaps some of them hearsay, I let what memory I had of the disappearance of Father Douglas tumble around in my head. Luzon and all that had transpired in the Philippines had all been shuffled into the back corners of my mind a long time ago. For the most part I had let it remain there. However, I could not dispel the significance of why a priest here in Limerick, Maine, with the same name, had suddenly appeared in my life out of nowhere and disappeared just as quickly, leaving me with an old memory, or at least parts of it. In the intermittent years since 1945 I had occasionally remembered a story that Father O'Reilly, another Columban Father whose parish was in Morong, had told me about Father Douglas when my outfit was bivouacked there.

That evening, while rocking on the porch, black and white cassocks began to dance before me in the moonlight. I went inside to escape the images and decided to draft a letter to the Columban Fathers in St. Columbans, Nebraska, requesting any information concerning the death of Father Douglas in Laguna de Bay in the Philippines. I had never given serious thought to the details concerning Father Douglas. He had been killed in 1943 when I was on Guadalcanal recovering from malaria. The few times when I had recalled the story, I did not dwell on it. I assumed the Church had taken care of the matter long ago. Now what once seemed of little concern began to disturb me more than that old lost dream or the incident at the church. There seemed to be a definite timing to it all. "But why should the memory of a priest I have never met before fill so many of my thoughts?" I dwelled.

Father O'Reilly, however, I remembered well. During World War II, my outfit, the 43rd Cavalry Reconnaissance Troop (mechanized), or *Recon* as we were known, had brought him out of hiding in the hills beyond Morong, giving him his first good meal in many days. We remained close to his church during that assignment, some of us attending Mass there whenever possible. The only other thing of note about Father Douglas also came from Father O'Reilly; it had something to do with the difference in their passports. Father O'Reilly had remained alive because of this difference.

I left the gurgle of the brook and returned to the city. Upon my return at the end of September I received a letter from the Columban Fathers in Nebraska. Their response fueled the fire of my determination to set sail across the Pacific for the second time in my life. At fifty-five years old and forever a member of the 43rd Cavalry Reconnaissance Troop (mechanized), I was going to make a second beachhead on the island of Luzon in the Philippines.

I would have to face the sea again. The very word made me shudder. I remembered the toss of it; I remembered the way the old troop ship *Grant* had turned its bow into the fury born in a storm in 1942; I remembered how it went under, and then came back up only by a miracle. Men were praying to die; that is how seasick they were. I remembered my own vow to never go back, never look at the white and bloodied beaches, never fear the silent and erupting nights, never hear the bamboo snap a man's mind back to reality. I had shoved it all behind me. Now there was a call, something reaching out and turning around my whole being. Like the moon pulling at the tides, I felt the tug, the hand on my shoulder, pulling me to the sea.

Enough sinew was left in me to climb a mountain. Every ounce of energy was at attention, ready. The love of a man on a crucifix had trimmed the sails, and the shadow of a cassock was beckoning me to reconnoiter the last trail of my life. I was prepared for one final assault on the past. I knew full well that it might be my last.

Within a week I sold my car, put my furniture in storage, gave notice to the apartment supervisor, notified the post office and left the city. I took a train across the country—the first 3,500 miles of my journey. In 1942 I had taken the same journey, only then I was laden with a full field pack, barracks bags and C rations and crammed together with hundreds of other soldiers on a troop train with shades drawn. This time, though, I slept soundly to the hum of the rails.

When I arrived in San Francisco I hailed a cab and gave the driver the name of my hotel. California was considerably warmer than my last habitat. The next morning I walked across town to a travel agency, where a ruddy-faced clerk stamped my ticket for passage aboard the *Matsonia*. The cruise ship would leave in two days for Manila via the Fiji Islands and Guam. I spent the time preparing myself mentally for the voyage. When the evening arrived I went down to the shore and tried to visualize just what it was that was beckoning me beyond the horizon.

Aboard the liner I heard the piercing whistle cut through the morning fog. Then the dock and all of San Francisco disappeared from sight. Once again I was in the grip of the sea, feeling like a piece of driftwood riding the crest of every wave, wondering if this expedition would find a fruitful destination. Below me on the lower deck the music heralding good fortune bounced over the rising and falling sea. The other passengers danced. Far into the night they whirled, toasting one another, while the ship cut the waves in two and the sea washed the champagned decks with a showery spray of salt.

Even with hundreds of people standing, sitting or lying on the decks, I continued to walk alone, living in the solitude I had chosen and keeping my cherished thoughts within, set apart from the clamor and din of the merrymakers. It was a vigil of sorts, for the thousands of soldiers who had perished in World War II. No one here would understand the waiting, desperation or thoughts of these men who had crossed the vastness of this sea. However, I knew the torment, the fear, the hidden tears lingering in the salt of the night. I knew the length and breadth of each man's shadow as he rode the waves toward the uncertainty of the horizon that stretched away from a man until he wearied of reaching.

When the liner docked in the Fiji Islands and Guam, I never left her decks. Remaining on board gave me time to think of both the positive and negative aspects of what might confront me in the Philippines. I also read a book I had brought with me on the culture and customs of the Filipinos. Anything I learned now might save unnecessary travel and wasted efforts later on. I also knew I would be faced by the silent Filipino tongue—unless a lot had changed since World War II. The silence would be a tremendous handicap to overcome.

Although conditions on board were not always ideal, between studies I managed to exercise and continued to walk the deck at every opportunity. Now and then the sea managed to gnaw at my stomach slightly, but I immediately retaliated by maneuvering around the decks. I intended to have my legs in shape. And despite the curious stares and gestures that came from the deck squatters, I also jogged around the liner from one end to the other: up and down the hatchways and the circling stairway to the lower deck, through the galley past gawking chefs and to the forward most deck permitted to the passengers, all in preparation for maintaining agility in the coming days southeast of Manila.

As we entered Manila Bay I momentarily reflected on the bottom of the harbor: the iron bottom, where so many remnants of warships, both Allied and Japanese, were rusting away, slowly oxidizing into oblivion. I shrugged off what had been and turned my attention to the future. My quest would commence far beyond the outskirts of Manila, somewhere in the towns, barrios and the stilt-raised bamboo huts and among the rural Filipinos and their snail-paced carabaos, which waded in the rice paddies and muddy rivers.

The ship's hostess had recommended the hotel Manila Royal to be of good repute for a few days. The hotel was only a few miles from the old walled city, the ancient Manila. After getting settled I immediately took the bus there and readily saw the old city was not as I had last observed it. During the liberation of Manila from the Japanese the ancient Manila had just about been leveled, scarred buildings everywhere. In the years since those devastating barrages most of the scars had been long since removed, and the old place was now mostly gleaming white.

Although there was a new look to the place a keen eye could discover the marks of the past. During the war the begging *batas* scurried through the streets and alleys, their small hands reaching toward us as we rode our vehicles southeast toward Laguna de Bay. The batas, ragged and starving, haunted us night and day for food and cigarettes. I wondered how much of this still existed. Liberation had brought change to the Filipinos, but the change seemed to be only in the faces of the new regime.

In some regard Manila had not changed. There were the same old alleys, still harboring the lonely, hungry and forgotten. Sure, there were new buildings, tall ones, white ones, but beyond them were the black shadows of discontent and poverty. All of the neglect that existed before the war in the Pacific was still there. I did not have to meander through the dirty streets just outside Manila, but I did, remembering how in 1945 we would throw oranges from the back of the six-by-six truck to the derelict batas running after the vehicle with all the strength they could muster from their scrawny legs. They were still chasing oranges, only there was not anyone throwing them into their outstretched hands.

Cars, buses and bicycles maneuvered rampantly through the old domain of Spanish origin, which was still evident in the old Spanish churches. Their influence was stone beacons, stalwart structures, bearers of an ancient heritage reaching into the skies. Their great stonewalls and towers were like sentinels guarding the memories of the past. Staring up at the stone crosses protruding from the arches brought me back to the intent of my sojourn to Luzon.

Luckily, many people in Manila spoke English; thus my search for the office of the Columban Fathers was accomplished without too much difficulty. One of the passing throng directed me to a building southeast of the city. It had been a long walk from the center of Manila. As the day's heat beat down upon me I began to ponder how the sun would affect me when I got out in the barrios and fields where there would be little shelter from it.

I discovered I had been initiated into the average Filipino style of travel—on foot. This, too, was a visible sign separating the two classes in Manila: one riding, the other walking out of the shadows of the alleys and seemingly entering the sunshine that they could not afford to live in. After plodding along for an hour, with my briefcase feeling heavier by the minute, I finally reached my destination—tired and perspiring.

There was no mistaking the four-century-old building. The outer walls were massive blocks and the peaked roof was slate. Stone slabs led to huge iron-banded double doors held upright by large gray metal hinges that had stood the test of time. The stone cross atop San Migual's projected into the heavens as one more protector of the ancient past. I ascended the stone steps, grasped the worn arched handle of ancient metal, and pulled open the massive door.

With a groan and slight shudder the door opened slowly, and I stepped into the silent interior. A few women who were kneeling in the pew did not bother to look up or stir, even though my footsteps sounded like the beat of base drums vibrating against the walls. I made my way to the front, looking for the stairway that led to the upper balcony where the priest would reside. Up the terraced steps I went until I reached another door. It was similar to the outside door but smaller and single. "Spanish-built doors were not constructed for the weak and frail," I thought. Yet the erectors of this house of God were small people. It made me wonder at the massive size of everything in the church.

After knocking solidly on the door it moaned as someone pushed it from the other side. A small, dark-haired priest, tanned and weather-beaten, appeared as he pushed once again on the archaic door until it swung far enough into the hallway for me to see his black cassock and pleasant smile. His eyes were smiling too. There was a hint of age, but that was difficult to assume because the tropical sun of the islands aged many people rapidly. It was easy to tell from the brown wrinkles across his forehead that he had been under the Pacific sun for a long time. Yet I had the feeling this man could easily walk over a mountain without any great effort, and probably had. He smiled again and beckoned me into his sanctuary. Above and behind his chair hung a picture of the Blessed Virgin and across from that was a picture of the Sacred Heart. We shook hands and his warmth was apparent. "I am Father Doyle," he said.

He walked over to an old rattan desk and seated himself in a rickety rattan chair; he then invited me to sit in a smaller rattan chair in front of his desk. He gazed at me with a quizzical expression and patiently waited for me to announce myself.

"I am Patrick Corbin," I informed him.

Father Doyle raised his eyebrows slightly and said, "I have been waiting for you."

"You have?" I replied.

"Yes. I have a letter here from the Order in Nebraska relaying your correspondence and the venture you propose. Perhaps you would like to give me a few more details before you enter into such a venture. No doubt you are unfamiliar with some of the situations here on Luzon since your last unpleasant experience here. I need not tell you that here, as in your own country, many ideas have been born and some of the old ones of the forties have disappeared."

He picked up the letter from his desk. I sensed that he had placed it there in readiness for some time, as nothing was on top of it. From his tone I could tell he was not enthusiastic about my proposal. He had many questions, to which I replied, "I am concerned only with circumstances regarding Father Douglas."

"This letter states that you never knew Father Douglas," said Father Doyle, "yet you are persistent in inquiring about him. Now you intend to pursue the events concerning his death—the death of a man who died for the cross over thirty years ago. It does seem strange, this interest, and I wonder if it would bring to light anything not already known to the Order. Perhaps there might be further harm in digging up the past. It might be for the best to let the dead rest," said Father Doyle.

"Perhaps it would be for the best, Father, but I have this gnawing feeling that compels me to look into his death even though I never met him." I then related to him all that had transpired between the incomplete dream and the car accident in Maine. I tried to explain the driving force that had brought me to Manila. Although he merely shrugged as if he were hearing a fantasy, I did not let it bother me; however, I could understand his attitude. I hardly knew why I was here myself; it must have been difficult for him to comprehend my reasoning.

"If you are going to pursue this still," said Father Doyle, "I will tell you what I know of the event and the investigation in 1948 by two priests from the Columban Order, if it will help."

"Whatever information you can give me about Father Douglas, I am sure will be a great help," I replied. I waited patiently until he was ready to reveal the findings of the investigation.

"It was just about dusk on July 24, 1943," he began. "While strolling outside his church, St. Mary Magdalene's in Pililia, Father Douglas was approached by several Japanese soldiers and then taken away in a military truck to Paete, twenty-five miles away. The Japanese were garrisoned in many sectors at that time, but these soldiers were believed to have come from Baras, no doubt carrying out a mandate—one of many that afflicted the inhabitants of Laguna de Bay—from Japanese Headquarters. There were many curfews imposed upon the Filipinos during the

Japanese occupation. Ordinarily seizures occurred without any justification; interrogation was almost a daily reality. Yes, Father Douglas had been questioned before, but this time he had been seized with such vigilance and haste. The onlookers in Pililia instantly sensed the significance of it and recognized this was not a routine process.

"The residents of Paete," he continued, "had been in the church when the Japanese, including a captain and a lieutenant, brought Father Douglas inside. There, in the baptistery of Santiago Apostol, he was interrogated and tortured. The captain, who spoke English fluently, belabored Father Douglas with a long list of charges. Father Douglas responded to their questions at first, however, he soon realized this was not the customary line of questioning, eventually avoiding their questions with silence, which infuriated the Japanese all the more. He never spoke again, even though his torturers inflicted greater pain and caused him to slowly weaken."

Father Doyle paused and sat back in his chair, the weight of the findings from the investigation pressing down on the rattan. "The torture lasted for three days. Several women had said the captain seemed very nervous, which, as you know, was not too common among the Japanese, who always maintained an air of arrogance. They also said the captain did not participate physically in the torture. When the Japanese realized Father Douglas was almost dead, they hastily carried him outside to a truck amidst the screaming and wailing of the Filipino women and children. As his tortured body passed them, some of the children ran down the stone steps and tumbled into the dusty street, where they put their heads between their legs and cried; the women fell to their knees and prayed. With this further display of anguish, the Japanese decided to move the priest away from the church.

"As I said, in 1948 the Order sent two Columban Fathers back to Paete to investigate the death of Father Douglas. You must remember this was five years after his death. They had little to go on, mostly the few stories they could gather from the inhabitants of Tanay, Pililia and Paete. After two months of extensive research that took them into the hills, where they hoped to uncover further evidence and remove the stoic silence of the local Filipinos, some of the witnesses in Paete confirmed that Father Douglas had been severely tortured beyond all human endurance, and they watched him suffer and pray in silence. Some of them are still alive today but refuse to give a full account.

"Both Columban Fathers readily admitted they sensed there was something unsaid and out of reach at times during the investigation, which left them with only frustration. The witnesses did, however, testify that it was the Japanese—and no one else—who had taken his life. But it was the disappearance of his body that became the most exasperating part of the investigation.

"The Laguna de Bay grapevine, then as now, moves swiftly within the towns and barrios; word rapidly reached the Filipino guerrillas about the episode taking place in the church. The rest of the findings I found hard to believe, maybe even fabricated, simply because there was but a remote possibility that the guerrillas could have infiltrated successfully into Paete under military conditions existing in the town at that time.

"There was a cemetery about a hundred yards from the church where the Japanese took Father Douglas and executed him. They quickly dug a shallow grave and buried him there. It seems that just as they finished the burial, the guerrillas made a daring attack, coming right up behind the cemetery using a bamboo thicket to conceal their movements. This by itself was a flagrant foray against the entrenched troops on all sides, but they used the oncoming dusk for camouflage. The unexpected and sudden attack, however, did not catch the captain by surprise; some of the onlookers said he had been nervously looking in every direction in anticipation. When the guerrillas first burst into the open, he immediately gave a warning to the others, and then disappeared into the far end of the bamboo thicket. It was too late for the others; the first burst of gunfire killed them immediately. There was more firing as the captain fled into the dusk, and witnesses said he seemed to stagger just before he reached the bamboo. The guerrillas vacated the area as silently as they had come—this was their method, and they had been using it for months.

"For a long time afterward the local Filipinos were subjected to brutal punishment and discipline for the death of the Japanese soldiers. Some of them carry the scars and memories of that period in Paete and Pililia to this day."

Father Doyle paused, shaking his head slightly, then continued. "When the spot that had been designated as the grave site was finally found, the Columban Fathers requested permission to have the remains removed for a proper burial, which involved litigation with town officials. The whole town of Paete became aroused at this point. The worst part was the verbal assault stemming from what suddenly became a united Filipino front. The two priests were beset with threats and were asked to leave. Father Morgan, who was assigned to Paete at the time, feared for their lives and notified the militia.

"Under armed guard and with a commission from town officials, the priests supervised the excavation. Those who had come to observe stood in a circle of silence. This sudden change from the hostility of the previous days caused the missionaries to wonder if something else was about to happen. After digging down six feet, even though they had been informed it was a shallow grave, they found nothing. Before the digging was completed, not a single Filipino remained at the site. It was as if they all knew there would be no body found that day.

"The body was never found, and further questioning of the Filipinos met more resistance and a determined reluctance. The priests maintained there was little doubt that someone, or even many, knew what the results of the investigation would be because of the sudden change in demeanor of so many at the same time."

I recalled the demeanor of the Filipinos and was not surprised by their united front or their stoic silence. Although it had been difficult to maintain my composure while Father Doyle related the findings, I tried to grasp all that he had said and how it all related to the dream and the incident at the church. Father Doyle noticed my distant look and asked, "Are you all right, Patrick?"

"Yes, Father, I am just trying to absorb it all." I did not want him to see how much the story had disturbed me and quickly asked, "And the two missionaries, where are they now?"

"With other assignments to attend to, they had sadly decided to discontinue the investigation and return to Ireland. There they gave a report of their activities to the Order, and the matter came to a close," replied Father Doyle.

I sensed Father Doyle might want to change the subject for the moment, and asked, "What brought you to the Philippines, Father?"

"I was in Pililia for three years in the 1960s, visiting various priests assigned there and in Paete. While there I had heard about Father Douglas, and I, too, inquired into his death. The Order sent me what information they had, which I have related to you. It was the death of Father Douglas that climaxed my decision to enter the Columban Order, as it has been for many other young men in the past thirty-odd years. I did not pursue the incident then or now. As a priest I am ordained to bring the sheep back to the pasture. If I had continued on with any kind of an investigation, openly or silently, I knew it would only provoke the people into further resentment. I could not afford to offer my hand to them and simultaneously probe into something they kept in complete secrecy. I, or any priest, would destroy years of progress, yes, even the progress Father Douglas brought to them. I suspect, as I am sure other priests who have been assigned to Pililia or Paete have suspected, there are Filipinos living who undoubtedly know the answer to what happened to the body of Father Douglas. Yet for some unknown reason they surround themselves with a wall of impregnable silence. It has yet to be penetrated. Every priest who has been assigned there soon learns not to dwell on the incident, because before long you will be listening to your own homily—alone. For some reason the residents maintain a vigilant silence on this matter.

"One must admit," I stated, "it sounds like a strong one."

Father Doyle replied, "They will not let go. It seems there is an existing anxiety, and even I, during my stay in Pililia, caught a glimpse of it. The Filipinos have not had favorable times, nor have their people before them. They have withstood degradation and oppression for centuries, even bending to them. One has to be very patient, very tactful in approaching them; if you are not, you will suddenly discover you are being avoided. They have little material wealth and very little hope of ever obtaining any. Perhaps, and this is only a surmise, with this atmosphere so prevalent in their present and dismal future, they are clinging desperately to whatever has motivated their silence. It is easy to see how tenacious an attitude they have. They know you are aware of it, yet they will not relinquish one bit of information. There is a tremendous amount of strength in their discipline and stature, which makes it that much more difficult to penetrate their wall of silence."

Father Doyle shook his head ever so slightly, and I sensed there was a bit of frustration in the movement. Then he continued, "Only once did I hear—and unintentionally—any reference come to the surface concerning the plight of Father Douglas. Do not misunderstand me. The residents have never stopped thinking about Father Douglas even though he is seldom a topic of discussion—at least not openly. They are very devout people and associate him and the Church as one."

"I sense they have maintained a deep admiration for him."

"Yes they have," responded Father Doyle. "I recall one Sunday after Mass, while standing just outside the doors at the front of the church in Pililia, when I overheard two women discussing the problem of growing flowers. One of them said, 'We must become like the rose.' This expression is seldom heard in public. It was not just the discussion of the merits of the rose, but their tone, very subdued, which seemed to indicate they did not want anyone to hear them; I pretended at first I had not.

"Ordinarily I would not pay much attention to these conversations, but the mentioning of the rose caught my ear instantly, as it is well known Father Douglas often mentioned the rose in his sermons. Although I barely turned in the direction of the conversation, my movement seemed to cause the two women to immediately scurry down the steps.

"So there you have it," sighed Father Doyle. "There is something there, yet out of sight. Now you say you intend to delve into a past that at times seems to be far away and at other times seems to be within reach. I do not think you really understand the complexity of it all."

Here he paused and threw his hands out to his sides in a sort of futile gesture. His frustration was evident.

I responded, "I have searched my soul and mind, Father, and, as I have said, I do not understand why I am here, but I have not traveled all these miles to get discouraged this early in the quest. That is what it is, a quest, strange as it may seem, to uncover a truth but also a reason. I also suspect my presence here could be an intrusion into the lives of people I have not even met. The question now is whether I have that right. I must admit, though, I do not understand the depths of these circumstances surrounding the events in Paete and Pililia. I can already see there will be more difficulties ahead."

Father Doyle looked up and said, "Then you intend to continue further?"

"I am here, Father, and besides, it is too early to put aside this commitment. I have to go to Morong, at least, now that I have come this far, even if only to feel the sentiment of these people. I certainly cannot turn around without going back to Laguna de Bay and the old church. Perhaps some of the Filipinos there will remember the old 43rd Division, especially the 43rd Recon. We camped for more than a month in the Laguna sector. Maybe some of the old friendships can be renewed. There is no doubt many of those I met there are gone, yet there might be some who will remember. We will see. Maybe it will be futile, but I am going to try to find out one way or the other. I just have to go as far with this as I can."

Father Doyle shook his head again with a slow motion, and then he walked over to the opened stained-glass window and gazed down at the people moving about in the street below.

"It is one thing," he said, "to stir up old memories and another to stir up a simmering bowl of soup. We who live here in Manila travel a different road than those in the towns and barrios—believe me, it is quite a different road. You can see for yourself that even here in the outskirts of Manila very little has changed since the days of the war. Yes, some things on the surface seemed to have improved, but one does not have to open his eyes too wide to observe the brewing emotions beneath the mask of progress.

"In the barrios you will discover poverty is a way of life; it is only one factor, though, in the lives of these people. Rice farmers are fortunate if they can feed their own, never mind make a profit. Too well they know they are slowly losing the battle of survival, which is why many flock to Manila, where, unfortunately, they wind up on the other side of the line that separates the classes—groveling in "sludge mountain," the garbage from which sustains them. They are proud people, but once they lose the land that has sustained them and their ancestors through monsoons and blight, the little dignity they have disperses with the never-ending promises by the government.

"So if you continue on, be prepared to meet the Filipinos on their terms. To be sure, you will be facing a unique experience, especially in the Laguna de Bay area. Perhaps the fact that you were with the 43rd Division might enable you to penetrate their code of silence. Who knows?"

Father Doyle was not very encouraging. His tenure in the Philippines did not lack experience, and there was in his advice forewarning. I could understand his anxiety; there was little doubt in his mind that I had no idea of what was ahead of me—and I did not. Although he had not mentioned my age, I could see that it was a concern; at fifty-five-years old the mountainous region, where the terrain was treacherous and flash floods were sudden during the rainy season, would be an issue. Yet I was determined.

There was little sense at the moment in trying to fathom why the Filipinos cherished their secret. I had to get out into the rice paddies, hills and stilt-house towns. Unlike Manila where there were two schools of thought, two economic classes clashing as they had for centuries, in the towns and barrios they were all on similar ground, grinding out a living in knee-deep mud or slashing bamboo shoots. This is where my real challenge would be.

I began to wonder if Father Douglas were more than a martyr: a beacon of hope hidden beneath the veil of silence prevailing in the winds and minds of Laguna de Bay.

Father Doyle must have sensed that my thoughts had carried me away. He continued as if they had not. "Here in Manila there is a monument dedicated to the 43rd Division. There is also a cemetery containing many from it."

"They were gallant men," I said, "dying for freedom—their own and that of the Filipinos."

"Freedom is priceless and a worn-out phrase," replied Father Doyle, "but that is just what it is. Father Douglas, like the Son of God, died for the freedom of the soul. He took his flock out of captivity and liberated them from the thorns he was so fond of removing from their souls."

"It is sad to think his grave is unknown," I commented.

"Perhaps his grave is in the winds, and that is why his shadow and words still move and echo through the hills and valleys and above the waters of Laguna de Bay," he replied.

Father Doyle gave me the impression there was a living spirit stalking the memories and bamboo groves. Just from listening to him, I intuited that the residents of Laguna de Bay had needed a staff to lean on and that Father Douglas had given them it, which aided them in keeping his memory and his image alive. He had been their support for years when they really needed him, and they did not want to fail him. He had not failed them. Only the elders could still hear and remember his words. When they died, the words and memories would leave with them. The greatest challenge to those who carried the memories would be to see that they were not lost.

I, too, had memories. Memories of men who shouldered rifles, toted musette bags and marched into the hills. Men who patrolled a seventy-five-square-mile front on Luzon in sixteen days as the eyes and ears for an entire division of men who had put complete trust in them—a division of heroic men who knew the 43rd Recon was somewhere out there constantly watching the flanks. Recon, the guardians, spreading a protective veil through mountains, across rivers, into ravines, and into the shadows of caves—ever watching, ever listening. They were proud but cautious, silent and steady, tired and lonely—and they walked from one dawn to another as thousands of men relied on their vigilance and ability and stamina. In sixteen days they had accomplished an unbelievable mission with a little over two platoons and without the loss of one man. It was a commendable feat and they were commended.

My memories were reborn, as I knew they would be. I wondered how many dreams of men Recon had kept alive because of their silent marauding through the bamboo and heat, from the Munda Trail in the Solomon Islands to the depths of New Guinea and to the Lingayen Gulf, Urdinetta and Ipo. I had a strange feeling as I thought of those days and how the memory of a priest had brought me back to Luzon, a man who had dedicated his life, all of it, to the protection of the oppressed who longed for a better life. Recon had come to free and save their lives; Father Douglas had come to free and save their souls—the man in a black cassock, a man without a face, who kept looming in my thoughts.

I thanked Father Doyle for his insight and knowledge and tried to reassure him about my venture. "You know, Father, I am aware you are not fully with me. But I promise you, if this becomes more than I can handle or more than the residents can handle, I will abandon the idea and let whatever has transpired be buried in the hills. But I have to give it a try."

He offered to give me further assistance if needed, but I knew the unforeseen would just have to be experienced one way or another. We parted, and I started the long walk back to the hotel. It was hot and I took my time, reflecting on the conversation with Father Doyle. One thing was plain: I would have to plan every movement around the sun, especially avoiding the heat of the day. It was difficult enough when Recon moved from Lingayen through Luzon in 1945, in nine months of rain and heat waves, but we had youth on our side then. At my age now, just the thought of the heat brought discomfort. It would be a test, perhaps the severest of all.

Morong would be my first stop after Manila. I needed a few more days in Manila to purchase a canteen, poncho, backpack and other necessary items that I might not find in the towns. There was also the matter of transportation to Morong. However, what I needed most at this moment was a rest and, above all, a bath.

It had been a restless night. After breakfast the next morning I followed the directions of the day clerk to a secondhand store a few blocks away. The clerk, short of stature, was also short tempered. After I had gone around the store several times, he suddenly confronted me, "Do you intend to purchase something?" He spoke good English. Although there were several other people in the store at the time, he seemed to ignore them. I sensed distrust in his voice, which the others could plainly hear, although they did not look up. I became uneasy but remained calm, remembering the Filipinos had been born in an age of mistrust. After assuring him I intended to buy several items, he went back to what he was doing, although I was aware he was watching me all the time.

When I had finally made all my selections I deposited them on the counter. This precipitated a hassle of how many pesos I needed. As I paid him and gathered up my purchases I caught slight grins on the faces of the onlookers. Evidently my money had calmed the storekeeper's temper, and he was at peace with the world again. However, I left not knowing if I had paid more than I should have and vowing to learn the dollar-to-peso value, or I would soon be broke.

Upon returning to the hotel all I cared about was how good another bath would feel. I reflected on my first real interaction with a Filipino, other than the casual nod of the head; it was not much, but at this point it was important, as it gave me some insight into the way things might be down the road and off the road.

In the morning after I checked out of the hotel, I set out to find the bus terminal. I had abandoned the idea of buying a bicycle; Morong was too far, about thirty-five miles away, and I had no way to carry all my paraphernalia. I knew it would be foolhardy to take up the challenge at this time. One breakdown on the road and I would be stranded in unfamiliar surroundings, an inconvenience I did not need at the onset of my quest.

The bicycle was the main mode of travel aside from walking, although walking was better and faster than riding the carabao. I recalled too well the dusty roads Recon had traveled during the war. Dusty roads would make peddling difficult, and I was not quite ready for eating my peck of dust.

At the bus terminal I received my first setback. Today was Tuesday and the next bus did not leave for Morong until the following Monday. I had hoped to leave the city before the weekend, but this now seemed to be out of the question. With six days on my hands I decided to inquire about lodging and stores in Morong. This information could have been gathered from Father Doyle, but I did not want to put him in an awkward position of having to give me names of local Filipinos who could offer accommodations. I checked back into the hotel, and then spent the day wandering around the city observing the ways of Manila life. I sauntered along with the crowds. There were many other Americans, all purchasing as if there were no tomorrow. I knew it would be an entirely different scene in Morong and even more so in the smaller barrios. Pesos would be hard to find there, which reminded me that I had to find a bank.

I located one near the hotel and made arrangements to have my account come through their office. I did not want to carry a large amount of money, especially beyond Manila where I did not know where I would be lodging. The trip to the terminal and bank had taken up most of the day. I returned to the hotel and took another bath.

The next day I went back to the terminal and approached the driver, Juan Peralto. He was pleasant enough, a little rough on the edges, but his English was excellent, which made conversation between us easier. He said, "I have been on the Morong run for five years. I know every bend in the road and some that are not there!" He laughed. "It did not take me long to develop a sense of humor; the passengers, especially on trips to and from Morong, can test the patience of any man. They are passive, quiet people, those from Morong and along the shores of Laguna de Bay, and you can never be sure of what is on their minds."

"Do you know where I could lodge while in Morong?" I asked.

"I know several families in the town, some more reliable than others," responded Juan.

He wrote down a list of names, six to be exact, and handed me the list. "I cannot make any further recommendation for accommodations; that is up to you," he said. I wondered if there were some way to approach these families but decided to deal with that when the time came.

"Juan, can you give me directions to the 43rd Division Memorial?"

"It is a bus ride to the northeastern side of Manila," he replied. I decided I had done enough for the day and went back to the hotel.

The next day I slept until nearly noon. Actually, I needed the rest, and there was not any hurry. I still had Friday and Saturday to ponder any issues that might arise. Early afternoon found me on the bus again to locate the 43rd Division Memorial.

It had been an hour's ride. The huge cemetery came into view before the memorial did. I left the bus and entered the cemetery through a large metal arch atop two large gray pillars. Miniature flags flew from the length of the arch. Down the center of the cement lane I went, rows of hedges lining either side. At the end of the lane, erected in the center of a walk-around circle, was the memorial. It was thirty-feet high, pure white and glistening like crystal in the Philippine sun. A dedication was cut into the pillar four feet up from the base, and a few feet from the top was the 43rd Division insignia, a black grape leaf on a red patch with arched white stripes on the black-trimmed outer edge. As I gazed up at the weatherworn insignia, nostalgia overcame me. I could hear the feet of marching men from Guadalcanal to the shores of Japan. I could hear the bugle cutting through the dawn and dusk, bringing men to their feet, and now, echoing through the crosses—row after row—before me. Above all I could hear the breathing of the men of the 43rd Division drifting through the vines, the dew, the shadows, and the silence and sounds of the jungle. I listened to it once again, here where the breeze gently caressed the flag. I knew I would hear these sounds forever—the mental journey would never end.

I lingered for some time among the white markers, wondering how many lives these deaths had saved. Once again I thought of the unmarked grave of a man who had carried only a cross and of how many souls he had saved. Did his shadow still move within the shadows of Laguna de Bay? Did his breathing console the downtrodden and the oppressed? Were his words lingering in the hills and valleys? Like the bugle, would its echo never die? Were there still Filipinos following the trail of roses where he had cast them? Surely, somewhere in those hills someone was listening. Someone must be following the shadow of his black cassock and, like my own incomplete dream, be searching for the Bamboo Shepherd.

I spent Friday and Saturday in the hotel, not venturing out once into the heat of the day or the milling populace. I had enough of that; instead, I left the room only to get meals in the hotel restaurant. On Sunday I went back to St. Migual's for Mass and spent half an hour visiting with Father Doyle. He was still apprehensive about my undertaking.

I left Father Doyle knowing I would see him when I came back to Manila for supplies. Tomorrow I would look to the mountains concealing a thirty-three-year-old mystery. But tonight I looked forward to what could be my last full bath for some time to come.

In the morning, with suitcase in hand, I took a cab to the bus terminal. I took the seat directly behind Juan, whom I already considered a friend. My real purpose, however, was to get as close to the windshield as possible to have a few more seconds to see how much change had taken place in the towns and barrios where Recon had ridden through so many years ago. By the time we pulled out of the terminal the bus was jammed with people, all returning to the towns and barrios along the route to Morong. They were a quiet group, and most of them carried a fully laden sack on their back or head. Although they gave little indication they were aware of my presence (I was the only American on the bus.), it was obvious they were. I suspected they were curious about my conversations with Juan too. If the Filipino grapevine was still as effective, I had the feeling my entrance into their realm would move inland and spread to every corner of Laguna de Bay.

The condition of the road had not changed; the dust swirled around the bus all through the ride. Those walking the road held white bandanas to their faces until the bus passed by. Their numbers decreased as we traveled farther away from the city, and after ten miles their numbers had dwindled to only a few. We rode past rice paddies and carabaos on both sides of the road. Water in the paddies was halfway up the shinbones of the slouched-over men, women and children moving along in lines in the fields. Their backs were braced, and wide-brimmed head coverings shielded them from the sun. It seemed as though I were still riding in the back of the half-track in 1945—the picture was the same. They did not look up, and that had not changed either. Even when the dust settled over them and clouded the paddy near the road, they did not alter their movements. It was as if there were no dust and no bus on the road—an attitude informing or reminding me, or both, that this display would be a way of life I would have to reckon with. Father Doyle's words were already ringing true about the difference between city life and barrio life. I began to understand the meaning of Juan's words when he mentioned the people in the barrios could "test a man's patience." I shook my head when suddenly I realized I was beginning to form opinions about people I had not met.

Antipolo suddenly appeared through the dust. In 1945, after the artillery shelling was over, only one building remained standing. I remembered that scene well: there was nothing on the main street but a row of rubble, every house and store with their tin roofs leveled to the ground with the exception of one defiant structure. There was not a soul in Antipolo when Recon wheeled through it. Every occupant had fled the town before the 43rd Division moved through—the Japanese, who had retreated all the way from Manila, fled in haste before them. The 43rd had encountered them along this very road and pushed them deep into the hills. Antipolo was now a bustling town without a visible sign it had been devastated.

We made one more stop in Teresa. We then left the flat land, and off in the distance I could see the outline of Mapalug Mountain. Morong was to the south of Teresa, and off to the east was Baras, the closest town to Mapalug Mountain. In the middle of this formidable hill, more than halfway to the top, were the Kalinawan Caves where hundreds of Japanese had perished in a futile attempt to defend the southern Shimbu Line.

I glanced behind me. We had left another wake of dust when we left

Teresa. Ten passengers were all that remained on the bus, which meant I would be seeing some if not all of them somewhere in the vicinity of Morong. One well-dressed passenger had an exceptionally large sack beside his suitcase and was the only one beside myself who had luggage. Another had a cardboard box; all the others toted their white sacks and guarded them cautiously. They all seemed to know one another. The five who boarded the bus with me in Manila received nods from the other five. Had I not been on the bus there might have been more cordiality among the passengers. I realized I was prejudging, but I could not eliminate the feeling completely. There was something just a little strange in their behavior after we left Teresa. Perhaps their composure had been diminished somewhat when they realized I was definitely going to Morong. I quickly turned my attention back to the front of the bus, fearing they would see me glancing too long. Uneasiness remained with me all the way to Morong.

Morong was not a strange place for me. I had spent many days there in 1945. As we approached the outskirts the first thing I noticed other than the rice paddies was the Morong River; the road ran above it, and then it crossed over a dilapidated wooden bridge before entering the town. Looking down at the river from the bridge I could see several women pounding clothes against the rocks, beating them steadily until the fabric became glistening white. Although the river was sometimes muddy from irrigation and wallowing carabao, the women somehow got the clothes clean. This ancient custom had not changed since I last rode over this bridge. Many a shirt, pants and skirt had felt the flailing from the flat side of a bamboo board. It was a never-ending chore.

Working the rice fields, a task the entire family participated in, was not any different either. The clothes could be washed anytime, but the rice had to be harvested and dried at the right times. These chores were like family rituals, and just as automatic. Every family member knew that growing rice was a livelihood and was life sustaining.

There was a slight upgrade after crossing the bridge, bringing us into the center of town. Juan pointed out the home of Raul and Alvita Reyes, the couple I had selected from his list as my first possible provider of a room and meals. Juan reminded me that they were elders of the town and very prominent citizens; both were town officials. It was my intention to contact them before I looked for the pastor of St. Jerome's, whose name had not been mentioned in my conversations with Father Doyle in Manila.

During my conversations with Juan I was careful not to disclose my reason for returning to Morong except to state I wanted to see the town where I had spent so many good moments with Father O'Reilly. There had been other casual acquaintances from those days, as Father O'Reilly had introduced me to some of the residents. But I could not recall their names now, and they were probably no longer alive.

I stepped off the bus and the other passengers followed. Several more boarded for the return trip. As I waved good-bye to Juan I tried not to look where the others were going, but I soon discovered it was I who was under scrutiny. I was the stranger here, and my every move, slight or significant, would be noticed. I knew the residents would not be openly curious, and I had to perform similarly. I could not afford to let them catch me observing them. I was on their ground and perhaps not even welcome.

I retrieved my suitcase and headed for the home of Raul and Alvita Reyes, wondering how many other visitors had been directed to their home upon arrival in Morong. Only the well-dressed man did not look in my direction; he was engrossed in struggling with his large suitcase as another passenger offered to give him a hand, which he accepted.

I turned my gaze upward to the huge Spanish church on the incline above the town. I could see in one quick glance that St. Jerome's had not changed at all. The large stone slab steps came right down to the road—steps that once had felt the weight of the redheaded Father O'Reilly. For a brief second those terrible days of war flashed before me, but then my thoughts were interrupted by a jeepney speeding past. I instantly recognized the possibility of additional transportation out of Morong and into the barrios and places a bicycle would meet with difficulty.

The Reyes's house was well constructed. Beneath the bamboo floor, which was high enough off the ground for the rainy season and high enough to crouch under, chickens squawked and poked away at the dusty earth. At the top of the stairs was a bamboo-framed door, whereas houses in the remote barrios had no doors. The exterior had board siding, another sign of prosperity. It was clear Mr. and Mrs. Reyes had prospered from some enterprising venture, and with this in mind I knocked on the front door.

It opened almost at the knock, as if someone were deliberately waiting for the sound on the other side. The woman standing there was about five feet tall with grayish white hair. She was slight of build, and she wore sandals, a light-colored dress and a nice smile.

"Mrs. Reyes?" I asked.

She nodded in assent.

I continued nervously, "Juan Peralto, the bus driver, recommended your residence for room and board. If you have a room available, I would like to stay here for a month or so, with meals of a sort. I was with the 43rd Recon Troop, which passed through here in 1945. We camped on the outskirts of town in the cemetery just above the shores of Laguna de Bay. I knew Father O'Reilly quite well; perhaps you remember some of us came back to town and visited with him on the weekends?"

I caught her reaction, a quick glance in the direction of the church, when I mentioned Father O'Reilly.

"Yes, I have room," she said in fairly good but broken English. "Remember Recon and all 43rd soldiers quite good. Very good soldier. Save Morong and protect all Laguna de Bay from Japanese. Very good. Remember Father O'Reilly who good priest. Cook food for you two times day."

She seemed to reflect on her words as she looked up the street to the church again and gave a little nod, as if she were reminded about something back in those days. I took a liking to her because she seemed to have a quiet nature. She invited me in, and then went through the kitchen, into a hallway, past the living room and to the two bedrooms at the rear, one with a small porch. This one she offered to me. I could come and go through the porch without passing through the front of the house, offering me some privacy. After a brief discussion over how many pesos a week it would cost, I piled my belongings on the bamboo bed. This room was to be my home, although I had no idea for how long.

I already knew where my next bath would be: in the Morong River, and I had to walk to it. Just before dusk that is just what I did. Without hesitation I walked right into the water. The many people who were already gathered there caught me by surprise, and I think I caught them slightly off guard. Some good resulted from my sudden entrance into their domain, however, because for the first time some of them nodded to me. I quickly returned their gesture with a smile and hoped this would be a breakthrough, minute as it were.

When I arrived back at the house, Mrs. Reyes was standing in front talking with a man. He was not much taller than she was. As I approached her, she said, "Mr. Corbin, this my husband, Raul Reyes." After extending his hand and shaking mine, he beckoned me to follow him to the porch at the rear of the house.

"Please have seat." He pointed to an old rain-stained rocking chair, which I sat upon. He seemed eager to talk, which was comforting.

"We Filipinos here think much time of Recon," he said with a gentle nod of his head, just as his wife had done and in the same broken but understandable English. His wife had evidently briefed him on my background. "Some people not think good of those times, but most old people in Morong remember Japanese bad times. Now much forgotten because some die and some forget. Alvita and I not soon forget. 43rd bring freedom from bad times. We offer thanks many times and think of Father O'Reilly too. Very good priest and kind man."

He paused, and then seemed to reflect on those days when he was one of the young of the town. "You see, not change much. Only now, not like before when young stay, now try to run away to city and not work in rice field and tobacco field. Some come home and follow life of family. Some go away far to school and only visit family. This good, but leave not so many for work. Young not remember war, only old people remember. Young only read about war time, so sometimes do not understand."

"The young in America are not so different," I said, "they only read about the war or see it in the movies. They do not know it, have not lived it, as we have. There is a world of difference, though, between the American and Filipino youth—Americans have so many more opportunities."

"Yes, Americans have much. Alvita and I have much too, how do you say, opportunities. We elders, long time in Morong."

I could detect in his voice and attitude the importance of the position. Family disputes, land rights, town policies, even bridge repairs were settled by the elders. Every town had its elders, and although their policies were not always popular, all decisions were adhered to and carried out with authority.

It was difficult to guess the age of Raul and harder to guess his wife's age based on looks alone. I assumed that because they were elders and had known Father O'Reilly, they were at least in their fifties.

"I not keep you longer, Mr. Corbin. Have nice stay in home and in Morong," he stated, looking pleased I had chosen his home to stay in.

"Please, call me Patrick," I said. Before ending our conversation I asked, "Mr. Reyes, do you know where I can buy a bicycle?"

"Please, I Raul," he grinned, "Yes, Alfredo Rican, down road past bus stop. Repairs and sells secondhand ones."

The next day I decided to take a walk around town. As I left the house I now understood how Mrs. Reyes almost had the door open before I knocked when I first arrived at her doorstep. She had a clear view down the street and could observe every passenger getting on and off the bus, which allowed her to keep an eye open for possible tenants.

As I walked down the street I noticed a few curtains moved in windows as I passed, but I did not acknowledge the interest I was causing. There had to be as much difficulty in concealing the curiosity as there was in concealing my awareness of the probing eyes. I began to wonder if this would become a game and speculated what I would have to do to end it. There had been several visitors to the Reyes' household since my arrival, leaving no doubt the grapevine was working. Perhaps when word circulated that I had been here years ago with the 43rd Division the reception might turn more cordial.

On the northeastern side of Morong, about a mile from the center, I found the garden and fruit tree grove where Recon had bivouacked after we had rolled through Morong the first time. It was here on March 17, 1945, St. Patrick's Day, that a platoon brought Father O'Reilly and a band of Filipino guerrillas out of the hills, where they had been hiding from the Japanese for days, half starved. When I gave Father O'Reilly my mess gear and his first real meal in days, his Irish eyes sparkled with joy and thanksgiving. He then recounted the events that led up to his hiding in the hills.

"I came close to saying my last Mass as the Japanese fled through Morong. During the confusion, just about the time I was reciting the offertory, I turned to face the congregation and saw three Japanese soldiers nervously standing at the front entrance—I then recited the longest offertory of my priestly life. Finally, when I could no longer prolong the

Mass, and the silence in the church began to dissipate, I turned around again and looked down the length of the aisle, but the Japanese had vanished. Other Columban Fathers had been killed during the Japanese retreat from Manila, and I had no doubt they had been ordered to execute me."

Later on, when I returned to visit Father O'Reilly on the weekends in 1945, he told me of the sad death of Father Douglas in July 1943. Father Douglas had been the first Columban missionary to die at the hands of the Japanese on the shores of Laguna de Bay.

All this ran through my mind as I traipsed around town. I thought of the distance between Morong and Paete, the town where Father Douglas had been tortured. It was approximately twenty-five miles down and around the Jalajala Peninsula from Pililia. Santa Cruz, where the Japanese were supposed to have taken Father Douglas, was twenty miles or so south of Paete. It was unlikely he ever reached Santa Cruz alive, as indicated by the report from the Columban Fathers. It was also doubtful there had been witnesses in Morong, simply because residents did not travel that far away from their homes during the Japanese occupation. In addition, transportation in those days for such distances was nil. I did not recall ever seeing buses or bicycles in Morong in 1945; they were therefore less likely in 1943. Any Morong residents who were discovered in Pililia or Paete in 1943 would never have returned home alive; also, they would probably have been considered guerrillas and been promptly done away with or at least subjected to physical or mental abuse. These factors alone suggested I would have to go beyond Morong to discover where Father Douglas had been buried. Somehow I had to work my way along the shores of Laguna de Bay until I reached Pililia. I wondered how long it would take to cover all the ground between here and Pililia—ground that I would be taking the bicycle over, if I managed to procure one. I chose the morrow as the day to go in search of a bicycle.

Alfredo Rican spoke fairly good English and had two bicycles to offer—for a price. Two prices to be exact: one for the bicycle with tires and one for the bicycle without. He reminded me of real estate agents back home who had just sold the best buy of the year just before you inquired about it but always had another available at a slightly higher price.

Smilingly I explained to Alfredo, "I have little use for a bicycle with-out tires!"

This, in turn, brought a smile to his face. "I give you good price for bicycle with tires, and Auriela Agpalo buy extra tires and parts for you in Antipolo or Manila," he replied.

"Who is Auriela Agpalo?" I asked.

"Agpalo, businessman with large suitcases on bus when you come to Morong; he take bus route for things like bicycle parts," said Alfredo.

It then occurred to me that Alfredo had given a hand to Agpalo when he got off the bus, which left little doubt they operated together. I sus-pected Alfredo did not miss much.

I rode my new acquisition up the main street to Raul's house and brought it in my room. I did not know if this gesture appealed to the own-ers, but I did not want my bicycle to appeal to anyone else either.

I now had a means of transportation, at least for this locality. There was not any hurry to plunge into a hectic bicycle-riding expedition. Although I knew I had to get to Pililia some way or another, it was not going to be by bicycle—at least not all the way. It would take too much out of me to pedal those fifteen-odd miles. Most importantly I could not afford to strike out immediately for that town. I had to work this venture in phases, visiting as many towns as I could without arousing suspicion. My next target would be Baras, six to seven miles away. First I had to pay a visit to the church and then the cemetery, two miles out of Morong.

The next morning I rode my bicycle to the old Spanish church. I noticed it was a replica of the church in Manila. I wondered if it had ever been filled to capacity. As I walked down the aisle the women preparing the altar looked up. I nodded to them and asked, "Is the priest in the sac-risty?"

"He go to Baras, meeting; back late evening," replied the woman nearest the aisle.

I hesitated, but dared to ask anyway, "Can you tell me his name?"

"Name?" she frowned, "ah yes." She then smiled, "Father Cannon." Then, having answered enough questions, she turned away and busied herself with the others. I was beginning to learn when a Filipino had been asked enough questions.

The morning sun greeted me when I wheeled the bicycle out of

Morong toward the cemetery where Recon had spent its final days in this area. Off to the right was the little knoll where six Japanese had died for the Rising Sun. Just beyond the knoll was the shore of Laguna de Bay, where the early sunlight was glimmering on the ripples of the water. Another half mile brought me to the cemetery, where, on its farthest side, I had lived for weeks in a foxhole, sleeping on a stretcher a few inches off the ground. My poncho had served as a roof, shielding me from sun and rain. From the foxhole I faced a bamboo grove three hundred feet away—machine gun and tripod my steady companions night and day, rosary beads in the palm of my hand through the long and weary nights, and the crackling of swaying bamboo to keep me alert. I sat there for a while, remembering it all. Then I got back on my bicycle and rode slowly back to Morong, wondering again if there were others, somewhere, remembering the trail of a cassock in the hills of southeastern Luzon.

For the rest of the week I pedaled across the bridge and one to two miles beyond it to get my legs back to the shape they were in while I was in Maine. I wondered if the entire town knew by now that I was from the old 43rd, because I was receiving more nods and a new grin once in a while. When Sunday came I walked up to St. Jerome's Church along with the other parishioners. Every day I was becoming a little more acquainted with their mode of living and resolved to meet them on their terms.

Father Cannon was outside St. Jerome's greeting his flock one by one as they came up the stone steps. From the way he greeted me, I could tell he knew who I was—I was not exactly a secret in Morong anymore. I went past him into the church and prayed with the residents of Morong.

Father Cannon mentioned the 43rd in his homily, praising the men who had given their lives in the Luzon campaign and especially those who had fallen during the liberation of the Laguna de Bay and Morong Provinces. He did not mention my presence; there was no need for dramatics.

After the Mass I waited in the last pew until the parishioners had left the church. Father Cannon stood outside the Spanish doors and bid good day to all who approached him. Finally, when they had gone, I went outside and greeted him.

"Hello Father. I am Patrick Corbin," I stated as we shook hands. "I am staying at Mr. and Mrs. Reyes' home here in Morong."

He smiled, almost laughed, "As I am sure you know, I already know! And I am sure by now you know I am Father Cannon."

"Yes, Father, I came by the church the other day."

"Would you care to join me up on the veranda, Patrick?"

"Yes," I eagerly replied, "I used to sit and talk with Father O'Reilly there."

We walked to the veranda together, and he beckoned me to sit. Father Cannon appeared to be an amiable man. He reminded me of Father O'Reilly, jovial with laughing eyes, yet the same humility. I liked him right away. I also knew I had to remember to harness my eagerness and let him talk.

"I received a letter from Father Doyle in Manila," he began. "He mentioned you were with the 43rd Division. What brings you back to the Philippines?"

"Yes, Father, I was with the 43rd. I intend to venture around the shores of Laguna de Bay as far as the 43rd had penetrated in 1945, and if possible, trek across the hills to the Kalinawan Caves, one of the last places of resistance by the Japanese."

"I have never been to the caves," said Father Cannon, "but I have been as far down the coast as Santa Cruz, attending church affairs in all the barrios and towns when time permits."

I suspected Father Cannon had visited Paete and Pililia and might be familiar with the Father Douglas episode. No doubt he had been briefed in the seminary about the events of the war, especially in the Laguna de Bay area. Nevertheless, he did not mention any particular Columban Father or event. If he had any feelings or thoughts about this time he did not disclose them to me. I also noted he did not mention one word about my reason for coming to Luzon; Father Doyle, I surmised, had left that up to me. Perhaps when the proper time arrived, I would confide in Father Cannon.

Father Cannon continued, "The Kalinawan Caves, I am told, is a long, hot, grueling journey, although numerous excursions have been made by hardy, youthful climbers. Outside Baras there is an old, unused road that is the closest striking point to the caves. It is wide-open country out there across a six-mile valley with many rice paddies. Beyond that is the huge Black Swamp, stretching to within a few miles of Mapalug

Mountain. In the monsoon season the swamp, also about six miles long, swells to a large lake. Whether rainy or not, you have to make a choice: slog through the swamp or tote a boat from Baras to cross it. The alternative is to travel northeast of Baras to the left of the swamp."

He then looked me straight in the eyes and said, "You will never make it through the swamp without assistance." He shook his head and with a stern look on his face continued, "A man of your age must have a very good reason for considering such an attempt."

I reflected a moment on what Father Cannon had said, especially the emphasis he put on *hardy, youthful climbers*. The interior of the swamp would bring the coolness of the soggy maze; the alternate route, exposure to the blistering sun. Taking the safest way of travel, to the northeast, eventually would bring one to the northern slope of Mapalug Mountain, which was not much friendlier than the swamp.

Before I could reply, Father Cannon interjected, "During the war the Japanese believed the Allied forces would never pursue them beyond the swamp to the caves; but they did, closing in from two sides. It was during this action that Recon patrolled the divisional flanks, keeping them open and secure from any counterattacks."

I was impressed by Father Cannon's knowledge and asked him, "How do you know so much about this campaign?"

He only laughed and said, "Not all trips I make around the shores of Laguna de Bay entail just religious discussions. Much of the information I have received about the Luzon campaign is not in history books. Only the local Filipinos who lived through the war are familiar with the actual facts, including the accounting of collaborators who, depending upon who was offering awards at the time, often operated on both sides."

Our visit concluded. I thanked Father Cannon for the visit and information, although I already knew a great deal of it. Before I took leave of him I said, "I assure you I have no intention of crossing swamps or climbing mountains. Biking along the Laguna de Bay shore roads will be enough for the moment!"

I did not walk or ride up to the church that week. Instead, I rode around town. On one occasion I visited Alfredo and asked him to order tires and tubes for the bicycle. Another evening I casually asked Raul about the owner of the jeepney, which I had not seen since that first day.

He informed me that a Mr. Luis Estes, the owner, charged fares that the average Filipino could hardly afford.

The following Sunday I attended Mass, as usual. I met Father Cannon afterward and told him I was riding my bicycle to Baras in the morning to give my legs a tryout. He talked for a short while, mentioning the never-ending political rhetoric and painting a bleak picture of living standards in the Philippines. "The Church is their only hope," he said, "and has been for generations. They cling to it tenaciously because it is all they can call their own." His words burned in my brain all through the night.

I pumped the two-wheeler out of Morong on Monday morning, scattering the dust into miniature puffs along the road. Carabao wallowed in the mud holes, getting an early jump on the sun. I pedaled slowly, leaning forward into the sun. My pith helmet, which I purchased in Manila, deflected some of the glare from my eyes. It was a bright day with wispy clouds drifting lazily above the bay. Some of the children had run after my bicycle for a short distance, but now their childish giggles faded in the dust behind me. I thought, "Children are the same everywhere, unconcerned with the hidden trials of the world because they never bother to look for them. Little mars their innocent beliefs; consequently, they never create doubt about one another. Instead, they develop a firm attachment to thousands of fancies, which they fervently believe until the day arrives when their childhood realm is shattered."

Once past the cemetery the road climbed up and down, hugging the shores of Laguna de Bay. Occasionally it gently leveled. I was already farther along the road than I had been in 1945, although there was nothing new. The many rice paddies formed a checkerboard pattern for as far as I could see, eventually meeting the base of the mountains. Here and there, close to a paddy, was a granary.

Every now and then a rectangular field, which did not have the customary banks that line the rice paddies, came into view. Elongated rows, hundreds of feet long, ran the length of these fields, but no water was running through them. Later on I learned they were tobacco fields, the tobacco from which had been a good source of income since the aftermath of World War II. Even the tobacco did not greatly change the Filipino lifestyle, and it had not kept the young from escaping to Manila.

My thoughts momentarily kept me from thinking about the sun—no one escaped the sun. It was constant. I was beginning to feel its effect after traveling only about three miles. Although this was only a trial run I was already concerned with my effort. I could have hired the jeepney, but that would hardly have kept me in shape. If I had to travel where it could not, things could become difficult for me.

I regulated my pace, traveling at one speed on the level road then ped-aling faster so I could coast up the inclines for some distance before resorting to the harder pace. I coasted down every decline, and on every stretch of the road kept my head down. The pith helmet had a tendency to shift, so I pulled off the road into a small thicket of bamboo to fix it. It was cooler in the thicket where the sun could not penetrate; it glim-mered in and out between the swaying trunks in sudden bursts. I unfas-tened the waterproof musette bag, took out a bandana and tied it around my head. It took up the extra slack in my helmet and absorbed some of the sweat that had been running down my face. I resolved to buy a small towel at the first opportunity. I chuckled to myself for not having thought of this before now.

Back on the road again I came upon a rise, the highest point thus far and also my severest test since I sat on the bicycle; however, I appreciat-ed the long descent on the other side and coasted until my wind returned. This brought me to a bridge, which crossed the first river I had seen since the Morong River. In the distance I could see houses and a bend in the river that appeared to circle back, winding around to the north of the town I assumed was Baras.

After another mile and a half I rode into Baras. Suddenly the jeepney I had seen in Morong sped past me, leaving me gasping in the settling dust. I looked up just in time to notice what appeared to be a Japanese passenger. Then the jeepney was gone, heading back toward Morong. I dismissed the incident at the time, not realizing how many more times my path and that of the passenger would meet in the mystery that shadowed the hills surrounding this very town.

Including the time to fix my pith helmet, it had taken almost an hour to bicycle to Baras. Knowing how far I could push myself on this two-wheeler without overdoing it gave me some satisfaction. I also knew it would be impossible to maneuver a bicycle over these roads during the rainy season, which lasted almost six months.

After wandering around this small community for an hour I came across a roadside stand that had sweet potatoes and eggs for sale. It took me several minutes to negotiate a price because the vendor was more interested in me. Although I was not sure how much English he understood, I explained, "I was with the 43rd Division when it passed through Baras in 1945. Recon had driven their vehicles through this town and patrolled by foot into the hills." Just when I thought the English barrier was too much of a hassle, a middle-aged man sitting on a bench on the side of the road suddenly looked up; grinning from ear to ear, he stretched out his hand to me.

"Are you Whitey?" he asked.

I was astonished. No one had called me by that nickname, which I received in basic training in 1942, except the men of Recon.

"Yes, I am Whitey," I replied. As I extended my hand he grasped it and shook it with vigor equal to the elation on his face. "But I cannot recall having met you before. Do you remember the 43rd Division?"

"I am Rafael Gonsalves. Ah, yes. I used to live in Morong but now I live in Baras. Many years ago I was a guerrilla during the war. Do you remember when we took Father O'Reilly out of the hills and gave him food? I was twelve years old then."

From the first days of the Japanese occupation, thousands of Filipinos formed separate small guerrilla units and embarked upon a hit-and-run tactic that gave little peace to the invaders. The younger guerrillas, barely reaching their teens, began participating in the Luzon campaign when the 43rd landed in the Lingayen Gulf.

"I am surprised you still remember me," I said, "being only twelve at the time!"

He only grinned and replied, "Do you remember the evening when you passed by my house in Morong and Father O'Reilly had to call you back to make a visit? I remember well. My mother is Amanda Gonsalves." He grinned again as he recalled how I had embarrassed Father O'Reilly and his mother by passing by his house—a slight unacceptable to the Filipinos.

I had felt embarrassed myself and wondered how he could have such a keen recollection after all these years. I was twenty-four at the time, but at the moment I did not remember seeing him in Morong or with the band of guerrillas who had brought Father O'Reilly into camp. I did, however, remember a *dilag* with the group; although young, she had been armed to the teeth when they straggled into Recon's camp.

Although I wanted to ask about the dilag, I thought it safer to first inquire about his mother and casually ask a few general questions. Again, I knew better than to rush into any inquiries that might arouse suspicion.

"Rafael, how is your mother?" I asked. "Does she still live in Morong? And you? Are you married?"

"Never married," he laughed. "I live in Baras but go back to Morong once a month to visit my mother and relatives. She still lives in the same house on road to the church."

"I promise to visit her, then, when I return to Morong."

He grinned again and asked, "Are you staying in Morong?"

"I am not going to remain in Morong much longer and intend to go around Laguna de Bay, at least to Pililia," I explained.

"I have friends in Pililia. Do you need lodging? I will contact them for you."

"Thank you Rafael. If you could locate a friend there who could offer me board and lodging, it would be a great help." Actually, this was a tremendous break, knowing it would be difficult to obtain sleeping quarters on my own in the towns surrounding Laguna de Bay.

Then he grinned again and asked, "Do you remember a young dilag guerrilla, Hilaria Filio? She lives in Pililia too."

I thought this worth remembering.

Talking with Rafael eased some of the tension I had been experiencing since I left Manila. I had the feeling I could have taken him into my confidence, but I resisted the temptation. It was still too early to jeopardize any chance I had of coming up with some answers about Father Douglas. I wanted to pursue the conversation about the dilag, but I had to be content with letting things follow their own course.

The day was waning. Rafael pointed out the direction of his home and then assisted me in purchasing the sweet potatoes and eggs, which he seemed to enjoy with great enthusiasm.

"I had better attend to my return trip to Morong, Rafael. I will visit you upon my return," I assured him. He waved as I shoved off. Looking back I could see he was still flashing his cordial grin.

My first push on the pedals signaled a tightness and stiffness in my legs. Up to this point I had not realized how exhausting riding on a dirt road could be. With my head down but eyes looking straight ahead, I was able to avoid the ruts, of which there were many. This dodging was taking its toll. I would have to make frequent stops on the way back to avoid getting leg cramps. The sun had begun to descend in the west, which was a relief. On this excursion I had managed to avoid the heat of the day— a sound philosophy and good old common sense I would have to adhere to. Nevertheless, I was exhausted when I wheeled into Morong just before dusk, having covered approximately fourteen miles all told.

Fortunately I arrived back in Morong before complete darkness, which eased the worry of Raul and Alvita. They came around to the back porch and I could see the consternation in their faces. Of course they did not ask any questions and I was thankful. They were appreciative of my offering of potatoes and eggs and promised me a hearty breakfast. The bamboo bed was a welcome sight, and without hesitation I flopped upon it. I slept well that night even though I had not gone down to the river to bathe.

I had been on Luzon for almost a month and had made some friends. With the exception of Rafael, most of them appeared to have little connection with the events that had taken place in Paete or Pililia during the war. I hoped to be established in Pililia before the rains arrived, dreading the thought of being caught on the road in a steady downpour. Only the carabao enjoyed the weather then and the crops flourished.

I remained in Morong for a few more days despite the impending season. I still could not afford to arouse a sense of urgency or haste. I rode all over Morong. The clothes beaters on the banks of the river began to lift their heads and smile when I approached. When I purchased fruit and vegetables at their local stands, smiles of appreciation appeared. Some of the batas continued to chase my bicycle, and I began to recognize some of them by name. When they fell down in the chase, I stopped and wiped the tears from their eyes. In fits of laughter they held hands and scampered down the road. Yet, there was still a sense of apprehension in the adults, and I knew trust was a long way down the road I was traveling.

The sudden appearance of Rafael in Morong that Saturday afternoon surprised me. I had taken a spin west of Morong, intending to go to Cardona, a town I had passed through on the bus; however, I never

reached it. The sun would have become a torment long before I completed the trip, so I wheeled around and returned to Morong. The jovial
Rafael was talking to Mrs. Reyes at the front of her house as I
approached. I had not expected to see him until next week sometime, and
I almost revealed my delight at seeing him. However, I was quick to
recover before I displayed too much excitement in front of Mrs. Reyes, or
any of the others within earshot. I knew Rafael would be able to open
doors for me elsewhere, but I had no idea what the people of Morong
thought of him. I greeted him casually.

Rafael and I went to the back porch and into my room, where he sat
on the edge of the bed and I in the rocker. I became aware of Mrs. Reyes
lingering within hearing distance and never entering the kitchen all during his visit. The explicit questions burning in my mind would have to
wait. The situation demanded, once again, I remain patient. I would have
to get Rafael away from the probing eyes and out of earshot. Actually I
feared he might mention Hilaria, the dilag guerrilla, again, so I suggested we take an evening stroll around town. Even if I had innocently
quizzed Rafael or any Filipino about that particular band of guerrillas,
eyebrows would have been raised. Discipline against too much questioning in the early stage of my investigation might keep me from being completely shut out by the residents. Over and over again it would prove to
be the only method that netted positive results.

Mrs. Reyes offered Rafael her husband's bicycle, but he graciously
declined. He wanted to spend a few moments conversing with old friends
as we strolled around the town. He did not have to introduce me; by this
time everyone in Morong knew who I was.

I had casually mentioned to Mrs. Reyes that I had met Rafael in
Baras. She had briefly told me she knew he had been a member of the
guerrilla band that had brought Father O'Reilly out of the hills in 1945.
As she mentioned the word guerrilla, I saw in her eyes a flame of hope; I
sensed something in her expression, but I dared not ask her what.

Just before darkness we turned up the street that led to St. Jerome's
Church. Rafael's mother lived a few houses up on the left. A short,
unpainted bamboo fence faced the dusty road. Between the fence and the
house was a garden, all flowers. In the right corner, growing against the
bamboo slats, was a carefully tended tall red rosebush, which dominated

the garden. Rafael was curiously watching my admiration of it. His usual outgoing way became distant for a few seconds, but only when he gazed toward the roses. "My mother never picks roses from that bush. She just lets the petals fall to the ground. No one touches her roses, not even I," he sighed. It would be many months before I found out why. He called through the doorway to his mother, and she appeared in the doorway. No doubt she had recently watched me pedal past her rosebush, and I wondered how I could have been so preoccupied to have missed it.

Amanda Gonsalves was one of the most pleasant and devout women I had ever met. She was not any taller than the other women, but her carriage, even at sixty-two, made her appear as if she were. She walked erect and barely spoke above a whisper. She waved off the introduction with a slight flick of her hand. I recognized her instantly as one of the women I had seen in St. Jerome's. It was in this second meeting that I began to faintly recall being introduced to her by Father O'Reilly. Rafael mentioned my social error, when Father O'Reilly had to call me back to their house for fear of slighting his family. The three of us had a good laugh over it. It was ironic that after such a span of time the incident actually brought us closer together. I knew I was as welcome now as I had been thirty-two years ago when conditions were not as kind. When I mentioned Father O'Reilly she immediately blessed herself as she nodded her head. Some of her traits were noticeable in Rafael—they both had endured the Japanese occupation.

She smiled her faint smile as she recalled the Sunday when some of the men of Recon came to Mass and received Holy Communion. "Father O'Reilly," she said in broken English, "receive great pleasure you come. He spoke many times of it. Remember Mass when Japanese come in church. Wait for Father O'Reilly to end service. Feel much relief hearing guns of 43rd Division enter Morong. Japanese go from church fast." Mrs. Gonsalves watched me as I, too, recalled that Sunday with fondness.

"You come have good meal tonight," stated Mrs. Gonsalves. And go to Mass on Sunday with us." I gladly accepted. Rafael grinned again, "If I do not go to Mass with mother, she will not feed me! Same for you, too, Whitey!" and he laughed even harder. Their friendship increased my enthusiasm, although I held it to a minimum. I began to feel their trust in me increasing. It was a beginning.

No doubt Mrs. Gonsalves was eager to relive a little of the past and the old ways, and my chance meeting with Rafael in Baras had opened the door to communication all around. I spent a good deal of the evening with them, but before leaving I had to promise Mrs. Gonsalves that I would attend Mass on Sunday with her and Rafael. I then returned to the Reyes' house, where I prepared myself for my second entrance into St. Jerome's Church the following day.

I walked up to the great doors of the church with Rafael on one side and his mother on the other. Father Cannon greeted us at the door and we exchanged salutations. I felt a bit of relief being in the company of an elder of the town. Those in attendance appeared as if nothing unusual were taking place, even though I was blatantly noticeable. Father Cannon must have sensed my uneasiness and also that of the others, and he seized the opportunity during his homily to call for all to be neighborly. I think he was calling for acceptance on my behalf, but I was not convinced the others interpreted his homily in the same manner as I. When Mass was over I walked with my two new friends to their house. Mr. Reyes passed by and gave an abrupt wave, then hurried on. Not to be outdone, Mrs. Gonsalves rendered a noticeable wave as I left and headed down the road.

That evening, just before dusk, I went back to Mrs. Gonsalves's house for an enjoyable dinner of rice, sweet potatoes and chicken. During the meal I realized Rafael was watching me, and I sensed he knew there was more on my mind than routine conversation. After dinner he walked me back to my room, and I invited him to stay for a while longer.

"I have upcoming business in Pililia; I will find lodging for you," he said.

"I would appreciate that, Rafael."

"You can stay at my home in Baras, then take the jeepney to Pililia."

We decided to meet in Baras on Friday and finalized plans for the coming week. Knowing Mrs. Reyes was listening, I pretended to tap on the bamboo wall when we finished talking; Rafael did not have to be told she had an ear against the wall. We just grinned at each other, which improved our relationship that much more.

In the morning I informed Mrs. Reyes of my plan to leave for Baras on Friday, and thus not reveal her eavesdropping. I could not afford to offend her or Raul, as they were my source of shelter and possibly information in Morong. An elder in Morong, Baras, Pililia or Paete could be harboring knowledge of happenings that had taken place during the war, and one irresponsible word or misguided intention on my part could silence lips in towns and barrios.

I continued to ride the roads of Morong, trying to keep in shape as best I could. Twice before Friday arrived I had to seek out Alfredo for bicycle repairs, which became a concern—the bicycle being my only mode of travel. If the answers to my questions were farther down the Santa Cruz road, I had to maintain and coddle the bicycle the best I could; there were just too many lapses between jeepney connections in the towns and barrios.

That night I sought out Mrs. Reyes and paid her the rent. I said, "I do not know just when I will be returning, but I would like to stay here again on my return, if I may." She just waved her fingers at me in agreement. In the morning, after a satisfactory night's rest, I struck out for Baras again. There was no need to hurry this time; I would not be returning for a while, although I did wonder how long it would be. Hospitality was beginning to surface in Morong, and I hoped it would still be there when I returned.

I met Rafael at the *dampa* in the center of town. He had ridden a dilapidated old bicycle three miles from his house on the other side of town. Smilingly, he said, "I thought I might have to carry the bicycle!" He had a good sense of humor.

The dampa no longer had the esteem and importance it did prior to the war, but some of the town's elders still frequented the rough hut. I had been receiving the stoic treatment until Rafael arrived; when they realized we were friends the tension decreased. For the present Rafael served as a barrier against some of the hostility, but he would not always be at my side.

After a short conversation we pedaled back to his house, which was a typical Filipino structure set well back off the road. A minor stream trickled lazily through his rice paddy from a large bog. He pointed to it and said, "Black Swamp. The water comes only in the rainy season when the swamp swallows the rains from the mountains."

"I know of the Black Swamp," I replied, but did not go into any detail.

From his porch, looking northeast, I could see a line of hills. Beyond that, piercing the sky and sometimes with its crest lost in the clouds, loomed the largest pinnacle on Luzon, Mapalug Mountain. It towered over all its surroundings. The sun had already stretched over its peak, and from its flooding rays I could see the Laniti Valley, a long indentation stretching south of the great sentinel.

Rafael, standing beside me on the porch, suddenly became withdrawn as he gazed at the mountain in the clouds. In the short time I had known him, this was the first time I had caught him in anything but an outgoing mood. I sensed his sullenness immediately, but almost as quickly he sensed my awareness of it and made a slight gesture, a little wave of his hand similar to the motion Mrs. Reyes had made. He had waved in the general direction of the swamp and the mountain. For a few seconds I wondered why this scene had provoked him. Although I did not pursue his change of attitude, I did not forget it.

We went to Mass on Sunday in Baras. To my amazement Rafael served as an altar boy. On Monday Rafael caught the jeepney to Pililia. Between Baras and Pililia was another town, Tanay, which he suggested I visit before he returned. I accompanied him to the jeepney stop and waved to him as it pulled away. I also noted the same Japanese passenger I had seen in Morong on board.

The road between Baras and Tanay was flat, so I seized the opportunity to ride back and forth a few times. I also cycled several times in and around Baras to keep my legs as nimble as possible.

On Wednesday Rafael returned from Pililia, where he had looked up an old friend and established lodging for me if I decided to remain there for any length of time. There was an air of excitement about him. Rafael said, "I talked with Hilaria, now Mrs. Hilaria Augustine. She spoke of the time when the guerrillas brought Father O'Reilly out of the hills. She is anxious to meet you again."

"I would like to see her again, too," I responded. Then I casually asked him, "Do you know the Japanese passenger on the jeepney when you boarded on Monday?"

He replied, "I do not know his name, but I think he is with the Japanese rice contractors in Pililia." I added this information to storage.

Every morning for the next two weeks I sat on Rafael's rear porch and watched the violent storms buffet the mountains in the distance. It was late January 1977, months away from the monsoon rains, but there were still many cloudbursts and thunder reverberating through the high country.

In those weeks I began to understand Rafael and his mannerisms more fully. He was hesitant to discuss the plight of his people; he had accepted his lifestyle long ago. Rafael was a hard worker. He worked his rice paddy, which was much smaller than the others in the area; during the harvest, he hired himself out to the neighboring farms. He never mentioned why he had not married, and I did not intrude. He also gave me the impression that something lingered just out of his reach. He went out of his way to make my visit as pleasant as possible, and I knew that offering him a direct payment would be an affront to his generosity. I was most fortunate to have him as a friend.

During the second week in February we rode our bicycles into Baras and waited at the dampa for the jeepney. Leaving on Friday for Pililia meant the vehicle would be crowded with traveling relatives. Fortunately there were only a few bicycles tied to the rear and roof of the vehicle, and I was able to find a place for ours.

Emotion began to grip me as we left the Tanay stopover and headed toward Pililia. I escaped into silence and tried to prepare myself for the scene where the parishioners had last seen their white-cassocked padre, Father Douglas, alive. It was better to organize my emotions now rather than give them away under the surveillance of Rafael. Control was of the essence before the eyes of my seemingly unobservant company. I managed to keep an outward calmness—within I trembled.

A few miles out of Tanay we crossed over the great Laniti River on a bridge that had seen better days. Rafael said, "The Laniti begins many miles inland behind Mapalug Mountain. During the monsoon season the bridge shakes from the thunder of the Laniti. Many people and carabao have been swept down river into the bay; no one survives the current."

"Well I am glad it is not monsoon season, then," I replied.

Pililia was several times the size of Morong. In fact it was a miniature Manila, bustling with a throng of Filipinos and shops. The majority of the houses were raised three to four feet off the ground. Many had tin roofs, which outnumbered the bamboo roofs. Bicycles were everywhere, twisting in and around the pedestrians. Now and then a vintage auto rambled down the road gasping for life on the dusty thoroughfare. There was turmoil on the main street, or so it appeared. Dirty-faced children ran pell-mell, and carabao lumbered through the center of it all. I could see the squalor in some areas, again reminding me of Manila. The farther we penetrated into the heart of the town the better its appearance. I had no idea where the church was located in Pililia, but I began to watch for it. Most of the buildings were located east of the coastal road, fanning out toward the ever-silent Mapalug Mountain and the hills. The Black Swamp and Mapalug Mountain were twelve miles or so to the north of us, yet I could still see the great sentinel through the morning haze.

Vendors were everywhere, trying to eke out a living. Chickens darted in front of the jeepney. *Binatilyos* pedaled their bicycles in chariotlike races, reeling and rocking them in circles. "Boys are the same everywhere!" I thought. Women wore scarfs to shield their eyes, ears and hair from the road dust. Autos that still had a horn barked continually, but no one paid much attention to them. It was a busy Friday afternoon, but Luis carefully and patiently guided the jeepney through the noisy throng. Through the droning Filipino voices, barking dogs and bellowing drivers, I heard the chimes of the bell, the bell Father Douglas had rung from 1938 until the afternoon of July 24, 1943, the last day he had been seen alive by the inhabitants of Pililia.

It rang through the squalor and fervor of Pililia. High above the din and dirty faces it pealed into the day. I was not the only one aware of it, though, as I saw some women make a quick blessing. I listened to the last chime settling into the water. I was more mesmerized by the bell than the havoc around me and noticed Rafael was intently studying my expression. I avoided his stare. I wondered, "Was this the bell that had been calling me for thirty-two years?" I was not about to let the call go unheeded.

I did not see any church in sight, and I was sure we had not passed one. My thoughts were interrupted by Rafael, who pointed to what seemed to be a more elaborate section of the town, at least compared to the outskirts of Pililia. He said, "That is Hilaria's house, you know, the dilag guerrilla I mentioned before." Her home was on the bay side of the road, facing the Laniti Valley and the massive sentinel above it. The waves lapped at the shore beneath her porch to the rear. On we went, passing another rundown dampa whose purpose had withered with the passing of time. Still, there was no sign of a church.

Luis managed to edge his jeepney to the side of the road near a ramshackle building with an open front. When I stepped out I could see the back was also open and there was a clear view of Laguna de Bay. We retrieved our bicycles and turned them back toward Hilaria's residence. Children began to dart in front of my bicycle in a daredevil manner, tugging at my legs and waving fruits and vegetables at me. Rafael half-heartedly scolded them, but they paid him no heed. I saw their tattered clothes and thought of their tattered dreams. I wondered, "Did not all children dream of a better way? Did not a young crusader in a white cassock offer a better way to the children who were now the adults of this thriving community? How many of those adults, who were at this very moment jostling their way through the heat, remembered the vision of the man who had begun to put meaning into their own young lives." I succumbed to their wishes and pleading eyes and got off my bicycle and purchased a few items from them. Several binatilyos were chasing each other, arms pinned behind their backs and yelling something in Spanish.

"What is this game they are playing?" I asked.

Rafael replied, "They play the one-armed guerrilla, Clastres Bulatao." As usual, he did not go into any detail, but I recalled various references to a one-armed guerrilla who had established a herolike reputation long before, and which remained long after, the Allied invasion of Luzon. His clever tactics had astounded the Japanese Command to such an extent they had offered incentives to the Filipinos to betray him. The Japanese had called him "the shadow" and they had lived in fear of him.

Rafael urged me down the road. Until now he had not interfered with my transactions with the children, and I think it had amused him somewhat. He knew what it meant to earn an extra peso before the sun went down; he had traveled that road. We came to a stop in front of Hilaria's well-constructed bamboo-framed house, which I noticed did not have a tin roof, as many of the others had. Hilaria was an elder and therefore resided among the better houses close to the center of Pililia. There were three steps to her front door, which was open.

I had not dismounted from my bicycle when Rafael came quickly to my side, leaned close to me, and whispered, "It is better not to think out loud because she will hear you!" I thought this to be a strange comment but made no reply.

I braced myself, mindful of Rafael's words, but before I could place my foot on the first step a woman whose carriage was reminiscent of Mrs. Gonsalves's appeared quickly in the doorway. It almost seemed as if she had heard my step before I had taken it. I had never seen a woman with such quickness. She stared down at me, her dark eyes piercing mine.

"You are Whitey," she said, with no doubt apparent in her voice, and beckoned both of us into her bamboo dwelling. There was a litheness to her; it seemed as if she would disappear if I did not keep my eyes upon her. She lacked the gentleness of Rafael's mother but not the kindness. Despite my protest she prepared a meal for us, so I offered her the produce I had purchased, which was received graciously. She had a good command of the English language; to avoid being rude she addressed Rafael in English.

Hilaria, whose age I was finding difficult to determine (Rafael informed me later that she was fifty-one), was married to Ramon Augustine, who owned and operated a rice granary with Juan Demala in the southern end of Pililia. "I am sorry my husband is not here to join us," she said. "He will not be home until later this evening." This is all she said. She did not seem to want to converse before or during the meal, so I patiently waited until we were through eating.

"Rafael," she demanded, "you and Whitey go sit on the rear porch until I am finished cleaning up here."

"Please, let me help you; it is the least I can do after such a delicious meal," I pleaded.

"I will have no part of that," she politely but sternly insisted.

Rafael and I went to the porch. I welcomed the protection from the midday sun and enjoyed the breeze coming off the water of Laguna de Bay. I did not envy the occupants of the bobbing skiffs, which were too numerous to count.

Finally Hilaria came out to join us and we thanked her for the meal. She gave that little characteristic wave of her fingers, a signal she was pleased, then sat facing the bay. After several more minutes, which to me was an awkward silence but not to a Filipino, she turned to me.

"I am glad, Whitey, you have chosen to come back to visit our people. I remember well the good padre, Father O'Reilly, and those days when he hid in fear for his life. Sometimes it seems like only yesterday, and sometimes, when I cross the road and see the hills, it seems so long ago. Perhaps I should never go back to those places and the memories that live in them. Many times I think of your friends, the Recon men, and many times in the hours of the night I remember the brave soldiers of the 43rd who drove the arrogant ones out of our lives."

She paused as if something else had crossed her mind, and I saw a slight eye movement in the direction of Rafael. It was just a flicker but enough to convey another message. It was also enough to make Rafael scan Laguna de Bay without purpose; he was pondering, and not over the lazily drifting vessels. Hilaria arose, and in one flowing motion was standing beside the screen, gazing at the shimmer of the spreading ripples.

"Over there," she said, pointing with a quick motion northwest across the water toward Morong, "was the place where we found joy for the first time in over three years. We waited patiently in the hills until we heard the echoes of the guns coming across that peninsula, and we raised our rifles to the sky for the first time since the armada landed in Lingayen. We did not sleep well for many nights until we heard the fall of Manila over the radio. Not a bamboo pole remained standing in Antipolo. Poor Antipolo. Such sacrifice was made there. It was then we knew you were coming and it was no longer a dream. We slept beneath the sun and in the shadows until the arrogant ones fled into the hollows of the mountains. In the hours of darkness we took Father O'Reilly, the gentle padre of Morong, and hid him in the bosom of the hill so there would be no more sacrifices. We guarded him with our lives because he saved our souls and listened to us under the point of the bayonet. What more can I say except this man with the red hair was good."

Then she gazed wistfully again toward the shores of Laguna de Bay, where, at that moment, the women of Morong were pounding clothes against the rocks. "There are not many who know," she said. With this Rafael glanced quickly at her. However, this time she did not give him that slight eye movement.

"We had traveled many miles from our camp," she continued, "far, far above the Laniti Valley where the eagles fly. Preparations had been made for what had to be done long before the Americans arrived in Lingayen. Day by day there was more danger for Father O'Reilly, but he did not tremble, which brought great admiration from his followers. Our friend here, barely a binatilyo then," and she gestured toward Rafael, "sought us out and asked us to rescue Father O'Reilly from under the noses of the arrogant ones. One of our guerrilla runners also came and told us the Japanese soldiers had waited for Father O'Reilly at the front of the church. We agreed, of course, to rescue him; otherwise, he would have been in great danger from the Japanese when they reached Morong. Rafael was sent back into Morong to prepare Father O'Reilly for the hour and place of his escape. He had much fear for his parishioners; his love for them was so great. The Japanese, however, were too occupied in escaping into the hills, where they had many implements, to be concerned about the priest or his parishioners. There was much joy because no one suffered because of this action."

Some of this I knew through other guerrillas when we had met them on patrol in 1945, but I had no idea of the part Rafael had played in the rescue. I wondered, "What else did these two loyal Filipinos know that I did not?" When the guerrillas brought Father O'Reilly back to Morong several days later, they remained in camp only a few moments and then were in pursuit of the fleeing Japanese. There had been little time to talk, and I only vaguely remembered this band of guerrillas. I would probably never have paid any attention to them at all except one of them was a young Filipino dilag, laden with a rifle, grenades and determination. Even now, after all these years, Hilaria had not changed except in age. She moved as quickly and her eyes and mind were just as alert. There was still a determination in her manner, as there was in Rafael's. I suppose this quality was instilled in them, stemming from the days when they were guerrillas who were prepared to give their lives at any given moment. Perhaps there were other motivations that had inspired their determination, even when they knew capture would have meant torture and sometimes, slow death. On the other hand, maybe the persecutions of the centuries, and pending ones, kept their spirits alive in a frail culture. They were not void of the hostility simmering out of reach; it was an inherent heritage. Their past experiences, however, taught them how to subdue the urge to release anger—not to do so would have meant bitter subjugation.

Curb and control was their policy, even to the taking of one unnecessary step on the way to freedom.

In the final stages of the war on Luzon, guerrillas were activated into divisions as the curtain began to close on the Japanese defenses, but there were many groups of guerrillas that acted independently. Hilaria's band was one of them, and they finished their marauding and harassment only when the last Japanese defender had been sealed in the Kalinawan Caves.

During our conversation I sensed Hilaria was controlling her thoughts. I thought of what Father Doyle had told me about the reticent attitude of the Filipinos concerning the burial of Father Douglas and their mute response to any reference to it. Maybe it was just my sensitivity to this reticent attitude that was causing me to overreact. Perhaps they were more suspicious of me than I of them. I had the feeling they were searching me out. I wondered what their reaction would be if they discovered the real reason why I was in Laguna de Bay.

Rafael had avoided entering the conversation to any degree. Hilaria, being an elder, had the right to speak. I was convinced Rafael did not want to participate in any discussion about those hectic days anyway, the memories being enough.

Rafael had mentioned to me earlier that he had told Hilaria about the close relationship I had with Father O'Reilly and my numerous visits to the church when Recon was camped in the cemetery outside of Morong. Undoubtedly this had inspired her to elaborate on the rescue of Father O'Reilly more than on the other guerrilla activities.

In turn, I talked about the part Recon played in the defeat of the Shimbu Line and the overall drive of the 43rd Division through the Morong and Laguna Provinces. Hilaria kept nodding her head in assent as those memories were reborn, and I could see the pain and fierceness in her dark eyes. She appeared ready to spring into the shadows, as she must have done so many times during those vague and doubtful years. When she moved around the porch, she was as quick as the burst of a sunbeam. She was brisk but not abrupt, sure but not arrogant—and she had beautiful carriage.

During our conversation, with the exception of Rafael, she referred to no other guerrilla involved in the movement, and I thought this quite strange. She also used "we," which aroused my curiosity again, but I continued to bite my tongue. The words of Father Doyle in Manila were beginning to haunt me, and his warning about the Filipino impassiveness was ringing true. I had the feeling it was even stronger here than in Manila.

More than a month had passed without progress in my quest. I had managed to meet only five Filipinos who might have an awareness of what happened to Father Douglas in Pililia and Paete, and not one of them had given me an inkling. The very fact that nothing was being said about Father Douglas convinced me the subject was being avoided. What was it going to take to pry up the lid of secrecy in Laguna de Bay and defuse the suspicion of those whom I already considered my friends?

Rafael noticed me wandering off in my own thoughts and suggested we all take a walk down to the shore. "You go on without me," said Hilaria, "I have a few things to attend to before I prepare the evening meal, which, of course, I expect you both to stay for." She then got up and went into the kitchen. We both knew it was futile to argue and went out through the porch doorway and down the steps. To the right of the steps I saw a rosebush identical to the one in Rafael's mother's garden. It was just as beautiful. Rafael was ahead of me and did not observe my hesitation; however, when I looked up, Hilaria, who had gone into the kitchen, was now standing silently behind the porch screen and instantly caught my interest in the bush. She had reinforced my suspicion of her suspicions. I did not mention the rosebush to either her or Rafael, and I also did not pretend I had not seen her reaction to my hesitancy.

She must have been a formidable foe to the Japanese.

Standing on the shore Rafael asked me, "Do you remember the day when the Japanese soldiers came up the bay in a skiff and landed on the west side of the upper peninsula, just below Morong?" He shook his head as if in disbelief.

"I recall it well," I replied, "and the excitement it caused, especially in the eyes of Father O'Reilly, with whom I had spent the day. The Japanese had burrowed behind an embankment, and even though Recon had them surrounded within minutes, they refused to surrender."

Rafael shook his head again at the stupidity of it and murmured something about the Rising Sun. As we turned back toward the house Hilaria instantly appeared, and I looked at Rafael quickly. Jokingly he repeated, although softly, "Not good to think out loud!" Hilaria, who had heard him, gave a flitting smile and once again was gone before I could put my foot on the first step.

We came back into the house and found a light meal had been prepared for us. Rafael had informed her earlier that we had to establish lodging for the night and would have to leave before dark. In the middle of the meal she raised her head slightly. I then heard the bell of St. Mary Magdalene's for the second time. It was as if she knew the exact second of the day and heard the twang of the rope as the bell ringer pulled on it. This time I gave no indication I had heard the bell and concealed my feelings over the sound of it.

After thanking Hilaria and saying good-bye—with a promise to return, of course—Rafael and I returned to the marketplace. The hubbub had not diminished in the least, but my friend knew his way around it. I followed him onto the coastal road and up a side street where the noise of the vendors and buyers was not as loud. He stopped in front of a fashionable-looking house with a tin roof, and then we went inside. There I was introduced to Mrs. Temporado, whose manners were similar to Hilaria's but not as brisk. She was as considerate, though, and Rafael and I came to terms with her on a room for both of us. Rafael would not return to Baras until the jeepney made the final run late Sunday, which meant he would be here to attend Mass with me and thereby eliminate my having to locate the church on my own. Again Rafael's presence prevented me from being too obvious in the eyes of the local residents, at least temporarily. A time had to come, sooner or later, when I would have to be more aggressive in my search.

Saturday morning we rode our bicycles back to the coastal road and mingled with the weekend throng, which had grown larger than on the previous day. I did not mention the church; I knew that Rafael, in his own good time, would lead me to it. Once again I wished there were some way I could penetrate the barrier that was hindering a solid relationship with these people. This difficulty was on my part, not theirs. They had established a firm commitment through the years and shared this secret for more than three decades—the longer they kept it the firmer it became.

My hope of seeing the church this day never materialized; however, I heard its bell peal at five o'clock, and the sound came from the south of

Hilaria's house. While in her house I was not sure of the direction, but out in the open, there was no mistaking it. Tomorrow I would put the print of my shoe in that of Father Douglas's.

I spent another restless night in my new abode. Toward morning there was a sudden deluge of rain pounding the roof relentlessly, but by early dawn the storm had swept into the bay. It was a reminder of the upcoming season; there would be muddy roads this Sunday in the town of Pililia.

I was awake when Rafael called out to me, but I pretended I was not. I did not want him wondering why I had been awake half the night. He offered no explanation for the early awakening and probably figured attending Mass was understood on my part. His call triggered my anticipation of seeing St. Mary Magdalene's Church for the first time. This church would become the center of my search, and I was now convinced the answers that were eluding me were hidden in the shadows of Pililia. Rafael shoved off on his bicycle through the muddy puddles, and I likewise. We went south, passing Hilaria's house on the way. We rode into the first ring of the bell that was calling the Filipinos to Sunday Mass.

We had not ridden very far beyond Hilaria's home, about a half mile, when St. Mary Magdalene's Church came into view. The sight of it was depressing. Unlike the stately St. Jerome's in Morong, the deteriorated old outside walls contained many cracks and hurried patchwork. Some of the slates were missing from the roof, and there were visible cracks in the stained-glass windows. Two steps led up to the usual heavy plated doors. Directly above the front of the church, where the roof came to a point, protruded the cross. It hovered over the parishioners entering through its portals, just as the Mapalug poised above the Black Swamp. St. Mary Magdalene's also served as a silent sentinel, gently summoning all to seek refuge. Above and to the rear of the cross, its roof shielding the bell, was a forlorn-looking belfry.

As we passed the right side of the church, I glanced toward the place where I had been told Father Douglas had last been seen alive in Pililia. There, thirty to forty feet from the side door, conspicuously nestled in a mud puddle, was a weather-beaten bamboo wreath. People passed it silently and carefully; some of the elders gave it a quick glance, but no one went within five feet of it. It was as if it were on sacred ground. The report from the Columban Order had never mentioned this and it caught me by surprise. To see that Father Douglas was still alive in the hearts of some of these Filipinos, and had been kept alive for years, was most gratifying. Whether or not the wreath was placed there every year made little difference. It was there at the moment, proving Father Douglas was still lodged in the minds of the Filipinos in Pililia, or at least in the mind of one of them.

The bell began tolling steadily, signaling the approach of Mass. I gazed up to where the bell was shuddering in the confines of the belfry and could barely see one arm of the bell ringer, who, I assumed, had a clear view up the street directly across from the church. This street was lined with better-than-average homes. Whatever affluence existed in Pililia seemed to be centered close to the church.

Rafael and I parked our bicycles and approached the old doors, which were being guarded by Father Jose Demato, who was introduced to me by Rafael. We did not converse because there were too many parishioners crowding into the church. After taking seats halfway down the aisle, I suddenly became aware there was very little eyebrow raising, but figured it was because there were several other foreigners in attendance. We stood up when Father Demato approached the altar. He had a limp that was as noticeable as his piety. I found myself wondering about the limp and the age of this pious man who was telling us, "We must all have hearts as soft as a rose even though we, too, are beset by the thorns in life."

After Mass we whiled away part of the day, seeing some of Rafael's friends. He waved to many others, and I could not help but notice how popular Rafael was in Pililia, not only with those his age but also with many older than he, although he did not reside here. I suddenly realized his popularity had been as great in Morong and Baras; here in Pililia, though, it exceeded that of both those towns.

"Rafael," I exclaimed, "you are as popular as the elders in town!" He grinned with embarrassment and replied, "Do not let them hear you say that." We both laughed, and I looked around and expected to see Hilaria, remembering Rafael's words about how well she could hear. Actually, I was hoping Rafael would make mention of her, but as usual he said nothing. His silence only left me with more speculation. Perhaps his activity in the guerrilla movement had something to do with his popularity.

"I am going to catch the jeepney soon; I have to go back to Baras," he said.

"I enjoy our friendship, Rafael, and it has certainly helped me adjust in Morong, Baras and here in Pililia. Because you are by my side others have let me in, even if it is only a little. Meeting Hilaria and some of your friends has made me feel welcome in this town. This would not have been possible without you." I did not want to embarrass him too much and said, "I have no definite schedule and will wait until you return."

"You are a good friend, too, Whitey. I am glad you came back to the Philippines. I will be back soon." He extended his hand and I grasped it and shook it with vigor equal to the elation on both our faces.

Rafael caught the jeepney back to Baras, and I was on my own again. I decided to wait until morning to venture out into the thoroughfare of Pililia.

In Rafael's absence I tried to conceive some sort of strategy for penetrating the silence surrounding the death of Father Douglas, although I hardly knew where to begin. Returning to the scene of the wreath was out of the question for now. If I approached the bamboo wreath, there would be little doubt that its maker, or those connected to the dedication of it, would be advised of my curiosity within a short time. I strongly suspected Hilaria would hear of it first, and Rafael before his return. With this in mind I rode past the church without turning my head and headed south on the coastal road.

About a mile beyond the edge of town the road suddenly swung sharply to the right in a more direct southerly direction. Heading straight ahead at this bend was an old abandoned road, which ran a definite course across the top of the lower Jalajala peninsula in Laguna de Bay. I could not recall seeing it on any of the maps. Perhaps the cost of maintaining the derelict swath was too much of a burden on the already oppressed inhabitants. I made a mental note to study the maps a little more closely when I returned to Manila.

Ahead there was nothing but a long ride beyond the bend in the main road, so I decided to return to the center of Pililia. I would accomplish more by being observed looking at sights in Pililia proper than wandering around. I began to think I was becoming paranoid about being seen doing anything.

The weekend hustle had virtually disappeared from the center of town but the muddy roads had not. In some places the milling populace had turned the road into a quagmire, and I knew I would have to face the same when the rainy season began in earnest. Present conditions did not seem to bother the civilians. Children were running through the mud in ecstasy, the "professional cyclists" were maneuvering without the slightest difficulty.

I headed up the street directly across from the belfry of St. Mary Magdalene's; it was a mile-long straightaway with fine houses lining it. As I rode in the direction of the Laniti Valley, shacks and shanties replaced the houses. Nearly a mile from the church the street died abruptly, directly in front of a cemetery. Both cemeteries of Morong and Baras could be placed easily in one corner of this burial ground, and some of the gravestones were much more elaborate. I dismounted and entered the consecrated resting place. There was no gate at the entrance, just a simple arch made of bamboo stretching across the beginning of a twenty-foot-wide unpaved walkway that ran through the center of the hallowed ground. Rows of gravestones lined both sides of the path. Looking down the walkway, which appeared to be about a hundred yards long, I could see a white picketed circle at the end of the path. My curiosity brought me to it. I walked into the circular fenced area to find a beautifully masoned stone with the finest glazed surface I had seen on Luzon. I had seen none like it in Morong or Baras, nor was there another in this cemetery. More surprisingly than the memorial itself were the thirty-four red-tinged wooden rose replicas, all magnificently hand carved and circled around the headstone. The inscription read, "Francisco Gonsalves, 1913—1943, A Bell Ringer, Died July 29, 1943."

Roses, hundreds of them wilted and some of them fresh, were strewn around the memorial. Plainly, there was more than one rosebush in Pililia. Father Douglas had presumably died on July 27. This epitaph surrounded by roses indicated Francisco Gonsalves had died two days later. I wondered if there were a connection between the deceased and Rafael; if there were, it may become my first real opportunity to get beneath the masks camouflaging the secrecy of Laguna de Bay.

Francisco Gonsalves was thirty years old when he died. I was curious as to why "bell ringer" was important enough to have been inscribed on his gravestone, a very select one, and one which had been definitively erected as to remain in constant view. It was not only the name Gonsalves that sparked my interest, but the number of roses that seemed to be sprinkled ceremoniously within the enclosure. Not another gravesite had such an exhibition, although there were a few roses placed on some of them. The words by Father Demato in Sunday's homily, "We must all have hearts as soft as a rose even though we, too, are beset by the thorns in life," echoed in my ears. The Columban Order had told me Father Douglas had also reflected on the flower in his homilies for years until his death.

Further investigation revealed a path, which was wide enough for two people to walk abreast, hidden beneath the roses. It was a miniature esplanade running around the inside of the picket fence. A weatherworn bamboo cross rested at the foot of the monument, looking forlorn and lost in the dismal surroundings. When I turned to exit from the shrine, I observed a woman standing fifty feet away at another site, silently watching my every move. I was sure the grapevine would be well informed of my interest in the memorial.

By the end of the week I had the boundaries and sights of Pililia firmly implanted in my mind. It was the mental attitudes that I could not grasp, for they were without boundary. I missed Rafael and the connection he gave me to the communities we came in contact with. I waited for his return, and that did not happen until he caught the last jeepney run out of Baras on Saturday night.

As soon as I greeted him I detected a withdrawal. His joviality was subdued enough for me to tread lightly.

"I am glad you have come back to Pililia, Rafael. Bicycling around town is not the same without you."

"Hello Whitey. I visited with Hilaria again. I have some business to attend to now, but I will be back later and we can make plans for Sunday Mass."

"Ok, I will see you when you return," I replied. Although Rafael was usually of few words, it was unlike him to be curt.

He left me alone with too many questions whirling around in my head: had the grapevine sped to Baras? Did he know I had been to the cemetery and had seen the gravestone with the name Gonsalves inscribed on it? Instead of letting his mood irritate me I was inwardly ecstatic over his behavior.

I had retired for the evening when Rafael returned. Without turning over I could tell he was sitting on the edge of his bed, but I was too tired from the day's cycling to begin a conversation. After Mass tomorrow we could resume our relationship on a friendlier note. Perhaps during the day I would discover what was bothering him and thus put an end to my insistent speculations.

In the morning we bicycled to church. During this homily Father Demato did not refer to roses, as he had in his previous discourse. When Mass was over I said to Rafael, "I would like to wait at the entrance of the church and converse with Father Demato." Rafael looked surprised. "I will join you, Whitey," replied Rafael.

We approached Father Demato, who greeted us in English. "It is a pleasure to see you attend St. Mary Magdalene's, Rafael. And you have returned with your friend who has attended Mass in your absence."

"Yes, do you remember Whitey? I mean Patrick Corbin? Father," asked Rafael.

"Please Father Demato, call me Whitey. I am becoming accustomed to hearing the sound of my old army nickname."

"Yes, I heard mention that you were with the 43rd Division when they came through Morong. Of course," and he sighed, "this was before I was ordained into the Columban Order." This statement brought on my own brow raising. If either Rafael or Father Demato had noticed, they did not let on. He continued, "I was originally assigned to Leyte until 1959, then was reassigned to the Pililia parish the same year; this is my eighteenth year at St. Mary Magdalene's."

"I do not want to keep you any longer, Father. I will be back next Sunday, as usual; hopefully, Rafael will be able to accompany me again."

Rafael and I parted from the congenial priest and went back to Mrs. Temporado's house. Rafael's eyebrows had not settled back as yet, and I was hoping he would ask me about the cemetery. He did not. I had a strange suspicion we were both waiting for the other to give a definite sign of our intentions. Still, his avoidance and curiosity could not be restrained forever.

I waited, but in the waiting there was a lot of biking and waving. He did not have to return to Baras for a week, so he decided to keep company with me during his stay. During the week we managed to visit Hilaria on two occasions, and in her usual manner, gave no indication she had heard of my rendezvous in the cemetery. Rafael's mood improved as the week wore on, and he sounded surprised yet impressed to learn how much I had discovered in Pililia.

It was now the latter part of February. Rafael had come and gone many times over. I reached the point where I did not care how many times I was seen at the cemetery. I visited it often—each time I would find a fresh rose in front of the memorial, which puzzled me that much more. I decided to arrive just before dawn one morning, but even then the rose was already in place. "There is a light sleeper in Pililia," I thought.

Mrs. Temporado had been watching me closely since my arrival in Pililia. This was not unusual; after all, she was my landlady. She was also a devout Christian, president of the Legion of Mary, and Father Demato's laundress. Moreover, I was getting accustomed to this scrutiny. She seemed to become markedly nervous when I returned from my frequent visits to the cemetery, especially on the day when I left before dawn. Eventually I gave up trying to solve the mystery of the rose, as there were no answers coming from the silence of the stones.

One day in the middle of my frustrations, Mrs. Temporado gently knocked on my bamboo door and beckoned me into her spotless kitchen.

"I am old," she said in her broken English, "and tired this day and unable to carry box of clothes to rectory. Please take it. Tell good padre, still one cassock missing. We must find soon, or moment be gone forever."

With these words she scurried out to her garden, leaving me startled and surprised. I realized instantly the concern, desperation and definite appeal in her voice. Mrs. Temperado was aged but far from immobile. At the river, which was a mile from her house, she would pound the clothes incessantly at the side of the others. She knew I was well aware of her capabilities. Whatever her reason for sending me on this errand, I seized the opportunity, one that would bring me to the church, and perhaps, closer to the wreath of bamboo and the burial site of the young missionary who once sat on the bench near the church listening to the snap of the bamboo while he dangled the rosary beads between his calloused fingers.

Father Demato was not in the rectory or anywhere in the church when I arrived. One of the ever-present women in the church finally motioned out the window and to the grounds outside. I saw him sitting on the bench with a set of rosary beads in his hands. A surprised expression appeared on his face when he noticed what I was carrying, but he recovered quickly.

"Hello Whitey, how are you this day?" he asked.

"I am fine Father. I apologize for interrupting your prayers."

With a smile he gave the usual flick of the fingers. Somehow I sensed my opportunity.

"Father," I began, "Mrs. Temperado says she is old and unable to deliver the box. She also said to remind you there is still one cassock missing, and the moment to find it will soon be lost forever."

Father Demato was not good at hiding his feelings, as another surprised expression was triggered from this seemingly simple request from an elder. "I see Mrs. Temporado has a need for a new messenger," he said. "But it is unlike her to include someone from outside the community in the mystery of the missing cassock."

"Maybe this simple request is her way of telling you, and me, I am finally being accepted here, Father."

He looked away, knowing as well as I that she was not too old and could have taken the box to him. He turned his head back and looked over my shoulder and up the street toward Mapalug Mountain and the Laniti Valley. "Perhaps it is time," he said with a sigh.

"Time for what, Father?"

He lowered his head and blessed himself. "Time to find the cassock."

Although Mrs. Temporado had spoken similarly of the cassock, his words still startled me. For a brief second a little grin spread over the face of this pious man. Then in a more serious mood he motioned me to follow him. We went up the walk on the side of the church to where the bamboo wreath was now covered with dust. There was a fresh rose in the center of it. The words and phrases of Father Demato's homilies began to echo in my ears. Upon reaching the wreath we both paused, and the padre gazed upon it for a minute or so. I did not interrupt his thoughts and waited for him to make any overtures about the content of the message or about the symbolic wreath.

None was forthcoming. After contemplating the soiled garland and making certain I had observed it, he put his hand on my shoulder. "Please tell Mrs. Temporado I will do my best to find the missing cassock," he said, "and if I am fortunate to do so I will make it known to her. Tell her to inquire of the others if they might know where it has been misplaced."

"I will give her your reply, Father."

I took the message back to Mrs. Temporado, who was outside tending her rose bush. She only gave me a nod but also displayed a sense of relief. I assumed the "others" to whom Father Demato referred were the women who performed various duties in the church. His reference to being "fortunate" left me in a quandary. Mrs. Temporado must have already contacted the other church workers about the missing cassock, so there would be no need for him to do so. I was convinced further developments would have to come through the padre.

The lack of information about the missing cassock frustrated me as much as the mystery of the roses that appeared in specific locations. I was certain Mrs. Temporado knew who placed the roses, which is why that person knew when to visit the cemetery.

On my bicycle excursions I saw many rosebushes, most of them blooming beside the houses of the elders, although not as elegantly as those of Mrs. Gonsalves's, Mrs. Temporado's or Hilaria's bushes. "There seems to be a sense of purpose in cultivating such exquisite plants," I thought. "Is the rose serving as a reminder of something from their youth, when uncertainty reigned from dawn to dawn and Father Douglas's words of roses their only hope? This man of the cloth, had he salvaged their dreams with his oratorical courage, uttered beneath the rattle of the sword? Do they cultivate and cherish the thoughts he had bequeathed to them, even under the cloud that greets them in the gray dawns? Roses, hopes and memories will survive if there are lifelines; hopefully, there are those who were inspired by Father Douglas still in Pililia and Paete."

It was time to see Paete. I had to decide whether to go there with or without Rafael. My interest in churches and bells thus far coincided with my ventures with Recon; however, since Recon had not traveled as far as Paete, I wondered if my going to Santiago Apostol, the church where Father Douglas underwent the torture by the Japanese, would arouse his suspicion. To exclude him from my endeavor at this stage of my search would do me more harm than good. Moreover, the grapevine would inform him within a day or two—such a visit could not be kept a secret.

After a few nights of tossing and turning, I decided to inform Rafael of my intention. Because his visits had been tapering off, I had begun to wonder if he had not already concluded that I was on a private mission and had thus begun to shun me. This might well be my last opportunity to hold on to Rafael. Come what may, I was going to Paete to see the last place where Father Douglas had been seen alive.

Another week went by and still no Rafael, so I went to the jeepney stop to see if Luis would leave a message with the elders who still gathered at the dampa in Baras. On a return trip he brought back the news that Rafael would come. He arrived a few days later in a jovial mood, although I thought it a bit strained. To ease some of the tension I felt between us, I said, "Paete will be the last town I intend to visit. Will you go with me?"

"I have friends in Paete, too. I will go with you," replied Rafael.

"I assumed you had friends there, since you have them everywhere else!" I exclaimed. He gave me that big grin, which I had not seen for a while.

Rafael said, "We can be there and back in one day. We will take the midmorning jeepney run to Paete and leave our bicycles in Pililia. It will be dark when we return."

"I will ask Mrs. Temperado to give you lodging." I replied.

Rafael continued, "I will be catching the early morning bus back to Baras." I tried not to show my disappointment in his having to go back so early.

We caught the midmorning jeepney run. When we passed St. Mary Magdalene's at the beginning of the ride, I glanced at my friend, wondering if he had been informed of the meeting with Father Demato and my first close-up view of the bamboo wreath. He gave no sign that he had, which of course did not mean he had not. He did not look toward Hilaria's house when we rode past it either. When we came to the bend in the road where we would turn directly south toward the point in the peninsula, Rafael pointed to an abandoned road that ran through the bamboo growth across from the bend and nonchalantly explained, "This road was made across the top of the peninsula by the Japanese during the war. It saved them time in bringing ammunition and equipment to Pililia, Baras, Tanay, Paete and Santa Cruz. Heavy air bombardment and artillery fire demolished the makeshift road; it was then no good for the Japanese. After the war, it cost too much to repair the road; it is no longer any good."

The road to Paete was dusty and potholed. Rice farms were visible to the left as we headed south, and Laguna de Bay was visible to the right through the bamboo. Down the coast we rolled amid the jabbering of passengers and drone of the motor. Some of the riders seemed to know him well, but he did not leave his seat beside me.

I said, "I am glad you could make the trip with me, Rafael. I hope you get to see some of your friends in Paete."

"Maybe on every corner," he laughed.

When we reached the southernmost point of the peninsula, it appeared the jeepney would run straight into the bay, but the hairpin curve shot us up the coastal road in a northeasterly direction. After traveling several miles, the shore to the right began to curl inward, and Rafael explained, "This is the narrowest place on this side of peninsula."

I could see the tall nipa grass becoming thicker on the side of the road. I said, "The nipa grass could easily conceal a man." He made no comment.

Soon we began to pass the customary walkers, indicating the approach to the town. Carabaos plodded along here and there, and some of the cyclists waved to the occupants of the jeepney. As usual, several people waved as they recognized my friend.

Once again the disparity of outlying nipa huts and homes on the outskirts was evident. The antiquated church, Santiago Apostol, suddenly appeared. It had stucco top sections setting on huge slabs of stone that supported the main body of the church. As with the church in Pililia, this one was badly in need of repair, and the belfry hardly seemed strong enough to support the suspended bell. The patched slate roof had also seen better days. Yet, in its dismal appearance, there was also a solemnity.

The better-built homes were located within view of the old Spanish doors. On the other side of the road was the usual dampa. I wondered if the elders still recalled those days when the fear of Japanese troops kept the church doors closed as they huddled within the interior, the only refuge existing during the occupation.

The jeepney stopped in front of the church and we got off. Near the front doors two pieces of bamboo, shaped into a crude cross, were lying almost buried in the dust. I had no doubt about its meaning: lying in the back of a truck, this was the last place Father Douglas was ever seen alive.

Rafael made certain when we left the jeepney that he was behind me. I quickly realized he wanted me to see the dust-covered memorial. I was being scrutinized. Without hesitation I walked through the open doors and into the echoes of muttered prayers still drifting within the walls of this old Spanish church. The memories were still here. The altar and the figure of Christ above it were silent witnesses to what had transpired here many years ago. However, the post immediately to my left became the center of my attention. This pole, splintered with age, had secured the young Columban missionary to an ordeal that had lasted three days and three nights. It was now within my reach. This pole and another to the right ran fifteen feet up to a beam that supported the choir loft directly above the hallowed site. Ten feet up the pole of sacrifice a bamboo branch was fastened in a horizontal position, forming a cross. In the center of the cross, a bamboo wreath (a replica of the one beside the church in Pililia) was another reminder of the past. It was secured to the cross with thorn-laden branches in a crown-shaped appearance; it was decorated with roses. Tied to the post and dangling waist high, was a symbolic piece of rope trembling in the shadows as the breeze caught it.

I imagined I could hear the gentle sounds of rosary beads as they rustled and fell between the fingers of the man who prayed for the souls of his tormentors. I reached out and my fingers embraced the sacred pillar— and my being was humbled here where the blood of the martyr had called to all mankind to put the sword back in its sheath. It was then I betrayed my inner emotions by bowing my head in sorrow.

I could hear Rafael's breathing. When I turned to look at him I saw understanding in his eyes. At that moment I was convinced he knew I was searching for Father Douglas. Kneeling to the side of the post, Rafael at my side, I thought of the agony that coursed through the veins of the Savior as he looked out over the world and of his disciple who tried to bring salvation to all in these towns and barrios. I felt a new strength come into my life beyond all accounting, and I trembled in the experience. My determination to penetrate the wall of indifference was solidified in the sanctity of this archaic structure.

Perhaps Rafael read it in my expression, but if so, he remained silent. Neither did I speak one word to him about my feelings. His grim silence only confirmed my belief he would not be the one to release any facts about the disappearance of Father Douglas.

We had not spoken a word since we entered the church, and we left in the same way. I was never to enter this holy place again and took this cherished experience—a gift from a town southeast of Manila—with me.

He did not display one bit of intolerance toward me that day, only curiosity. Little was said on the depressing ride back to Pililia. I thought, "Thirty-four years is a long time to harbor a secret and to quell the urge to betray it. It is a miracle in itself." I wished I could have shared my feelings with Rafael and wondered if he had similar thoughts. Although Mrs. Temporado had opened the door, someone else would have to offer me entrance.

In the third week of March, almost four months since my arrival on Luzon, the young binatilyo who delivered the laundry for Mrs. Temporado brought me a message from Father Demato. The single-line message read, "Come. Let us remove the thorns from our hearts and find the beauty of the rose."

My spirits began to soar in anticipation that this call might lead to a gratifying solution. I sent the young binatilyo back with the message, "I will see you after Mass on Sunday."

During Mass I listened intently to Father Demato. If there were to be any signals for the parishioners, I wanted to be sure I heard them and deciphered them. They were there, and they were much stronger and more open than in his previous homily. At one point he said, "If we cannot see the rose, then we must look for it; otherwise, the thorn in our lives and the pain of it will pursue us to eternity." He had placed the problem directly into the minds of the parishioners, at least some of them. There seemed to be a faint plea in his words, and he sounded as though he knew exactly what he was doing and saying.

Looking at the parishioners with their masked expressions made me think there could be pain behind their stoic appearance. They seemed to be facing the difficulty of hiding some memory just as I faced the difficulty of uncovering it. Yet they were immovable, like the Mapalug Mountain hovering in the distance.

At the end of Mass I waited on the steps of the church. Father Demato did not turn to me until the last parishioner had disappeared from view, making sure no one eavesdropped on our conversation, although he knew full well that many parishioners were conscious of my lingering. We moved away from the church, passing the ragged bamboo wreath, to the bench at the side of the house of worship. We sat down on the creaky bench, and I courteously waited for him to speak.

"Whitey," he said. Hearing him say my old army nickname startled me again. "You have not remembered me from the days in Morong where I, too, was one of the guerrillas who brought Father O'Reilly to you. Now, after all these years when our courageous friends, the 43rd Division, drove the Japanese from the towns and hills of Luzon, we are dignified with a visit from one of the same men from whom we sought protection for the red-headed padre of Morong. We Filipinos are much indebted to those men who carried on our struggle until the moment of liberation. Sometimes when I am called to Manila I visit the magnificent shrine dedicated to your friends who had the courage of the saints and carried their crosses through the islands of loneliness. Surely, they must have felt as lonely as the crucified Christ.

"We have always had a great desire for the same freedom your country has shown to the world. Every guerrilla had such an enormous admiration for the willingness of sacrifice born in the days of your earlier patriots who refused to be subjugated to aggression and the strike of the whip. We look to the great Mapalug that casts its strength to every corner of Laguna de Bay, reminding us never to succumb to the sword of tyranny. We cling to this strength because it is a source of hope, yes hope, the magnificent survivor when all else has failed. That is all we really have, so we carry it into the rice paddies, along the river, into the mountains and finally, to the feet of Christ, our spiritual strength.

"The very fact that so many of your fellow men laid down their lives on the soil of the Philippines in order to preserve our freedom, and theirs, further reminds us that hope never dies. We cannot relinquish our hold on this unseen force even though there are times when it seems to have vanished from our existence. This we know even when it is difficult to feel its presence. Hope must never be neglected."

I sensed there was either a reprimand about to be administered or a rosebud about to bloom. I did not alter my expression, but silently opted for the latter.

"Whitey, you and I are as one. You came in wartime to drive out the arrogant ones, and I came to destroy the works of the devil. As Father Douglas said, 'We must become as soft as the rose and as gentle as the heart of Christ, who is the hope of all mankind.' These are the words of hope that flood the minds of these people at the sound of the bell. These are the words that greet them as they greet the morning sun. These are the words they hear when the last cry of the Mapalug eagle pierces the first shadows of the rising moon. These are the words of the man for whom you search."

Had the moment come? The shove Mrs. Temporado had given the door had now been opened further. The symbolical words, originating here thirty-four years ago, were reborn where Father Douglas had looked to the great mountain, where he had listened to the snap of the bamboo, where he had walked beside the waters of Laguna, where the Japanese took him away. His memorial, a simple bamboo wreath, was lying several feet from me, and his words were echoing in my ears like thunder. A circle of splintered, shattered bamboo sprouts were beckoning me to meet the thrust and not betray the challenge of a man who had talked of roses, a tolerant man who had labored in a white cassock beneath the hostile sword.

"Is this the memento to where he was last seen in Pililia?" I asked without looking at the wreath.

"Yes." Father Demato answered quietly, "From that place Father Douglas was taken."

The dialogue had begun and some of the uneasiness disappeared, even without my mentioning the name of Father Douglas. I did not have to. Father Demato might have known my intentions for some time; by verifying them he contributed to a better relationship between us. We would have no need to fend for words, because we were now on an equal basis.

"It has been a long time since that day, Father," I said.

"Yes, and we have known the sorrow and also the hope it instilled in Christian and non-Christian throughout the valley. There has not been a day without remembering the life of our martyr. He held a cross against the sword. One man against many, but as you can see by that symbol decorating the plain earth, he has prevailed in death, just as our beloved Savior did."

"Yet no one talks of him," I replied.

"No," he said, "not in the streets, not in the dampa, not in the marketplace. They honor him in silence. He is alive in their hearts because, for those who remember, he is the torch of hope in the darkness of abjection. They cling to his memory as if he were still speaking to them in his homilies about roses. Perhaps someday he will be on the altar again."

"What a startling statement!" I thought. And he made it with only a passing reflection and the typical flick of the fingers. I knew better than to challenge him about it though. Then he did a complete turnaround and asked: "Why are you so concerned with the disappearance of the Columban missionary from New Zealand?" I told him everything from the dream to my resolve to find the burial site of Father Douglas, if it were possible. I continued, "The refusal of the Filipinos to even mention the name of the slain priest convinces me they are shielding the location of his burial and that time is running out for those who know."

I could easily see that it was an irksome subject, and it bothered him. Father Demato began his defense of the prevailing silence in the lives of his people. "You know, Whitey, these people have but three things to counteract their meager existence: There is heavenly salvation, the hope of a good rice harvest, and Father Douglas who offered them hope through his own sacrifice. He is their hero. His gift of hope during oppression and tribulation was there with the rising and setting sun. He called them to him when he first rang the bell after all its years of silence. Slowly but surely they heeded his pleading until he united them with love. It is this unification that exists within the hearts of these people who knelt before the altar and listened to the comfort of his words, words they still carry with mute expression from morning until night. They believe that as long as they can persevere with their silence, he will always be with them, though he is dead. They do not want anyone, or the church, to take him from them. He is immortalized with reverence, and they believe if they bring him into the light they will have lost an inspiration. The time is approaching when only one will remain with a living memory of Father Douglas's sanctuary. Perhaps Mrs. Temporado is correct. Perhaps it is time to unveil the missing cassock. Still, all of this is out of my hands."

He said this with a negative shake of his head and without the usual toss of the hand, which meant it was almost a certainty. This just about climaxed any hope I had of influencing the inhabitants of Laguna de Bay in any way. My frustration only deepened.

"The significance of the refusal to unveil the place where Father Douglas rests is justified in their minds," continued Father Demato. "There is no doubt the church desires to give Father Douglas a proper burial, and it, too, has consternation over the thought that he might never be found. The solution of the entire affair will come only from the Filipinos themselves, and this will not happen until they realize time is beginning to run out and that only good can come from the revelation of that which can be lost forever. I can only hope their love for this man is strong enough to make them see his love cannot remain hidden forever. Love is asleep when it is not shared. They must release the selfishness of their love before it is too late."

"I believe, Father, that since my arrival on Luzon I have learned to accept the ways of the Filipinos, fully understanding that their acceptance of me is due mainly because of my affiliation with the 43rd Division, especially the 43rd Recon. With the exception of a very few Filipinos, I have had little conversation with them."

"You would be surprised by the respect these people have for you, although that, too, is hidden."

"I sense this respect, Father, but behind those curtains and doors and on the streets I am still under observation, more so since my visits to the cemetery. I would have to be blind not to realize the memorial at the end of the walk, and this wreath at our feet, have a connection to the death of Father Douglas. I have no one with whom I can confide concerning my desire to complete the search. You are the only one who has openly discussed it. Yet even in this conversation I believe there is something not being said. With Rafael, Hilaria and Mrs. Temporado I get the impulse to probe deeper, but do not dare to be that aggressive. There has to be a reason why those I have come in contact with have never broken their silence in all these years. If you are not at liberty to unravel more of the legend of Father Douglas, I will not pursue this with you further. It hardly seems likely for me to uncover in a few months what has been sheltered all these years. Time is running out for me too, because the rainy season is only a few months away and I do not care to be negotiating the roads with my bicycle. Perhaps it will be for the best if I leave empty handed and let the matter rest."

Another disturbed look appeared on Father Demato's face as I mentioned the monsoon season. I caught him quickly glancing toward the mountain, as if that were the direction in which the rains would come.

Father Demato interrupted my thoughts, "I can understand the discouragement you are experiencing. There is no doubt you consider Father Douglas a martyr, as the church does, but you must realize he is *their* martyr."

Father Demato continued, "He rang their bell, dried their tears, blessed their children and died for them. They see him on a cross when they close their eyes and look into those of Christ. They still hear his footsteps on the paths and trails, the swish of his cassock in the shadows of the church, and the rustle of the beads in his hands."

"I am beginning to understand this wreath at our feet is both his and theirs. He is buried in their hearts and in their earth. It will be difficult for them to give up this vigil. I only hope they do so before it is too late," I sighed.

"We can only hope," replied Father Demato. "Yes, the time will come when they will have to give up the vigil. It will not devastate them, but there will be regret in that they will have to make one more sacrifice when they have made so many."

Father Demato had merely called me to relate the position of the parishioners and those beyond who revered the martyrdom of Father Douglas. It was well past noon when I left him. I rode back to Mrs. Temporado's and found Rafael waiting there on the back porch. I was sure the grapevine had informed him of my visit with Father Demato.

He greeted me in what seemed to be a more jovial manner than usual. I asked, "How come you arrive on a Sunday afternoon; this does not leave too much time to visit."

He said, "I am going to take a vacation. No one deserves one more than me!" We both laughed.

We spent most of the time talking about events that had occurred during the war and the plight of the Filipinos under the Japanese occupation. He betrayed a deep resentment toward that period of time although he abstained from dwelling on it. He casually mentioned, "I am going to pay a visit to Father Demato tomorrow morning." This brief but definite announcement I accepted with mild elation.

The sun had barely topped the mountains when he left the house. He returned later that morning on a bicycle, so I knew he had visited others. I seldom questioned him as to his whereabouts, so I did not bother to now.

For two days I patiently waited for something to happen. For want of something to do, I resumed the bicycle riding while Rafael visited friends or relatives. I did not ride beyond the limits of Pililia, and on these local tours the residents did not seem to be regarding me as closely as they had previously. Even this little touch of insignificant nonchalance on their part showed acceptance of me.

During one of our late afternoon rides amidst the weekend vendors, who were setting up their carts and booths, Rafael swerved his bicycle up the road across from the church. He did it suddenly. At first I thought he was reacting to the growing crowds, which he could have easily avoided by taking the side road. I could not tell if his action was spontaneous or deliberate, but I realized there was nothing for us at the end of the road but the cemetery. Either way it momentarily caught me off guard, and I nearly ran over a grinning bata who was waving vegetables at me. I recovered after a wobbling of the wheels and pursued him up the road. Rafael arched his arm in the air in front of me, beckoning me to follow.

When we reached the cemetery archway we dismounted, left the bicycles at the entrance, then walked beneath the arch. I was invading the solemn graveyard of the Pililia ancestors once again. Rafael was somber. We set off toward the white picket fence surrounding the shrine. Rafael walked slowly, becoming more solemn as we approached the opening in the fence. It had been painted since my last visit, giving the site a much brighter appearance in the late afternoon sun. Momentarily the freshness of it seemed to liven up my friend, but this did not remain once we entered the circle of pickets. Without saying a word he walked up to the beautifully glazed memorial and stood before it in deep silence. He seemed to be in the depths of prayer, and there no longer was any doubt the man buried here was his father. Courteously I waited for him to speak. He turned and looked toward the sun beginning its descent into the western sky, shrugged his shoulders slightly, and then, as if he could not endure any further remorse, motioned me out of the circle to one of the benches along the walk.

"You have seen the name," he stated, even though he knew I had been there many times before.

"Yes," I said.

"And the roses?"

"Yes," I said again.

"Do you know who is buried there?"

"I think so. I believe the man interned there is your father. I have little doubt the roses signify he was a man of great importance. A new rose every day can only mean this to be true."

Behind Rafael's usual mask of joviality I could see a river of sensitivity welling up in the corners of his eyes. He seemed relieved I knew the honored man was indeed his father.

With a tremble in his voice he asked, "You saw the date and the inscription?"

"Yes," I answered. "It is the second day after Father Douglas disappeared."

At the mention of the name he looked up inquisitively, but I no longer had any qualms concerning the issue. By his manner and mode of questioning, I was now positive he had discussed my meandering and inquiries with Father Demato.

I thought the date on the memorial had some connection to the death of Father Douglas. Nevertheless, the inscription about the bell ringer was still mystifying. Any parishioner could be assigned to ring the bell if the parish priest were preoccupied. It must have been a deed of spectacular significance to so honor a ringer of the bell.

Rafael interrupted my thoughts. "Whitey, I have taken you here today because I have never met so much persistence in finding answers without asking. I have studied your actions for some time now and am sure of your intentions. Yet you never disturbed the privacy of one Filipino in any of the towns. Many admire your patience." Rafael paused before he continued.

"Father Demato has praise for all of the 43rd Division and especially the men of Recon. We all feel the same way too. We remember the excitement when the 43rd secured the Kalinawan Caves and all of Laguna de Bay. We also remember the sadness of those hours. True, I was only a binatilyo when I helped Father O'Reilly escape the Japanese. At the time

I was the youngest guerrilla in all of Laguna Province—and the proudest—but I was already a man with a rifle slung over my shoulder. I helped Father O'Reilly into freedom even with the sword dangling overhead because rescuing him was my own personal revenge for the death of my father, now buried beneath roses. I, as well as many others, will never forget the bitter days and anguish. We will live with the memory shackled to us until we, too, die."

I was amazed. This was the most Rafael had ever revealed to me since our first encounter. I remained silent, hoping he would reveal the mystery of the legend of Father Douglas and also that of his father and the courier of the roses.

"So many times I have wanted to talk to you, my friend. But it cannot be. I cannot explain why roses decorate the resting place of my father. This is why I came here today so you would understand I cannot even though I want to."

There it was again, the boding obstacle. Rafael was apologetic about it. What was this entity imprisoning the legend of Laguna within the boundaries of the mind? Rafael did not offer any further explanations and I did not try to find any. Both he and the padre seemed to be in a predicament, and for now I would have to accept their partial explanations. They seemed to be meeting me halfway, but it was not enough to curb my appetite. I was downhearted at not finding out the reason for the death of Rafael's father and who the courier of the roses was. Rafael must have noticed my disappointment and interrupted the awkward silence. "Let us go back to the marketplace and buy some vegetables for Mrs. Temporado."

I tried hard to hide the disappointment in my voice when I said, "Mrs. Temporado will be pleased." I am sure I did not fool Rafael.

When Sunday arrived and Father Demato found himself short of altar boys again, I was not surprised this time seeing my friend serve on the altar. I began to wonder just how long Rafael had been living in Baras and how long his mother had been living in Morong. His father had been buried in Pililia, which implied he had lived there in 1943. Father Douglas was known to have organized a group of altar boys and Boy Scouts, and at the age of ten Rafael would have lived in Pililia, although it had never been mentioned in any of the conversations I had had with him. As an altar boy

Rafael would have had a close relationship with Father Douglas. Perhaps my friend was concealing much more than I thought.

I decided to confront him. I had to do it soon because he was going back to Baras before evening, but first I had to listen to the words of Father Demato at Mass and observe the expressions of Rafael as he sat beside the altar.

Father Demato once again brought the rose to life: "Not one rose can survive unless it is nourished; similarly, the soul of man cannot survive unless it is nourished by the word of God. Jesus, the Living Word, came to feed the sheep that had strayed into the realm of apathy and ignorance. We must call the shepherd out of the hills and let him come back into our lives. We must rise and follow the shepherd to the garden of roses, nourishing our souls through the way of the cross and the body and blood of Christ.

"Here, in my hand, I hold the thorn. When I thrust it into my skin I understand his pain and the love offered to me by he who bore the crown of glory. He has nourished us through his life and with his death; by his resurrection, raised us above Mapalug Mountain. If we hear his words and feel the softness of the rose, they will destroy the thorns of anger and indifference we have toward the words of our heavenly Father. No individual or group can shield the shepherd from our brothers because he came to love all of them. Let us take him down from the cross, let us open the tomb, let us raise him up in our lives—for he belongs to all who would be as soft as the rose."

There was movement in the pews when Father Demato mentioned the rose and the tomb, and when he stated no one could claim the right to keep the shepherd to himself. Rafael might be able to control the effect the homily had on him without the flicker of an eyebrow, but he could not control the effect it had on the other parishioners. At any rate, the parishioners and Rafael had something to think about once again.

After Mass Rafael and I went and sat on the bench that Father Demato and I had occupied previously. Time was eluding me and the monsoon season was not; I therefore immediately challenged him directly, although I tried to use a little finesse.

"You were an altar boy when you were young." It was more of a statement than a question. My openness did not seem to shake him, though.

I guess he had prepared himself for this eventuality.

"Yes," he replied.

"Then you must have lived in Pililia in 1943," I continued.

"Yes," he said, but he did not elaborate.

"Your father died that year," I countered. "And you were almost eleven years old at the time. Did you serve Father Douglas as an altar boy?"

"You have calculated that too!" he answered, still not offering any additional information.

I did not retreat, although any one of my questions could send him into complete silence.

"You were close to Father Douglas, Rafael." Again, it was more of a statement than a question.

"Yes, very," he said in a melancholy manner.

There was a pause, and in this interlude I carefully pondered my next question. I wondered if he would answer, because we both knew the ultimate question was unavoidable if our conversation continued in the same vein.

"Were you in the church when he was taken?"

"Yes," he replied.

"Did the Japanese realize you were a guerrilla at the time?"

He bristled. "I was not a guerrilla then."

Knowingly or not, he had provided me with a connection between the death of his father and the disappearance of Father Douglas. I was now sure he knew, or had a very good idea, where the body of the man he once served as altar boy was buried.

"My good friend," I said, "I am not going to ask you the very thing you fear. I am quite sure you would not answer anyway. I value your friendship far more than that. I will do my best to wait until the answer is found elsewhere or from someone else. This might never come to pass, but surely you and I and all those who do know have to realize the location of the body of the martyr must be divulged to everyone very soon or it never will be. Mrs. Temporado's words ring true. Father Demato's anxiety over it worsens, and the church could not bear the loss of its martyr. The elders are becoming older and the children will be deprived of the meaning of his sacrifice." I did not deem it necessary to enter into further details. My message was clear to him.

We parted again; he caught the jeepney and I returned to my lodging, wondering just how much my interest would affect those who governed the outcome of the saga of Laguna de Bay. I wondered, "Would anyone be concerned about the interests of someone who did nothing but ride a bicycle on the roads of Pililia, Baras and Morong?"

It was now April 1977, and the angry clouds were beginning to gather, sometimes without warning. I found myself waiting and watching for the winds and rain. During the murky evenings I began to trifle with the notion that my words to Father Demato about giving it all up might become a reality. Hundreds listened to him at Mass and during the Lenten services, yet it seemed as if his sermons were falling on deaf ears. He faced a sea of stoic, placid and apathetic faces from one week to the next. Perhaps they could go on to the end of time this way, bringing just a memory with them of what had occurred in Pililia and Paete. It would be a buried memory, buried in the hills and in their hearts. The bamboo wreath and the sound of a bell would no longer turn the heads of the villagers, because the monsoon rains would wash the memory out of their lives and thus the chronicle of mankind.

From the mist and floating clouds came the rain. Slowly but steadily it began to descend from the hills. Mrs. Temporado's roof rendered a patter of sounds in a melodious rhythm, a gentle warning of what was waiting in the winds. The urge to vacate and the urge to remain rambled through my thoughts in a seesaw contest.

The sounds of thunder became more numerous and flashes of light burst upon the Mapalug. Maneuvering the bicycle became more hazardous, which prompted me to take one last ride north to the bridge between Tanay and Pililia where the Laniti River finished its run from the mountains. Beneath the supports of the old bridge the Laniti was coming to life. It had already climbed a few feet up the embankments, signaling once again it was preparing to threaten the existence of the structure. I heard the river's rage thrashing against the beveled rift and over the stones laid bare and smooth from the torrents of ages.

My thoughts were interrupted when the jeepney roared across the bridge. A huge gray cloud hovering between the sun and me suddenly unleashed a deluge of rain, which rapidly filled ditches, rice paddies and potholes, forcing me to walk my bicycle most of the way to Pililia.

Although the flash shower subsided within minutes, it took hours to cover the distance.

When I reached the outskirts of Pililia, I saw the jeepney hung over the side of the road, stuck in a muddy ditch. Luis and several farmers, who left the rice fields to help, were pushing and shoving. The woman stood aside watching with passive interest. One of the passengers, who had only one arm, watched me with great interest as I approached the vehicle. I peered inside and saw the Japanese passenger again. He was seated behind the wheel, and he knew exactly what he was doing.

"Luis, do you need an extra shoulder?" I asked.

"Gladly" he replied.

I put my shoulder to the back of the vehicle, which was still embedded, while the others stood ankle deep in mud. Together we heaved the jeepney while the Japanese helmsman steered it back onto the crest of the road.

"Thank you everyone, thank you," Luis beamed, relieved to be out of the mud. The jeepney then sped on its way again.

The Japanese man appeared older than I, and there was something about him that was jogging my memory. The exertion of bicycle riding, walking and shoving had also jogged my muscles and ligaments again, so much so I had no difficulty in getting to sleep that night. Nor did the downpour arouse me. I was too tired to dream.

Mrs. Temporado's description of the storm the following morning, which arrived shortly after I had gone to bed, brought an instant recollection of the man with one arm, who had placidly scrutinized my efforts of assistance with the jeepney. "Could this be the legendary one-armed guerrilla, Clastres Bulatao?" I wondered.

It was the middle of April and Rafael had not returned since the cemetery rendezvous. I figured he was busy with the rice crop, and I was sure he was avoiding my inquisitiveness. I decided to try another source, his mother. By now she and all of Morong knew my intentions and no longer had to secrete themselves behind the shades and shutters. Besides, it had been some time since I had left Morong, and I did not want Mrs. Gonsalves to think I had forgotten her.

With the inclement weather so unpredictable, I put my bicycle aside and caught the jeepney to Morong. As soon as I stepped into the vehicle

Luis said, "Cannot thank you enough for aiding me on that rainy day."

"I only hope there are others around when your jeepney gets stuck and I am a passenger!" We both laughed.

I sat up front and conversed with him all the way to Morong. As we crossed the bridge in Tanay, he said, "If it ever collapses, those living north of it in Tanay and Baras will have a difficult time getting their goods, crops and vending carts into Pililia."

I replied, "Those who own carabao are fortunate, but I suspect even the carabao are unable to maneuver the crossing during floods."

He nodded in agreement and said, "Pililia is the center of commerce above Santa Cruz, and many people coming from the north and south of it, some ten miles either way, depend upon the town for their livelihood and for the goods brought in from the surrounding villages. The ten thousand or so inhabitants, in turn, rely on these farmers not only for food but also for hemp, tobacco and fabrics. It is a great interchange of mutual dependency, which would be immensely jeopardized if the bridge went into the river."

I saw Luis shudder at the thought—his existence was also dependent on the survival of the structure. Unfortunately, the bridge spanned the widest and most ferocious section of the Laniti, where it emptied into Laguna de Bay. One could easily see that the bridge controlled the destiny of many, and the lack of funds controlled the bridge. It was just a matter of time before it would topple into the Laniti. After safely crossing the bridge I asked, "Luis, do you have a jeepney schedule for my return to Pililia?"

"Whole stack of them on the dashboard. Everyone around here knows the schedule by heart," he replied. He handed me a piece of paper, the ink having faded somewhat from the sun.

Back in Morong I went to see Mrs. Reyes for accommodations and found my room was unoccupied. I made arrangements to stay for a few days, which seemed to please her because the oncoming season kept visitors at a minimum. I felt in my pocket for the slip of paper Luis had handed me but it was not there. I asked, "Mrs. Reyes, do you have a jeepney schedule? I must have left mine in the jeepney." She replied, "No need for bus and jeepney schedules, carved in memory."

I did not go visit Mrs. Gonsalves this day. It would have been too obvious if I had hastened to visit her and beset her with a sudden line of questioning. If she suspected I was trying to deceive her she would divulge little to me. I felt inhibited without Rafael's presence. I wished Rafael were here so that I could make the visit with him to his mother's, but I had no idea when he would show up. Therefore, I walked around Morong for three days listening and talking to some of the children who recognized me from my previous visit. Some of them were playing the one-armed guerrilla game, but mostly they kept asking me, "where is your bicycle?"

"Carabao ate it!" I kidded, which brought screeches of laughter from them.

Finally I decided to take my chances and confront Mrs. Gonsalves as tactfully as I could and let the aftermath take care of itself. I just could not wait for her son any longer. For the moment I was facing the possibility of losing the confidence of both Rafael and his mother, a situation that would be most disadvantageous to me. Even though I realized they might never assist me directly, they might indirectly channel me in the right direction.

Tossing all caution aside, I turned my steps in the direction of St. Jerome's. The magnificent Spanish structure loomed down upon me, and the ponderous doors seemed to be beckoning my entrance. First I stopped where the splendid rosebush of Mrs. Gonsalves vied to be the most beautiful of all rosebushes. The brilliant red flowers, dancing in the breeze coming up from the waters of Laguna Lake, brought joy to the heart of the beholder. It was perfection in a nonperfect atmosphere by someone I deemed as soft as the rose itself.

She had already seen me turn up the street. As I looked away from the rosebush I saw her standing in the doorway looking determined I should not pass by her house. "How are you Mrs. Gonsalves?" I asked. She flashed her quick smile in return.

"I wait for you, Whitey," she said, her manner implying the visit was a matter of fact.

I wondered how much Rafael had told her about our cemetery visit and if she knew it was just a matter of time before I would approach her with questions that no one else would answer. Perhaps her eyes and ears were not as keen as Hilaria's, but her perception and intuition were.

"I have been busy riding and visiting in the towns," I said, "but just last week I received a visit from Rafael. He had visited me more in Pililia than I have him in Baras, but I know he is busy in the fields and perhaps I can see him on my return to Baras."

"Rafael visit me first of week," she said in return. "He is troubled in his mind, and I make him eat better or he fall down in rice paddy. Not good to grow rice and not eat some. I worry for him."

"A mother should care for her son, no matter what age," I said. We both laughed because Rafael was forty-four years old.

"I suppose," she said, smiling again.

"Whitey, you come many miles. Many American soldiers come back since wartime. Filipinos remember days of struggle. Only you stay. Look to hills. Search for more than scars of battle.

"Many eyes follow you. Rafael and Father Demato tell us why you stay, even though we know some time ago. Why you try to take from us what buried in hearts? Very difficult to surrender this love of many years. You must understand."

"Mrs. Gonsalves, I do understand and please understand I mean no offense. Perhaps this love you cling to, as Father Demato has reminded us, should be shared, as was the love of Christ. Perhaps this love, which is held captive in the secret of Laguna de Bay, might protect the innocent batas who splash in the puddles. Perhaps the greatness of this invisible love of which you speak may then enter the hearts of the ignorant and those who rattle the sword. Mrs. Gonsalves, I know who is buried in your hearts, and he is buried in mine also. I would regret leaving this rosebush behind knowing its flowers would never adorn the missing cassock."

For the first time in all these weeks I saw a tear wash away the will of apathy and fall at my feet, burrowing a hole in the Philippine earth as big as the Mapalug. Mrs. Gonsalves had finally released her hold on the past, conquering this grip with a single tear. Not another tear escaped her, one being enough to shatter her veil covering the pain and anguish of thirty-four years.

I politely waited until her composure returned.

"Father Demato know difficulty. Elders not want to talk about past," she said. "We in the Morong Legion of Mary hear whispers near altar. Some agree. It time to wash old cassock and replace with new, but not up to us to say. I meet with others before I say more to you. Women only say few words in administration building. We are elders but we are women. We pray harder. See if we can open eyes of those who do not want to see. I talk to Hilaria and Rafael."

I took note of her mentioning Hilaria's name. This reference made it certain the guerrillas were somehow responsible for the concealment of Father Douglas's body. I thought it best not to pursue further questioning of the guerrillas at this time and said, "Mrs. Gonsalves, I hope I have not caused you any trouble. I know the difficult position you, and also Rafael and Father Demato, are in. If there is any way I can help, please allow me."

"We have meeting, Legion of Mary, Friday. Wait, please," she concluded.

"I will wait in Pililia, Mrs. Gonsalves." I went back to Mrs. Reyes's house to spend the night because I had missed the jeepney.

I wondered how much sway the Legion of Mary in Morong would have in convincing whomever in Pililia that something had to be done about a proper burial for Father Douglas before it was too late. I was convinced Mrs. Gonsalves had lived in Pililia because her husband was buried there. I hoped his past prominence and her being an elder would have some influence on those in Pililia, especially since they would control the outcome.

I woke up the next morning to find Mrs. Reyes excited about something. While preparing my breakfast she casually stated, "Amanda Gonsalves go to Pililia." I was surprised by this bit of information, which I suspected had been prearranged by Rafael's mother—Mrs. Reyes would never have declared such news to an outsider. I wondered if she, too, were inwardly awaiting the results as anxiously as I. After the noon hour she sought me out again, "Amanda take large bouquet of roses with her." I was now convinced this information had been considered beforehand, and I knew which grave would be adorned this day with the most beautiful roses in all of Luzon. The timid Mrs. Gonsalves had gone on a crusade, and she was armed only with roses. I caught the next jeepney out of Morong and followed her to Pililia.

Within hours the grapevine went to work, and Rafael answered it with a visit. He showed no animosity toward me but was concerned about his mother's role in this newly developing crusade. He feared it could be devastating to her position in the Legion of Mary and as an elder. He said, "She goes beyond the limits in the community. People are talking about her actions, even the men in the dampas."

The wife of the bell ringer carried her roses wherever she went. She dedicated herself to the task in a quiet, steady, unyielding performance that began to shake the walls of the administration building and dampas as well as the stained-glass windows. She shed the cloak of timidity and took her individual parade all the way to Mrs. Renya Florintino, president of the Legion of Mary in Paete, who placed a wreath every July 27 at the spot where Father Douglas had been taken away. In the valley where the Laniti cut through the villages, and where the delicate bearer of roses could not reach, murmurs about this crusader wafted through the evening dusk and early dawn, settling in the nipa huts. Into the towns and barrios she went, recalling the words of the martyr, and every Legion of Mary meeting was graced with her quiet manner. She went back and forth from village to town, reaching for the ears of the elders, trying to break through the barrier that had been put in place years ago.

One morning I overheard her talking to Mrs. Temporado. She said, "His love no longer theirs alone. Belong to everyone. World waiting for it to be released." I knew she wanted me to hear these words, because she spoke in English. She continued, "One not take beauty of rose and bury it. Rose no longer beautiful then." Mrs. Gonsalves walked and talked, stirring the complacent with her simple monologue and logic.

Rafael, still concerned about his mother's persistent crusade, frequented Morong daily and kept me informed as well. His connection to the grapevine was invaluable. At first he told me most of her listeners were the women of the Legion of Mary, but some of the men began to listen. When she was challenged by the elders she simply declared, "Everyone should be like the rose." She then challenged them with, "Francisco would want you to listen to my words." As softly spoken as she was, her words rumbled through the grapevine.

Her lily-clad manner began to penetrate those who knelt in the aisles of the church praying the Stations of the Cross, and especially those in Paete who encountered the wooden post after the last station—the solemn pole reminding them there had also been another sacrifice meted out by he who freed their souls during their darkest times.

Little by little the memory of those dreaded hours of Pililia and Paete returned. Those with failing eyes who could no longer see the summit of the great Mapalug began to long for their Bamboo Shepherd who had said, "You are all roses ready to bloom in the heart of God." Tears that had longed to be freed from beneath the mask began to fall upon the bamboo floors once again, until finally in the first part of May, the bearer of roses, who no longer had a single rose remaining on her rosebush, appealed to the women of the Legion of Mary to demonstrate in the streets of Pililia this coming Thursday.

Rafael was at Mrs. Reyes's back porch the following morning. He looked worn. "Whitey," he said, "Come with me to Pililia on Thursday, but do not tell my mother."

"I will meet you at St. Mary Magdalene's in two days." I hesitated a moment and then continued, "You know Rafael, your mother may appear to be as soft as a rose, but she has the strength of the Laniti."

"I worry for her. I have never seen her like this before. I hope her position as an elder in the town will not be shattered for all times." He frowned even more at this thought then continued, "I must catch the next jeepney run. See you soon Whitey."

Rafael left and I informed Mrs. Reyes that I would be returning to Pililia the following day.

"Not surprised you want to be in Pililia by Thursday," she replied.

My room was already prepared for me when I arrived at Mrs. Temporado's; again, the grapevine made it to Pililia before I arrived.

"Father Demato leave message. Be at church tomorrow," she said. "Oh yes," she remembered, "Rafael there too."

Thursday arrived and so too did the women of the Legion of Mary— and they assembled by the hundreds. I met Rafael and Father Demato at the church. Father Demato, whose words had fallen on deaf ears exclaimed, "My heart is pounding like the winds billowing against the wall on the eastern slope of Mapalug Mountain."

"I have never seen a woman, or women, behave this way," stammered Rafael.

"Then I am sure there are more hearts pounding besides ours," I stated.

We waited in the shadows of the church while the women assembled out front. Mrs. Gonsalves stood before them with her last spray of roses, telling them, "My rosebush, just like Father Douglas, will be a memory, and it, too, will disappear into the past and its beauty will be lost forever unless a caring, compassionate attitude is found to revive it." The women, all wearing black head nets, turned and went north up the main street and in silence faced the administration building of Pililia. Still, the doors of the administration building remained closed. Yet while the women stood their ground, no one chose to enter the building, not even the men. This was a sign of some support, as minute as it was.

The following afternoon Mrs. Gonsalves reappeared with a fresh rose bouquet, which she picked from Mrs. Temporado's rosebush. There were also other roses strewn on the steps of the administration building. The number of black head nets increased to over six hundred. The women mutely stood or sat throughout the day; only darkness budged them, forcing them back into the bamboo houses and nipa huts. The Legion of Mary was becoming a small army and getting larger by the day; by the end of the week their number had risen to nearly eight hundred. The heads of the men were turning.

Rafael did not go back to Baras, fearing for the safety of his vigilant mother. Instead, we watched her and the Legion of Mary from a distance. In her quiet resolve the memory of Rafael's father was rekindled. Rafael solemnly commented, "My father made quite a defiance in Pililia a long time ago, just like my mother is doing now. He, too, shook all of Pililia. He had said to me, 'There is no compromise if a man wants freedom.'" A price had to be paid, and Francisco Gonsalves had paid it with his life. None forgot that.

Rafael worried once again that this episode would be similar to the past. He fretted his mother would be destroyed. Nevertheless, there was no frown upon the comely face of the rose bearer when she returned to Pililia after the weekend. Instead, besides the roses, she carried a smile that glowed, because on the previous Friday the women had vowed unanimously to resume their vigil on Monday. Their husbands could go hungry and run after the batas if they could find them.

On Monday morning they were there, and others began to drift in from the villages, walking, always walking. Some of them had walked several miles out of the Laniti Valley in the torrid sun. The women in the

Legion of Mary from Pililia gave them haven in their bamboo and nipa huts. Once again a common cause had begun to surface in the towns and barrios, and even to Mrs. Gonsalves, the strength of it was a surprise. Nearly a thousand women assembled throughout the day on Tuesday, and just before dusk they watched Mrs. Gonsalves climb the belfry steps of St. Mary Magdalene's, look out over the sea of black head nets, and calmly reach for the dangling rope that had put calluses on the palms of her Francisco. Then gently, so gently, she began the swaying of the hemp until it arched up and then crashed the giant tongue against the inside of the ancient bell, almost sweeping the dainty rose bearer off her feet. The residents in the upper and lower valleys of the Laniti, bending in the shallow rice fields, were brought erect as the slow tolling continuously echoed to them and beyond into the hills that were already trickling the flood into the mighty Laniti.

Then there was a half toll as Mrs. Gonsalves fell exhausted to the floor of the belfry. Others clamored up the steps, nearly trampling her in their rush, and grasped the frayed rope in a state of exuberance—the tolling was kept alive for the entire afternoon. They alternated, each shift of women pulling for fifteen minutes right up to the hour of dusk. Then, just before the sun disappeared in the western sky, a low murmur swept through Pililia as a thousand angelic voices sang the refrain of a song that had remained in obscurity since the death of Father Douglas. It chorused slowly and gently at first, just like the bell, then floated into the ears of those who made the policy in Pililia. The crusade of Mrs. Gonsalves ended half an hour after dusk when there was just one clang from the old bell.

These vigilant, unnerved women, who had fled their kitchens, knew exactly whom they wanted to see appear at the doors of the building. It had become a battle of patience, and it did not end for two weeks, and only then because Mrs. Gonsalves, by ringing a bell, had sent a message that could not go unanswered. She knew this.

From the outset of Mrs. Gonsalves's unheard of public demonstrations, I remained clear of any involvement. I felt responsible for arousing a usually placid woman who was now creating a furor in the streets of Pililia. Therefore, I cautiously positioned myself well to the rear of the milling throngs during the entire episode, gluing my eyes upon the valiant form of the little lady who clutched her armor of roses. Every day I watched her as she confronted the front door of the administration building and marveled at her perseverance.

I was not the only outsider surveying the scene. Several times I caught sight of the Japanese passenger who had guided the jeepney out of the ditch. He remained well to the rear, as I had, but always to the opposite side of the crowds, keenly observing all that was taking place in the heart of Pililia. Even from a distance I could see he wore a frown on his face.

A silence of completeness settled within the shadows of Pililia. The music of the bell and the angelic voices drifted into the surrounding hills. They also found their way into the ears of Clastres Bulatao, who had been meeting nightly with Laudez Rosaldo, Ramon and Hilaria Augustine, Raul and Alvita Reyes, and Fredrico Guzan.

Rafael returned to Mrs. Temporado's and informed me he had approached Hilaria with his concern over his mother's performance. It was his third visit to her in two weeks.

"He said, "I am going to see Hilaria again. Will you join me Whitey?""

I hoped being invited to Hilaria's would clarify some of the mystery surrounding the turmoil that was going on in Pililia. I replied, "Of course."

As usual she was at the door before we knocked. We exchanged greetings then Rafael said, "I hope you do not mind, but I brought Whitey with me."

"Not at all," she responded.

"I am unable to sleep," he continued. "My mother has troubled my thoughts for many nights."

"How is Amanda recovering from her fall in the belfry?" asked Hilaria.

"She is improving," answered Rafael, "but the fall from public opinion will do her more harm than the bruises ever could. If she does not succeed in her quest she will perish quicker than her roses."

"It is a worry," replied Hilaria, "but I am only one of seven who can end her crusade. I will talk to Laudez and hear what he has to say."

Rafael was overflowing with anxiety and despair, but at the same time, he had to admire the nobleness in his mother's determination to put a quiver in the door of the administration building. Too well he realized his mother was on shaky ground, enough so that if her challenge should remain unanswered, her position as an elder would vanish. This by itself would be a disaster. She had crossed the line of no return and only success could redeem her. Hilaria fully understood the consequences.

"It means a lot to me that you will speak to Laudez and the others," said Rafael.

"I will see what I can do, Rafael, but I cannot promise you anything," commented Hilaria.

I remained silent during their conversation, hoping to obtain the slightest bit of information, but as usual, only small pieces came my way. We said our good-byes to Hilaria and Rafael returned to Baras.

Two days later he returned to Pililia. "I have been to see Hilaria again," said Rafael. "She related a comment made by Laudez the last time she met with him. He had said, 'At the Monday night meeting I will have some words to offer the others that will rattle their bones and render them speechless.' Hilaria appeared to be exceptionally nervous, something very unusual for her. She said she would contact me after the meeting and give an account of what transpires, but only if it can be disclosed. This is unprecedented."

Rafael was filled with exhilaration. I feared a disappointment now would be a calamity. I said, "Rafael, look to your mother, remember your father, and you will find the necessary strength."

We returned to Mrs. Temporado's for the night. Rafael slept very little; consequently, I slept very little myself. He was up first thing in the morning and said, "I am going to see Hilaria again. I will meet with you later." He returned after a few hours, and I immediately saw the change in him. He was filled with exuberance.

He spoke excitedly, "Hilaria and the other guerrillas have met, and she was granted permission to relate to me what transpired in their meeting. I will relate Hilaria's account of the meeting."

A revelation, provoked by a gallant and gentle woman, Mrs. Amanda Gonsalves, and relayed by Rafael follows:

"The last clang of the bell, just after dusk," said Hilaria, who was meeting again with the other six remaining guerrillas, "was just like the one I had heard many years ago when I was praying in the hills above

Pililia, one that I am sure none of you heard. It had the ring of mystery then, but this time I heard the cry of another love and it made me pray again."

Then, in a role reminiscent of one she had lived so many years ago, she confronted Clastres. "Did you hear the bell, Clastres?"

"I heard the bell, Hilaria." The others nodded in agreement.

"Until this very night," continued Hilaria, "Francisco was the only one who ever rang it after sunset. Now, one barely able to pull the rope has reminded us that we must share the love we keep to ourselves. The others wait patiently in the marketplace and along the rivers. They know what they are doing and this can be heard in their song. Did you hear them sing, Clastres?"

He responded, "I heard them sing." The others nodded in agreement again.

"Do you remember when we sang that song in the hills?" she asked.

Clastres nodded. "We have debated this issue many times, all seven of us, and we have known that some day this time would come. When there were fifty of us left we argued like the batas, but always we said it was not time. Do you think, Hilaria, the time has arrived?"

"We are the only ones who can accept the white cassock from the priest," she replied. "In your condition you cannot take it where it must go. Father Demato tells us the missing cassock will be lost forever, and Rafael's mother preaches we no longer have the right to conceal the love we have nourished all these years."

Laudez, quiet up to this point, turned toward Hilaria but spoke to those assembled as much as to her. "You are not answering the question, Hilaria. Is it time for us to break the silence we have vowed would never be broken?"

Hilaria looked at Raul and Alvita and asked them, "What are your thoughts on breaking our vow?"

"We have come to this point many times," said Raul, "and we have always settled it with the written vote. Perhaps it will have to come to that again."

"We always come this far, as you say," said Fredrico. "But each time we discuss this, there are fewer of us. Perhaps that should mean something. It will be too late when there are none of us left."

However, Clastres controlled the outcome, just as he had for as long as they could remember. They could vote forever, but he was their leader and they had never tried to take this command from him. It would be his direction they would follow ultimately, although they always liked to think they had influenced him, and he liked them to think they had.

"Have you asked the priest what the church has to say?" asked Clastres, who had asked this for years.

"Rafael has consulted with Father Demato many times over this," said Ramon, "and he has assured Rafael, on his bent knee, the church will only grant a blessing and in no other way interfere with any decision we make. But he cannot bless if there is nothing to bless."

Then Hilaria, who was not apt to display sentimentality, looked straight at Clastres and spoke once again, "Do you remember how he looked that last time?"

Clastres got up and walked around the room. "Yes, I have seen him many times in my dreams and when I kneel at the altar."

The others agreed it was the same with them.

"How can one forget?" said Fredrico.

Raul stood up and challenged the future prospects of the seven. "Rafael says Whitey, from the old 43rd Division, remarks one has to be blind not to see that it will soon be too late, and Mrs. Gonsalves says the children will never know how to pray for our beloved martyr. Are we that old and blind ourselves that we have lost sight of this, or are we blinded by the loyalty of those who are no longer with us? Surely we are not that old that we cannot reason this out. A secret is no longer a secret when it is lost forever. It is nothing."

"Are you saying we should listen to outsiders and those who gather in the streets demanding we sever ourselves from the honor of our word?" asked Clastres. "Would this not disturb our comrades in the grave?"

"Yes, Clastres," said Hilaria. "They are dead and we are almost the same. Who will keep the vow alive when all are dead, and why? The thought is ridiculous and without merit. It is foolish to bury the words of our martyr forever. Perhaps we will not be forgiven after we are dead. You have asked me and I say it is time to listen to our hearts and not our minds."

Clastres thought Hilaria had more opinions tonight than in any other meeting. Was she going to force the issue, this woman who had saved his life and who could still hear the rice grow?

"And what is in your heart, Hilaria?" Clastres asked her.

"You know what is in my heart, Clastres Bulatao," she retorted.

It was unusual for her to use his last name. It brought a stirring from the others to such an extent that Raul and Fredrico shook their heads in disbelief. Laudez did not even look to see the expression on his old friend's face; he knew Clastres had flicked his eyebrows at the one who could hear unsaid words if she so desired.

"You still have not answered the question, Hilaria," said Clastres, ignoring Hilaria's outburst.

"What does it matter about what lies in my heart?" said Hilaria quickly. "It will be a decision by all of us, not one. We are seven out of one hundred and ninety-five. That should tell us we are dying. Mrs. Gonsalves rebukes us with her words about the love we conceal. She says we are prisoners of it. It becomes a question of whether we have the right to withhold the beauty of the martyred priest from our own and from one another. We cannot take him with us. Nor can we let him be forgotten. We are bound by a selfish oath. Mrs. Gonsalves and the others, who patiently stand, are demanding we act before we no longer can. I think tomorrow the streets will be empty, and that will be worse than if they are not."

Alvita nodded in agreement. She knew what Hilaria was implying, and before any of the others could retaliate about Hilaria's remarks, she spoke out.

"It is true. There will be no marketplace tomorrow or through the weekend. The head nets will not be worn but hung on the walls of the bamboo dwellings and the pesos will not change hands. You will not see the women all day or smoke from their kitchens. There will only be men walking through the streets looking to fill their empty bellies. But there will be many roses on the grave of Francisco Gonsalves."

Her words had removed the focus being placed on Hilaria to commit to a verbal decision. However, Hilaria was not about to be singled out as the arbitrator for the other six. They realized she would not let this happen. They knew their collective agreement would affect the entire Laguna community immensely. There would have to be a unanimous decision, as originally formed into a covenant, to dissolve the content of the oath. However, there was a difference this time—the demonstrations.

The discussion continued for hours, all admitting the loyalty of the covenant besieged them and not the logic. It had to end before they died, but the imposing threat of betrayal had always surpassed clear reason. Pressure brewing in the streets could not be ignored. If the situation were not attended to now, it most likely would reappear in the future when they might be fewer in number. Should they all be the ones to disavow, or should they let it eventually fall into the hands of one? This could be a disastrous decision because who could say for sure that one would remain? Some said they could not hold out much longer but detested the pressure to heed the will of those who had no solemn vow to consider. They debated the reaction of the people, and the church, if the remains of the priest were brought to the altar for a proper funeral Mass.

Hilaria carefully observed Clastres as he eyed his comrades patiently, always seeking the point when they would finally challenge him. He said, "I have endured thirty-four years of continued badgering by the populace and my associates. I have heard the voices in the streets for nearly two weeks, and I have listened to every word relayed to me by the widow of Francisco Gonsalves. I know the day will inevitably arrive when I will have to concede the matter."

Each meeting was a little more vociferous than the last, and Clastres began to wonder if this one would be the last before they ended the drama. Hilaria was sure that if they decided tonight to cast a written vote, Clastres would have to throw open the doors of the administration building in the morning and give up the ghost of Father Douglas.

Laudez, who had said little so far, never interfered with the decisions of his old friend and wartime leader, but he also knew Clastres was a troubled man who maintained a vigorous attitude when it came to upholding honor. As an originator of the pact, Laudez had a similar attitude about such things. Being aware of this had been a source of conflict, and he had many sleepless nights because of it. He had supported Clastres with the silence through the years, but he, too, knew a time would come when it had to end. Listening to tonight's debate and conscious of the growing dissension in the streets, Laudez faced reality, knowing Clastres would never be the first to declare the end of the covenant for fear of forsaking the trust the others had in his leadership.

With this in mind, Laudez decided he, and he alone, was the only one in the room who was in a position to release the remaining guerrillas from the vow they had made thirty-four years ago and still allow them to maintain their honor, reputations and trust.

Laudez and Clastres had established their trust in each other since the days of their youth, and he hoped it would sustain him through what he was about to reveal. He waited for the right moment, just before he thought one of them would suggest settling the entire matter by taking a written vote.

"We are all men of honor and that is to be respected." Laudez began his monologue as familiar as the one he had startled them with thirty-four years ago. "Before we cast our votes, which could well be swayed by the circumstances in front of the administration building or by our devout determination not to undermine the oath we faithfully uphold, there is something I must tell you that might influence the outcome of this meeting. Perhaps you would like to hear it."

Although the evening was late, they were willing to listen to any possibility of ending the stalemate in the most argumentative meeting they had ever conducted. For a moment they thought Laudez might be testing them to hasten a solution to the quandary they were in, but this was quickly disregarded. Laudez did not jest.

"We would like to hear what you have to say, Laudez," said Clastres. "Let us pray your words will assist us and preserve our dignity."

"I have information that I have kept to myself for nearly two weeks. And although I have agonized over the thought of betraying our comrades who swore themselves to secrecy and were true to it, I believe if they could speak they would tell you what I am about to say. You can be sure they would do so."

"And what would they say, Laudez?" asked Hilaria.

Laudez gathered his wits, stood up to face them, then shattered their thirty-four-year-old covenant in a matter of seconds.

"They would tell you of one who knows our martyr is not buried in our hearts. One who knows exactly where he sleeps."

Hilaria heard the pulse of her heart pound in volleys against her eardrums. Raul's knuckles whitened as he grasped the edge of the table. Fredrico, who always had a smile, lost it. Ramon stood erect with the look of disbelief, then immediately sat down again. Alvita's mouth fell open and for the first time in her life not a word came out. Clastres, always under control, always prepared, always calm, merely flicked his eyebrows in the direction of Laudez. He was not about to refute the word of his friend who had been a lifelong ally. Laudez would not make such a statement if it were not so, even though he had just splintered the pledge of Laguna de Bay.

"Are you saying, Laudez, a comrade has broken the silence?" Clastres asked calmly.

"No," replied Laudez. "This has never happened, because surely one of us would have discovered it before now. The one with this knowledge has known as long as we have. He has stated to me that the waiting and the anguish of the people can be satisfied. We must bury our silence and open the grave he says before it is too late for us, because then he will be the only one who will know where the priest is buried. When the people hear this, they will never forgive us, even in our graves."

"And who might this man be, Laudez?" asked Clastres.

"He has been here for a few months now, a rice buyer," replied Laudez. "During the war he was a colonel on the Shimbu Line, which we all remember so well. He has not been recognized because he has aged and looks different. His name is Nikono Yashima."

Laudez sat down and let the group mull over the significance of what he had said. They all knew Nikono had been a Japanese colonel during the siege of the Kalinawan Caves and was the archenemy of every Filipino, guerrilla or not. He had been notoriously brilliant for his performance in the field and a strategist of emplacement installations. During the war his 27th Regiment went in relentless pursuit of the notorious one-armed guerrilla, Clastres, and his associates until the Japanese unit was relieved of the detail.

Nikono had returned to Luzon wearing a full beard, business attire and dark glasses. He was a quarterly visitor who treated the rice farmers fairly and would return to Japan when the harvest ended. At first no one recognized him, mainly because he had seldom been seen in the towns during the war. His passive attitude combined with his limp gave no hint of his old arrogance.

At the end of the rice harvest, while supervising the loading of the yield, Nikono's glasses were knocked off accidentally. Laudez, the overseer at the time who had already begun to recognize his old adversary, was convinced of his beliefs despite the beard. He never challenged Nikono even though there had been times years ago when he had wished the Japanese colonel were dead.

Laudez was not the only one who had recognized Nikono when his glasses fell off. Alvarez Guzan, a cousin of Fredrico, had instantly recognized him, even after thirty-four years. It was then Alvarez had been forced to carry the water bucket that was used in the torture of Father Douglas. Since that day Alvarez had been accused of being a collaborator but had persisted in proclaiming his innocence. No, this was a face, beard or no beard, he would never forget. Alvarez and Laudez were the only two who had recognized Nikono since his return, and they did not disclose his identity for fear of instigating riots and retaliation.

During one of their business arrangements, Laudez confronted Nikono. It was only through positive identification of Laudez as one of the original guerrillas did Nikono come forward—and he devastated the former guerrilla with the news that he knew where the priest was buried.

Hilaria waited until she was certain the impact of Laudez's news had subsided and the relief she felt had also taken hold of the others. She, who had not shed a tear for thirty-four years, refused to let herself become emotional. She confronted Laudez: "Has he told you where our martyr rests?"

"He has."

"He knows exactly the place?" Hilaria pressed on.

"Yes," replied Laudez.

"Why has he not made this known before?" asked Ramon.

"It was not until recently when he saw the demonstrations in the streets did he realize we had never returned for our beloved priest." Laudez hesitated a moment, knowing his next statement might not be welcomed. "He said he is willing to come to one of our meetings and relate to us what he knows with the hope that if we will listen to him we might be able to remedy our differences with the people."

Raul bitterly assailed the interference of outsiders. "Our soldier friend Whitey suggests we settle our problems now. Our old enemy makes the same opinion. Perhaps we should let everyone but ourselves tell us how we should conduct our affairs."

"Do not be angry, my friend," said Clastres. "Did not our shepherd forgive the arrogant ones while he was bleeding? Did he not free every one of us when he came to us when we dared not leave the safety of the hills? Is there not one of us who would not be full of joy to feel his presence once again? Perhaps we should listen to the American who has come from such a distance to seek someone he has never known. He survived the great effort to free us, and I believe we should give this some consideration. He could have died for the cause as our martyr did, and this, too, should be considered. Maybe Nikono Yashima has something worthwhile to say, and perhaps we should hear more of it. Now that we have been informed he knows where the good priest rests, surely we can all understand what that means to us, because he could have very well released this knowledge. It could be he respects our silence and our reasons for it. Before we make a decision, perhaps we should hear what he has stifled within his own conscience these many years. I bear him no unkind feeling, because I have tried to emulate the words of Father Douglas who said, 'We should be like the rose.' Would I be like this flower if I were to harbor unforgivingness? Was not his message to forgive, as he forgave us? How can any of us be forgiven if we do not forgive? If we do not remember his words, then we have been nothing but hypocrites. We will not be able to face the gray dawn or look for his courage if we do not remember what he told us. We must forgive or his words are meaningless."

They listened attentively, as they always did, to their old, dogged leader, which he still was to them. Clastres was their rock, the wall that turned back the tides threatening to drown them in their meager surroundings.

Clastres was wise enough to let them improve upon his suggestions and waited for their conversations to subside.

Hilaria asked, "If we decide to invite Nikono to our next meeting, should we also invite Whitey to be present?"

Alvita interjected, "If so, then Father Demato and Rafael, should they also attend?"

Clastres put these proposals before them, and they agreed unanimously to listen to Nikono and also invite the three others to attend. At this point they fully realized that if Nikono definitely knew where Father Douglas was buried, he would actually be making the decision—whether they liked the idea or not—for them.

Tired, disgruntled, and well past midnight, they elected Fredrico to notify Rafael and Father Demato. Rafael was to inform me to also attend, and Laudez was to notify Nikono. Hilaria had thought of requesting the presence of Mrs. Gonsalves but then reconsidered because everything hinged upon the words of Nikono Yashima.

It had been a hectic two weeks in Pililia. The marketplace was still in turmoil from the lack of women buyers, and the batas had more freedom than they had ever had before. The influx of those entering Pililia from the villages along the Laniti crowded the streets and hindered the progress of vehicles. Even the jeepney runs were far behind schedule. No one knew when the women would take to the streets again, but everyone knew they would if they did not receive a response from the administration building.

Meanwhile, Mrs. Gonsalves, with her bruised hip from the belfry fall, had returned to a roseless bush. She immediately went about the business of bringing new life into the thorny plant. The women, who had almost forgotten the words of the pilgrimage song, began to sing it once again. Hilaria heard them singing it along the shore; Laudez heard them singing it along the riverbanks; Clastres heard them singing it in the streets. These same women claimed the presence of their martyr could be felt in their hearts and therefore sent the batas to gather wild roses and cast them into the Laniti River so its anger would abate. Instead, the Laniti became angrier as the miniature monsoons entered the mountains and unleashed squalls, which pushed the river into the Laguna depths. Neither the river nor the song subsided.

Rafael, who had returned to Morong to comfort his mother, suddenly returned to Pililia in great haste. He brought with him the message that I had been longing to hear. With elation such as I had not seen since our first meeting, he said, "You—an outsider—are invited to the Monday night meeting. You should know only Filipinos have ever been permitted to attend. Father Demato has been asked to be there as well as Nikono Yashima. He is the man you saw in the jeepney."

I responded, "I am amazed, too, Rafael; since coming to Luzon I have been patiently waiting for this. But why is this Japanese, you say his name is Nikono, to attend?"

"We will have to wait until Monday, my friend. I only know he has been asked to attend."

The hundreds of women, inspired by the slim rose bearer, had opened the guerrilla's ears and hearts, and their effort had stirred the heart of Pililia. There were no head nets seen on the streets from Tuesday until Sunday morning, when they appeared by the hundreds again. Their effort had not deteriorated in the least. This was clear at Mass on Sunday, evidenced by the overflow, mainly women, that spilled out into the street.

Father Demato, during his homily, pleaded, "Be rational in your quest, and remember Christ is still having a problem in getting listeners." Some of the wearers of the head nets stiffened their necks at his words, as if they were bracing for a storm. These crusaders were ready to stand their ground again—the grapevine assured this. Tenseness lingered over Pililia, and the bamboo wreath was buried beneath a mound of roses. To my eyes this was an unforgettable gesture of beauty.

Directly after noon on Monday the women began to assemble, arriving by ones, twos and groups. Three busloads brought hundreds from Paete. Standing in the rear, I saw there had been some changes in the agenda. Mrs. Gonsalves, because of her hip injury, did not leave her home. More noticeably, there were more men within the ranks. Perhaps the empty rice bowls had prompted their resolve. At any rate they stood beside the stalwart women, signifying additional support for their vigil, which was not particularly enjoyable because they had to stand in the heat of the day. The drivers, who had to turn up side streets to get around the multitudes blocking the way, were becoming annoyed. The demonstrators stood their ground, though, refusing to be intimidated by the blasting of horns or shaking of fists. Some of them sat down, and when a shower fell upon them it was looked upon as a blessing to their cause. Still the doors of the administration building did not budge the entire day, and just before dusk the people trudged homeward.

In the cool of the evening Rafael and I went to Clastres Bulatao's house. After introducing me to the one-armed man of combat heroics, Rafael escorted me around the room to meet the other guerrillas, two of whom, Raul and Alvita Reyes, I already knew—their presence astonished me.

Clastres was intriguing. At fifty-six he moved quicker than Hilaria and was definite in his movements. He caught the slightest movement in the room and let you know it with a flick of his eyebrows. Before this night ended I would understand the depths of his determination and his incredible endurance. In the eyes of the Japanese, this folklore hero must have been a man to be reckoned with and a man who had commanded their respect.

Clastres motioned me to sit next to Rafael, who sat next to Father Demato. They were situated several feet from the six other guerrillas, with Clastres stationed to the front of the group. One vacant chair off to the side was for Nikono, who had not yet arrived. There was a sense of anxiety in the room, yet Clastres and Hilaria maintained their composure. I remained silent, assuming the position of a selected guest waiting his turn to be welcomed in out of the shadow of unimportance. I was the outsider and I sat there behaving like one.

Suddenly Hilaria motioned Clastres to the door (he seemed to be waiting for a signal from her). The renowned veteran opened the door for Nikono, who also had an air of assurance about him that seemed to be characteristic of all those in the room with the exception of Father Demato, who sat with arms folded on his chest and eyes closed, surely praying. How Hilaria knew Nikono was at the door dumbfounded me for the moment, but then I remembered the words of Rafael concerning her hearing ability. Perhaps she was the reason why no one had ever been able to get within hearing distance of their meetings. I was now sure she could hear my thoughts before I did.

Nikono Yashima, about five feet seven inches tall, wore a graying beard and dark glasses. He spryly moved to the seat Clastres had set aside for him. He did not speak when Clastres introduced him to me, but only bowed and nodded. Evidently all the others knew him, because there were no other introductions. His familiarity became more evident to me as he now sat across from us. Clastres went over to him and asked a question, and he nodded in assent, slowly removing the dark glasses, which aroused my interest in him even further. Something was nagging at my brain, and I tried to get a response from some old memory. The picture did not come.

"First," began Clastres, "I would remind all of you in this room that regardless of what is accomplished here tonight, we must refrain from letting the results be known until we seven guerrillas decide what is to be done. The execution of any decision must come from us alone, and not the eleven taking part in this discussion. We have asked our soldier friend Whitey to attend, because we seven remember that his comrades, his friends, accomplished much for us. We are grateful and indebted to them. We know of his quest concerning Father Douglas and have thus agreed to have him attend this meeting. We have also invited Nikono who has relayed critical information to Laudez that, once we have had a private conversation with him, may or may not change the course of our direction. If we find that his statement is not sufficient enough to satisfy us, then Nikono, Whitey, Rafael and Father Demato will be dismissed and the matter will revert to Laudez, Ramon, Hilaria, Raul, Alvita, Fredrico and myself. So as not to prolong the anxiety, we seven will escort Nikono from the room and take into consideration what he has to say."

They left the room. I had no idea what was transpiring but Father Demato and Rafael apparently seemed to. Father Demato unfolded his arms, bowed his head and prayed. In the quiet of the room the faint rustle of his beads could be heard. Rafael was sitting straight up, staring heavenward. He, too, was praying. I tried to keep my uneasiness hidden.

After several minutes they reentered the room and took their previous positions. It was plain to see something had happened in the lives of these hard-nosed Filipinos. Clastres stood up and spoke directly to the three of us. With the dripping of water from the trees onto the roof, breathing of eleven people and the sound of Clastres's voice, it came to me that these were the only sounds in the otherwise stillness of the night.

"My friends, it is because of Nikono's information handed out to us through Laudez that we have conducted this meeting. Therefore, I will let him relate to you the reason for this assembly."

He stepped away from the center of the room and occupied the chair of Laudez, who strode forward and diplomatically acknowledged the bid to speak.

"Thank you, my good friend. I hope I shall be worthy of your confidence. There is a trust we have endured together since the days of our guerrilla warfare. One that Rafael's mother and all our women near and far are challenging us to forsake. We have never been able to do this. We were positive this trust was completely in our hands and no others; however, two weeks ago Nikono approached me in the streets and informed me he also knew the content of the trust.

"We have verified what he claims to be true. We know he was present when the event occurred that put all of Laguna de Bay in great darkness. He says there is much beyond understanding on his part during the events of those days, and he asks if we will listen to what he has to confess. I hope after tonight we might be able to bring our martyr home and into the prayers of the children, and I hope every Filipino will hear the bell as it calls for our love of him to be shown to the world. If there is no objection, let us hear what lies in the heart of Nikono Yashima."

There was no comment from the other guerrillas. Laudez waited until Nikono moved to the center of the room, and then took the chair Nikono had just vacated. It was imperative for them to have Nikono tell his story first; then I, an outsider, would be a witness to the fact that they had not betrayed the honor binding them for so many years.

T he following is my version of Nikono's account of his trials and ordeals during the war. He begins the saga in the year 1933 and continues it to this night in Pililia, May 1977, when the tomb of the martyred priest would be disclosed.

Nikono Yashima was an exceptionally bright scholar. In 1933, at the age of eighteen, the Japanese Military Academy sent him to the San Diego Engineering College in San Diego, California. He graduated in 1937 with the highest honors in his engineering class, and he excelled in the English language. Due to the rumblings in China he was forced to put aside any desire and hope he had for his future in America. Official correspondence requested his return to Japan immediately following his graduation. He then enlisted in the military.

The military wasted no time with Nikono, placing him directly in the Engineering Corps. There he spent four months drafting blueprints and installing engineering equipment, but most importantly as the future would require, interpreting maps. In 1937 he found himself comfortably locating strategic positions of field artillery in China. There his map interpretation and coordinating abilities combined with the dispersing of personnel merited enough esteem to promote him to corporal. That same year he married Um Okada, whom he had known since his younger years. When his promotion to corporal went into effect, Um began to look to the future with optimism, hoping to settle away from the military base and in the country; however, this dream was short lived. Nikono Yashima's future was in the South Pacific.

In December 1941, immediately following Japan's attack on Pearl

Harbor, Nikono was sent to Rabaul by submarine. For three frantic months his expertise was utilized to the utmost. It included all strategic assignments from pillboxes, artillery emplacements, excavations, tunneling, study of high and low elevations, coral reef determinations, sea depths, and topography to channel entrances, where he expedited the laying of mines. Further promotion did not come despite his vast knowledge and ability to implement all the information he had available. He was invaluable, but he did not contest the conditions he was subjected to even though in those three months he was at the point of exhaustion. Nor did he question the effort put into the defense of Rabaul with all its war materiel and the latest firepower. Nevertheless, he knew, as some of his superiors must have known, any island could easily become isolated. Rabaul was a fortress, but it required a superior air defense, which never materialized.

At the end of February 1942, Nikono Yashima's name was placed on the immediate shipment of troops for Luzon, in the Philippines. Through official communiqués, which he had access to, he learned this island would be the final barrier in the Philippines confronting the Allied force. Therefore, elaborate networks of defense would be required. Nikono was ready, as always. Another frontier demanding his skills was calling; without reluctance or hesitation, he accepted this new tour of duty. The Allied forces, he surmised, would never reach the Philippines. The Japanese Imperial Navy would send them all to a watery grave long before they attempted such an undertaking. Clark Field on Luzon was stockpiled with Japanese Zeroes and bombers, and the pilots of the Imperial Air Force would devastate everything in their path.

Nikono closed out his career on Rabaul, finally getting the order that sent him under the sea again. When he reached Manila at the end of March he was still a corporal. Once situated in his new quarters another order was issued, which placed him under the tutorship of a Filipino teacher and a special course in the Filipino dialect, Tagalog. This involved a month of intense study, but his proficiency came to the forefront once more. His command of the English language served him well, as he soon discovered in Manila, where it was used extensively. Somewhere during the tutoring he began to realize his duties would take him beyond the masses in Manila. It began to look as if he would be relegated to what he considered to be his most favorable position, the survey of the interior and the further implementation of war materiel. If Manila succumbed to conquest the main line of defense on Luzon would not be in the hundreds of barrios but in the territory beyond them. English was seldom, if ever, used in these isolated barrios, where Tagalog was the main language. Within a month Nikono understood enough of the dialect and notified his command he was ready to pursue further activity. His request was received, and he was notified he would be activated to his new field of duty: the 27th Imperial Infantry Regiment of the 13th Division. His destination was the barracks of the 27th Regiment in Pililia.

In his five years of military life he had developed a tremendous zeal to excel. There was little opportunity for this in Manila; all its defenses had been installed before his arrival, and most of that was in the old walled city. The buildings themselves made up the bulk of this defense, which he did not consider adequate. His military instinct warned him that the city was, for all practical purposes, dangerously vulnerable to both aerial and naval bombardments. He was positive the defense of Luzon had to be installed beyond the city's limits.

The new assignment was therefore welcomed. In the few remaining days he pored over every map available in the corps that referred to Laguna de Bay. He utilized every moment to the fullest. It was during this interim that he received the news from Um that their first child would be born in September. It had taken almost three months for Nikono's mail to catch up with him since his transfer from Rabaul. He was elated, and the news only increased his aggressiveness.

In the middle of April 1942 he boarded an army truck with two trunk loads of classified maps and hundreds of documents pertaining to the regions in the Laguna Province. Two lieutenants and a colonel accompanied Nikono, who was still a corporal. It was a long ride over isolated roads to Pililia, and they were well aware of the Filipino guerrilla activity in the Laguna hills. The officer's truck was carefully positioned in the center of a seven-vehicle convoy: three weapons carriers in the front and three to the rear. It would take a considerable amount of guerrilla firepower to prevent this convoy from reaching its destination. All through the ride Nikono studied the terrain between conversations with the officers, who were inquisitive about his accomplishments on Rabaul. Nikono

was at ease in discussing his tactical expertise with them; however, he
soon realized when talking with them that his skills greatly exceeded
theirs. His strength was his ability to immediately distinguish what went
where and how. He could invariably recall the height of a mountain or the
depth of a ravine without ever climbing the mountain or crossing the
ravine. In his work patience was his virtue, and he never let ambition
interfere with it, although his resentment toward their rank grew.
Performance would eventually merit reward; he was sure of this.

The dust generated by the convoy filled his lungs. At times the vehicles in front were invisible. Goggles became coated with silt, and Nikono
wondered how the drivers, especially the rear three, could even maintain
direction. When the convoy left the outskirts of Manila behind, the vehicles suddenly increased their speed, and the rapid run to the garrison in
Pililia began. Increasing the speed lessened the chance of a surprise
ambush and could prevent the timing of one. The convoy sped through
Antipolo, Teresa and Morong; as they approached each town, the vehicle
throttles were wide open until they had passed through them. Chickens,
dogs and civilians scampered off the road in fear for their lives. They were
used to it. The Japanese had been here for months and seldom had they
been kind. In these towns beyond the fringes of Manila, civilian life was
a day-by-day existence.

Nikono had received several briefings on the Filipinos and was readily prepared to deal with any situation. Here on Luzon, unlike that on
Rabaul, the Japanese were faced with constant ambushes and sabotage.
Nikono's objective was to distribute his talents where necessary and mil-
itarily important. He had no desire to become involved with the guerrilla ground war, and he believed this involvement was under the jurisdic-
tion of the infantry regiments.

It did not take Nikono long to discover life in Pililia was not the same
as in Manila. The Filipinos did not look up when the convoy entered
Pililia—a clear indication of their hostility toward the Japanese. When he
stepped out of the army truck he caught the resentment immediately.
However, it did not alarm him. In his studies in Manila he had been fore-
warned by his Filipino tutor, who said, "For the most part, Filipinos trusted only Filipinos." Nikono read of the domination they had endured since
the invasion of the Spanish. Hours of research from the time of King

Philip up to the Japanese invasion had been in his curriculum. Nikono realized he and those with him were the immediate danger, not the past. This, in turn, became his danger. Under the Japanese occupation, which brought about severe restrictions and punishment, he had little fear of the inhabitants. Lack of cooperation by the civilians was dealt with by precise action, none of it ever beneficial to the people. Nikono was confident the real danger was beyond the towns: it would come from the hills, or on the isolated roads, or on the river crossings. The inhabitants had to contend with him and his superiors, which minimized his concern about them, although it did not lessen the tension in Pililia. "It will not be a friendly place," he thought.

Pililia, with more than ten thousand inhabitants, was situated at the most northern tip of the Jalajala Peninsula, the larger of the two in Laguna de Bay. The southern end of the peninsula almost came to a point. By traveling down the road that hugged the bay, one would eventually reach Paete. Below Paete was Santa Cruz, one of the largest towns on the shoreline. Nikono was not interested in Santa Cruz, although he had included it in his studies and briefings while in Manila. His greatest attention, however, would be focused to the north and northeast of Pililia. Rugged mountains were in either direction; just back beyond the flat lands, rice paddies and the lesser hills. It was in these surroundings his assignment would be fulfilled: a defense far to the east of Manila, without the use of roads, beyond the plateaus, and into the foothills to the partially established Shimbu Line, where he would put into effect his greatest accomplishments. What he did not have on paper was already secured firmly in his mind. He was going to install a defense beyond penetration from either the ground or the air; as on Rabaul, the plan would utilize elevations. He intended to get the use of the Filipinos to accomplish this, but first he had to go into the mountains. He was going to get a silver bar on his shoulder yet.

He was assigned quarters with the other cadre of the Engineering Corps. Colonel Ogawa, the division staff officer, immediately informed Nikono of his first assignment, which was to occur this coming morning. "You will be going toward Baras," he ordered, "then striking eastward toward the base of Mapalug Mountain. Circumstances permitting, you can climb the mountain and explore the caves. You have studied this area on maps; I now want you to know it first hand."

"Colonel Ogawa," and Nikono bowed, "I request two hundred men to keep any guerrilla activity from interrupting this reconnaissance."

"You shall have them."

"I request to handpick them myself."

"I grant you this also," responded Colonel Ogawa. "You will start this mission by three o'clock in the morning." With this said, Nikono was dismissed, overjoyed at the possibility of exploring the Kalinawan Caves.

Nikono immediately went about handpicking his men, who were all veteran infantrymen, but not accustomed to taking orders from a corporal. They had been under the immediate command of Lieutenant Yajiro Miyomoto, who was now being pushed aside.

"You will be prepared at 12:30 in the morning," informed Nikono. He saw no need to tell them about the destination. This was the beginning of their discipline.

Nikono was going to make sure the guerrillas could never be sure of him. Once he got a foothold in the mountains, the guerrillas would have to have an army to dislodge or disrupt his plans even though they knew every foot of the terrain. Nikono was aware of the approximate number of active guerrillas in the Pililia hills and how dedicated they were. He lived by facts and figures. The guerrillas had to eat and there was not any food in the mountains. Sooner or later, in or out of disguise, they would have to return to a source of food and ammunition.

Most of these well-experienced soldiers had seen active duty in China. Untested personnel could not jeopardize this assignment; it required men who understood the mind of the guerrilla and the importance of establishing a superior defense at the southern end of the Shimbu Line. Facts, figures, blueprints, maps and surveys were one thing, human error was another.

When the early call, a whispered one, awakened the men out of a half-night's sleep, they had no idea a man with a rank just above that of a private would be leading them through the shadows of Mapalug Mountain or that a lieutenant would be taking orders from him. After countless patrols and searches, they would learn why the lieutenant listened and why the corporal was indispensable.

The convoy of trucks, one containing all the maps available on the territory north to northeast of Pililia, left Pililia under the cover of darkness hours before dawn. There was no deliberate attempt to pass through Pililia unnoticed. There would always be an observer lurking in the shadows, and he had no doubt military movements were keenly scrutinized. They went north, traveling over the old bridge toward Tanay and Baras. The wake of dust clouds left eerie formations as the truck lights illuminated them in the darkness.

When Nikono had been on Rabaul he experienced a short period of anxiety over his ability to perform to expectations. This was soon overcome as he undertook the missions that would eventually prove his capabilities. Those days had transformed him into a cold, determined, calculating machine. He no longer allowed one ounce of personal incompetency to disrupt his program or alter his attitude toward success or failure. This attitude would create a bond between the two hundred men and him and would bring total submission from these seasoned troops. In the months to come they would seldom see him smile, but they would see his comprehensiveness and his ability to adjust under the most taxing circumstances. They would become comfortable under his command.

Nikono could have commenced this first venture with a series of daily and nightly bivouacs, but he knew the Black Swamp and the lesser hills on the slopes of Mapalug Mountain were ahead of him. He also wanted to abolish the routine of such maneuvers, thus creating a confidence in these men so that eventually they could and would depend upon him no matter what the occasion, even death. Meanwhile he would nourish their individual aspirations into a concrete solidarity and mold them into a unit filled with explosive loyalty, devoid of individual performance and egotism. He would lead and they would follow.

Nikono was well aware of another individual, Clastres Bulatao, watching the stars in the Philippine sky. This crafty guerrilla had also handpicked each of his comrades, calling them out of the bamboo thickets, rice paddies, nipa huts and from the anguish of the Japanese occupation. Nearly two hundred men, without rank, uniforms, enough ammunition or food surrounded him. They, too, were bonded and firmly dedicated to their cause and had committed themselves to the struggle their leader had chosen them for. If he climbed a mountain, so, too, would they, and they would continue until their blood ran down the slopes and into the Laniti River. The determined Japanese soldier grinned amidst the thought of the challenge of crossing paths with the guerrilla leader.

The sun was a long way from coming out of the east to scorch the mountain ranges when the Japanese convoy reached Baras, where Nikono turned the trucks to the east. Even in the mantle of darkness he knew where the edge of the Black Swamp began. He also knew he was but a month away from the beginning of the rainy season. When the wheels of the vehicles began to churn and every chassis shuddered, Nikono ordered the soldiers to dismount; their boots were immediately initiated into the dank undergrowth of the swamp. They could barely see this new corporal, but they could hear his quick, sharp commands and wondered how this new arrival with only two stripes was demanding more of their attention than Lieutenant Miyomoto.

The edge of the swamp was several miles from Baras. The swamp itself was six miles long, ending only because the foothills below Mapalug Mountain kept it from reaching the base of the mountain itself. When he was in Manila Nikono had decided to challenge the swamp head on before the rains could prohibit a crossing. He knew where every village was located, north, east and south of its fringes. There would be staples there for his men if necessary. His mind was a map, and the length and breadth of the Black Swamp was etched carefully within the channels of it, so much so that before this company of selected personnel reached the opposite end of the quagmire, they would marvel at the man leading them even though he had never come this way before.

Nikono went over the supplies taken from the trucks. Satisfied, he ordered the men to sit down while he assigned them the various duties and system of portage. Again, he did not instruct them about their destination. He wanted them to trace his steps in the still of the night so that on this first expedition they would be following him blindly, and would do so from this time onward.

They marched into the depths of the swamp. They stumbled but never grumbled. Some of them sank to their knees and even hips. Others thumped their helmets on the branches of trees that had succumbed to the yearly flood of water. Many of the men had been on Luzon since Pearl Harbor, but only a few had ever been engaged in a swamp maneuver. In the darkness of the swamp they soon realized they had to depend upon one another for survival, yet as a unit they had not been together for twenty-four hours. Nikono was creating a mold they would never break out of.

Sinking to their knees became routine but tiring. The suction of the gripping swamp drained their stamina, yet not one of them questioned why the man ahead of them had not circled the swamp. They dared not ask. They were confronted with entangled vines, soggy thickets, quicksand and semiquicksand, bottomless pits, tormenting mosquitoes, fist-sized spiders and numerous snakes. By the time they reached the far fringe of the swamp, they had struggled for four hours. They slumped onto the solid earth at the base of the hills and watched the sun break over the crest and glisten in the drifting vapors. The steam escaped from their soaked and muddied uniforms, then evaporated in the heat of the sun. As they plodded out of the maze, they witnessed the corporal place his hand on one of the soldiers shoulder. This gesture convinced them they had overcome some sort of test. Nikono knew how to strengthen their bond when he did not even know their names.

There were several hills of various heights between this end of the swamp and Mapalug Mountain. Nikono, along with Lieutenant Miyomoto and three other men, climbed the first hill that was hindering his view of the elevation that was embedded in his mind—the aperture that led into the heart of the mountain and the Kalinawan Caves. When they crested the hill the tireless Nikono looked up to the opening in the mountain, which was over four thousand feet above them, yawning out over the hills and the stagnant swamp. For several minutes he scrutinized the scene, then a slight smile escaped his concentration, one of the few times this would occur in the presence of his men. The only area that Nikono had little information of was the interior of the caves, which had not been recorded on the maps.

After they had climbed back down the hill, he assembled the men on the moist edge of the swamp and stood beside Lieutenant Miyomoto. Finally he offered them his name: "I am Nikono Yashima." They already knew his rank. The lieutenant was there to train these men for combat, but Nikono was there to implement the instruments of combat.

With the introduction behind him, he and the men set out to climb the hills that defended the mountain. He was careful not to forge ahead of the lieutenant but also cautious enough not to let his superior outmaneuver him. For the moment Nikono was willing to settle for even terms. However, he was aiming for that silver bar on his own shoulder and a star after that.

They did not encounter any problems with the hills. Only the sun affected their effort on the six-mile trek to the base of Mapalug Mountain. He brought them through the bamboo thickets, trying to maintain as true a course as possible. Every time they emerged from the sheltering treelike grass and its crackling song, the sun was there to greet them. It could not be avoided. It was late afternoon when they dragged themselves to the foot of the massive mountain, which loomed over them as they slumped at its base.

Nikono had no intention of herding them up the mountainside right away. He told them, "Do not look up. The slopes will be awesome enough when we are on them." He let them wallow in a stream like carabao for the rest of the day. He knew tired men would accomplish little and develop complications when exhausted.

There was a gradual rising at the base of the slope that would enable them to work their way upward without too great an initial effort. The area beyond the first fifteen hundred feet would pose the most difficulty. It was not as sheer as the wall that surrounded the mountain to the south, but there were many overhangs to impede the ascent. Scaling each one of them would be a severe test.

They began the ascent without the ropes they had portaged through the swamp, but several hundred feet into the climb the footing became less secure. At this point twenty men wrapped a rope around their waists; likewise, the others did the same. In this way each man had the support of the others.

Eight hundred feet into the climb there was a sudden change in the terrain as the foliage gradually disappeared and a solid-rock formation became more evident. Nikono did not use the rope because it prohibited him from maneuvering on the wall of the mountain. He had to show them how. The soldiers cautiously watched him and his acrobats; his actions brought confidence. They would go where he went. He led them up the rock until they came to where he had marked with his eyes from his position on the base—a bald spot almost a thousand feet above the swamp.

Nikono knew the unwelcome ball of fire would catch them some-where on the mountain no matter what time they began the ascent. Climbing at night was out of the question and would endanger the lives of his men unnecessarily. He had a thousand other plans for them as well as the thousands of feet to the mountain aperture.

Just before high noon, moments before the sun topped the peak, he brought them to rest beneath a series of overhangs. They were still a thou-sand feet below their target, the Kalinawan Caves. He walked among them, making sure the ropes were securely fastened and handing out gauze and bandages to bind their cuts and bruises. Then he went off by himself to study the ordeal that would have to be faced before they gained entrance to the caves, none of which could be seen from this position on the mountain. After an hour's rest he returned to them and cautioned them, "Do not look down until you reach the eye of the mountain—the doorway into this sentinel of the Laniti Valley."

The men began the final leg to the ledge above, a fifty-foot-square span that awaited them at the mouth of the caves. The thousand feet above their heads would be the most hazardous climb they would ever encounter in their military careers, and it would have little to do with sol-diering. They scrambled and crawled their way up the slope, resting atop each overhang that hindered their effort. They lost sight of the hole in the mountain more times than they saw it, and only on the overhangs could they observe it, and even then it was not always possible. Always above them was the man who seemed to have more arms than a spider had legs. Where he dared to venture they came after, and their confidence in him became immeasurable. He seemed to know just what route to take, as if he were part of the mountain itself. Lieutenant Miyomoto eventually sub-mitted his position to the aggressive Nikono.

Nikono led them to the top of the narrowest overhang of the climb. He was thirty feet beyond it and cautiously working his way toward the next precipice when he heard the rock dislodge from the side of the mountain. He looked down to see it hurtling and crashing into space like a gigantic cannonball. One hundred and fifty men had reached the ledge that Nikono had just mastered, all working their way upward on an angle, when suddenly the rock that had been bearing their weight released itself from the slope of Mapalug and cast five of the men into thin air. They dangled below those who had secured footholds on the overhang. Swinging like pendulums they were helpless. The men on the ledge immediately felt the pull of their weight, and instant reflex against the tug collapsed them to prone positions on the ledge. Nikono immediately commanded, "Do not move until the drifting momentum of the dangling men has subsided."

They listened to him, sensing the calmness in his voice. Nikono waited until the initial thrust of their bodies had come under control and they were dangling straight down, then slowly and carefully he instructed his men on the ledge: "One man at a time, rise to a standing position; this will hold the weight of the pull. Then secure your heels in the crevices of the ledge. When this is done drag each man up and to the top of the overhang." They listened to the firm directions of the man thirty feet above them.

When they were all on the ledge they looked up at Nikono. He threw a salute in their direction, which raised their morale again because they knew he was saluting them, not the lieutenant. But they did not dare return the salute, not only because it would have embarrassed Lieutenant Miyomoto, whose back was to them, but also because it was not protocol. Nikono was only a corporal, and no one salutes a corporal but an officer.

After a half-hour's rest they resumed the climb, but a little more cautiously than before. They had five hundred feet yet to conquer. It was now early afternoon, and a sudden shower swept across the apron of Mapalug, drenching the men just as they were about to turn into the final assault to the opening above. A black cloud, as well as the downpour accompanying it, came in from the eastern side; however, it was shielded from their view by the width of the mountain. The unexpected event caused them to hug and cling to the face of the shale in a precarious position as the winds and rains deluged them. Once again, Nikono commanded them, "Do not look down into the sweeping rains." They could hear him despite the howling winds and pelting rain all around them. Losing the sun briefly was the only welcome aspect of the deluge. When it had passed they readied themselves once again for the ascent. They slung their rifles behind them, the butts inside their bandoliers at the lower back so they could keep both arms free to grasp what fissures and cracks could be found. The search for these clefts commenced.

All eyes were trained on Nikono as he searched for the safest and securest seams on the rocky promontory, always moving back and forth across the face of it until he was sure of the course. The only overhang remaining was the ledge in front of the Kalinawan Caves; it was the table-land that would offer rest to the climbers.

The day wore on and the sun and the struggle wore them out. There was little to cling to now except their reserve. Nikono snaked his body up the final hundred feet slowly, cautiously, painstakingly. They found his bloodied fingerprints staining the stone above them, and they followed the spattered trail to where he was perched like an eagle on the ledge four thousand feet above the Laniti Valley. He hauled the first man over the ledge with his bleeding hands, then another, until enough of them secured a position on the overhang and then together literally dragged the last twenty of them up the incline and onto the shelf. They cheered, and then they collapsed simultaneously before the gaping aperture with the eagles circling overhead. Tired as they were, meeting the mountain on its terms had given them an inner strength.

For an hour they remained there. Lieutenant Miyomoto, wise enough not to enter the chamber before Nikono, waited for him to make a move. Nikono, on the other hand, was not about to flaunt the authority of his superior before the eyes of these men who already held him in high esteem. It was still imperative for him to influence these men in a manner that called for military protocol. Therefore, he made a gesture permitting the officer to proceed first. But Lieutenant Miyomoto also was not about to overplay his authority before these men, so in turn he signaled Nikono into the caves ahead of him, although he made certain he was only a foot behind the corporal. They were almost abreast when they went into the darkness before them.

The sunlight that had penetrated the fifteen-by-fifteen foot opening had fled, leaving Nikono's flashlight to reveal a chamber two hundred feet square. The sight of it brought a glow to his eyes and a thousand ideas into his mind. Lieutenant Miyomoto saw Nikono smile in the shadows of the beam, but he did not see the fortress in Nikono's mind. All Nikono needed now to accomplish this fortress was time and the will of two hundred men.

Nikono moved to the center of the chamber and instantly became motionless. Above him, and above the sound of the shuffling men behind him, he heard the faint sound of running water trickling through the ceiling of solid rock. He could tell by the expression on the lieutenant's face that he had not heard it.

What they all needed now was rest, and the lieutenant ordered them to do so. Some of them slept in the cave and others on the Mapalug ledge.

Before the dawn lit the entrance to the cave, Nikono was up and exploring the tunnels that twisted away from the huge chamber. He let the weary men sleep; they would need additional vigor to get them off the mountain. As he moved into the interior of the cave, he was keenly aware that the trickling sound of the water began to fade. There was complete darkness in the tunnels, broken only by his searching flashlight. Only the shuffling of his boots broke the eerie silence.

He never lost his way, although the passages ran in all directions, crisscrossing one another with some of them passing over others. He did not draw maps or make markings of this cavern of elevated chambers and corridors, all capable of storing enough supplies to create the fortress of his imagination into reality.

One tunnel, leading away from the main chamber to the southern slope did arouse his curiosity, but when a draft from it penetrated the acrid smell of the interior he knew it was a vent to the outside of the mountain. He decided to investigate the next morning.

After a good night's rest Nikono and ten soldiers wended their way around to the southern slope where they discovered the entrance to the tunnel. The opening afforded excellent screening of the Laniti River and the rice-paddied valley. In the sharp eyes and keen mind of the corporal, who stood watching the soaring eagles, he knew immediately what he would implant at the entrance of this nest.

Bearing farther to the east, they surveyed this treacherous slope and the elongated wall of solid rock that wound around to the northeast. The farther end of this wall was obscured by an overhanging ledge and heavy foliage. It disappeared into an impassable abyss. These natural obstacles would hinder any attempt to scale this slope in full force. Feeling secure with this observation and satisfied with the day's excursion, he led the men back to the Kalinawan Caves—and to the future challenge that would eventually absorb his every moment.

For three days they remained on the ledge, catching the crystal clear water that ran down the natural tiny sluices. They took advantage of the forenoon heat to escape the coolness of the caves, and then returned to the interior to escape the tormenting afternoon sun. In between Nikono took them into the maze of corridors to familiarize them with the interior network. Only when their rations were depleted did he announce they would begin the descent.

They left the ledge on the morning of the fifth day. To their surprise Nikono traversed around the ledge to a plateau overlooking the lower northern flank. The foliage here was much thicker on this side of the mountain because the sun was not as searing as on the western and eastern slopes.

As the men gazed down the northern slope they were surprised to find it was not as strenuous a challenge as they had previously overcome. They were convinced Nikono could just as well have taken them up this way as not, and Nikono realized they knew it. They also knew the catlike man had merely put their merit to the test in order to safeguard their own future. He and the mountain had prepared them as a complete unit, not individuals, and the rope had proven it.

They reached the barracks in Baras at nightfall, tired and disconsolate. The lieutenant dismissed them to their quarters, where the sagging cots were a welcome sight. They were content to slump on the twisted canvas, using their laced sacks as pillows and trying to block out the image of the mountain they had half conquered.

The following morning Nikono submitted his objective concerning the Kalinawan Caves to Colonel Ogawa; he also requested thirty men be sent to Japan for a six-month training course that included the assembling and dismantling of all types of winches, cables and specifically the 105mm and 120mm artillery pieces. Colonel Ogawa advised the ambitious engineer there would have to be a confirmation by the Engineering Corp to conduct a military project of such magnitude. A week later, mindful of the exemplary status of Nikono's accomplishments in the field, his request was granted.

The task Nikono faced was arduous but never complicated. He implanted formidable pillboxes, he concealed entrenchments, and he utilized every cave he could find to house artillery and machine guns. He made portable bridges with the empty gasoline and oil drums. Ninety percent of these projects were located in the hills from San Miguel in the north to Paete in the south. He made roads accessible for vehicles with supplies, ammunition and manpower. Lieutenant Miyomoto, a line officer, drilled the selected two hundred men on every piece of equipment available so they could respond immediately to any situation. Ultimately they became skilled craftsman. At any given moment they were prepared; Nikono, ever present, reminded them what they were preparing for. They marched and drilled as a solitary unit. When Nikono received his first bar in May 1942, he celebrated his promotion to lieutenant by taking them to the hills on a night bivouac amidst a torrent of rain. The silver on his shoulder did not separate him from this well-trained and seasoned contingent; it only completed the circle he had begun on the mountain. It was the link that closed the ranks.

His promotion was greeted by a guerrilla attack on two ammunition trucks on the shore road between Paete and Pililia, an isolated area that extended down into the Jalajala Peninsula. Both vehicles were destroyed when two expertly thrown grenades detonated the vehicles into fiery balls, lighting up the waters of Laguna de Bay clear across to Morong. Only one soldier survived the attack. The guerrillas then slipped silently into the interior of the peninsula. The following night, on the outskirts of Pililia, the guerrillas attacked an outpost guarding a supply depot; again the marauding guerrillas fled into the shadows.

There were several other forays by the guerrillas, but Nikono was quick to note none of them occurred above Baras where the extensive emplacements were more numerous. The attack areas were always confined to the districts of Tanay, Pililia and Paete.

Nikono, although seldom involved directly with militant action, requested another meeting with Colonel Ogawa. Permission was granted.

"Colonel Ogawa," Nikono began as he bowed.

"Lieutenant Yashima." This was the first time Nikono had been addressed by a superior as lieutenant and he liked how it sounded.

"I am here to convey my annoyance with the guerrilla activity in my zone of operation."

The colonel answered, "We have been gathering intelligence to plan our course of action. Have you heard of Clastres Bulatao or of a priest named Father Douglas, whom the division staff is certain is in contact with the guerrillas?"

"I do not get involved with civilians or their names," replied Nikono.

The colonel continued, "There are reports of the guerrillas secretly entering Pililia. This is where Father Douglas's parish is. Apparently they enter at night, communicating with the priest, and then return to the hills. We also believe the priest visits them in the hills, attending to the wounded guerrillas."

This information astounded and baffled Nikono, who could not understand why a priest would jeopardize his own welfare in such hostile surroundings.

"This provocation has prompted the silencing of all church bells in Laguna de Bay," continued Colonel Ogawa.

"How will this action curtail the guerrilla activity?" asked Nikono, unaware of the ways of the Christian faith.

"We believe the residents use the bells to inform the guerrillas of certain activities."

"My men would be more than anxious to retaliate; it would be a welcome deviation from their present assignments," suggested Nikono.

Colonel Ogawa listened to the request with interest, knowing of the reputation being established by the men under Nikono. "The matter will have to be presented before the division staff before this kind of action can be undertaken," responded Colonel Ogawa.

Nikono, always patient, diplomatically heeded the colonel's advice. He also knew he would not participate in any foray to oust the guerrillas from the hills. That would be an assignment for Lieutenant Miyomoto, who was just as anxious as the men to participate in a field activity that had the possibility of them seeing some kind of action.

Nikono's men recognized the hostility in the towns, just as Nikono had when he first arrived, and they fervently resented the guerrilla attacks plaguing the entire Laguna de Bay area. At first there had been little to upset the Japanese occupation, only the initial resentment, but after January 1942 the resentment became hostile, although individual defiance was not as common as in the previous month. The Filipinos were dealt with severely—forced labor, beatings, even death—and head counts were taken in every town. In February the Japanese Intelligence Corps began to notice here and there a male Filipino was no longer found within the family circle. The division staff was certain they had become part of the main guerrilla force.

Prior to Nikono's arriving in Pililia, a group of twenty guerrillas had attacked a storage building. The following week thirty guerrillas destroyed a small ammunition dump in Baras. It was evident the guerrillas were well trained and well organized and that someone very capable was in command. There had also been two simultaneous attacks, one in Pililia and the other in Paete, which gave further evidence the guerrillas were not acting in separate groups but were coordinated in guerrilla warfare. Thereafter, all patrols and details were on high alert and prepared for an ambush at any time. All outposts were placed under strict guard and a military code was established. All suspicious Filipinos caught day or night in these areas would be shot. The wily and cautious guerrillas always seemed to know the vulnerability of every site, and with precise action, accomplished every mission with minimal loss to their ranks.

Eventually every military site, whether rations or ammunition dumps, doubled or tripled the guard; upon their arrival, Nikono's contingent was also assigned this duty. Nikono had raised a slight objection to this, although it was never discerned degrading by his "men," as he liked to think of them even though they were not under his direct command. When division staff finally informed Nikono to prepare for a counterattack, his men were relieved to escape the boring guard duty and go into the field again.

There was some grumbling when they learned Nikono would not be involved. Division staff was not about to send a man with such expertise so essential for the preparation of war into the maze of hills surrounding the towns. He was needed for more important commitments.

In June the detail went into the hills above Tanay and Pililia and across the stretch between Pililia and Paete. Reconnaissance reports indicated these sections were the main locations in which the guerrillas were operating. There were a thousand and one signs of guerrilla presence but not one guerrilla. Every time the force entered one of the guerrilla camps, they were gone like thieves in the night. The Japanese realized they were facing an adversary with extreme capabilities. Frustration turned into impatience and anger. The entire Japanese occupational force in Laguna de Bay was on constant alert for any information that would enable them to capture the determined freedom fighter that was in command of the southeastern guerrillas. Hundreds of interrogations took place within the towns, but none of the civilians seemed to have any connection with the unseen foe, which brought further frustration to the Japanese because they had no one to punish.

Thus far the Japanese intelligence reports indicated only the priest had any open contact with the guerrilla band. They were unable to observe any direct contact, which was usually made at night, between civilians and guerrillas. Every Filipino knew what it meant to be caught having anything to do with the guerrilla movement. Many of them suffered greatly through interrogation concerning a relative who suddenly disappeared from the town; however, the relatives would only say, "They have probably gone into the hills." Such statements often infuriated the Japanese, which brought further beatings and in some instances the oriental water cure.

Some of the civilians had but a slight connection to the guerrilla insurrection. Regardless, they never knew at what time the soldiers would drag them out of their household and submit them to terrible punishment. Even the storing of rice in the nipa huts would subject them to the death penalty. The Japanese rewarded collaborators with food rations; these individuals were sometimes found floating in the rivers or hanging upside down from trees, usually miles away from their town.

Nikono remained in Baras while his men, under the command of Lieutenant Miyomoto, searched in vain for the guerrillas through July and August, returning for rations either in Tanay or Paete. Through radio contact Nikono always knew exactly where his men were and when they would return to Baras; occasionally, they would return to the barracks. Nikono always made sure to address the men when they returned.

In the first week of September 1942 Colonel Ogawa summoned his two lieutenants to his quarters and said, "Division staff, combined with the Intelligence Corps, has agreed to relieve the company from its detail and consider another method." Colonel Ogawa did not explain further, and Nikono did not question the decisions of the higher command. The matter concerning the guerrillas would no longer be of any concern to him or his men. Nikono relayed the decision to his men, who were satisfied to be excluded from the frustrating drudgery of trying to round up a shadow in the hills.

Nikono and his 27th Regiment returned to fortifying positions all over Laguna de Bay. A few of these positions were placed within the towns themselves, but for the most part they were installed in the outlying areas, usually in the hills. A few machine-gun emplacements were scattered along some of the roads leading into the towns and barrios, but these were meant for delaying purposes only.

When these minor positions were implemented, Nikono was never present at the installations and did his best to avoid the general population. He was as elusive as the already legendary guerrilla Clastres Bulatao, for whom Nikono had developed a slight admiration. This guerrilla's name had become synonymous with, a fox; a ghost; a daring, courageous, sometimes foolish man. He represented a way of freedom to the Filipino people, yet there were indications he was a lunatic.

Simultaneously, Nikono was becoming a legend among the Japanese troops, a legend laden with confidence. The troops were secure in that nothing could surmount the effort of this genius in the field. Nikono made the plans, the blueprints, and let others do the installing. To them he was a mastermind with a master plan.

In late September 1942 Nikono was promoted to the rank of captain. He now maintained absolute authority within the ranks of the two hundred men whom he had selected to follow him.

The monsoon continued, pelting the mountains again and again as Nikono and his men labored furiously in the hills, battling the winds and rain that arrived in sheets. They excavated artillery and machine-gun positions, placing some of them in concealed locations where they first entered the Black Swamp and along the six-mile stretch that ran through the lesser hills beneath the apron of Mapalug Mountain. Meanwhile, Nikono kept a watchful eye on the tributaries as they emptied into the six-mile basin of mud and mire. With his field glasses he could see the pelting rains rushing down the ravines, drowning the nipa grass and vines that had been flourishing in the marsh. He constantly monitored the depth of the incoming surge of water and was awed at the force of the bulging Laniti as it carried debris out of the hills—trees, logs, bushes and sometimes the bodies of the unwary carabao caught in the fury it mustered. In its raging power it almost severed all contact between Tanay and Pililia. The old bridge separating the two towns trembled above the surge of the river, and truck convoys became bogged down on either side from the sudden downpours.

Nikono never tired of his dedication. He and his men traveled the length of the Shimbu Line over and over, constructing and reconstructing. The Shimbu Line was dug out and dug in—an underground fortress—through the hills from Pililia to San Miguel. Only the stretch between Pililia and Paete above the Jalajala Peninsula was the least defended, because Nikono reasoned any forces below this stretch could easily be nullified and isolated. The only access and egress would be by way of the bay itself, and Japanese launches would be sufficient to handle this attack. Originally he had considered cutting a road across the neck of the peninsula, but the Engineering Corps had decided it would require too much manpower and too much time. For now they would have to continue to use the shore road, an important and fortunate decision for the guerrillas and an unwise one for the Japanese.

The rains hampered Nikono tremendously, but he and the men wallowed through their first monsoon season of muck and mire unflinchingly. Occasionally between assignments he would take the men back to the swamp, assuring them they were going to climb Mapalug again but not empty handed. They could not imagine the Shimbu Line, the result of their captain's artistry, crumbling, so few of them entertained the notion. Mapalug would dissipate before the shield of the Shimbu Line yielded. There was no doubt about that.

When the swamp reached capacity, Nikono had empty oil and gas drums brought to the edge of the Black Swamp, along with enough logs to construct a platform fifty-feet square. Hundreds of drums were piled up at the swamp's edge, and Nikono had them repaired so they would float. He wanted to give the Filipinos the impression that this was just another dump for discarded materials.

In October the rains began to ease and the Laniti began to return to normal. Tributaries no longer accepted water, and the Philippine sun returned to its tormenting ways. The eagles of Mapalug Mountain glided gracefully over the hills and swamp searching for unwary prey. Mosquitoes bred by the millions along the edge of the Black Swamp.

Nikono was going to thrash his way once again into the caves, and the hand of nature was going to assist him.

The end of the heavy rains signaled the beginning of guerrilla activity. Renewing their aggressiveness also renewed the agitation it brought. The Japanese increased the infantry patrols twofold and tried to drive the guerrillas deeper into the hills, where the food supply was limited. Even with a massive patrol mounted throughout Laguna de Bay, an element of the guerrilla band always seemed to break through the barriers and create some form of sabotage. The patience of the Japanese Imperial occupational force ebbed to its lowest point in January 1943, when one hundred guerrillas overran a 40mm antiaircraft position on the outskirts of Pililia, destroying the weapon and annihilating the crew. The Japanese Command, infuriated by the ability of the insurgents to penetrate their defense security so easily, called an emergency session. Before it ended they decided someone would answer for the daring incursion. They also decided whom it would be—the man who sat on a bench in a white cassock dangling his beads in the sound of the swaying bamboo; the man who was seen going into the hills, conversing with and attending to Filipinos who were never seen in the towns; a man who was a servant of God but one who the Japanese were now sure was the servant of the guerrillas; a man who was the heart and soul of the parish in Pililia—Father Francis Vernon Douglas.

From the middle of February to the middle of July 1943 the Japanese stalked the priest. A soldier in every detail was designated to observe his every movement, whether he wore the white cassock or the black one. Father Douglas was observed going into the lesser hills, always carrying a little brown leather bag and conversing with the Filipinos whom he met. The information gathered was handed over to Colonel Ogawa, who became convinced the priest was relaying military information to the guerrillas. If Colonel Ogawa could obtain the names of these hill climbers and saboteurs, he could stifle the insurgents once and for all and perhaps get a promotion. He also needed someone who spoke English as well as Tagalog to interrogate the priest.

Colonel Ogawa braced himself when he summoned Nikono to his quarters, knowing this task was completely out of the realm of this intelligent, skilled engineer. The colonel did not waste any time, and as soon as Nikono entered the room he began, "As you know, Captain Yashima, the guerrilla activity in the Laguna de Bay area has to cease, and it is going to be accomplished through an investigation of the priest in Pililia. Division staff has resolved to move quickly in order to expose the priest publicly and set an example that will deter the guerrilla movement." Colonel Ogawa hesitated a moment before he continued, "You are the only one within the ranks who has the qualifications to carry out this interrogation."

"I am an engineer," stated Nikono, "not an interrogator."

Colonel Ogawa pressed on, "Under direct orders from division staff we are to eliminate the guerrilla menace completely, regardless of how we go about it. If the priest will submit the names of the guerrillas with whom he has contact, he will receive no punishment. This should be a simple procedure. I must also inform you the responsibility to obtain results rest with me; however, I will leave the method by which you receive the necessary information from the priest up to you and Lieutenant Miyomoto, who will assist you in this order."

Nikono realized the magnitude of the mandate, which was not a routine company order. To refuse meant a court-martial, but even worse, in the mind of Nikono, he would be insubordinate in the eyes of his men, incapable of following orders as he demanded of them. He could not let this happen and jeopardize all his effort, as well as his own merit. He reluctantly submitted to his superior's command, of which he had little choice.

Nikono returned to the barracks in Baras and informed Lieutenant Miyomoto, who saw it as an opportunity to climb the military ladder. Nikono, as the company commander, realized he would bear responsibility for the outcome. He also realized it would be the first time he would be exposed to public scrutiny on Luzon. That irritated him.

Nikono made one final effort to convince his colonel he was not the man for the assignment and went to his office. Nikono bowed to his superior and then directly asked, "Will you mete out this mandate to an infantry officer?"

"Father Douglas," responded Colonel Ogawa, "is from an unfriendly country, New Zealand, that has troops scattered throughout the Pacific. He also has a British passport, which officially makes him a British subject, therefore an enemy of the Japanese people, as are the guerrillas with whom he is befriending. This matter is out of my hands except to see the order properly carried out."

On the morning of July 24, 1943, Nikono ordered a heavily armed weapons carrier along with eight well-equipped men and enough rations to last several days. Lieutenant Miyomoto carried out these orders, and late that afternoon they left the barracks in Baras, passed through Tanay, and arrived at St. Mary Magdalene's in Pililia just before the sun went down beyond Laguna Lake. Nikono remained in the truck with four of the soldiers. The lieutenant and the other four intercepted Father Douglas outside the old church and brought him to the truck. This was the first time Nikono had seen the missionary. He ordered a return to Tanay, the nearest outpost of military importance, to see if there had been any changes in his orders. The mandate remained.

Nikono was well aware of the excitement and anger caused by the seizure of the priest; therefore, he did not stop on the way back through Pililia but continued on to Paete. He knew better than to interrogate the priest in his own church, which could provoke possible demonstrations or even open rebellion.

Nikono's only affiliation with religion was Shintoism, the ancient religion of his ancestors. He was skeptical about any god dwelling on an altar; consequently, he had never seen the inside of a church. He did not want to enter the church in Paete, Santiago Apostol, but it did afford him a place for questioning and keeping the majority of the Filipinos from witnessing the interrogation. They dismounted and went into the church, passing a group of Filipino prisoners. Lieutenant Miyomoto, one soldier, and a Filipino carrying a bucket of water and a coffeepot escorted the priest into the sacristy. Nikono did not follow them; instead, he stood observing the parishioners moving about the church. Then he went back to the door of the church where the other soldiers were standing guard.

At the front of the church Nikono heard the oriental water cure begin. Nikono went back to the sacristy to see water gurgling, rushing back out of the mouth and nose of Father Douglas and spilling on the floor. The priest was stretched out on the floor, a board across his stomach and a soldier pressing down with all his weight while the Lieutenant Miyomoto poured water from the coffeepot into his mouth. Father

Douglas lay there clutching a cluster of beads in his hand. His lips moved, but he did not utter a word of protest. He was not alone in this suffering; several other Filipinos were given the same treatment that day.

Before Nikono left the priest's side to go to the baptistery, he informed the lieutenant, "I and no one else will conduct this interrogation." It was the first time the captain had ever raised his voice in front of any of his men, and immediately the lieutenant and the soldier stood at attention. Nikono turned and looked directly at Father Douglas, who was still trying to recover from the water cure.

"This is a simple matter," Nikono told him. "You are required only to offer the names of those guerrillas you have been seen associating with. There will be no further affliction if you cooperate, and we will return you to Pililia, where you can continue your work undisturbed."

Father Douglas did not answer the captain but instead fingered the black beads he had managed to conceal in the palm of his hand. Nikono did not look at the beads, but he was well aware of them. Nikono tried again.

"There is one guerrilla who seems to maintain control over the others. As I said, and have been so ordered, if you release his name you will be released. Until you give us this information, I have no control over the consequences."

Nikono waited for the priest's heavy breathing to subside, but no answer was forthcoming. He tried again.

"Do you know a man named Clastres Bulatao?"

Still no answer. If the priest had said he knew the man, then he certainly would have known the names and hiding places of the other insurgents harassing the Japanese positions. Nikono tried for the fourth time.

"We are concerned only with the insurgents. If you would release the location and names of these belligerents and their leader, I promise many of the restrictions imposed upon these people will be done away with. Once more I will remind you that if you do not oblige the Japanese officials with this knowledge, which we are certain you have, I will have no recourse but to obtain this information for the division headquarters by other methods. I am trying to make this whole matter as easy as possible. It rests with you. I will leave this room, permitting you time to consider what course you should take."

From the first moment of the questioning, Nikono was quick to note the passive man he was confronting was concentrating more on the dangling beads than the questions. However, Nikono did not reveal his irritation with the rustling beads or the priest's uncooperative attitude.

As before, Father Douglas did not respond. Before Nikono left the room he signaled Lieutenant Miyomoto, who remained behind with the other soldier and one whom he had beckoned from the front of the church.

In the baptistery the silent, unflinching man of the cloth was now facing the ambitious lieutenant, who did not have the patience of his captain. The lips of Father Douglas still moved but he did not utter a single word out loud. This taxed Lieutenant Miyomoto's composure to the extreme. He assumed the docile, resolute man quietly trembling his lips was mocking him. (Unbeknown to Nikono and the other Japanese, Father Douglas was reciting the rosary.) The lieutenant would not be mocked and ordered the soldiers remove the priest's white cassock, and then he gave them a signal. They responded by severely beating him. The other prisoners, as well as the remaining parishioners in the church, realized instantly what was taking place and dropped to their knees and began to pray out loud in front of the altar.

Nikono did not recoil at the disturbance; he had expected this kind of retaliation. Inwardly, he felt a tinge of admiration for the priest, who had not made a sound during the beating. Nikono returned to the room and saw the slumped priest, his discarded cassock on the floor, and his splattered blood on the marble cover of the baptismal font and on the candlesticks. He also saw the bruises on the arms of the priest, the blackened and swollen eye, and the blood running down his face. He also saw the lips of the priest were still opening and closing, but still no sound came forth.

Here was the same steady determination he had instilled in his own men when he had punished them on the mountain. Nikono began to wonder who could command or demand such obedience and humility from this man, who was neither defiant nor angry and was without an army to sponsor him or protect him from the shedding of blood. What manner of man was this who was so insolent but did not appear to be, who seemed as arrogant as his own countrymen but did not display it? These thoughts irritated Nikono, and through them came the sudden realization that this man who had not spoken a word was willing to accept his lot, even death.

When the impact of this notion fully lodged itself in Nikono's mind, he realized for the first time in his military career he did not have an answer. He knew the quality of every man in his company and just how much they could withstand, answering to him from sunrise to sunset, all subordinate without question. However, he did not understand this man. He was a man without assistance and resistance. There was no outcry, only the echoes in the church from lamenting and helpless parishioners and prisoners, all keeping their mumbled prayers to a steady drone. This, too, irritated Nikono and the soldiers with him; he therefore ordered the Filipinos to maintain silence. They immediately followed the habit of the priest, their lips moving in unison with his.

Nikono refused to let this irk him and continued the interrogation. If he had been able to understand the suffering priest, he would have discovered the strength of a man who would not betray the confessional or his friends. Here was a man who was preparing to die for all of it, broken in body but not in spirit—a power or substance the Japanese could not shake from him. Father Douglas was on a vigil, standing guard over his people and ready to make any sacrifice to restrain the sword from sweeping across Laguna de Bay. Before this ordeal was over Nikono would have more respect for this solitary man than he had for his entire company of two hundred men.

Nikono decided Father Douglas was in no condition to answer any more questions and was now convinced he never would. Nevertheless, he had a mandate to fulfill and a colonel who was waiting for results. Just before dark that Saturday, Father Douglas was taken from the baptistery and tied to a wooden post at the rear of the church, one hand dangling like the dangling beads, unable to even rest or reach the harsh comfort of the floor. When a bowl of boiled rice was brought to him, it was placed just beyond his reach. These conditions continued from Saturday evening until dusk on Tuesday, during which eight guards were constantly present.

Father Douglas was tied in such a way that he was facing the altar, praying steadfastly and moving his lips in prayer. Nikono resumed the interrogation but to no avail. It was as if Father Douglas did not see his tormentors and was oblivious to the questions.

As Lieutenant Miyomoto stood before Father Douglas his last ounce of patience left. He drew his sword and thrust the point of it into the face of the priest toward his eye. The blood ran down the cheek of the unyielding priest and into his mouth. One of the soldiers struck the priest in the back with the butt of his rifle. The Columban Father, now almost blind, looked to the altar once again and resumed his vigil.

Neither Nikono nor the others could reverse the will of the nearly unconscious priest. Then Father Douglas broke his silence and requested permission to have his confession heard by the parish priest, Father Nicomedes Rosal, who consented, but only if a Japanese soldier who understood Tagalog would be a witness, thereby ascertaining Father Douglas was not informing his confessor of anything but sins.

On Tuesday evening Father Douglas was released from the wooden post, both hands tied behind him, and placed face down in a truck surrounded by Japanese with fixed bayonets. Nikono was well aware of the resentment building in Paete. When a parishioner came abreast of the truck and peered at the still conscious but weakened priest, a soldier immediately placed a canvas over the battered face. That was the last time any Filipino saw him alive. Back in the church in the quiet of the baptistery, the white cassock lay crumpled and stained at the base of the font.

Amid the hushed, smoldering indignation of Paete, Nikono directed the truck out of town as the Filipinos watched it head south toward Santa Cruz. As the truck sped away Nikono received a radio message warning him guerrilla activity had been observed not far from Pililia, which reinforced his decision not to return there. Alarmed at the proximity of the guerrillas in Pililia, and knowing too well how swift the grapevine traveled, he stopped the vehicle at the barracks in Paete and received a motorcycle escort. Another truck was added to the convoy, and Nikono detailed Lieutenant Miyomoto and four of the men to the vehicle, which was actually a vanguard protecting the superior officer and also a prisoner of the Japanese Command. The motorcycle proceeded out of Paete followed by the new weapons carrier and then Nikono's vehicle, in which he occupied the rear seat with two other soldiers. Father Douglas was prone directly behind Nikono's seat. Just before they left the barracks, Nikono made one last radio call to Baras, getting his final instructions from Colonel Ogawa. It was a simple and precise order: Father Douglas was to be executed somewhere between Paete and Santa Cruz.

Nikono was not familiar with the barrios or the terrain beyond Paete, but he did know there were guerrilla bands roving the hills below it. He therefore cautioned the entire detail to be vigilant in the arriving dusk. Momentarily, he reflected on the episode in the church and his dissatisfaction with it. Nothing had been accomplished except to arouse the temper of the Filipinos, and he felt sure there would be repercussions. The results of his new instructions would surely kindle another flame in Laguna de Bay, something the Japanese did not need. The thought of this caused him to turn around and remove the canvas covering the face of Father Douglas, whose eyes were closed. In the twilight Nikono could not see if his lips were moving, but this was the least of his concerns at the moment.

The guerrillas southeast of Manila had been meddlesome enough without furthering their ambitions. No doubt the interrogation would incite them to greater lengths. He could well imagine the flame becoming an inferno when the priest was never heard of again. He shrugged his shoulders, but this did not banish the uncomfortable thoughts surging through his mind as he turned around—thoughts that were suddenly and violently interrupted in the flickering shadows on the road.

The gunfire blasted the windshield of the weapons carrier into smithereens, felling everyone in it. The searing pain in Nikono's knee toppled him backward over the body of the priest and into the flying dust. Before he hit the hard surface of the road the second volley echoed in his ears, and he saw his vehicle careening off the road as he tumbled into the brush, rolling over and over until he could barely hear the sound of voices. He then heard a single delayed shot, followed by a voice yelling, "The other one, the other one." He knew the guerrillas had reached their objective. He listened to the shuffling in the road. When he heard someone approaching through the brush, he flattened himself to the earth, motionless. The guerrillas then went into the night as quickly as they had arrived.

Then Nikono heard the sound of the returning motorcycle and crawled out to intercept it. He managed to get to his feet, hailed the rider and sent him to investigate. The soldier returned and informed him all were dead and the body of the priest was gone. He had also heard the sound of a boat engine as it raced across Laguna Lake. Using the motorcycle radio, Nikono sent the grim news back to the barracks in Paete.

The disastrous events numbed the pain in Nikono's knee momentarily. Sitting sidesaddle on the motorcycle, because he could not get his leg over the frame, he bitterly ordered the soldier back to Paete. He had lost a lieutenant and eight others, all to be stated in a report he would eventually fling onto the desk of his colonel who had sent him on a mission he had reluctantly accepted. He had been an arbitrator and lost, not only his objective but also the answer to it. Moreover, he would never forget the courage of the man beneath the shadow of a cross.

When Nikono arrived in Paete he found the Japanese had alerted the patrols on the Jalajala Peninsula and along the stretch of guerrilla trails between Pililia and Paete. The men of the heavily armed launch on the lake had been alerted, and a road was being hastily constructed across the peninsula. From his bed in the field hospital, the captain was further embittered by the failure of his effort to have the road developed months before. If it had been constructed when he proposed the idea, the guerrillas would never be able to get off the peninsula, and it would have nullified any notion of creating an ambush below it. Any guerrilla activity within the peninsula could only be isolated encounters.

On July 29, 1943, his thoughts were further interrupted when he was informed the old bells in the church lofts of Paete and Pililia began ringing. Nikono instantly recognized the meaning—something nearly every Filipino already knew—the guerrillas had come out of the peninsula. Neither Nikono nor the entire Japanese military force knew that a new white cassock had replaced the bloodied canvas in a coffin made of bamboo. What they did know, however, was the Filipinos had disregarded the order that had silenced the bells. To the Japanese this was an insurrection with the most deliberate intention. To Nikono, it was a matter for other authorities, and he dismissed it from his mind. It would give Colonel Ogawa the opportunity to follow another avenue in compensating for the dismal failure of the interrogation. Nikono was more interested in returning to his command that had been abruptly interrupted.

Colonel Ogawa silenced the bells that evening in both towns, but he could not silence Nikono, who demanded his release from the field hospital despite the excruciating pain in his knee. The colonel was cognizant of his impetuous subordinate's frame of mind because of the incident in Paete, and he obliged by discharging the captain back to the barracks in Baras. Because Nikono had to return through Paete and Pililia en route to Baras, he asked to be released in the early evening in order to avoid the grim circumstances that were now taking place in both towns. He had received radio communications, several of them, about the demonstrations conducted by the Filipinos of both towns, and he did not need to become involved. He wrapped a blanket over his knees to keep the Filipinos from detecting his wound. His destination was the Black Swamp, and he wanted to have as much time as possible for the building of the barges that would be put afloat there as soon as the monsoons flooded the area.

As he passed through Paete he opted not to look at the church, but the moon was bright behind the cross on the spire of the old church. The shadow of it fell on the road until the vehicle brought it up, dancing on the hood and in the eyes of the captain. For a brief second it flickered before him hauntingly, and then the vehicle ran through it.

He wasted no time in Baras. After dropping the report about the interrogation on the colonel's desk, he left for the swamp. There he would supervise the construction of the first barge from the seat of a weapons carrier. The first phase of the Mapalug defense of the Shimbu Line had begun. This reserve fortification would bolster the morale along the entire line, supplying tremendous support for the ground troops. His selected contingent had declined to less than two hundred because of the ambush, but Colonel Ogawa had assured him the men would be replaced. Despite the loss of Lieutenant Miyomoto, Colonel Ogawa was certain Nikono was well qualified to continue the training of the men, most of whom were as capable of exercising the nomenclature of the field pieces as Nikono. The lieutenant was never replaced, which left Nikono in complete charge when the men were in the field. This brought exultation to his charges, who would now answer to their captain only.

The rains were increasing and beginning to lash Mapalug Mountain, sometimes in furious gales and cloudbursts. Before the first barge was completed the rainwater had begun to creep toward the edge of the swamp near Baras. The storms had been late in arriving, but Nikono had patience and dutifully crafted the floating armada that would carry the

120mm through the treacherous confines of a temporary lake. It did not take long for the tributaries to fill the swamp to capacity, allowing Nikono to conduct his first test to float a barge. Each day it received a heavier cargo until, on August 5, he made the decision to have the 120mm secured to one of them, then sent it out into the swamp, where it floated in perfect balance. All of his calculations of weight, buoyancy, depth of the swamp and size of the engine had proven accurate. The mammoth weapons were ready for the first voyage across the sea of nipa grass and strangling vines.

He had purposely left several feet at the front of the barge void of drums so the vessel could reach the embankment without hindrance, making it that much easier to unload. He employed the same pattern on the other five barges that were under construction. A special cradle was welded together, having an upturned bow with a doughnut-shaped hole at the top of it. The cannon barrels were not only going to sail across the swamp, but were going to sail up a mountain and disembark hundreds of feet in the clouds on a fifty-foot ledge that overlooked the Black Swamp. This attempt was going to surpass all of his endeavors on the Shimbu Line. His greatest requirements would be manpower and strong will. Not one of his men questioned his sanity. They knew Nikono Yashima finished every military endeavor he attempted.

The six-mile swamp awaited the deadly cargo on the barges: artillery, mortars, machine guns, ammunition, winches, jackhammers, cable, generators, fuel, engines, bulldozers and a thousand soldiers. Traversing the body of water would conserve energy and fuel and eliminate the many miles it would take to traipse its boundaries. The specially selected and well-trained men under Nikono would lead the way and he would direct them. In the first week of August the first barges set out across the swamp loaded with bulldozers. The beginning of the defensive Shimbu Line was under way; the armada of equipment and men would follow.

During these weeks of preparation Nikono had little time to ponder the incident in Paete and the demonstrations in Pililia. He avoided Pililia as much as possible and never returned to Paete, but indirectly Pililia did not avoid him. As captain of this separate segment of troops, he had greater access to the communiqués on the progress of the war in the islands than when he had a lower rank. Many radio and local bulletins that reached his desk referred to the insolence of the Filipinos over the Paete incident and the near uprising in Pililia. Some of them mentioned the drastic measures taken to extract the whereabouts of the missing priest; other bulletins constantly referred to a phrase, "He is buried in my heart," now being commonly used by the inhabitants of Paete and Pililia and occasionally in some of the other surrounding towns. Nikono could not understand how a collaborator with the Filipino guerrillas could be defended so staunchly by a people subjected to restrictions that, when disregarded, could sometimes lead to death. He brushed any connection with the interrogation from his mind and focused upon his task.

However, he could not ignore the military communiqués that disclosed the disaster in the Coral Sea, defeat on Guadalcanal, and movement of the American 43rd Division to the Russell Islands in February 1943. The 43rd Division then made beachheads on Rendova and New Georgia in the Solomons. The Munda Airfield had fallen to the 43rd Division on New Georgia on August 5, 1943, the very day Nikono had floated the barge in the Black Swamp. These campaigns did not upset him, because he reasoned the Imperial forces were overextended in the South Pacific and his own fortifications on Rabaul and those on Truk were capable of halting the Allied advance in the Pacific.

The bulletins also reported guerrilla activity had lessened in the past few weeks, but Nikono was sure this was due to guerrilla preoccupation with secreting the body of the priest. Since the ambush on the shore road to Santa Cruz, there had been a strange silence in the hills as well as in the streets. The sullen attitude of the Filipinos was obvious, and Nikono recognized this as a forerunner to more sabotage. The bulletins stressed the use of extreme caution when dealing with them; therefore, Nikono had a mandate posted outside of Baras forbidding any Filipino to venture within one mile of the depot at the swamp. Disobedience to the order would be execution. He was going to conceal as much of his project, the largest buildup of military supplies southeast of Manila, as possible.

Prior to the first floating of the barge, advanced elements of the infantry from the 27th Regiment had hacked their way across the swamp, moving all obstacles in the path of the barges; depths were also set. Nikono had originally deployed soldiers along the Shimbu Line, but he had them removed from this duty and requested they be detailed to his project and work in conjunction with his own company. An engineering unit along with a signal company was also attached to the infantry battalion. This completed the team that would serve in the field. All other ordnance would be barged across the swamp and also handled by the infantry.

After the first barge reached the far edge of the marsh, the bulldozers, a priority cargo, fanned out over the hills at the base of Mapalug Mountain searching for the two trails that ran up the northern slope, trails Nikono had carefully noted on the descent from the Kalinawan Caves. The assault on the sentinel of Laguna de Bay had begun, and a sudden whirl of howling winds and rain greeted them. Mapalug was going to defend itself.

From his seat in the truck Nikono guided the earth-crushing vehicles through the lesser hills, always directing them toward the best route possible until a road from the edge of the swamp could be carved to the most accessible trail. The medics were constantly dressing his knee wound and repeatedly warned him of its condition; he would lose his leg if he did not heed their admonition. Nikono listened and heeded to a degree, wise enough not to over extend the bounds of his limits.

Nikono avoided the lower ledges of the hills, and kept the vehicles clear of the soft terrain as much as possible. Some of the vehicles following the bulldozers sank in the mud, but these areas were soon lined with logs by the engineering unit, which worked through every cloudburst and blustering the monsoon had to offer. The road began to stretch toward the base of the mountain.

By the end of October as the rains abated somewhat, there was a crude but passable way around the base of the western slope to the slope slightly northeast of the swamp. There it met the trail running up the slope where it ended in a nightmare of ledges and jutting overhangs. Here would be the real test facing the captain.

Most of the lighter equipment would be hauled over the road by truck, but the bulldozers, which could grind through the low spots, would slowly move the heavy artillery. Everything was stacked at first near the base, but the 105mm and the 120mm, which were still secured in their cradles with noses to the sky, rested at the end of the road. They would be the last pieces of heavy equipment to ascend the mountain.

Every ledge, gully, rivulet, crevice and obstacle from the end of the trail skyward was cataloged in the memory of the mastermind. Nikono was satisfied many of the obstacles would be removed before the attempt was made to bring up the gigantic cannons, thus making the drag that much easier. The other pieces of equipment and the crates would be test enough.

The test began in November when the monsoon fled across the seas and the Black Swamp had filled to capacity. Nikono, ever planning ahead, had already made use of the temporary lake. Every fieldpiece required for this defensive position had been ferried across the six murky miles of ripples to the edge of the swamp. The only items remaining to be ferried across were the crates containing nonperishable food rations; this would not be done until Nikono had estimated the troop strength required to be perched permanently on the mountain. Field rations were to be used during the excursion to the caves. The thirty soldiers, having trained for six months in Japan, rejoined his select company and began to disassemble and prepare the cannons for the ascent.

The bulldozers went up the incline as far as they could without toppling over, hauling the winch components to the highest elevation possible. However, these two hundred feet would not be part of the stubborn ascent, and Nikono, with three months of knee recuperation behind him (although he carried himself with a limp), looked up and faced the trial of his career. There, in the mist, four thousand feet into the sky, he was going to build an immortal battlement that would defy the might of man. This would be the labor of love in the life of Nikono Yashima, a soldier with the grit of the dragon, a man who stood rigid and embittered before the greatest challenge of his lifetime. Only that morning he had received a bulletin notifying him that Rabaul and all his creations were being destroyed, day, by day, by day.

Nikono did not smile this day, and the soldiers who were carrying fuel for the winches saw the glint in his eyes and stepped aside to let him pass on his way up the mountain. This attitude Nikono displayed at times did not deter them, and a thousand of them were ready to follow him to the eagle's nest.

He spread them on the slopes up to the first ledge where they reassembled a jackhammer and a winch that would be used to emplace three heavy-duty winches at three-hundred-foot intervals when possible. Holes were drilled and bolts inserted in the rock to support the winches. These tactics would be employed all the way to the lip of the Kalinawan Caves. By the end of the first day three winches had been installed with attached cables.

When the sun was almost beyond Laguna Lake, Nikono abandoned the day's effort. There was no need to endanger the lives of weary men even though they could have brought light to the mountain by using the generator below. They rested in the coolness of Mapalug Mountain, finding sleep difficult on the side of the great hill. Mist blocked out the valley below.

There was plenty of time to do what they had to do, only their will was required, and Nikono showed them how to use it. The experiences of the first day would make the second much easier. Tomorrow they had to get the first crate to the top of the ledge.

Before the sun came up they were already moving on the mountain. One detail climbed around the ledge and primed the motor; the winch went into operation. The first test would be the crate with metal runners on it. It was a struggle; the dead, dragging weight threatened to snap the cable. On command Nikono ordered a slow, steady, crawling pace, keeping the cable as taut as possible until they were able to balance the crate on the edge of the overhang where it was eased over and onto the ledge. The first endeavor had been accomplished. It had taken two days of laborious maneuvering of winches, cables and manpower to get one crate on the first ledge, but the learning process would enable them to cope more readily with whatever obstacles faced them in the days ahead.

Eight more ledges and outcrops loomed before them and were all overcome. It took two more weeks before they were able to scale the final ledge, the platformed level of rock in front of the entrance to the Kalinawan Caves, where a heavy-duty winch was set into position, ready to haul up the other implements of war.

The crate had created an irregular furrow that all the equipment could follow. The long drawn out drama of transporting the paraphernalia from the base began. It became a continuous effort that lasted months. During this time Nikono stocked the tunnels and corridors in the belly of the mountain; everything was systematically put in place. The caves became an arsenal with an inventory of destruction. The shells for the monstrous cannons were ceiling high in several of the tunnels.

Meanwhile the heavy-duty winches and cables replaced the smaller ones on the slope and were ready for the task of hauling up the artillery. The wheels, pedestals and barrels of the 105mm were dragged slowly to the caves. Although these components were not as burdensome as that of the 120mm, they were still a strenuous test for the winches and the will of man. A deadly firepower would soon be poised to reign havoc and death across the Black Swamp—with little chance of hindrance.

Occasionally Nikono had the engineers blast sections of overhangs in order to straighten the crevice carved into the mountain. The 105mm had a tendency to roll over, but Nikono, ever alert, soon solved the problem by welding stabilizing fins at an angle to all the cradles, thus giving them greater balance.

In December, a time when Nikono felt sure of the weather pattern, he began to prepare the way for the 120mm, the next to the last phase that would bolster the fortification of the Shimbu Line. He cut the task force to seven hundred, alleviating some of the congestion on the slope. Then he instructed his men on the necessity of safety, especially the danger imposed by the threat of a snapped cable. They listened with all sincerity, as obedient as ever to a man who had just been promoted to major in the 13th Division.

Nevertheless it happened. During the elevation of one of the heavier crates to a ledge, a cable from one of the winches had become frayed because of the constant grinding against the solid rock. It snapped without warning. Two soldiers, standing off to the side and guiding the crate away from the wall, were killed instantly when the cable recoiled downward. The crate tumbled down the mountain for two hundred feet, barely missing several other men.

The pedestal and the components that supported the 120mm had already been dismantled and hauled separately up the mountain on the cradles that had carried the 105mm. The barrel of the 120mm weighed three tons, was sixteen feet long, and fired a ninety-five pound projectile within a range of six to eight miles. It required an eighteen-foot cradle.

With the accident in mind Nikono decided another heavy-duty winch and cable would be necessary, especially for the weight of the barrel when it was coming up over a ledge or overhang. This would be the time when the weapon would become dead weight, suspended without earth or rock support. It took two more days of safe preparation to install the winch and cable. With this done he looked up the mountain into the eager faces of the watchers, and then he gave the command that would commence the four-thousand-foot pull to the eagles.

The slack ran out of the cables slowly, and then they went taut. The immense barrel began to inch upwards. In the initial two hundred feet, progress was fairly smooth, but the major kept the men well to the sides, quite conscious of the recent accident. Only when the cradle became lodged or threatened to capsize did he permit them to venture close enough to rectify the problem, but always from the uphill side when the cable had been slacked off.

They managed the two hundred feet without incident, and then the pull of gravity began to test the endurance of the cables as the nose of the cradle curved slowly toward the summit of Mapalug Mountain. The cradle had been holding true to the furrow and the fins were maintaining a balance. The winch operators on the slope began to sense the increasing gravitational strain so the tow was cut in half, which was slower but much safer. Slithering up the face of the mountain the cradle dipped into the fissures and gullies, then emerged on another level. Every half hour the winches were shut down to let the heat escape from motors that were ready to explode.

It became a long, slow, tedious grind. By the end of the day they had overcome the first minor overhang, a precarious moment filled with frustration and anxiety. At this pace it would be a week before the wall in front of the Kalinawan Caves would be reached. Patience, once more, became the order of the day. With this in mind Nikono granted the men more respite, although it was difficult to rest on the apron of the mountain. It was not practical to descend the mountain and then have to climb back up the next day.

After ten days the crucial moment confronted them. Nikono stationed himself on the ledge, advising those controlling the winches to carefully interpret every motion he made. They dared not stray from the sides of the winches, knowing the military career of Nikono hung in the winds just as the barrel was going to. The major raised his hand, held his breath, and then gave a slow batonlike movement. The lowest gears went into motion. The dramatic moment of the will of man against the will of nature was exercised. The two cables cut into the shale of the ledge, grinding it into fine dust, and the doughnut-shaped hole on the curved cradle eased upward inch by inch.

The men guiding the cradle with the ropes were struggling to keep it balanced and prevent it from bouncing against the lower wall of ledge. Nikono's moment of truth had arrived, and he was well aware of it as the bulky 120mm approached the lip of the ledge. There the soldiers had stacked four feet of nipa grass to prevent the cable from snapping when the cradle began to topple over after getting halfway above the lip. The arched bow had prevented the cradle from catching on the jagged wall and lip as the cannon went up until the nose of it finally cleared the rim. When it was hanging over the ledge the massive weapon became suspended in midair, then slowly eased over and came to rest, cushioned by the crushed grass. The test had been met.

In a rare moment the soldiers nearby caught the flicker of a smile from the man who had constantly focused his eyes upon the nest where the cannons would finally rest.

The two other 120mm barrels were pulled up in the same fashion, taking but a week due to the lessons learned on the previous haul. All three were hauled across the ledge to the aperture where the thirty-man team reassembled the five artillery pieces. Rises in the interior were built in order to roll them out to the ledge. With careful preparation they installed heavy-duty winches, cables attached, to the rear of the opening to pull the weapons back in.

Two fifty-caliber machine guns were placed to the left and right sides of the Kalinawan Caves, and two at the tunnel opening to the south.

The soldiers on the Shimbu Line were ecstatic over the success of their major.

In February 1944 Nikono received a communiqué that read, "The 43rd Division has left the Solomons for New Zealand." He did not have to read between the lines and knew this veteran division would not return home until hostilities came to an end. The bulletin also mentioned "Butcher's Bridge," an incident that had taken place on the Munda Trail during the New Georgia campaign (led by the 43rd Division) on July 17,

1943, ten days prior to the death of Father Douglas. There was also another communiqué noting the 43rd Division had returned to combat along the "Bloody Driniumore River" in Aitape, New Guinea, supporting other military units and eventually replacing all Allied forces there.

However, Nikono's agenda continued unattested through the spring until one night when the guerrillas boldly attacked the restricted southern section of the depot outside of Baras. Four soldiers were shot. A wreath of roses was found draped over the muzzle of a 75mm howitzer, and there was not a thorn in the cluster. The Japanese could not single out the owner of the flowers, as they were growing everywhere—a constant reminder of the silent but simmering anger of the Filipinos.

The following day four Filipinos suspected of guerrilla activity were taken out of Baras and never seen again. Nikono had no intention of being a patron of the conquered.

The sky was cloudy on the morning of July 27, 1944, and the monsoon season was in full swing again. The Japanese awoke to discover thousands of roses strewn on the shore road in front of the church in Pililia. There were reports of the same in Paete. Shortly after the noon hour the rain began to fall on Pililia, spattering on the feet of the women who had begun to gather in the street in front of the old church. At first there were just a handful, but by mid afternoon there were more than a thousand Filipinos silently staring at the house of God. At dusk there were more than three thousand men, women and children almost motionless in their vigil. They stood docile, unmindful of the rain that splashed on their faces. Yet not a tear fell in the mud of Pililia.

The Japanese were uneasy, this being the first anniversary of the death of Father Douglas; they kept to themselves, mindful of the episode that had taken place a year ago. There was not a sound in the marketplace or on the riverbanks. A deathly silence prevailed in every shadow and on every corner of the town. Just before the mantle of darkness reached the waters of Laguna de Bay, a woman quietly shuffled her way to the side of the church and gently placed a rose-laced bamboo wreath on the ground. Then three thousand Filipinos broke the silence by singing the haunting refrain, "My Everlasting Rose," to the memory of a man who was still their Bamboo Shepherd and who remained buried in their hearts. In the rain and darkness they drifted back to their bamboo structures. They would not let the arrogant forget what they could not. The message was clear in the streets of Pililia, and it played with the thoughts of the Japanese.

Its significance found Nikono listening to the radio announcer telling about the gathering in the town. "At least they had not rung the bell," he thought, "although they might just as well have." They were protesting, as the priest had, without saying a word, and it made him wonder again about the hold this priest had on the people and what presence had so dominated the man who could not be shaken. The aftermath of the interrogation came to Nikono one night after dreaming he could not outrun the shadow of a cross. The dream had startled him at the time but was soon forgotten.

The handwriting was no longer on the wall—it was on the desk of Nikono, now a colonel following the climatic accomplishment on the mountain, and on the drawing board at division headquarters. The war in the Pacific had floundered, and the Japanese were making desperate but futile efforts to stem the tide that was swamping the islands. The thought that the new colonel once had about his defenses possibly becoming the last bastion was becoming a reality. The Imperialist Empire no longer commanded the seas or the air, and the isolated troops became just that. The Rising Sun was sinking, and not only into the sea. The American forces were no longer island hopping but island skipping, flying over them to shatter the dreams of Tokyo itself.

The final phases of Nikono's expedition commenced in August when the rains were beginning to subside but with the swamp still at capacity. Food rations and water were barged across the swamp before it began to drain. In the middle of these operations came the message that Leyte had fallen. Nikono wondered about Rabaul, unaware the message had never been sent that would have informed the occupational forces of their ships that were lining the ocean depths off Truk Island. The defenses on Rabaul and Truk had collapsed.

A steel door was winched up the mountain in sections and installed at the entrance of the caves, controlled by pulleys and a winch. Nikono knew one of the tunnels on the north side penetrated to within ten feet of the outer wall of the mountain; therefore, he had the solid wall blasted, bringing additional ventilation into the interior. It also offered surveillance all the way to Antipolo, which was north west of the caves. A fifty-caliber machine gun was placed at the entrance. All slopes were now protected with the exception of the one directly east, a rugged treacherous terrain that did not concern the wily colonel. The weapons of war were masters of the hills and valleys below.

Fifty-five-gallon drums were brought up to the caves, and soldiers were assigned to catch the water that flowed off the edge of them and ration it in case of a dry spell. Quinine would be added at all times to prevent malaria. Then Nikono decreased the number of troops on the mountain to two hundred, his own original company.

The company was assigned to all weapons in the caves and on the mountain as well as all the winches. Platoons were rotated for guard duty. All of these operations became a daily ritual and were practiced to perfection under the supervision of the tactician who left nothing undone. The swamp made an excellent target for the artillery pieces. Filipinos in the hills shuddered at the booming.

The 43rd Division arrived on January 9, 1945, a dull gray morning, and ran up the beaches in the Lingayan Gulf. They brought the implements of war and the memory of the Munda Trail with them.

The Japanese on the Shimbu Line listened to the radio blurt out the news of the American beachhead. Nikono, confident his underground emplacements could never be penetrated, left his men in the caverns of Mapalug Mountain and reported back to his superiors in Baras. His rank and an order from Colonel Ogawa compelled him to be on the line of battle with the 13th Division. He had no qualms about the conduct of his men in his absence. With or without him they would not abandon their positions. He had been preparing them for two years.

The Shimbu Line waited. The 43rd Winged Victory Division did not. Nikono kept abreast of the movements as the 43rd left the beach and went into the hills, always the hills. From January to the middle of March they overran the Japanese in Rosario, Fort Stotsenburg, Clark Field, Pozorrubio, Alacan, Urdaneta, Mount Alava and countless other towns and barrios, rooting the Japanese out of their holes and into the hills, never stopping to catch their breath in a relentless effort. Then in March the Shimbu Line felt the tremble in the depths of their pillboxes and dugouts, followed by the plodding boots of the 43rd. The storm that came with them spit fire and havoc upon the helmets of the underground hermits.

The memory born on the Munda Trail in New Georgia flourished in the bamboo and nipa thickets, driving the 43rd on and on through the hills of the Santa Maria and Laniti Valleys. The Shimbu Line trembled from San Miguel to Pagsanjan, and the thunder from the hottest guns in the entire Pacific buried the Japanese wherever they chose to die. Every hill and knoll became a cemetery. The elite Japanese 13th Division began to dwindle into isolated pockets of resistance. Nikono miraculously survived the months of artillery and aerial bombardments that raked the Shimbu Line, scurrying from one emplacement to another, shouting encouragement and orders to the beleaguered and doomed soldiers. The handwriting was now in his hands as officers and enlisted men could no longer be accounted for. He began to look for the refuge of the mountain. The guerrillas, now cooperating with the advancing Americans, began to look for signs of the retreat to the Kalinawan Caves. They knew it was a question of time, and they waited for this in the bamboo thickets and nipa grass within the swamp, lying quietly in the mud and the rustle of the singing bamboo.

One night in February Nikono and the three thousand remaining troops of the 13th Division, with their wounded, little ammunition, no medical supplies, and exhausted rations, fled the Shimbu Line and what was left of it above Baras and sought the shelter of Mapalug Mountain. They had no choice but to take to the Black Swamp because of the military action north and south of it. A division of both Filipino and guerrilla personnel, who had moved six miles closer to Mapalug, crossed the Laniti the same night, working in conjunction with the 43rd Recon, which was extensively patrolling the entire Laguna de Bay. The guerrillas, familiar with the terrain of the swamp (as most of the fleeing Japanese were), were also coordinating with the artillery units of the 43rd Division and waited in the middle of the marshy terrain. The unsuspecting Japanese forward echelons walked into the deadly fire of the unseen guerrillas, and the confused troops scattered in all directions. The guerrillas fled after they had relayed their coordinates to division artillery personnel, and the Japanese, caught in the fire, mud, bog holes and vines, were almost annihilated. Only three hundred men along with Nikono were able to reach the emplacements in the lesser hills below Mapalug

Mountain. The others who survived the swamp ambush and the battery of fire escaped into the hills north of the swamp. Many of them died from wounds or starvation or were eventually captured.

Nikono put the cadre in charge of those now at the base of the mountain. In the pitch of night, amidst the pounding shells from the 43rd Division artillery and his own scorching fire across the valley, he circled the base of Mapalug Mountain. Eventually he found the furrow running up the northern face and began his climb to the tunnel overlooking the slope. It took him all night and half the next day. He had miraculously survived the Shimbu Line attack and the swamp ordeal—he was once again in command of his own unit; they considered him indestructible.

The stalemate began. Nikono's massive cannons would belch death across the hills, driving the Filipinos out of the towns and barrios and harassing the forward elements of the 43rd Division. The five artillery pieces kept the Allied infantry units at bay for a month. Air strikes and constant barrages pounded the slopes of Mapalug. The foliage disappeared off the apron of the mountain, and the smoke from the shells settled on the terrain like a cloud. Rainstorms became more numerous, hampering the artillery units of the 43rd but not the enemy on Mapalug. Nikono and his charges were restraining an army. With the supplies available in the caves, they could hold out for a year.

The American forces knew it was time to call upon the guerrillas again. These hill nomads knew the mountain and what was in it.

It was a moonlit night. There was a sudden flash of an explosion just after dark as the metal door was being raised to the ceiling of the chamber; the explosion rocked the interior of the caves. Neither Nikono nor his men in the caves knew what happened. Shots and shouts echoed in the semidarkness of the chamber, then there was a complete blackout except for the moonlight flickering through the cave entrance. Through the beam of his flashlight Nikono rushed to the winches to discover all three of them were jammed with metal rods, expertly placed through the gearboxes, hopelessly locking the gears—the door could not retract. The caves were now vulnerable and his men were in a state of confusion. He hobbled to the ledge only to see a signal flare burst below the two artillery pits; he knew it had not come from the valley. Then he heard the aircraft circling and the familiar high-pitched whine of the dive, followed by another, then another. A ball of fire crashed below the ledge, lighting up the side of the mountain with a fiery flash and dancing flames. It was a napalm attack launched by American bombers, common along the Shimbu Line, exploding gasoline that could search out any living thing in its path. The Kalinawan Caves became coffins of death for many of the followers of the Rising Sun.

Nikono made for the corridor that exited on the south side of the mountain. Just as he cleared the chamber, a napalm drum found the main entrance of the caves, exploding in a blazing inferno in the middle of the chamber. The concussion killed half the remaining soldiers in the chamber and blew Nikono thirty feet into the tunnel. Confusion was rampant. Another napalm drum found the entrance, detonating the ammunition stacks, resulting in massive explosions. Fire and smoke filled the huge chamber, and the draft from the front entrance forced the smoke and gases into the corridors. Those who had not perished in the flames died in the tunnels from suffocation.

Nikono landed on his back, his uniform in flames. After rolling on the ground until the flames had subsided, he half ran, half dragged his battered body to the opening where four guards had been stationed. Behind him echoed the incoming explosives. When he burst out of the mountain, stumbling and gasping for breath, blood streaming into his mouth from gashes on his head, he found all four guards dead and stripped of their uniforms. Both machine guns were missing as well as their rifles and grenades. In the dancing shadows of the moonlight, amidst the whine of diving planes and echoing artillery, he saw the bayonet stuck between the rocks positioned like a miniature cross, draped with a bamboo wreath of roses.

The guerrillas had skillfully penetrated the armor of Nikono Yashima. In the horror of the moment, dizziness and bitterness seizing him, he thought he heard a church bell above the din. He staggered to the crosslike image and crushed it with the rocks that held it in place. Then he made one of the few mistakes in his life. Blinded with a conditional rage, the sure-footed Nikono slipped on the ledge and fell off Mapalug Mountain, plunging and tumbling one hundred feet, landing on his already bruised back in a crevice. He did not hear the hurtling napalm still blasting away at his crumbling fortress. He was unconscious and almost dead. The last bulwark of the Shimbu Line was smoldering in the skies over Baras and Pililia. All through the night the caves shook and thundered, and the mighty Mapalug trembled as the exploding ammunition and flames belched out across the Black Swamp like an erupting volcano.

When Nikono regained consciousness before the break of dawn, he knew it was all over. Smoke and fire discharging from the minor exit above told him that. He could hear the artillery shells pounding the western slope, but there were no answering volleys.

He did not attempt to move until there was more light on the mountain to guide him off it. He knew exactly where he was and was abashed at the thought that his lack of composure had put him in such a position. He closed his eyes again, waiting for his head to become clearer. The sound of voices suddenly drifted through the mist. Opening his eyes slowly he looked directly above him; in the early light he could make out the forms of about twenty Filipinos talking in the native Tagalog. They were perched on the ledge he had tumbled from. All were armed. One of them came to the edge of the rim and looked down in his direction. If he had not been wedged into the fissure, she would certainly have seen him. She was still peering over the rim when she spoke to the others.

"The replica of the cross is broken, Laudez. These stones have crushed it; obviously it has disturbed someone. Perhaps some of the infidels managed to escape and are now going down the mountain."

Another guerrilla came to her side. "Perhaps this is so, Hilaria," he replied, "but we do not have time to pursue them. It is dangerous here on the mountain. We must go up to the bald face first and cross over to the eastern slope and see if the basin there still conceals the priest in the chamber. Clastres has ordered this."

The name of the guerrilla leader tormented the crippled Nikono. Another guerrilla came to the edge and looked down.

"We have waited almost two years for this moment," he said. "We shall go and see if our shepherd sleeps while the others drive the arrogant ones from his resting place. Only four hundred feet separates us from the pool of water, so let us go there now while we are able to remain on the mountain. We will see for ourselves if the priest has not been disturbed and if the water is still contained."

"You are right, Ramon," answered Laudez. "When we come down we will see if the water is still locked within the mountain as we secured it. Everything must be the same as we left it. Then we will return to Clastres and hear what he has to say about it."

Laudez was evidently the leader of this band. Nikono heard them scrambling up the mountain in the direction of the bald-faced wall he had first observed from the base of Mapalug. Then it became quiet on the mountain; the bombardment had ceased. He realized the missing priest had been hidden behind his back in the seclusion of a pool of water. The basin and chamber the guerrillas were referring to must be hidden and beyond reach as long as the water was contained within the mountain. Somewhere on the mountain the guerrillas had cleverly restrained the flow of water so the basin would not empty. Then Nikono remembered the early days in the Kalinawan Caves when the sound of the running water above the ceiling could no longer be heard.

For a brief moment a sense of admiration for the guerrillas passed through his thoughts just like the moment of wonder he had felt toward the man in the white cassock. These same wanderers, who had buried the priest where the eagles nest in the clouds, had almost buried him in the same mountain. He grimaced at the thought of how close he had come to discovering the inspiration that held the Filipinos in awe, and how close he had come to ending it. Then the thought of his predicament superseded all others and he instinctively reached for his sword. The infantry regiments would soon be on the mountain in search of life.

Nikono's labor of love had gone up in smoke. The guerrilla's labor of love was in the heart of the mountain, hidden under the protection of love. Father Douglas had stood in the face of adversity, and Nikono had fled from it. The man in the white cassock had not been afraid to die for his labor of love; he had lived to die for it, and the guerrillas had died to live it. The fruits of the vine were indispensable and the fruits of the sword lay in ashes.

Nikono had to get off the mountain. He would die on the slopes if he did not. He also had no desire to be taken prisoner by the guerrillas because of the possibility of being recognized. Twisting around with care he managed to remove his sword from the scabbard, then use it as a prop to haul himself out of the cleft. However, thirty-nine hundred feet fell below him, and he was unable to walk downhill.

Even in defeat Nikono was a determined man; the blood-spattered braids on his shoulders attested to that. If a man could not walk or run, he would have to crawl. Nikono did just that.

Sheets of windswept rain concealed his movement as he rolled and crawled his way down the precipitous southern slope. Gales lashed through the near darkness, hurtling him into a flash- flooded ravine, nearly drowning him fifteen hundred feet above the Laniti. Excruciating pain and the tremendous effort he had to make weakened him considerably. With the gullies running wild around him, he stuck his head beneath the ledge and listened to the rain pounding on the mountain. The drumming of it put him to sleep for two hours.

He awoke and continued. Lightning began to strike the mountain, and he used this source of light to gauge his descent. Thunder crashed and the echoes of it rolled and rumbled, exploding in his senses. The contours of the terrain told him he had crawled twenty-eight hundred feet down the southern apron. He was seized with shaking and dizziness, and for the first time he wondered if he were going to die on what had now become for him a mountain of terror. It was no longer a refuge in his life but a sign and signal of death. The Mapalug had drained him of everything but his will, the only thing that was keeping him alive.

Sometime during the night the storm began to weaken. Nikono awoke in a drizzle. The eastern sky began to grow brighter, which prompted him to renew the descent. It had already become clear to him that he would spend the entire day struggling to reach the base beneath a parching sun. He knew that to survive he had to get off the mountain as quickly as he could, reach the Laniti half a mile from the southern slope, and find a rice granary.

It was a long and tortuous day, but Nikono was a soldier born with a will that could not be defeated; in that sense he did conquer the mountain. It had drained his blood and his energy, shattered his labor of love, and annihilated the bond he had developed with a select group of men who were all lying dead above him. Yet despite all this he reached the foot of Mapalug Mountain even though he had to crawl into the veil of darkness to accomplish it.

Then he found the river and slowly slid into it. After an hour of drifting, a granary became silhouetted against the sky. He crawled out of the river and flattened himself against the dank embankment, then he crawled to the first handful of food he had had in two days, raw rice. He crammed his pockets with it, and then returned to the river the same way he had come. The raw rice knotted his intestines, almost making him sick, but it kept him alive.

For ten days and nights he hid in the bamboo thickets. Americans patrolled the mountain. He soon realized he was watching reconnaissance patrols, not an infantry unit.

During the nights he left the protection of the bamboo in search of rice, each foray becoming more laborious as his head laceration began to throb and his back pains became unbearable. Then the night came when the pain in his back caused such distress that he was unable to crawl to the granary. Without food he faced a slow, painful death, and a painful decision. Nikono Yashima, the artist who laid out the Shimbu Line from Antipolo to San Miguel, was traumatized and now bleeding to death in a bamboo grove five hundred feet from his enemy, the 43rd Recon. On the night of April 14, 1945, Nikono temporarily put aside his will and resigned himself to the inevitable. Early the next morning the maimed soldier of the Rising Sun Imperialist Japanese Army pulled himself erect with every remaining ounce of strength, drew his sword, brushed his tattered uniform, took one last look at the pinnacle domineering Laguna de Bay, and walked out of the bamboo. For the last time he laid down his sword, held his hands at his sides, informed the astonished men of Recon who he was, then pitched headfirst to the earth.

For a week he was lost in a coma, then delirious, then tortured by misgivings as he recovered in a field hospital in Cabanatuan, sixty miles from his military demise. Manila was in shambles. The war wound down after the 43rd Division recaptured the Ipo Dam. The sounds of turmoil waned on Luzon as they did all over the Pacific. Colonel Yashima underwent four operations to mend his ailing back; none was completely successful. A scar ran across his forehead, a visible reminder of the drama that took place in the mountain. Eventually he recovered well enough to be sent to the hospital in Manila; he was there on August 15, 1945, when Japan surrendered unconditionally to the Allied Command. The echoes of war would never leave him entirely. He was repatriated to his homeland in November, three months after all hostilities had ceased, and then spent one more month convalescing in a nursing home in Kamakura, the town where he had been born.

After his convalescence he chose to live on the island of Kyushu for its serenity, which offset the harshness of his military career. He grew to love the island, especially in the southern area where his house overlooked the Kagoshima Bay and a few rice farms. He would watch his daughter, Kieko, perform miracles in her flower garden.

It was a pleasure just sitting there and watching the results of her work. She had been three years old when he was discharged from the army. With Um, her mother, she planted her first flowers that year. She developed an insatiable desire for gardening. Eventually her skill attracted attention throughout Kagoshima Bay, and people began to arrive on weekends to observe her artistry. In time her project became a business venture, and she was the envy of competing florists throughout Kyushu. This brought Nikono a quiet pride, which blended with the serenity he had come to Kyushu to enjoy.

Nikono had never been as gentle in his work as Kieko was with hers. She kept her distance in her own way from the regimentation that had dominated his life in the service of his country. It was her way of showing there was another way to prove one's aptitude in the world. She was doing it with flowers, thus creating joy. When he thought of the years he had given to his country, and the years he had lost for it, he realized it was still not enough. To him the giving had been the reward, whereas Kieko received the joy. The whole town could attest to that. Nikono considered her the mother of flowers. She planted them, nursed them and raised them to stand tall and graceful in the eyes of Kagoshima Bay. Research and study were rituals with her. Plants became her life's work.

There were no roses in Kieko's garden at first because she believed it would be a constant struggle to grow them. Roses had been grown with great success in the northern sections of Japan because of the cooler climate, but growing them in her subtropical climate was something else. However, being determined like her father, she decided to seek all the information she could gather on growing them near her home.

Her flower garden was filled to capacity, and she had no desire to remove any of her flowers to make room for a venture that could be a failure. The Extension Bureau of Kyushu, which recognized her gardening prowess, granted her request to plant flowers on public land close to Mount Sakurajima. Kieko purposely neglected to inform her father of the project. It was to be her secret, although she did explain she ultimately wanted to establish a public garden for all the people of Kyushu.

Kieko had the entire layout of the garden in her mind long before she received permission from the bureau. She had thought of every detail, just as her father would have done, with the exception of one. It had never occurred to her that she needed her father's approval to grow roses.

Kieko studied the landscape. The lava surrounding the mountain had been the subject of some of her research and would be a key to growing roses. Most of the gardeners in her town had been using lava for years, because it was excellent for retaining moisture. However, it was like clay and almost impossible to crumble by hand. For the moment Kieko needed only a few buckets of lava to perform the initial tests to unlock its components. She took the samples to the Extension Bureau, then read everything she could on the culture of roses.

The test results were not encouraging. Lava was fertile by itself after years of weathering, when it gradually disintegrated into fine soil. It held moisture, but Kyushu received more than eighty inches of rain a year, far too much for roses. Only a minimum of this fine soil could be used. Kieko had little choice. It was either break down the lava in its present form or travel great distances to obtain additional soil. She decided to find a way to use the lava, in combination with something else. She had made up her mind to grow roses; nonetheless, the roses took a long time to make up theirs.

It was the summer of 1975 when she began the process, using everything from bamboo roots and leaves to pine needles—anything she could mulch. In the beginning she used just a few rose seedlings, trying different varieties in different mixtures. Weakening and strengthening the formula were a constant process, causing her to work late into the nights. There were months of failure. Several times she thought she had the correct formula, but the seedlings withered. Maintenance crews dumped truckloads of leaves on the lava beds. They were mulched with bark, rice fodder and bamboo shoots; however, the roses would not grow in the mixture.

After months of experimenting with different combinations of soil ingredients, one of the seedlings survived and began to grow. Kieko held her breath.

Her first rose to bloom went on display in the summer of 1976. Within a year roses enhanced each flowerbed in the public garden. Horticulturists along with thousands of visitors from all over Japan came to admire her garden and the spectacle of roses. A young Japanese woman had accomplished single-handedly what the most prestigious laboratories could not.

Nikono made little comment about her success. He missed her presence in her own garden. When she brought home a spray of roses, he was both infuriated and consoled. He began to understand she was the bouquet in his life, and if he lost her he would have little else. One night he dreamed Mount Sakurajima erupted, and the lava buried all the flowers except one—a red rose.

The roses blooming in the public garden upset Nikono so much that he made a silent pledge not to visit the display. Um had no inkling as to why a rose was such a thorn in the life of her husband. It was now 1977 and he was sixty-two years old; for more than three decades he had tried to suppress the misgivings he had about the events of Laguna de Bay—the roses would not let him forget.

Due to the lack of tillable land, Japan, itself a rice-producing nation, needed additional rice for its increasing population. Two rice dealers, Kesaki Takeshi and Koji Yoshida, owned a rice refinery in Kyushu and had representatives in every rice-producing country in Asia. When they discovered Nikono's vast knowledge of the Laguna de Bay area, where they had never established contact with the rice growers but where several other countries were purchasing rice, they immediately offered him a position.

For the first time in their marriage, Nikono consulted Um and together they decided he should accept the offer. She and Kieko had penetrated an unseen barrier.

Kieko's roses were awakening Nikono's curiosity about the role the flowers had played in the lives of the Filipinos. He wanted to discover why one man died so others could live, and why he lived and the others perished. Just before Nikono left for the Philippines, he shocked both Um and Kieko by growing a beard. Dark glasses were concealed in his pocket.

A company car and a company representative were waiting for him in Manila. They drove northeast to Cabanatuan, where he was given a two-week course on every aspect of rice growing on Luzon. His intention was to establish himself in the rice market long before he reached Laguna de Bay, thereby eliminating a sudden entrance as a rice merchant in the area.

In his negotiations with the rice farmers, Nikono listened to every conversation within earshot about the towns below Antipolo, but not a word was uttered about what had transpired in Pililia or Paete thirty-four years earlier, or the roses that had played such an important part in the episode in 1943. He contacted the office in Cabanatuan and expressed his desire to enter the rice market in the Santa Maria Valley and the surrounding towns and barrios in Laguna de Bay.

He drove directly south to Baras, observing Mapalug Mountain long before he reached the town. He knew he would never climb that wall of stone again and wondered if the Filipinos had ever taken the body of the priest out of the crypt. A gradual approach to Pililia revealed many roses. What possible reason could these people have in continuing a cause that died many years ago?

When Nikono entered Pililia, he located a boardinghouse half a mile from the marketplace and a mile from the church. There was a jeepney stop on the corner, which made Manila accessible in case the car became disabled. An old carabao road connected to the boardinghouse road curved through the outskirts of Pililia to the Laniti River. The Laniti Valley had what Nikono believed to be the most fertile soil southeast of Manila. The river, carabao, road and soil all contributed to the largest rice market in the area. Nikono needed to be as close to the center of the competition as he could get. Although he might be recognized, he had little choice if he wanted to purchase the finest rice.

He did not deal with any of the rice farmers for two weeks but sauntered around, letting his presence be observed in the marketplace. Although he did not hear one word about the circumstances that occurred previously in Pililia, the roses said it all. The residents in Pililia had not forgotten, and Nikono was already observing the mask covering the face of the town.

Nikono had a keen ability to distinguish the varieties of rice and the quality of each kind, which was quickly noted by the farmers and the competition. He maintained a strict policy of fairness in all his dealings, which deterred close scrutiny. Consequently, he avoided any unscrupulous dealings that might otherwise cast suspicion in his direction. The beard, dark glasses, civilian clothes and straw hat were in stark contrast to his old military attire. Only his limp gave any hint of his former self.

The rice farmers were coming in from the valleys in droves with their carabaos and carts laden with precious grains. As usual it became a week of frantic bidding, buying and weariness. It was well worth the effort, because the harvest was nearly exhausted.

One day he observed the batas as they kicked up the dust with their hero worship and fantasizing of the legendary guerrilla, Clastres Bulatao. They ran through the crowded thatched pavilions that lined the marketplace, one hand held behind their back, blessing themselves as they pretended to defend the "Ghost Priest" of the hills. Nikono did not dare seek them out with questions.

In the last week of the rice sales, the shadow of Alvarez Guzan fell across the path of Nikono. For two weeks Alvarez had been bothered by the appearance of the bearded rice purchaser and followed him. He saw the Japanese buyer remove his hat and glasses to wipe his brow and recognized the man he had hoped had been killed during the war. Alvarez was sixteen years old in July 1943 when the bayonet at the end of a Japanese rifle prodded him, with a water bucket in his hands, into the church in Paete. Now it was Alvarez's turn to prod the antagonist who had caused all his misery.

Alvarez cautiously approached the bearded buyer on the final day of the rice market, just before the bell rang at dusk. At first Nikono thought he was a rice farmer arriving late to the market, but when Alvarez identified himself (although the name meant little to Nikono), Nikono immediately understood he was being confronted by one of a few who could recognize him as the interrogator of the priest.

Nikono motioned to a bench in the pavilion and they sat down. Alvarez looked toward the sun as it began disappearing beyond the shores of Laguna, then he spilled forth the anguish long locked within.

"It has been many years since the point of the bayonet pierced my rib bone, but that was only my flesh. I only regret it was not plunged into my heart. Being young and weak at that time, I did not have the courage to meet the test. Instead, I have died a thousand deaths when I could have died but once. How may times have you died, Nikono Yashima?"

"I had never given you much thought until I saw the church again," Nikono replied. "I thought perhaps you did not survive. It did not occur to me that one day I would return to Laguna de Bay. There have been many times when the strength of that priest diminished anything you or I could have done. In those days I marveled at the strength of the sword. You and I followed orders, or it was death. Perhaps we did not have the will to die as he did."

"When I first heard of the ambush," said Alvarez, "I prayed you and all the others with you were dead, yet I feared in this death I could never be freed of the taunts and the accusation of being a collaborator. So I prayed for the survival of the one who escaped, because he was my survival. Only he could become my witness to the thrust of the bayonet. When I saw you in the marketplace, my prayers came true. Do you ever pray, Nikono?"

"Prayers are nothing but hope, are they not?" replied Nikono. "Is that what the priest was doing? What was he praying for?"

"He was praying for you, Nikono," replied Alvarez.

"Praying for me? Why did he not pray for himself when he certainly was sure of the consequences?"

"He prayed for you because you did not know what you were doing and also because you did not know what he was doing. Did you ever look upon the man on the cross, Nikono? Father Douglas and the many you put under the sword did likewise. Perhaps he will become your intercessor and you will be forgiven as the man on the cross forgave."

Nikono shrugged his shoulders. He had heard about the man on a cross, his foolishness and his foolish followers. He also remembered the orderly, disciplined clicking of the handful of beads. The memory of them revived the irritation he had felt on that day.

"Are you saying the Filipinos were following the priest because he was some kind of God?"

"In a sense, yes," replied Alvarez. "He was a representative and a follower, and we followed the man on the cross through the guidance of the priest who took us to him with roses. This rose you took from us lived according to the words of the man on the cross who was also pierced with the touch of steel. We all must follow orders or there will be nothing but darkness."

"There was that talk of roses again," thought Nikono. "Why did he not speak?"

"Would you have listened to him?" asked Alvarez. "You would have listened only to what you wanted to hear, a betrayal. You would have ignored his words that had meaning and life for those he loved. His was a true labor of love, a compassion one man had for many. You received the ribbons of valor, and then you bestowed upon him the ribbon of death, yet he accepted it freely and humbly. You would do well to remember he shed not a tear, only his blood, and he shed it for you."

"Are you telling me he died for me? He was a man who collaborated with those who refused to follow the decrees applicable to their own welfare."

"Yes," said Alvarez. "He died for you and the rest of us. Do you see anyone guided by the edge of the sword? It is a fallible tool and turns to rust. You can cut the heart out of a man, but you cannot destroy what is in it. That is why we still hear his words in our own hearts, so he really is not dead for us. If you had listened to him you would never have drawn your sword except to throw it in the river."

"Are you condemning me because I followed a mandate handed to me by my superiors?" asked Nikono. "It would have been an invitation to death."

Alvarez merely smiled at this defense. "You sound like a man called Pontius Pilate. He, too, had the support of an empire, but the man he condemned died only in the body, not in the spirit. It is also true of the righteous man whom you were the last to see alive. Have you not seen him in your dreams? How could you not remember his face?"

"I remember his courage and also his foolishness," replied Nikono. "We all have causes, but I never understood what that man died for. He appeared to have nothing of worthiness yet appeared to be defending something beyond reach. It was strange behavior."

"Did not the men you instructed lay down their lives for you?" asked Alvarez. "And willingly? Did they not believe in the words you spoke? How can you condone this behavior and not condone that of the priest who died for the guerrillas and all the people he had instructed? You gave every ounce of strength you had for your cause, but he gave his life for his. Perhaps if you had been able to read his lips, you might have known he was condemning your cause because the cut of the sword is never right and reaps nothing but pain. Perhaps he was praying for you to become as gentle as the rose. Does anyone remember your words, Nikono?"

"You talk as if he were still alive."

Alvarez smiled again, aware of what Nikono was searching for. "He is alive in every heart that beats in Laguna de Bay. He has never died except in body only. Your cause perished with the sword in the hills. Father Douglas walks beside the river and the shores of Laguna, and his shadow sleeps within the bamboo, and we know it is there."

"I have seen the roses that seem to foster some sort of inspiration both here and in Paete," said Nikono. "A week ago I managed to get away from the rice market and visited the cemetery where the bell ringer is buried; there are many roses at his grave. I have also noticed the many roses growing in the surrounding towns. Are these roses all for one Filipino when there were thousands of your countrymen who died for similar causes? Was he so special and such a celebrity that he should be paid such homage, or are these roses destined for another grave, perhaps that of the priest? If this priest holds such an important place in the hearts of your people, how come a monument has not been erected for him for all to visit? This, too, is strange behavior after all these years."

"Yes, he does have a grave, Nikono. He is buried in our hearts. As long as we keep the rose alive, he cannot die. It is only if we forget its meaning, his words, his sacrifice, and, above all, the love and compassion he had for us when we have received very little, that the rose will die in the dust."

"Alvarez, I can see something else is bothering you besides that for which I seem to be the blame."

"I have suffered these many years because of that terrible day in Paete," said Alvarez. "Now I face a ghost of the past, one that holds the memory of those hours and who alone can untie the noose that chokes the life out of me. I do not put a bayonet in your ribs to obtain justification for what I had unwillingly been forced to do, which only you know to be true. In your hands lies my redemption from this unjustified stigma. So I ask you, Nikono Yashima, if you will go before the elders in the administration building and swear under oath I was under the sword and did not participate in the torture under my own volition."

Nikono got up from the bench and began to pace back and forth across the pavilion. After a few moments he returned to the bench. "First, I want to stress I had never been commissioned with an officer's rank in the Japanese army to impose a mandate upon others outside of the military. I was promoted for work in the Engineering Corp, in which I fulfilled my entire career. I was obliged to follow orders no matter what the mandate. This Father Douglas represented himself as an enemy to the Japanese military. It was of no consequence to me at the time about his activity. You, too, can give testimony that I was only an interrogator. One can exonerate the other if he so chooses. In a sense we were both carrying out orders under the threat of the sword, as you put it. Admittedly, I was not, and still am not, familiar with the personal life of that strange and unemotional man you call a priest. Now after all these years, I find myself becoming anxious to understand the meaning he exuded and why it has created such endless dedication. Which brings me to the question that has both bothered and intrigued me. Perhaps, if you choose to answer it, it will solve many other questions. With regard to Father Douglas, what are your people waiting for?"

Alvarez requested an overnight delay before responding to Nikono's question. Nikono agreed. They met the following day in the rice pavilion, which was now barely frequented. The season was over.

"Nikono," began Alvarez, "I have sought advice from an elder, Laudez Rosaldo. He is also a legendary guerrilla as well as a rice farmer and seller."

"I have had several dealings with him in the rice market; he seems to be a man of integrity," replied Nikono.

"You should know Nikono, I have told Laudez who you are."

Laudez, one of the few residents who had given Alvarez any support concerning the episode in Paete, had advised him to answer Nikono's question cautiously but honestly.

"I will go before your elders, if it will help you Alvarez, and present an argument on your behalf concerning your participation in the church in Paete."

Alvarez composed himself, hoping finally he would be exonerated of any deeds that had branded him a collaborator. "Yours was but a short answer, Nikono, but I cannot be that brief. I have many considerations before me, some of which I have no right to express; therefore, I cannot commit myself to great detail. You must understand this. To answer your question, Nikono, 'What are your people waiting for?' I must first explain.

"Father Douglas, when he first came to us, came empty handed but full of love and faith. He sowed the seeds of love in every heart that opened to him and into the ears of those who would listen. He told us many times Laguna de Bay was a garden of flowers and we were the roses in it. He said we should never become thorns in the lives of others, and must bury the thorns with the chaff. He labored tirelessly in this garden, and he cradled us with his love, wiping the tears from the batas who ran through the bamboo by the church. On July 27, 1943, a day that lingers in every soul in Pililia, even in those who had not been born, he was accused of collaborating with the guerrillas, and his breath was taken from his body, but not from his spirit. His words are still ringing in the hills and valleys of Laguna de Bay, even louder than the bell that echoes his compassion. Compassion so great he offered it to the wounded and dying when he dared to stand against your sword. He sent them to God, where he said they would find fields of roses and they would be home. He did not speak that day, and how well I know, because he knew you would not understand. So he prayed for you, and I know he prayed for me because he saw the tears in my eyes and the sword in yours. He died for his roses, but we were unable to embrace him. You who thought he was a perpetrator of death did not understand he was only bringing love into the hills.

"When he stood before you, did he appear to be a wielder of the sword? Was he not passive and relenting? Did he not have the same right to bind the wounds as you did for your followers? I will say to you now, Nikono Yashima, you did not take him from us, because the love he fostered dwells forever in the minds of those who remember. It is the only real thing we have ever been able to say is ours, and no one can take it from us. So here in Laguna de Bay we cherish what we find in his memory and wait for his return."

Here he paused and glanced at Nikono and saw there were still questions on the rice merchant's face; Alvarez proceeded in removing the mask of Laguna de Bay.

"When you were ambushed on the shore road and the body of Father

Douglas was snatched from your clasp by not only Clastres Bulatao, but also by the love of the liberators against tyranny and arrogance, we wept in the nipa huts and beside the rivers when the bell told us he was dead. Clastres and nearly two hundred guerrillas, seven of whom are still alive, carried our benefactor into the hills. Not one of them, in thirty-four years, has ever betrayed the burial site of our martyr because of a vow of silence they agreed to at that time. So now you know that in all these years the roses of Laguna de Bay have not known where our beloved priest is resting. They are waiting for the day when they will be told."

Nikono could not conceive of the idea that the guerrillas had never brought the body of Father Douglas out of the mountain. He realized there had to be an important reason, if not several of them, for not doing so. He also realized he was the only one besides the guerrillas who knew where the priest was actually buried and that the guerrillas had no idea he knew. Nikono had the means to shatter a thirty-four-year-old covenant and accomplish what thousands of Filipinos were waiting for: a resurrection that would crack the bells in the belfry towers of Pililia, Paete and every town and barrio in Laguna de Bay.

Nikono surmised Laudez Rosaldo was one of the original guerrillas. He decided it would be Laudez, not Alvarez, whom he would approach with his startling news. "I would like to meet with Laudez; can you arrange this for me, Alvarez?"

Alvarez was surprised by Nikono's request but assumed it was to speak to Laudez on his behalf. Alvarez was ecstatic. He arranged for the meeting to be held in the rice pavilion just before dusk. Nikono asked Alvarez not to be present. Alvarez, satisfied Nikono was going to clear his name, agreed, although he was slightly resentful.

The marketplace was practically empty when Nikono arrived for the meeting. Laudez was prompt with his arrival. After cordial greetings they retired to the pavilion bench, where Laudez opened the conversation.

"Alvarez has informed me you are willing to approach the elders of Pililia with a statement declaring he was forced to carry the water bucket, the water from which was used in the torture of our martyr, Father Douglas. To offer this information would be to declare you were also present, and it also informs me you were the one who escaped the night of the ambush. Is this all true?"

"Yes," answered Nikono. "I was a captain and in charge of the interrogation. I was carrying out a mandate handed down by the division staff."

"Do you understand the implication of what you are saying?" asked Laudez.

"Fully," returned Nikono. "I understand perfectly well. If I did not understand the consequences, I would not have returned to Pililia or any of the towns in the Philippines."

"I recognized you some weeks ago as the colonel who had diligently established the Shimbu Line and the one who had brought the great cannons to the mountain, but I did not realize you were one of the men involved in the interrogation.

"I am somewhat mystified," continued Laudez, "as to why you have come forth after all these years. Surely the position you hold in the rice market is but a pretense; this confession tells me so. You must have another reason, or we would not be here talking."

"Yes, there are other reasons, but first I want to clarify my position. I will swear on oath concerning Alvarez, and I swear on oath my duty in the interrogation was strictly that of asking questions. Those who were following orders other than the ones I received are all dead. Alvarez can attest to all that took place within the baptistery because I had removed myself to the front of the church. Alvarez remained there under the threat of the bayonet. I am not making an effort to vindicate myself, but I do want it understood just what the circumstances were. In addition, I cannot speak for my comrades who died in the ambush. I will not be their judge.

"This brings me to one of the reasons I am here today. For months I have witnessed a silent devotion, if you wish, that has prevailed for many years. The impact of it has astounded me, because I had assumed the body of the priest had been recovered a long time ago. I will admit the events of thirty-four years ago have begun to enter my conscience more so because of what I am now witnessing. In Japan, and indeed here, I have endured many unwanted flashbacks because of the happenings in Paete and Pililia, but because of my life in the military it has been difficult to be remorseful knowing I had only been carrying out a mandate.

"I am the last one who saw the priest alive, and this was just before he was taken out of Paete when I removed the canvas covering his face. In the dusk I could not tell if his lips were moving, and after the ambush he was in the hands of the guerrillas. I have wrestled with this many times, in all honesty, and believe he died somewhere between the church in Paete and the ambush.

"Alvarez surprised me with his words when he said the body of the priest and its location have never been divulged by the guerrillas due to a vow of silence. This is also difficult to understand. I can see there is a great concern about this just from witnessing the demonstrations going on at this moment. I, and perhaps every Filipino in Laguna de Bay, would have to be somewhat naive to believe that love is the complete reason for such behavior. Alvarez has also informed me only seven of the original guerrillas, of whom perhaps you are one, are still alive. Therefore, before I give you the main reason why I summoned you here, I must first find out if you are one of the surviving guerrillas who have cherished this thirty-four-year-old covenant. If you are not, then this discussion is ended."

Laudez had been listening attentively; however, it was not until Nikono mentioned removing the canvas from the face of Father Douglas did he sense the arrogance had abated in the life of the rice merchant. Perhaps the former commander of Laguna de Bay was human after all, and his disciplined attitude was beginning to strain in the face of a compassion he could not quite understand. Was the master of Mapalug Mountain seeking reconciliation?

"Yes, I am one of the seven remaining guerrillas," said Laudez, "and one who participated in the ambush. Father Douglas was dead when we reached him, and his soul had gone to its reward." He blessed himself in front of Nikono, who had seen this gesture many times in Luzon, even though he never understood it.

Nikono stood up, walked to the side of the dusty road, and looked up the full length of the street to where the inhabitants, young and old, thousands of them, were milling in front of the administration building. Others were in front of the church. He came back to the bench.

"There are many, from what I can see, who are longing for an end to the waiting. When I came back to Luzon I did not know what they were waiting for until I confronted Alvarez. The information I have to offer will help end this drama that has besieged Laguna de Bay—and in such a way that the remaining guerrillas will not have to betray their covenant."

Laudez was on his feet in an instant. There was only one way to break the grip of the oath, yet here was a foreigner stating he knew how.

"Are you saying you know where the body of Father Douglas lies?"

"Yes," answered Nikono.

Laudez wished Hilaria, the one with the sharpest ears, were here, because this time she would not believe her ears. Laudez's pulse was racing at the suggested revelation. Was Nikono serious, or was there some sort of ploy being instigated to trick the guerrillas into a betrayal of a most solemn vow? Laudez was well aware of Nikono's familiarity with the terrain from one end of Laguna de Bay to the other. Now, this onetime nemesis of the guerrillas was declaring, after all these years of silence, knowledge of the burial place of Father Douglas. Laudez was more than skeptical.

"How could you know this?"

Nikono's answer opened the way to the crypt guarded by eagles and angels.

"If he has not been removed, which seems to be indicated by the gatherings we are both witnessing, the remains of Father Douglas still rest above the pool of water contained within Mapalug Mountain. When I was lying below the opening on the southern slope, critically injured from the explosions within the Kalinawan Caves, the voices of the guerrillas who had come to verify the concealment came clearly to me, and I heard them tell of the location. I believe it was your voice I heard in that terrible moment, and that event has been instilled in my being for all time. They did not know of my presence. I crawled off the mountain and was captured a few days later by Recon, of which I believe your American friend was a member."

Laudez was both agonized and relieved by the revelation. The covenant had never been really sealed, and the guerrillas had subjugated themselves to criticism unnecessarily for more than three decades; now the yoke of it had been lifted from their lives. In a sense Laudez was downhearted, because it meant the culmination of the obligation that had bound the guerrillas together in one of the greatest exhibitions of loyalty and love they had and would ever experience. Seven nomads of the hills would be free to relate their epic story.

Laudez requested Nikono to be present at the next guerrilla meeting and to relate to them all that he had disclosed. The bell in the tower of the church rang just as Nikono gave his approval. This ends Nikono's story.

A fter Nikono finished telling his story he did not return to his seat immediately. He merely bowed his head, as he had done when he first sat down in the center chair. He remained with his head bowed for the greater part of a minute. We all waited courteously.

Nikono had maintained the same vow the guerrillas had for years, but he did so unknowingly. Nikono was learning much about things that at one time in his life were as remote as Mapalug Mountain. He was finding his own answers now just as his daughter had when she grew a rose.

When Nikono finally raised his head, Father Demato, spellbound by Nikono's story, limped across the room to embrace his onetime adversary. Then the others shook hands with their old archenemy that had suddenly entered their lives like a ghost from the past. I did not do so immediately, because I had another, more pressing matter that needed attention, and only Nikono had the answer.

All during Nikono's account an image out of my past began to take shape. As Nikono unfolded his saga I had studied him as intently as I did his words. I looked beyond his beard and age, because there was something about him that brought me back to the shadows of the past, back to when I, too, was walking the hills southeast of Manila. There had been a bitter engagement there and its climax opened the door to the contested hills that Nikono had desperately defended with the 27th Regiment of his 13th Division. It was here on Mount Morling, which the 43rd Division had captured, that Recon set up its command post. Some of the fiercest fighting of the entire Luzon campaign took place across the valley east of our bivouac. When the battle ended that sealed the fate of the

169

defenders, we saw elements of the defeated main division of defense, and we knew it was only a matter of time before they were eliminated or died from starvation. There was one Japanese soldier who I had never completely forgotten—Nikono Yashima.

When I last saw him he was more dead than alive. His sudden appearance startled the men on the hill. It seemed as if he had come out of the ground right in front of us. It was in the latter part of April 1945, and the hill had been cleared of all resistance the previous two weeks. Nevertheless, there he was, coming toward us, limping, unarmed and unafraid. Weariness and hunger were apparent, and his uniform, or what was left of it, was saturated with blood. He said nothing to us as he came forward. Gaunt, solemn, unemotional, he just stood there. There was a trace of military bearing still evident in his carriage, but he also carried an expression of resignation, or perhaps futility.

Every man on the hill watched him carefully, well accustomed to the fanatical mind of the Japanese soldier. He stood there quietly, docile, and for a brief second he appeared to stagger slightly, as well he might, considering the condition he was in.

When asked his name and rank, he replied in perfect English, "I am Colonel Nikono Yashima of the 27th Imperial Infantry Regiment." Then he collapsed, pitching headfirst to the earth.

I thought Nikono's story remarkable. Now, after returning to our seats, I approached the onetime military commander. I surprised them all with my question. I did not surprise Nikono Yashima. He surprised me.

"Do you remember me, Nikono?"

"Yes, I remember you well, but only your face."

"Do you remember that day in April 1945?"

"I remember it well," he said. "It was your reconnaissance troop of the 43rd Division to which I laid down my arms."

"Were you treated well?" He understood that I meant after his surrender, although in his testimony he referred to it as being "captured."

"Yes, very well."

"Back in my home I have a regimental flag of your 27th Regiment. When I return I will send it to you in Japan. We found it in the valley below Mount Morling."

My words caused him to bow his head. When he looked up there was a soldier's sparkle in his eyes, and we both understood each other as we reached out and shook hands.

I never told him I gave a young Filipino binatilyo a can of corned beef for the blood- stained emblem of the Rising Sun. I could not tell that to a man who had lost his standard-bearer in the hollow of Mapalug Mountain. There is always pride in every soldier.

Laudez returned to protocol and let Clastres continue the agenda.

"We have listened to Nikono," said Clastres, "and we believe his words, as they seem to be emptied of anger and mistrust. He has had many misfortunes, for such is the way when one man is tested against the other in warfare. The man we have defended for so many years carried nothing but a cross, as even Nikono will attest. In death he had no fear except the fear of the Lord. Years ago we all put aside our implements of war, for they accomplish little. Tonight we find reconciliation in one another's words—this is the way to solve everything.

"Now that we have listened to Nikono, who alone is the only one among us to last see the bearer of our sins alive, we will also reveal the reason why we so diligently refused to dishonor the agreement we undertook those many years ago. As you have heard, the bond no longer exists, and never really did, but believing in it has kept us as one. It is over, and we, although never wearied by its burden, are free to open the doors of the tomb.

First I will read to you the words of Isaiah 53:4—9. (In the last line, Clastres changed the word wicked to eagles, and the word evildoers to God.) Clastres had read this at every meeting held during the vow; they understood its meaning well and listened to it reverently with bowed heads.

Yet it was our infirmities that he bore, our suffering that he endured,
While we thought of him as stricken, as one smitten by God and afflicted.
But he was pierced for our offenses, crushed for our sins;
Upon him was the chastisement that makes us whole,
By his stripes we were healed.
We had all gone astray, like sheep, each following his own way;
But the Lord laid upon him the guilt of us all.
Though he was harshly treated, he submitted and opened not his mouth.

Like a lamb led to the slaughter or a sheep before the shearers,
he was silent and opened not his mouth.
Oppressed and condemned, he was taken away, and who would have
thought
any more of his destiny?
When he was cut off from the land of the living,
and smitten for the sin of his people,
A grave was assigned him among the [eagles] and a burial place with
[God].

When Clastres finished he summoned the other six guerrillas into a semicircle, and sat Nikono, Rafael, Father Demato and me slightly apart from the others.

Before the guerrillas released their account to us, Clastres turned to Father Demato and requested a blessing upon the words of their narrative for consistency of truth and intention. Then, lost in awe for the second time that night, I heard another incredible story, the one of Clastres Bulatao, Laudez Rosaldo, Raul Reyes, Alvita Reyes, Fredrico Guzan, Ramon Augustine and Hilaria Augustine, all members of a contingent of guerrillas who had carried a bamboo coffin to where the eagles fly. The following is the story of Clastres Bulatao and the roses of Pililia.

On July 24, 1943, Fredrico Aurileo ran six miles from Pililia to the guerrillas' encampment above the town, bringing the news to Clastres that the Japanese had taken their priest from St. Mary Magdalene's in Pililia. Father Douglas had been suspected of collaborating with the guerrillas in the hills by carrying military information to them.

Clastres and his contingent of guerrillas could do little but wait. Other reports reached the camp, all giving evidence of the gruesome account of the ordeal taking place in Santiago Apostol, the church in Paete, a town heavily garrisoned with Japanese combat troops and one impossible to infiltrate. Any attempt to enter the stronghold would have been suicidal. It was the strongest fortified position all the way to Santa Cruz, further south.

Ten Japanese soldiers were holding the priest captive, one of them a captain and another a lieutenant. These troops were heavily armed and hostile. The priest had only the spirit of God for protection.

During the afternoon of July 26, Laudez, Clastres's second in command, suggested the priest might not be taken back to his parish in Pililia, and as a precaution perhaps a patrol should cross Laguna Lake to prevent the Japanese from taking the priest south to Santa Cruz. It was a dangerous suggestion, but Clastres trusted the judgment of his lifelong friend.

Clastres selected a ten-man patrol, including Laudez and himself. On the night of July 26, the group stole down into the peninsula with their dilapidated radio, and then they stationed themselves close to the shore road where it swung up the eastern side of the peninsula. The place afforded the shortest route across the bay if they were forced to take that course.

The main reason for the undersized unit of ten was the size of the boat they had hidden in the nipa grass along the shore; it was only sixteen feet long. Hopefully, it would enable them to get across the water so they could set up an ambush if the Japanese decided to head south to Santa Cruz. The ploy of the guerrillas left them extremely vulnerable. Any Japanese patrol could easily cut them off if they were detected that close to the water or that far down in the peninsula.

There was little sleep that night, mainly because of their location. They remained under cover throughout the daylight hours of July 27, keeping movement at a minimum and monitoring the cumbersome field radio.

Just before dusk the radio blurted out an erratic message: "Japanese truck, shore road, Santa Cruz." It was the message they had been waiting for. Clastres concealed the radio in the thicket, then rapidly moved the patrol out. They had fifteen minutes to run the quarter mile to the shore, get across the water and organize an ambush, all before dark.

Clastres turned around on his way to the shore to see how Hilaria was handling the run. She was seventeen and only a week ago had joined the band after her brother had been ambushed by a Japanese patrol in the hills above Pililia. Now, clutching a rifle, grenades bobbing from her ammunition belt, she was running silently in the desperate haste to reach the water. She did not smile; she ran with determination. Running through the slicing grass, she was not conscious of the blood running down her arms. Clastres marveled at her spirit. The dilag had only one thing on her mind: the recovery of the man who said, "You are a rose in the garden of Laguna de Bay."

Only death was going to keep Hilaria and the others from reaching the shore of Laguna Lake. Clastres veered to the left, spreading the grass with his machete while holding the rifle in the other hand. If the boat were not there, the priest would be gone forever.

Clastres suddenly felt moisture squeeze into the cracks in the soles of his boots. He veered to the left again, sensing the dampness of the lake although it was still out of sight beyond the tall grass. The ground became softer, but they neither slowed the pace nor broke stride.

The boat was there, and the guerrillas raised the vessel together. Not a command was uttered. Hilaria stayed right with them, refusing the silent order of one of them to follow behind. One tremendous shove and the boat glided into the ripples. Clastres was in the bow in one quick bound. Laudez reached for the pull rope; on the third tug the engine sputtered, coughed then burst to life.

A simple plan was now in effect: cross the lake, ambush, take the priest out with them, retrieve the boat, and churn across the lake from whence they had come, no matter how many were left after the skirmish. They had come for the priest, dead or alive.

They reached the far shore and the first five sloshed through the reed grass, Clastres, as always, spearheading the grim task. After the grass came the brush, then a slight uphill. Panting, they ran up it and found the road; it was clear. Clastres and four guerrillas remained on one side of the road; Laudez and four guerrillas darted across the road to find sanctuary in the banyan trees and bamboo thickets further up the road. Both groups had a clear view of the bend in the road.

A good fifteen minutes had elapsed since they began the run. Had they missed the truck? Alternatively, had the Japanese for some reason or other reversed direction? They had to wait, and wait they did, watching the sunlight dissolve. Another ten minutes and they would have to fire blindly at anything coming around the corner. Patience was in order.

Clastres was wise enough to realize that a minute was beginning to become forever, so he watched for the first signs of impatience. Hilaria had shifted since he last looked at her. Now she was on both knees, the palms of her hands flat on the ground, her head cocked to one side. It suddenly dawned on him that she was listening. She was as rigid as a flag-pole. Her finger was inches away from the trigger, bolt forward, and she was pressing against the root of the banyan tree to ease the tension of her position.

They certainly could have been troubled over his selection of Hilaria. On a quiet day just a week ago she had walked into the encampment north of the peninsula line declaring she had come to wear her brother's only pair of boots. He had trained her with the use of the rifle, but she had no rifle of her own. If someone would lend her a rifle she would knock a stick off the end of a machete, that is, if someone would stick one in the ground. All the guerrillas knew her brother Rizal Filio because he had walked with them. His body had been seen half buried in the mud of the monsoon—a marker had been put there on the slope of the mountain to show where the Japanese weapon carrier had run over him although he was already dead. None of them would ever forget that ambush because a collaborator, who was now dead, had led it.

Clastres had nodded to Laudez who handed Hilaria a rifle with an empty chamber. She snapped the bolt back in an instant, startling Laudez who had not expected a seventeen-year-old dilag to be able to handle such a heavy weapon, and so easily and confidently. Standing there she said, "It will not fire without a bullet." Laudez handed her a twenty-five caliber from a Japanese rifle. In disgust, but unruffled, she calmly said nothing until another guerrilla had planted his machete in the earth. Then, without looking at Laudez, she strolled away from him, confronted another guerrilla with outstretched hand until he handed her a thirty caliber, which she slid into the chamber, rammed the bolt forward, and turned, bringing the Springfield to her shoulder at the same time, and blew the stick from the top of the machete fifty yards away.

Rizal Filio had taught his seventeen-year-old sister well. However, neither Clastres nor the others were convinced. Despite their show of macho arrogance toward a dilag, she would not be denied a position in the ranks. Walking up to Laudez, who had just challenged her capabilities and knowledge, she said, "I can hear the rice grow." Now she had challenged the second in command and only Clastres could do that. Laudez was cornered into some sort of retaliation and he could not turn from it in front of the waiting companions. Besides, he was curious. What lesson could this cropped dilag teach them that was not already known? Clastres kept his distance, considering himself a spectator in some sort of a guessing game. Hilaria was a long way from playing guessing games—she would stand these stalkers on their heads. Hilaria was clever enough to remove the embarrassment from the head of Laudez before he could answer by walking away from him for the second time and addressing Clastres, "Give me your best three point men." Now she was challenging the leader of nearly two hundred men and his most trusted scouts. What manner of creature was this rice gatherer of Pililia? He consented to her wish. She proceeded to walk among the ranks of the unimpressed guerrillas, taking one empty can, two bamboo poles, two rocks from the fireplace and one bayonet. She returned and dropped them all at the feet of Clastres whose curiosity was now greater than that of Laudez. She whispered into Clastres's ear then turned away, beckoning the three scouts to follow her. One hundred yards from the campsite she stopped behind a thick stand of bamboo, knelt and rested her head and palms of her hands on the ground. She instructed those with her to do the same. Then she threw her bandana out from behind the bamboo grove as a signal to Clastres. She stiffened her body like the cheetah before the spring and told the three guerrillas to listen. Five minutes passed. She relaxed then stood up, motioning the others back to the curious watchers. Once again she approached the leader and the second in command, and for the second time said, "I can hear the rice grow. Clastres has struck the can with the bayonet three times and the bamboo six times, banged the rocks together four times and, finally, stomped his foot on the ground ten times." All three scouts had heard metal against metal but not one of the other sounds. Hilaria had proven her worth, and some of them believed she could hear the rice grow. Others asked her jokingly, "Can the rice sing?" She knew she had proven her point to all of them. Laudez nodded his satisfaction to her with a grin, but no one shook her hand because she had yet to take to the trail. For a week they all talked in hushed tones, fearful Hilaria would hear.

It began to drizzle. Where was the truck? Suddenly Hilaria raised a hand to Clastres who relayed the signal across the road, and then a motorcycle roared past them. Shortly after this she raised two fingers to Clastres, who signaled the same across the road. Shortly after her signal, two vehicles became silhouetted in the blinking sunlight, approaching at a rapid pace. The first truck was approximately twenty-five yards ahead of the other. Not a guerrilla moved. When the lead vehicle was almost abreast of Clastres's split squad, he raised himself to a kneeling position and quietly said, "Let us defend our freedom."

In the next second he opened fire on the rear vehicle with his Browning automatic, shattering the windshield in the first blast and killing the two occupants in the front seat. One of the three in the rear seat toppled over backward, hitting the ground. Another went down behind the front seat.

Seconds after Clastres's opening rounds, Laudez stepped out in the open with his four guerrillas, spraying the lead truck. For a split second the occupants half turned to see where the firing had come from. Laudez's Thompson machine gun and another held low by one of his squad cut the five Japanese to pieces. By this time the truck to the rear had gone out of control, lurching and then smashing into the banyan tree to Hilaria's side, almost hitting her. She left the sanctuary of the tree in one immense leap, as if catapulted.

Clastres turned to see how his second in command had fared, and as he did, the soldier who had fallen behind the seat of the second truck suddenly stood up and aimed his rifle at Clastres. Hilaria, who had bounced back to a standing position, fired, hitting the standing soldier squarely between the eyes. Meanwhile, the first truck continued down the road for forty feet, finally coming to a halt in the brush. None of its occupants moved; two of Laudez's men pursued it while the other two covered them.

The ambush was over, the shooting and the commotion lasting less than a minute. The numbers were even, but the guerrillas had the element of surprise. Not one of the Japanese was able to open up with the machine guns. The guerrillas scrambled to the damaged truck, where, just behind the second seat, they found the body of Father Douglas wrapped in a canvas. Laudez, whose assignment was to recover the priest, rolled back the end of the canvas and they gazed at the man who was now at peace. He drew back the canvas and, as if in a trance, said, "Let us become like the rose." Then the guerrillas blessed themselves.

Three minutes had elapsed. Clastres suddenly remembered his blast had knocked one of the soldiers off the rear of the truck. He quickly ran back but saw no sign of him in the increasing darkness.

Laudez's four men, two on each side, became the pallbearers on the Santa Cruz road. In seconds they lifted the inert body of Father Douglas out of the truck and placed it on the ground. Three guerrillas quickly fashioned a makeshift bamboo stretcher while the others stood guard; they took off their shirts and slid two poles up through the sleeves. They wrapped three bandoliers around the body—one around the shoulders, one supporting the back and the other around the legs. They scrambled with the limp body to the boat.

With two pulls the engine kicked over in the darkness, and they lifted the body to Clastres and the others already in the boat. The water passage would be the most dangerous part of the trip. Every Japanese patrol on land, on water or in the air would be on the lookout for Clastres and his followers. The sound of an approaching patrol boat shattered the guerilla's thoughts. The Japanese, with their searchlight, knew the crossing as well as they did.

From his position in the bow Clastres watched his men closely in the dark. Rain washed down their faces as the boat maneuvered out into the bay. Some of their hope vanished without the light of the moon to guide them, and with bowed heads they silently prayed.

The roar of the patrol boat increased. Before long the beam would illuminate their crossing. Above the sound of the engine and the wind and rain, Clastres heard a sob swirling like a halo over the forlorn group. Tears were falling with the rain. All the grief, tension, desperation and anxiety exploded here on the waters of Laguna Lake in one quiet, gentle, uncontrollable sob. Clastres put his arm around Hilaria's shoulders.

"Cry," he said, "for the freedom of the man in the bottom of the boat and for Rizal Filio." It would be many years before she would permit herself to cry again. Clastres knew her tears had spoken for them all.

Suddenly the zigzagging searchlight found them and the beam remained stationary, holding them in its light. "Two hundred feet to independence," thought Clastres, as he trained his Browning automatic rifle in the direction of the approaching nemesis. He ordered everyone to fire directly into the center of the searchlight on his command. It was their only hope.

Clastres raised his weapon again, firing until the barrel singed his wrist. Hilaria and the others holding Springfields held the fate of all of them, because that gun was far more accurate than the Browning or the submachine guns. The glaring beam and bobbing boat made shooting difficult.

The light suddenly disappeared; one of the Springfields had found its target. It meant little, however, because the well-disciplined patrol boat crew had it repaired in seconds. The next burst of machine-gun fire raked the guerrillas' sixteen-foot skiff, killing two of the men in the bow. Just then the boat slammed into the reeds. The survivors were out of it in a second as the engine suffocated in the swampy ground. The patrol boat was less than a hundred feet away when Laudez and two guerrillas swung the keel around sideways as a temporary barrier.

In the pouring rain Clastres, with Hilaria at his side, grasped for the fallen guerrillas, but both were dead. Clastres gathered their rifles amid another intense barrage of bullets, and Hilaria unfastened their bandoliers and slung them over her shoulder. They lifted the body of Father Douglas out of the boat. With Clastres and Laudez leading the way, the eight floundered through the marsh.

There was another hail of bullets, and one of the guerrillas, Alphonse, staggered when he was hit in the right leg. Clastres fell into the muck, hit in the shoulder. As he stood up and staggered, Hilaria ran up to him and yanked his shoulder strap over his head to release the rifle to her; she slung it over her shoulder with the two bandoliers.

The remaining eight guerrillas staggered, fell, scrambled and crawled beyond the probing searchlight. By now the boat that had carried them across the lake must have been splinters. In the darkness there was an explosion as the gas tank erupted; by then, they were well into the disguising grass, hidden in the rain and darkness.

When they reached the edge of the grassy marsh, they collapsed onto the firm ground. Of the eight who had survived the ordeal, only six were uninjured; three would have to carry the body of the priest and three would have to carry Alphonse. With their machetes they cut bamboo poles to construct another stretcher. They placed Alphonse on it then staggered into the night.

It was a five-mile trek to the temporary encampment between Pililia and the end of the peninsula, then six miles to the main camp northeast of that. The first three miles were grueling because they had to avoid the open, level rice fields in favor of the sheltered bamboo thickets and nipa palms.

With pain draining his strength, Clastres thought of the far greater pain of informing the relatives of his two fallen comrades now lying in the tall grass at the edge of Laguna de Bay. The majority of the populace, even though they had to disguise their affiliation with the guerrillas, stood behind their counterattacks. Most of his guerrillas were in their late teens to early twenties. Clastres was twenty-two, Laudez twenty-one. Both slain guerrillas were twenty-one. For the first time in years he had lost two men on a patrol and was unable to bring back their bodies. Returning for them would be suicidal.

If the Japanese were not driven out of the Philippines, the guerrillas were well aware of the consequences—death if captured. For the prize of freedom they lived as nomads of the hills, constantly on the move because of the fear of discovery or betrayal, scavenging at night for food and jeopardizing their own lives as well as those who showed support. They were separated from wives and families, exposed to the elements, and forever dodging and hiding from the hated Japanese.

Clastres Bulatao prided himself in being one step ahead of the Japanese. He had summoned all his relatives together within a week of the occupation, and before a head count could ever be put into effect, he divulged his guerrilla undertaking to them. They immediately vacated the towns, fleeing to Manila in groups and then dispersing into the city.

Circling the rice paddies had taken precious extra hours and further sapped their strength. Sometimes they had to maneuver hundreds of yards off the true course because of the burdensome biers. Clastres had been fortunate; the bullet had gone through his upper arm and exited through the back below his shoulder. Alphonse had taken the bullet below his right hip; it shattered the femur and exited through his leg below the hip.

Clastres and Laudez sat apart from the others and discussed their predicament. They agreed Alphonse would die if he did not receive medical treatment in the next twelve hours. They patched him up and prayed. Clastres also discovered one of the guerrillas, Jose Demato, had injured his ankle during the boat skirmish but had said nothing.

At four thirty in the morning, just when the first streaks of dawn broke over the distant mountains, they reached the temporary encampment. It was deserted. Slumping to the ground in complete exhaustion they lay there as if dead. Alphonse barely recognized Clastres when he put the canteen to his lips. It was a pathetic scene; haggard, weary and bruised bodies sprawled upon the ground, and they had another six miles to go.

Clastres lay on the cold, damp earth unable to ease his mind of the problems that were facing them. Expecting aid when he reached this camp, he was disappointed more than startled to find it vacant. Something apparently had called out the thirty-odd guerrillas he had left here when they made the run down to Laguna de Bay. It had to be important enough to cause a complete retreat. Clastres searched the camp but found nothing to indicate the reason for such a hasty departure.

Laudez and Clastres sat down once again and planned what had to be done. They decided they could no longer carry the wounded guerrilla and the body of the priest. Someone would have to leave the squad and go ahead to the main camp to report their condition and situation. Furthermore, they would have to bury Father Douglas in a temporary grave.

They decided to awaken Hilaria to inform her of the plan. She would become the third person to know the location of the body in case something should happen to either one of them.

Laudez gently woke her and they informed her of their decision. The three of them chose a temporary burial site in the center of a bamboo thicket three hundred feet from the camp. Using their own machetes and four bolos they found in the camp, they hacked a swath in the middle of the grove, being careful to save every bamboo pole. Then they dug a slot two feet wide, six and a half-feet long, and two feet deep. To retard decomposition of the body, they lashed together a coffin from the bamboo poles.

Swiftly but gently they lifted the body of Father Douglas into the crude coffin. After they lashed on the cover they knelt, prayed and then lowered the coffin into the shallow grave. They covered it with the loose earth, burying the four bolos a few inches above it, then covered the grave with leaves and splintered bamboo limbs. They had plenty of practice in camouflage.

Two hours had elapsed since dawn. Clastres and Laudez decided to awaken the others. They did not disclose the burial site, and no one questioned them about it.

With just one stretcher now to be handled by five men, the pace was increased; however, when they arrived at the foothills the advantage was lost. It became clear that Laudez would have to depart for the main camp and return with assistance; he was also to send a runner to Pililia to summon Dr. Mansang so he would be at the camp when they arrived. Laudez was to return with four or five other guerrillas to continue the portage.

Laudez was exhausted when he left, and the three-mile trek took all his strength. He staggered up to the main camp on the side of Mount Cordillo. He could not help but notice the lack of activity and the absence of many guerrillas who ordinarily would be stationed here. Fortunately, Fredrico Guzan, who was the fastest runner for this group of guerrillas, was in camp, and Laudez sent him off at top speed to Pililia to get the doctor. Then he briefly conferred with Alonzo Velasco, who was in charge of the guerrillas in camp, as all the other men listened.

Alonzo then told Laudez all that had transpired since the ambush. "The entire Laguna Province is on alert. Every Japanese patrol has been recalled to their garrisons in Pililia, Paete, Tanay and Baras. A new line extending from Pililia to Paete will seal off the whole peninsula, thereby restricting the guerrillas' access to a food supply."

"This explains the abandonment of the base camp," said Laudez.

Alonzo replied, "The thirty guerrillas from the base camp had been called back here when the runner, Fredrico, brought news that a Japanese rebuttal force of about three hundred soldiers, heavily armed, had left Paete immediately after the ambush."

"Round up five of the remaining guerrillas, Alonzo. We have to get back to Clastres and his squad and help them off the peninsula before the iron vise closes it."

Within two hours they met up with Clastres. He already knew the Japanese, by protracting their strength across the peninsula, would strangle a vital line of communication and curtail the use of numerous trails. It would affect every guerrilla operation on the peninsula. He also knew retrieving the body of Father Douglas would be extremely difficult and that he would have to return for it while the Japanese assumed they had the guerrillas on the run.

It was decided Laudez would direct and lead the trip to retrieve the body of Father Douglas. Complete darkness would be required to deal with Japanese encroachment of their old trails.

Clastres sent for Hilaria. "You must get all the rest you can," he said. "You have been selected to recover the body of a martyr. You have a gift, the ability to hear what others cannot. You will be the listening post when Laudez and eight others I have selected have to crawl hundreds of yards through the Japanese lines. You will remain close to Laudez and keep your ear to the ground, listening for sounds that do not belong in the night. Laudez and the others will unearth the body of Father Douglas."

When the guerrillas reached the temporary grave, they clawed at the loose dirt with their hands until they uncovered the buried bolos a few inches from the top of the coffin. They excavated rapidly, keeping a cautious eye on Hilaria who was standing guard. As they dug Laudez pondered as to where they would make the final commitment of Father Douglas's body once they returned to the camp. A marked grave was out of the question. The Japanese would not tolerate a venerated martyr buried under their noses in Pililia or any other town; otherwise, they would have handed the body over to the Filipinos instead of trying to secretly dispose of it somewhere on the road to Santa Cruz. If they buried the priest in some remote place in the hills, the site might be neglected or lost. That would be a disaster to the morale of the Filipino people, especially those in Pililia.

Laudez was seized with the impulse to see Father Douglas once more. He made an excuse to send the others away so he could pull back the canvas. He shone the light on the face of the dead priest. He gazed upon the features, blessed himself and said a short prayer, never taking his eyes off the body in the coffin. When he heard the others returning, he quickly closed the cover. He said nothing to Hilaria or the others about opening the coffin.

They moved out, four trailing Laudez and Hilaria at ten-foot intervals to protect the four bearers but mainly to encircle the coffin quickly. All of them had vowed that in case of attack the body of the priest would be protected to the death; however, they encountered no Japanese.

About a half mile from where Laudez was expecting the new camp to be located, Hilaria came up to him and said, "I hear the bell." The band came to a halt and stared at her; she was the only one who could hear the tolling drift through the hills from Pililia, some miles distant. Then they all knelt on the trail in midday amid the faint echoes of an ancient Spanish bell as it rang out the message that the guerrillas had come out of the peninsula. It was July 29, 1943.

When they arrived at camp, they rested the bamboo coffin on the earth amidst a great moment of exultation. Then the ten of them slumped to the ground and slept.

The Japanese had made a mistake. Punishing the proponents of insurrection was one thing, but plucking the rose from their garden was another. Father Douglas had come to Pililia with nothing but a crucifix, rosary beads and the Gospel. As the Filipinos plowed the rice fields with their slow-footed beasts, he cultivated their lives with the dove of peace. He prayed with them and for them. Where and when there was nothing, he instilled dignity into their lives and pointed them to the way of the cross. He quelled their anger, soothing it with patience. When there was no rain, he gave them the blood of Christ; when there was no rice, he gave them the body of Christ. When he gave them both, he gave them life everlasting. In the turbulence he ministered to them in the hills; in the shadows he consoled their fears. In their pain he held out his hand, and then he threw the cross upon their shoulders, reminding them love came through forgiveness and that was the greatest gift of all.

So many times he told them they must be like the rose, bringing the beauty of God through the thorns. So many times he told them they must remove the thorns and flower like the rose. So many times he told them not to let the thorns of life drain them of their compassion, but to be humble, and in their humbleness they would find humility; in humility they would find the soul of Christ.

In the ensuing years as they knelt at the foot of the cross, they would look up to see the face of their priest and the life of a man who was so much like the crucified Christ. Father Douglas was thirty-three when he died; Christ had been thirty-three when he died. Father Douglas was beaten by a rifle; Christ had been flogged with a lash. Father Douglas was tied to a wooden post; Christ had been tied to a wooden cross. Father Douglas said the rosary, eyes on the cross; Christ had prayed, eyes to heaven. Father Douglas was pierced by the sword; Christ had been pierced with a lance. They had no food or water; they forgave their torturers; they suffered for three days; they were stripped of their clothes; they were shepherds—and they both died for their sheep.

There was one dissimilarity: the whole world knows Christ died on the cross, but only God knows where and precisely when Father Douglas died.

Father Douglas had said, "Christ will come again, through his resurrection." Now, throughout the entire region of Laguna de Bay, there would be another resurrection, filled with determination and love because their priest told them, "Christ will always be with you, and I, too, will always be with you. My ghost will shadow your trails and shield you from the invaders and their arrogance. Bury arrogance in the roots of the rosebush and it will become lost in the beauty of the flower. Good fruit cannot bear bad fruit." Now they would carry his goodness upon their backs and shoulders, letting his words and the words of Christ comfort them in the cold nights and the torrid days.

The news of the death of Father Douglas stirred one parishioner of St. Mary Magdalene's, Francisco Gonsalves, to action. Francisco began his preparation for climbing the steps of the belfry, which he had not done since 1941.

On the afternoon of the July 29 a guerrilla runner brought the news to Pililia that the body of Father Douglas was safely off the peninsula. Francisco immediately went to the belfry as angry as a man could be. At three o'clock in the afternoon he began the tolling of the bell that would only end when his life did. He tolled like a man possessed until the blood ran between his calluses.

The anger of the bell rang up the Laniti River, and the rice growers wept in the muddied paddies as the wild river ran into the waters of Laguna Lake. Uneasily, the Japanese watched the residents of Pililia begin their vigil in front of the church. The Japanese, however, could not understand the strength of the love in the hearts of Father Douglas's parishioners—strength without a sword, a bell challenging atrocity, black headnets in the hour of darkness, a silence in the hush of sorrow—and not a tear falling in the rain-soaked streets of Pililia.

Rafael, Francisco's son, stood with his mother in front of the rows of silent throngs that were increasing by the minute. He watched the rope swing in and out, causing the bell to stifle the murmuring town of Pililia.

He feared for the life of his father. He began to tremble like the stalks of bamboo swaying beyond the bench where Father Douglas once sat and prayed. At one point he thought the old belfry might collapse from the thunder of the bell; it was older than anyone in Pililia. The shadow of the cross began to creep across the road as the sun began its decent beyond Morong. Rafael's mother, silent as all the others, gazed up at her husband vigorously tugging on the rope, and when two soldiers arrived with the dusk, she fell to her knees in the shadow of the cross. Amanda Gonsalves was sure there was nothing on earth that would bring her Francisco down from the belfry, only the sword. She was still kneeling when two lines of soldiers positioned themselves between the crowd and the doorway to the belfry tower. Amanda knew that to beg her husband to desert the rope would be an affront to him and a display of conformity to the Japanese. Francisco would never have forgiven her. She thought of how Father Douglas had climbed the hills, unafraid, attending to the guerrillas with only the Host for protection. Similarly, her Francisco, unafraid, had climbed the stairs to the belfry finding only the sound of the bell for protection. She tried to persuade him with unspoken prayers while the results of the torture in Paete tortured her silent vigil.

The irritation of the bell ringing had brought the captain of the Pililia garrison to his feet, a few hundred feet from the resounding tower. He ordered his lieutenant to post a notice declaring the bell ringing must end at the hour of sunset and never toll again. Sunset, however, did not fall on the hour—it went down on the half hour. Francisco tolled the bell at five o'clock and then flagrantly tolled it again a half-hour later, when sunset actually occurred—a defiant and dangerous act. The captain was infuriated by his own miscalculation of sunset.

The sun had gone, but not the soldiers. Amanda began to shudder, knowing her husband had not left the tower. Two soldiers were ordered to ascend the stairs, and then the ensuing shot shattered the silence of Pililia. The death grip of Francisco embraced the hemp long enough to send the tongue crashing into the hollow of the bell. The final toll of Francisco Gonsalves on July 29, 1943, sped out of Pililia into the encompassing hills, findings its way once again into the ears of Hilaria. She recognized it immediately as another toll of death in the lives of her people, but she did not weep.

Rafael and his anguished mother rushed through the ranks of soldiers to find the bell ringer crumpled at the bottom of the stairs. Others followed, pulling headnets over their eyes, showing the Japanese their arrogance was not worthy to be looked upon. The parishioners placed the motionless bell ringer onto a carabao-pulled cart and brought him home. Hundreds followed and prayed all night long beside the bier. Two days later two thousand Filipinos followed the wake of the casket, praying mournfully in a dreary procession to the cemetery. Pililia went into mourning for the second time in a week.

That very morning Clastres had welcomed the returning squad into the new camp with a great sense of joy. He commended them for the success of the excursion. Their youth had been severely tested as they carried the body of the priest through rugged and dangerous territory. Clastres had already constructed a temporary hut on the northern slope to shelter the body from the sun. He did not post a guard at the entrance of the hut, but he did deploy guards along the sides of the hill.

That afternoon Laudez approached Clastres and said, "I suggest we send Fredrico into Pililia to get another cassock for our priest, a white one. I want to make sure his body will always be adorned in the finest cloth, worthy of all the world to see."

"I agree," said Clastres, "but Fredrico is already under enough suspicion. Let us choose a new runner, Garcia Lopez, to go to Pililia to confiscate a new cassock."

Garcia left at dusk, returning long before the rising sun. Due to the hour he did not report immediately to Clastres but waited for the sun to appear, then he told his leader about retrieving the cassock from the vestry of the church and the unfortunate death of Francisco Gonsalves.

Clastres and Laudez prepared to hold a meeting to discuss where Father Douglas would be buried. He included Hilaria Filio, Laudez Rosaldo, Fredrico Guzan, Alonzo Velasco, Rodriquez Homamassa, and Ramon Augustine from Pililia; Juan Boniface and Emilio Florentino from Paete; and Raul Reyes from Baras. Clastres considered these guerrillas his finest, four of whom had participated in the ambush on the shore road. When they were assembled on the hill they politely waited for Clastres to open the meeting. However, Laudez, for the first time in his nomadic life, requested to speak first.

"We are here," he said, "to establish a resting place for our good shepherd. It has been four nights since we took him from the hands of the arrogant ones and carried him with our arms to the bamboo thicket. On the night of the ambush I pulled back the canvas from the head of our beloved martyr. Hilaria, Clastres and myself looked upon the face of the good priest. We gazed upon his wounds, and we saw the deep wound close to his eye. There was no need to look for further torture. Even with his dried blood, he was angelic and beautiful. Through my unseen tears I knew he was in heaven, just as our fallen companions were on that same night.

"On the night when we brought him back out of the earth, I stood alone at the side of the bamboo bier and shone my light on the face of our beloved and for the second time gazed upon him."

His voice was now trembling, and he held his head in his hands. They all patiently waited until he had regained his composure. With great care he organized himself, took a deep breath then continued speaking.

"When I gazed upon his face for the second time, his wounds were gone."

A stunned silence prevailed. Surely their second in command would not utter such an untruth. Father Douglas was their martyr, their inspiration, their shadow on the trails. Surely Laudez would not make a mockery of these things, and brazenly do it before their eyes.

Clastres spoke for them all, "What are you saying, Laudez?"

"I am saying before God and you that when I looked the second time, the blood and the scars had vanished."

"Have you looked again since such a vision?" asked Clastres.

"I did not see a vision. I saw the same face that prayed for me at the altar and handed me the bread of life. I have not dared to look again. I slept but very little this night. All night long I could find no explanation." His head went into his hands again.

Some of the guerrillas did not believe what they had just heard. Did Laudez know what he had implied? Raul and Juan thought the exhausting nights had beleaguered him with nightmares. Perhaps the sun had affected his vision or the shadows had altered his perception.

However, Laudez was steadfast in his convictions. None of the questions could shake him. Clastres was not about to challenge him openly;

he would leave that to this select group, which is why he had picked them in the first place.

He did not have too long to wait. Emilio Florentino, who was considered a reckless but brave guerrilla always trying to fashion his exploits after the legendary Emilio Aguinaldo, was the first to stand.

"Perhaps," he said, "all of us should enter the nipa hut and see for ourselves, especially Hilaria and Clastres, as they also saw the face of our padre at the ambush. Surely they remember how he was that night. Rodriguez was there also." Clastres and Hilaria nodded in assent. Rodriguez nervously nodded with the others.

Clastres decided to ask Laudez to go alone and look into the coffin again. Laudez realized Clastres was giving him the opportunity to gracefully admit he had made a mistake in the dancing moonlight.

"I will look for the third time, with your permission," said Laudez, "but I ask Hilaria and Rodriguez to accompany me." In this way he had cleared Clastres from all doubt and also gave the doubters their moment, because with either an affirmative or a negative response from Hilaria and Rodriguez, the issue would be settled. The two agreed to accompany Laudez into the hut.

The three of them entered the nipa hut and Rodriguez lifted the cover off the coffin. Then he stepped back, allowing room for Laudez to approach. He pulled back the canvas, then motioned for them to come to his side. When they gazed into the casket, they knew this death had conquered the aggressors. There was neither a mark on the priest's face nor a trace of blood on the canvas, and there were no signs of deterioration. He seemed to be asleep.

The truth of the priest's words was staring them in the face, and the serenity on the face of their priest forced them to their knees. Laudez knelt beside them, and the three prayed for the soul of the man who talked gently about roses.

Meanwhile, Clastres and the others waited patiently; then he beckoned them to follow him. They entered the hut and found the other three on their knees. None of them had to be told Laudez's description had been confirmed. They all knelt together, unable to fully comprehend why this had occurred in their midst. No longer were they just followers of the padre's words; they were the guardians and were obliged to shield and protect the marvel that had been granted to them. From that moment on the face of their priest remained uncovered. Clastres let them take their time inside the nipa hut.

Laudez was the last to leave the nipa hut after gently closing the cover over the body. When time permitted they would have a magnificent weatherproof liner made out of mahogany and encase it with the finest bamboo in all of Luzon and decorate it with hand-carved red roses.

It began to rain in torrents. Clastres recommended they all return to their tents and rest. For the remainder of the day he pondered where they could conceal the body from the Japanese and have it still remain accessible to the Filipinos.

That night Jose Demato lit the only candle he had left and let his thoughts drift back to the days when he was spellbound by the words of the martyr who now rested a few yards from him. Jose's tears splattered in the rain that found its way into his tent. Tears also stained the paper on which he composed the words and music to, "My Everlasting Rose," a song that would resound for years within the echoes of Laguna de Bay.

The next day Clastres asked Laudez, "What do you think of the previous night's event?"

"I am not sure. It is not a sign of hope as I see it. We have always had that. Perhaps it is a sign that we must live better lives."

"We are poor," said Clastres. "Is he telling us that as children of the earth we must always struggle to grow?"

"I do not know what he is saying," replied Laudez. "None of us may ever understand what lies in his silence."

"I think he is the rose," said Clastres. "I think he has blossomed despite the thorns. Was it not a sword that pierced him?"

"Yes, a sword in the hand of the devil."

"What do the others say of this?" asked Clastres.

"Some of them do not understand," replied Laudez. "They are bothered by what they have seen, but they are glad our priest is at peace and his torturers will pay with their death. We need be careful to control their feelings, or it will be us who die."

"You are right," said Clastres. "We must warn them not to endanger the lives of the rest by rash impudence. We must remain disciplined."

"Shall we permit the entire band to see the body?" asked Laudez.

"We cannot deny the sheep of the nomadic flock the chance to behold their shepherd."

"No, we cannot," responded Laudez, "and we must decide where to conceal the body of Father Douglas for as long as necessary without placing him in the ground. His beautiful face should be exposed for those who choose to see him."

Clastres suggested, "How about the Kalinawan Caves?"

"That is a terribly long journey," replied Laudez. "There are many miles of rocks, tributaries, hills, ravines and swampland."

"We will find a way, Laudez," said Clastres.

"Some of the openings in the caves face to the south and southeast," continued Laudez. "The main one faces directly west toward Baras and the Shimbu Line just a few miles away. During the monsoon the great swamp will be full to transport the Japanese by boat to within a few miles of the base of Mapalug below the caves. We would be under their noses. There are thousands of Japanese gathered in the entire area, and before long they will winch their weapons of destruction up to the caves."

"They will not move before the rains," said Clastres. "We have time. It will be weeks before the swamp overflows from the tributaries, and they would be foolish to cross the swamp before it reaches capacity. They have no reason to do so now."

Laudez replied, "Only with the help of heaven will we be able to hide the body in the caves. The Japanese have the manpower to funnel men and lines within the entire mountain. We do not have enough guerrillas to infiltrate every tunnel under such direct observation."

"We will not go to the Kalinawan Caves," said Clastres. "We will go above them."

Now the plan was clearer to Laudez. "You mean to the cavity and the basin?" It was more of an exclamation than a question. "It is forty-five hundred feet up to the cavity. We cannot be there before it is filled by the monsoon. We will not be able to get Father Douglas across the water and into the room above. It will be overflowing and running back out and down the side culvert to the bottom."

Clastres responded, "If we get to the opening and it is filling with water, then we shall float the bamboo bier across the cavity. We shall do this even if it costs us our lives. We owe this, at least this, to our confessor.

Once the cavity is filled to the opening, we can rest secure in the awareness that Father Douglas is safely hidden in the room above the cavity and
no one will see him until the monsoon has passed."

Laudez had begun to accept the plan. There was no other secretive
place southeast of Baras where the body could be placed. Only a betrayal
would reveal the mystery of the missing priest.

In the hot noonday sun Clastres, accompanied by Laudez, walked
into the center of the circle of guerrillas and gave the longest speech of his
young life.

"My companions, my comrades, my men of the hills. We have traveled many miles and accomplished many things together. Beneath the
moon and the sun we rest far from our friends and loved ones. The morning dew and monsoon rains wash our hair and bodies, and our sweat runs
into the rivers and the bay, and we are cleansed once again. Some of our
own are prisoners of tyranny. Some have died because we dare to ring a
bell. The echoes of the bell will never leave the hills. We will never have
it any other way. For we are brothers against the arrogant ones and we will
walk upon their graves or perish in the hills. It is our cause and we have
chosen to follow it. Our closest comrades are at peace amongst the crosses because they believed this to be so. Yet we are not free, and that is why
we gather today to hear the echo of liberty reminding us of our cause. A
bell of silence hangs unmoving in the belfry in Pililia, but we must
remember it tolled until the death of one and because of the death of
another, a man who was not one of us yet was one of us. Silence prevails
in his chamber, for he but sleeps. Tomorrow he will be adorned in white,
and then those who so choose will carry him yet further into the hills.

"What I am about to say concerns loyalty and comradeship. You are
all free to make your own decision on what I am about to suggest. Go to
the nipa hut and gaze upon the body of Father Douglas. Form your own
interpretation of what you see, and then leave. At the same time I ask
each one of you to ponder whether you should take part in the portage of
over thirty miles to the Kalinawan Caves. In addition, I ask each of you
to make a personal vow, a covenant as a unit, to never reveal the burial
place of our beloved martyr until it becomes appropriate. In time you will
understand this is in the best interest of our people.

"As you visit the body, Laudez will tie a hemp rope between two trees.

I will retire to my quarters, and at the hour of one o'clock I will come before you again. Those who stand on the west side of the rope will have chosen not to go, and those who stand on the east side will have chosen to accept the burden and the covenant."

Then he handed the rope to Laudez, turned his back to them, and went into his quarters. As he sat there gazing out through the open door of his bamboo hut, he heard the first strains of "My Everlasting Rose." A contingent of ill-clad, ill-fed guerrillas with choirlike voices softly sang. It was their tribute to a silenced man who was not one of them yet was one of them.

Alphonse, who had been wounded on the shore road, was no longer in the hands of the doctor. Gangrene had set in and because of it four guerrillas had to carry him on a stretcher to view the martyr of Pililia. Amidst the pain he requested to stand erect on the east side of the rope, supported by two others—where he sang the last words he would ever utter.

Hilaria sat alone on the hillside, her eyes and ears keenly aware of conversations. She had only been with this band of tattered shirts and rude manners for a little over a week, and despite her inner admiration for their gallantry, she felt isolated. She gazed off to the east and then to the west and north, considering the unknown that lies before the contingent of nomads, until her eyes found the crest of the great Mapalug Mountain.

The Japanese had killed Rizal, her brother. He had become a man before he had become a youth. Her thoughts wandered to Alvita Aquino, Rizal's devoted girlfriend, a dilag with a broken heart. Hilaria gazed toward Clastres quarters. She decided she would confront Laudez immediately and present her suggestion. Laudez was standing beside the bamboo coffin, and they conversed for several minutes. They then went to see Clastres.

Laudez said, "Hilaria has a concern," and he motioned for her to speak. Hilaria gathered her senses and confronted the guerilla leader. She did not beat around the guava tree.

"Alvita Aquino has a broken heart. It lies shattered in the cemetery beside Rizal. For two years she was taught how to fire the rifle and the pistol. The runner says she is patiently waiting at the bench beside the church, waiting for the message that will call her into the hills."

Clastres merely looked at Laudez, who almost appeared to be

grinning, but gave the characteristic twinge of the eyebrows—which was enough for the leader. He consented to her request, although Hilaria had not really asked for the company of Alvita. Clastres was forced to grin at the ingenuity displayed by this reliable dilag and encouraged her by saying he would inform one of the food gatherers to bring Alvita to the hills and join them. However, she was to be given no information, and Hilaria would take her into her confidence later. This settled, Hilaria returned to the hillside and continued watching the mists envelope the upper slopes of Mapalug Mountain.

Laudez came to inform Clastres that the men were ready. Clastres looked down the slope to see his entire band, with backs to the sun, singing in a hushed tone. All were standing on the east side of the rope. He walked toward them.

"My comrades, I thank you. Let us prepare for the task at hand."

They had accepted his wish and he had accepted their answers. There had been no command or any resemblance to an order. The song was still softly echoing around them when Alphonse collapsed and his soul drifted through the echoes to where the eagles circled Mapalug Mountain. They buried him in front of Clastres's hut, facing the mountain he had longed to climb.

Ten guerrillas would remain on the hill in the absence of the main contingent: Jose Demato, with his sprained ankle, seven others who had been wounded slightly, and two runners who would be needed to go between the camp and Pililia. They would be the rear guard, maintaining constant vigilance around the camp until the return of Clastres and the others. The runners were to keep a close watch for any enlarged Japanese infiltration into the hills or the Laniti Valley.

Before dark Clastres sent twenty men down into the villages along the river to procure enough food to feed them for two weeks and to inform the relatives of the circumstances concerning the deaths of Alphonse and the two others on the shore road of the Jalajala Peninsula. That evening the altar women of St. Mary Magdalene's discovered one white sheet and one white cassock had disappeared from the top drawer in the sacristy bureau. They simply went outside to where Father Douglas was last seen standing, blessed themselves, and then looked toward the hills miles away. They knew more than the Japanese.

While the men were in the village Clastres visited Jose in his tent and asked him about the guerrillas' response when viewing the body of Father Douglas.

"We all see things differently," said Jose, "but not so much this time. I looked upon him the first night and what I saw made me very sad. When I looked upon him today I felt nothing but joy. I instantly knew my beloved confessor had returned from a journey. It is to let us know he will always be with us. Many of the others have the same opinion. They say no man has gone under the stick and sword for three days and emerged without a mark. I think he is telling us he will never abandon us. I think he is saying he will be our shadow on the trails. I think he is beyond all suffering and has shed the thorns and now he blooms like that rose he wants us to be."

"We think alike, Jose," said Clastres. "Pray this night we can find the strength he has offered us."

In the morning an exhausted runner arrived in camp to inform Clastres the Japanese were beginning to build a well-constructed road from Baras to the Black Swamp. Barges were being installed on oil and gasoline drums. There was no doubt these barges were going to cross the swamp. Clastres felt certain the guerrillas could reach the caves before the completion of the road, although it might involve taking a wide loop far to the east of the Black Swamp that would provide numerous places to bury the body if it became necessary.

Meanwhile, one of the food gatherers returned with Alvita Aquino. She and Hilaria embraced on the hilltop amidst the well-wishers. They knelt in prayer. Hilaria took her into the nipa hut where Alvita gazed upon the face of the Bamboo Shepherd, donned her black headnet, and blessed herself with the name Rizal Filio on her lips. She did not shed a tear, but the agony of the moment, and the joy of it, would remain with her for the rest of her life. Father Douglas had called her a rose.

Alvita returned to the hilltop and became the one hundred and eighty fifth guerrilla who would carry the Bamboo Shepherd into the clouds. At that time Clastres detailed the two runners, who were to remain on the hill, to adorn the body of Father Douglas with the white cassock. It was the last time the coffin would be opened until they reached their destination.

Clastres called upon the men to shoulder their haversacks, sling their weapons, remain disciplined, and remember who they were and whom they loved. "Let us be like the rose," he said, and they set out in the direction of the Kalinawan Caves.

It was a long line of pallbearers. Every guerrilla carried the bier over and over. When the sun beat upon their backs they watched the shadow of the coffin dance over the earth, and they were all sure their martyr was walking with them and letting them know he would always be with them. They harnessed themselves with a dedicated determination just short of obsession, believing that when a man dies out of love for you, the perils in the mountains cannot be of any consequence.

All that day they walked solemnly and slowly. It would be their easiest day. Pacing would be essential and regulated. When the rain subsided enough to let the sun find them, they resisted the temptation to hasten toward the welcome coolness of the trees.

Clastres kept Mapalug Mountain in view as much as possible. Looming majestically above the distant hills it was his beacon in the sea of foliage. It cut through the clouds and jutted through the squalls of rain. He lost sight of it when in the depths of the ravines, but on the next rise he would find it again. Four miles behind them, resting on the hillside with his badly injured ankle, Jose Demato scribbled the words of a poem entitled, "Antrum."

> His shall be a throne of stone,
> Within the marrow of the bone,
> Unmarked by man, or thorn, or sky,
> Where eagles rest, and eagles fly,
> Where eagles go, and eagles die.
> His shall be a throne of stone,
> Within the marrow of the bone,
> Carved by the Master's hand thus blest,
> Hallowed round like an eagle's nest,
> His is the throne of silent rest.

Coolness greeted them at dawn, and the lowland mist left the hollows and swirled up the mountain. Ominous gray-black clouds were moving along the horizon. Clastres did not like what he saw. The bamboo coffin would not cast a shadow today and neither would they. If torrential rains were to come they would deal with it. The rains came.

The hills became steeper and the sky turned purple, then black. Clastres did not want to be caught in a gully or a steep ravine if the sky opened up. Suddenly, the flood left the sky. They heard the rush of water fifty feet below and knew it was barreling knee deep through the gully. No man would be able to stand up to it. Each guerrilla huddled with his own thoughts, fearful of sliding down the hill into the flooded channel.

There was no dry wood to start a fire that night, so they ate cold wet rice and wild guava and slept in their soaked clothes. When Laudez changed the dressing on Clastres's shoulder, in the darkness he did not see the redness around the scar. Clastres felt a twinge run the length of his arm but said nothing. He was on his way to an eagle's nest.

The following day the sun had not cleared the distant mountains when Clastres suddenly raised his arm and the two lines came to an abrupt halt. He kept turning his head right and left. A musty smell was drifting through the valley—a foul smelling stench that could only mean one thing, the swamp.

North brought them to the Japanese, south was away from their objective, west was where they had come, east was the only alternative, and that was through the swamp. It was midmorning when Clastres led them into it as the arm in the sling was beginning to throb. He told no one.

The guerrillas soon discovered they could not hurry in the swamp. It set the pace. As they moved in deeper Clastres signaled the guerrillas to close ranks to within an arms length of each other, allowing the rotation of the bearers to occur more often. Before long they were in water over their ankles. The hidden roots and decaying branches brought them to their knees. It was more difficult for Clastres, with the exception of those carrying the bier and ropes.

Suddenly a twenty-foot python descended from a banyan tree, landing on the shoulders of Rodriquez, who had been struggling to free his boots from the suction of the mud. Within seconds the python had him entwined in its coils, and the contractions began running the length of its sleek black skin. Just as quickly Laudez drove his machete straight through the oval head. By this time Rodriquez was almost under water. Laudez knew the contractions continued long after the snake was dead, and continued to hack at the snake until there was no longer any movement. They then dragged Rodriquez out of the mud to a high spot. Clastres called for a break; they were exhausted.

After the rest the entire cortege moved still closer to each other, maintaining the coffin in their center as much as possible. Keeping the coffin above the water was becoming extremely difficult.

A quarter of a mile ahead a widening gap appeared. Clastres warned them of the possibility of crocodiles in the pond. The reptiles, some eighteen-feet long, were there, lying motionless on the banks like fallen stumps. The pond was too deep to ford, so they would have to swing around toward the base of the hills, which were lined with boulders. Beyond the giant rocks was the clear outline of a rainforest.

They skirted the edge of the pond nearest the canopy of green. Keeping a safe distance from the crocodiles, they slowly made their way around the pond. Not a cloud sheltered them. They dipped their bandanas time and again into the discolored water; it was their only defense against the fiery orb as its rays danced on their heads.

It had been a tiring day. Clastres halted them beside the stream that was filling the pond. Guards were posted to watch for marauding snakes and crocodiles. Before slumping to the ground they cut wide stemmed nipa strips, sliced slits in them for eye openings, then wrapped their bandanas over them and their heads. Mosquitoes would not torment them tonight.

The third day found them in a rain forest, where only a flicker of sun made it through the thick foliage. It felt like a mausoleum with a vented ceiling. Pythons curled in the vines above them, and in the dark of the forest it was difficult to distinguish a vine from a snake. The mists hugged the moss-covered stones and rotted stumps. Four-foot lizards crossed their path, scampering into the thick undergrowth. This was the domain of the reptiles, and the guerrillas were the intruders.

They followed the course of the stream twisting and turning beneath the canopy. It was a gradual uphill ascent. Time after time they had to pass the coffin hand over hand. Their knees bled as they slipped on the grimy stones. At times Clastres could not scale the rocks and had to be pushed or shoved up and over them, protecting his arm the best he could. Their clothes became as drenched as the day before, sticking to them like the moss to the rocks. Chills penetrated to the bone.

On they plodded. They rested more often; however, it brought stiffness to the muscles. One of the guerrillas climbed above the vines to see the extent of the rainforest ahead. They had come approximately half way; a few miles ahead the mountains rose out of the valley. Slightly east were Lake Lampon, Mapalug Mountain and the Laniti River; but first Clastres had to get them through this jungle of gloom before the sun went down.

Hilaria suddenly stopped the group, "Listen," she said. "There is a cascade pounding down into a body of water, and a loud hissing sound." Of course the others did not hear it yet. They continued on to find a severe climb up to the water basin, but before they reached it, they discovered a waterfall tumbling two hundred feet onto a huge rock with a hollow core, which accounted for the hissing sound.

Relaxing before they faced the climb to get above the airborne spout, they enjoyed the spectacle of hissing spray as it caromed into the streaks of sunlight. The moment was short lived, though. The beams of light suddenly disappeared, and Clastres came to his feet instantly, "Get to the ledge above the pool as quickly as you can," he ordered. They spontaneously stood erect and formed two lines to pass the bier up the steep tiers of stone. They had to reach the ledge before the deluge reached them and caught them in the hollow below. Up went the bier, dragged over one rock after another. They received deep cuts and bruises as they slipped on the jagged pock- marked, rain-chiseled rocks. It was a treacherous climb, but they conquered the pile of stones just before the rain broke through the green ceiling. The forest was now pitch black. Clastres had to get them out of this dreariness before pneumonia set in. To guide his way he used the sound of the rippling stream, which, within moments, roared in its new momentum.

Clastres knew they would never find their way out of the rainforest without additional light, but he was hesitant to use the flashlights, which he was saving for the interior of Mapalug Mountain. He had no choice and the beam from the flashlight guided him, in fifty-foot intervals. For a half mile he herded them in groups. Not until the beam caught the outline of the mountain did he relax, knowing they had withstood the challenge of the rainforest. When they broke into the open, Clastres discovered Raul Reyes had torn off every one of his fingernails while slipping and desperately grasping the edge of the boulder to keep from falling. He had never uttered a sound.

They were misery at its lowest, and there were at least two more days of uncertainty before them. If the rains abated tomorrow they would repair and reinforce the battered coffin. For now they stretched out in the middle of the knoll. Weary nomads determined to fulfill the covenant; they closed their eyes beneath a starless sky. It rained all during the night. Fatigue shut it out.

Lake Lampon was locked high in the hills. They would reach it their last day on the trail. All this night and the following day would be for resting and sleeping, because crossing the Laniti and the approach to Mapalug Mountain would be under the cover of darkness.

They settled into a steady grind. The high altitude left them short of breath, but they never faltered. Sweat ran into their cuts and bruises. The hillside brush tore the bandages off their legs. Eagles soared above them, dipping between the hills, gracefully skimming the peaks over their heads. The guerrillas climbed, descended, climbed, descended, on through high noon until they met the bald hills. There, Clastres gathered them together away from the sun and told them Lake Lampon was a mere mile distant. They would reach it before dark.

While they rested they gazed with awe at their final challenge, Mapalug Mountain. It dwarfed everything as far as they could see. They were one night and one day from testing the power of this sentinel of the valley, where a secret opening for which they were struggling would shelter the Bamboo Shepherd. It was forty-five hundred feet to the basin, and only Clastres and Laudez had ever reached it. A good many of the guerrillas had never climbed a mountain before. They just sat there in the approaching dusk shaking their heads.

One barrier remained to the mountain, the Laniti River. Four of the strongest guerrillas would handle the coffin during the crossing. Laudez and Clastres discussed the crossing point and a site in which to rendezvous in case some of them were swept downstream. He selected what he thought would be the shallowest point and which had a supportive tree on either side. The Laniti was raging.

Clastres sent six guerrillas upstream; two would cross the Laniti with two ropes while the others held onto the other ends. After testing the current each guerrilla looped a rope through his bandolier then plunged into the unmerciful Laniti; its strength sapped their own, leaving them gasping for breath in the murky waters. They were swept downstream like splinters of wood but fought the river with every ounce of energy. Scrambling ashore they fell exhausted on the muddy soil. Their rest was brief, as they had to secure the ropes around a tree. Once both ends of the ropes were secure on both sides, they would have two lines stretched across the raging waters, enabling them to transport the bamboo coffin.

Clinging to the two lines they traversed the river supported by their bandoliers, which they hooked around one of the ropes. Hand over hand they crossed until only Clastres, Laudez and the bamboo coffin with its four bearers remained.

Laudez asked Clastres, "How do you expect to cross the river with one arm?"

"I shall tie myself to the rope and my companions will pull me across," he said.

"With one arm you will drown," said Laudez. "Those with two good arms are barely alive on the other side. Let the good shepherd carry you across"

"It is not fitting," Clastres exclaimed. "I could not do such a thing."

"It is better than drowning or swallowing what the others have left for you. We have carried him many miles, and I do not think he would mind carrying one of us two hundred feet."

Clastres had to smile at his friend and said, "You talk as if he were alive, Laudez."

"He is alive in my heart and in yours. You know it is so. You must let him do this one last thing for us."

"I will float across this terror of a river with *our* good shepherd!" replied Clastres.

Laudez took the rope and went into the river.

The remaining guerrillas untied the ropes from the tree and secured one end of the rope to the left front of the bier and the other to the right front. They could feel the force of the water pressing against the coffin. They assisted Clastres to the top, and he signaled those on the other side to commence pulling. The ark began its journey across the swollen river. The struggle was immediate.

The extra weight of Clastres pressed the bier deeper into the water and made the pulling even more difficult. Tugging on the rope the guerrillas fought the river and the fury of it. The bearers had all they could do to keep the coffin from tipping over and to keep Clastres from rolling off the top. Clastres clung to the side with his good arm; at times the coffin dipped and rocked in the angry, churning whirlpool of power. However, the bearers and those on shore hung on until the blood spouted from their palms like that of the bell ringer of Pililia. Finally, Father Douglas was brought ashore. He was another Noah coming to the mountain.

Clastres had swallowed a good deal of water, and his shoulder dressing had sailed to the bay. They carried him ashore and pumped the water from his chest. Laudez knelt down beside him, and in the light of the moon he saw the yellow telltale shade running from Clastres's shoulder to the elbow.

They gathered in their ropes, their wits and their pride. Together these nomads fell asleep at the foot of Mapalug Mountain. The tired but victorious guerrillas had won their tug-of-war. Clastres and Laudez looked to the outline of the mountain and knew there would be no shadows in the coming dawn.

The next morning Laudez decided to confront Clastres.

"The night conceals many things," he said. "When you were taken from the angry waters like a drowned rat, the moonlight revealed the condition of your arm."

"So you know, Laudez?" quizzed the leader.

"Yes," said Laudez, "and I know you will have but one arm for the rest of your life."

"Would you have me turn back, Laudez? If you had been with Father Douglas when he was being tortured, would you have begged him to appease his tormentors? You would not have succeeded in taking his moment from him. Did he not shield us from the thorns of sin, climb the hills, and pluck the thorns that were draining our wretched souls? That is why I must climb this mountain, so he can be hidden from the thorns that once cut his flesh. We all must keep his memory alive as he kept our souls alive. Do not take this moment from me."

Laudez now understood they would have to drag their leader up the craggy slope. He never criticized or mentioned the decision again, but for the rest of his life he never forgave himself for not being more alert to the condition of Clastres's arm before and during the journey through the wilderness.

Two hours before dusk Clastres assembled the guerrillas and unfolded the assault on Mapalug Mountain. Hilaria and her squad would go southwest; another squad, led by Rodriquez, would go around to the northern slope. Hilaria was assigned to listen to the mountain and discover the secret of its hidden stream. If they could control the water in the basin by blocking the outlet, the basin would fill up and seal the entrance to the upper chamber, preventing anyone from reaching the bamboo coffin that was to be secreted there.

After several hours Rodriquez and his squad finally reported back to Clastres.

"There are floating barges," he said, "carrying large crates in the Black Swamp. We could see trucks and bulldozers staggered along the roads, raising dust as far as you can see."

"Then the Japanese must be in the Kalinawan Caves, making additional preparations," replied Clastres. "We will have to wait for Hilaria to return to find out what she has discovered."

Hilaria's squad then straggled in.

"Clastres," she said, "I heard nothing but the screams of eagles. The hidden outlet will have to wait until tomorrow."

The next day Clastres gathered his caravan of nomadic guerrillas and remarked, "It will be imperative that we avoid all open areas until we reach our destination—and then only the shadow of God will conceal us."

They looked to the peak of Mapalug Mountain, which appeared ready to crush them; they prepared for its assault, booted and barefooted, with only their ropes and willpower to guide them. Visions of roses bloomed in their eyes, roses from a thornless bush. The sun would reflect the bloom of it over the mountains to Paete, Pililia and all the way to Laguna de Bay. This they vowed.

It was a precarious and unpredictable climb. They dug their heels and toes into the side of Mapalug, and the entourage headed into the heavens. Sometimes the bier, dangling from the ropes, swung in midair. Their shoulders burned and bled from the cutting rope. The mountain mists vanished and the sun found them. Sweat salted their cuts and bruises. At high noon they were half way to the opening, which meant they would have to spend the night on the side of the mountain.

A large cliff appeared above them, and this, too, they conquered. In their exhausted state they collapsed upon it. A jagged wall was ahead of them. A thousand-foot drop was below, laced with jagged miniature pinnacles. They would have to conquer the wall. Clastres, barely able to contend with the rope, called for a halt. "We will wait for the morning before we attempt to climb the wall," he said. Clastres then pointed to the clouds coming in from the east, they understood his gesture.

An ominous silence entered the valley and crept upon them. Far beyond the range of mountains to the east the sky turned an ugly gray. Clastres herded them together against the jagged wall. There was no other way to escape the coming storm. The wind slammed into the base of Mapalug, and then it swept the ridges and ravines in an upward draft, hurling its fury upon them. They suffered a whirlwind of cold rain. Eighty- to one-hundred-mile an hour winds had them locking arms and bandoliers to keep from being blown off the mountain. Black and yellow skies lashed at them, and they were sure they saw the horns of the devil emerge from the mass of rolling and howling death. Winds as wild and ferocious as they had ever experienced tried to elevate them out of the crevice and carry them into the clouds. All around them fissures gushed to overflowing, spouting up shoots of water. Stones and boulders went hurtling down the sentinel to the valley below. Locked in death grips they shielded Clastres and the Bamboo Shepherd with their lives—they clung to their prayers.

Then another blast of wind jolted them. It was the last thrust of energy before the storm abated. The band of guerrillas unlocked arms and bandoliers. Too tired to shiver they bunched as close as they could and went to sleep sitting up, heads in their hands.

Clastres hardly slept. His arm ached and so did his legs. His heels were black and blue and the palm of his hand was raw. They all had similar miseries, but he had to find one among them who would extend himself yet further. He selected Garcia to challenge the wall. They tied the rope around him, and Clastres said, "Do not look down." Some of the others tied their ponchos together, making a trampoline, and held it directly below the frail looking man, all the while calling encouragement to him. Slender and nimble, Garcia inched his way up the wall surface. The rope pestered his progress. Blood ran from his fingertips and the end of his toes.

Garcia tied the rope around a boulder and the guerrillas shinnied hand over hand to the ledge. When the bier was safely on the ledge a saddle seat was made and Clastres was hauled up. They took a welcomed rest while he pointed to the location where the opening to the basin should be. Then he motioned to commence the last climb of their agonizing trek. He walked to the bier and placed his hand upon it.

They resumed their ascent, but with an unexplained confidence. Suddenly, when they were all crawling, lifting and scratching at the side of the mountain, Hilaria dropped to all fours. Not a guerrilla moved as they watched her in suspense. She moved back toward the direction they had come, constantly falling to her knees, listening intently. Then she disappeared from view. Soon she came clamoring up the slope, holding her canteen, and emptied it on the rocks in front of them.

Hilaria had found what they hoped was the runoff from the basin above.

Clastres sent Hilaria and several guerrillas in quest of the runoff. After an anxious fifteen minutes Hilaria returned and reported, "There is a pool glimmering in a small crevice above us. All we have to do is clean out the crevice and fill the gap with a stone. A combination of gravel from the slope and slivers of shale packed on top of the stone will seal the gap. The frequent rains on the mountain will keep the basin filled to capacity forever."

Clastres urged them up the gully that ran from the mouth of the basin. At the hole in Mapalug Mountain they stood in elated silence. They had reached the belfry overlooking the Laniti Valley, a belfry in the clouds of Luzon.

The entrance, about three-feet wide, did not go straight in but dropped steeply to the floor of the basin. Clastres tossed a piece of shale through the opening. The splash echoed throughout the chamber. The flashlights were unwrapped, and with one in hand Clastres slid slowly through the opening. Laudez followed. At the end of the incline they beamed their lights across the surface of the hidden pool, casting ghostly images across it. They were standing in three feet of water, then they moved to where the water seemed the deepest, about four feet.

They turned back to the sunlit opening. Clastres designated Laudez and Hilaria to float the bamboo ark with him, assisted by two others. The five of them sailed the bamboo coffin across the limpid pool into the heart of the mountain. At the end of the pool they climbed out and dragged the coffin up the slippery incline to the chamber ten feet above the basin. Then Clastres raised the cover. For the third time on this journey he gazed upon the face of the Bamboo Shepherd. He saw nothing had changed.

They were the ones who had changed. Scarred and bleeding with most of their energy sapped from their bodies, they knelt on the side of the mountain amidst the screams of eagles; simultaneously, barges floated across the Black Swamp laden with the implements of war. One hundred eighty-five guerrillas waded through water shoulder high, soothed and bathed their wounds, climbed out of the baptismal font, then moved in a single line around the bamboo coffin to look upon the man who had no greater love. They had carried Father Douglas through the hills to a sanctuary in the clouds, hidden in the mist and shadows of eagles. As Clastres closed the cover over the Bamboo Shepherd the others waded out into the welcome sunlight. None of them saw Clastres reach into his haversack, turn off his flashlight, kneel in the darkness, and place a disheveled rose upon the bamboo coffin.

They gathered their gear and their wits and began the descent. Eight hundred feet down they came to the place of the escaping water. At the level of the gap they spread out until they found a stone about the size of the opening and rammed it in the slot. Then they gathered slivers of shale and pounded them along the edges of the stone. With their hands they mixed the gravel and fine shale into a claylike substance, then sealed the opening with it.

The descent was as harrowing as the ascent, and then they struggled with the Laniti River for the second time. Near the end of their journey, Laudez sent Garcia to strike out for the camp and send one of the men to Pililia for Dr. Mansang. Clastres's arm would have to be amputated. Meanwhile, Laudez dressed the arm of his tireless leader for the last time.

Clastres led them out of the valley. Through a starless night he paraded them into the hills below the camp. He had kept them hidden from the Japanese. When the rain abated just before dawn some of the early rising farmers saw the distant lines of men crossing the hills far from the shadow of Mapalug Mountain. The tired and ragged guerrillas had listened to their leader in the shadows of death and now were following him home. Once again they softly sang "My Everlasting Rose," which seemed to drift across the valleys and hills and into the crypt of the great mountain. They sang to the heavens because they had brought the man who spoke of roses, their Bamboo Shepherd, closer to God.

The next morning Clastres led the guerrillas into camp. Dr. Mansang and an intern arrived from Pililia. Clastres would not carry a rifle again.

For two weeks Clastres hovered in death's shadow. Every day the nomads of the hills opened the door of his hut to let in the sunlight so Clastres could see the great mountain. He had used it to get his bearing while crossing swamps and hills, and they wanted him to see it so he could get his bearings again. The light finally returned to his eyes, and Laudez told the men Clastres was with them once more.

Clastres and the shadow of the Bamboo Shepherd then began to plague the arrogant ones. The one-armed guerrilla roamed the peninsula with such vigor that the Japanese issued bulletins reminding the Filipinos there would be instant death for anyone caught associating with him. However, his men struck ferociously and relentlessly with him along the Shimbu Line as if driven by an uncontrollable force. Clastres was becoming a legend in Laguna de Bay.

The number of guerrillas who had carried the bamboo coffin began to decrease drastically. Many fatalities occurred along the Japanese defense line that had been hastily constructed across the top of the Jalajala Peninsula shortly after the guerrilla ambush on the shore road. Although the Japanese had solidly fortified this perimeter, the majority of the guerrilla attacks were carried out here.

Then in 1945 the Allied forces arrived.

They besieged the Japanese in the entire Laguna Province and especially during their assault on the well-dug-in Shimbu Line. The guerrillas could readily see the strength of the remaining forces of the Shimbu Line still within the Kalinawan Caves. They understood devastation would continue to rain down upon the towns and barrios if the caves were bypassed. Subsequently, Clastres and Laudez were summoned to attend a meeting by the Allied military command and asked to offer their service in penetrating this final bastion; the guerrillas agreed without hesitation. They were to make one last heroic endeavor in driving the Japanese from Laguna de Bay—assault the mighty Mapalug and the seemingly invincible stronghold of the Kalinawan Caves.

Clastres had already stationed an outpost within six miles of Mapalug and had assisted in the routing of the Japanese as they retreated to the Kalinawan Caves. From the hill they watched the frustrating attacks of the military forces for a month. Clastres knew there was but one way to remove the arrogance lingering in the hole of the mountain.

The artillery raked the western slope constantly while Clastres scanned the southern slope with his binoculars. For two weeks the guerrillas watched and recorded the changing of the Japanese guards at the two machine gun nests until there was conviction of a definite pattern. Still, Clastres waited another week before making a final decision and then informed the Allied forces of his mission. Twenty of his men, led by Laudez, would ascend Mapalug Mountain, destroy the two machine gun nests, and then enter the Kalinawan Caves through the southern tunnel. He requested there be no shelling in that area until his men sent up a flare signaling the mission was accomplished. The time was set.

They moved out during a steady drizzle and, that night, rested on the shores of the Laniti River. The following day, using the bamboo and other foliage to conceal their movements, they ascended Mapalug Mountain for the second time; they perched like eagles two hundred feet above their first objective—the machine gun nests.

Huddling on the slope they prepared themselves for the most dangerous assignment of their nomadic lives. Just before the shadows infiltrated the mountainside, Laudez split them into two groups. Prayers were said beneath the mantle of Laguna de Bay.

Patience became the format of the hour as they waited for the changing of the guards. Four minutes had been allowed for this procedure, then the pause until the replaced guards had cleared the tunnel. With the four new guards settling at their post, Laudez signaled the men down into the foliage within fifteen feet of the unsuspecting Japanese. When both groups were abreast of each other Laudez waved again, and the guerrillas leaped into the midst of the startled guards who were disposed of within a minute. Hilaria fled into the tunnel with her squad as the four guards were then stripped of their uniforms. Garcia, Raul, Rodriguez and Emilio put them on and hurried into the tunnel. The remaining guerrillas dismantled the machine guns and threw the ammunition down the mountain as Laudez jammed a Japanese bayonet between some rocks, reached into his haversack for a bamboo wreath, and looped it over the bayonet. Then he hurried after the others.

Both squads moved through the stacks of ammunition, stumbling as they negotiated the dimly lit tunnel, until they could see the light from the main chamber. The two squads reached the chamber just as the metal door was being raised. The four uniformed guerrillas walked nonchalantly toward the four winches, ignoring the crew preparing to roll the cannons toward the main entrance of the chamber. Rodriguez calmly pulled the pin on his grenade and hurled it as far as he could into a tunnel to his left. The explosion burst upon the arrogant ones like a sudden clap of thunder; shouting and commotion followed. By this time the four uniformed guerrillas had reached the winches and immediately jammed metal rods into the gearboxes. The cannons and the door would never move again.

Simultaneously, a Japanese soldier hurled a grenade into the pandemonium. It bounced across the rocky floor and stopped at the feet of Emilio, Ramon, Rodriguez and Garcia, who, without hesitation, threw his Japanese helmet over it, then his body. He died instantly. Laudez and the others emptied their sidearms, killing the crews of the cannons and several others who were trying to reach their rifles. Then they raced for the ledge where Laudez and Juan tripped flares and hurled them over the edge. The guerrillas then fled across the ledge amidst the distant whine of the Allied aircraft.

Twenty dedicated and disciplined guerrillas had accomplished in several minutes what otherwise would have taken the Allied forces months and the loss of many lives.

The remainder of the night they stayed on the mountain, listening to the explosions of napalm and ammunition destroying the last of the Shimbu Line. They did not mention Garcia except in their silent prayers.

By August 1945 the war ended in the Philippines. The number of guerrillas dwindled to less than a hundred. Some died of malaria; others never fully recovered from their wounds. Clastres made sure the remaining guerrillas were bivouacked near the Kalinawan Caves. He sent Laudez and several guerrillas, including Hilaria and Alvita, up the northern slope of Mapalug, the easiest ascent. They were to enter the caves to assure there was no sound of running water above the ceiling. Hilaria heard nothing except bouncing sound waves. Not completely satisfied, Clastres sent another patrol, led by Laudez and Hilaria, up the southeastern face of Mapalug, where they found the opening that had sealed off the escaping water. It had remained secure. Then they ascended to the mouth of the basin; to their joy they discovered it was filled to capacity. They were certain the basin was sealed forever.

Thus ended the epic in the Kalinawan Caves. Their journey was completed, ending two years after the initial ambush. Most importantly, their Bamboo Shepherd was asleep in the heart of Mapalug Mountain.

This ends the narration by the remaining seven guerrillas.

The testimony of the seven guerrillas, each testifying separately and unequivocally that the martyred priest was without a mark when they viewed him after the ambush and also when they sealed him in the mountain, could well have been the factor that continued the change in Nikono. I do not think he believed all they said, but I am sure their epic fostered a respect for their love that at one time he thought was ludicrous.

I asked Nikono, "Do you believe what the guerrillas have stated concerning the condition of the slain priest?"

"Not really," he replied, "But why would they fabricate something they claim one hundred and ninety-five guerrillas witnessed? They could easily have said only seven or ten had seen such an event.

"Following my return to Pililia," continued Nikono, "there came a slow, clear respect for the guerrillas who had held firm to their beliefs. Those who had been interrogated and threatened by the sword about the ambush and the location of the body of Father Douglas had answered only, 'He is buried in our hearts.' They guarded this with caution and determination."

I replied, "What they were really protecting was an undying love. Father Douglas had died for the right of others to live, and the guerrillas had died to keep his memory alive. The simple logic of both incentives is the right to choose, the basic desire in attaining freedom."

Nikono added, "For a long time I did not understand how one man without a sword could incite thousands of people, even more so after he was dead. It has mystified and angered me for many years after the war, becoming a thorn in my life. I did not find the rose the priest had spoken of until one bloomed in the life of my daughter, Kieko."

When the meeting ended it was two hours before dawn. A sense of relief was noticed in the seven guerrillas. A burden, one of silence, had been taken from them, and now they could discuss some of the episode without restraint. They were no longer bound by a covenant that had both guided and hovered over them for what must have seemed an eternity. I found myself wondering if they would have ever revealed the secret of Mapalug or died with it if Nikono had not told his story.

Clastres announced, "We will wait to reveal what has transpired tonight. Rafael, you will tell your mother to notify the women in every Legion of Mary that on the coming Sunday, Father Demato, who had assisted in the recovery of the martyred priest, will make an important announcement at every mass in Pililia."

It took me a few days to put together all the facts of the guerrillas' overland trek and what became of them after the war. Clastres, Laudez and Hilaria assisted me tremendously.

"The secret of Mapalug," began Laudez, "died with many of us because we vowed it would, although we were incessantly pressured by our business associates to reveal the secret location. After the war Clastres married and so did I. We both raised families and went together into wholesaling rice in Pililia. Clastres eventually became the mayor of Pililia. Hilaria married Ramon, and, as you know, they have remained in Pililia. Their rice paddies have made them prosperous."

"Raul married Alvita and settled in Morong," interjected Clastres. "They had owned many rice paddies at the top of Laguna de Bay, but then opened a room and board establishment, where you have been staying, in the center of Morong. They became prosperous citizens and elders of the town. Eventually Raul was elected mayor."

Hilaria continued, "Jose Demato, whose injuries from the war have left him with a slight limp, went into the Columban Seminary after the war and was ordained into the priesthood in 1954. He was eventually assigned to our church, St. Mary Magdalene, in Pililia. As you have heard in his sermons he often quotes the words, especially of roses, of Father Douglas. Every evening before dusk he says the rosary on the church bench, as did Father Douglas, then pulls the rope of the bell, which echoes across the valley into the nests of the eagles on Mapalug Mountain."

I absorbed it all, and then asked Clastres, "How, under the noses of the Japanese, did you accomplish these seemingly impossible objectives?"

"Clastres explained, "It is a simple answer to a simple truth. Father Douglas loved us and we loved him. With this kind of love all things are possible."

I stated, "Nikono had masterminded a defense that seemed impregnable. He had seen the invincible forces of the Rising Sun crawl out of the islands, or what was left of them. Then the Shimbu Line disintegrated before his eyes because men like him, brilliant as they were, were blinded by their arrogance and never fully understood the cry for freedom.

"The Japanese soldier was always ready to die. They were patriotic and dedicated, but they were not struggling for freedom. Their ambition was superiority laced with arrogance. They should have learned from the Spanish, who had the same unattainable aspiration. Nikono was different, though, because failure was not in his vocabulary."

Laudez replied, "Nikono must have realized, at some point, Father Douglas believed in a different set of values. This ideology is a different kind of freedom, one of the soul, and we and Father Douglas were ready to die for it."

In the interim I waited for Rafael to return from seeing his mother. He arrived at Mrs. Temporado's house with his jubilant face. He seemed eager to talk, which was uncharacteristic, and I let him.

"In 1943 I was only ten years old and an altar boy serving Father Douglas," said Rafael. "Being young I posed no problem for the arrogant invaders, but I knew what was going on in the hills and supported the guerrillas whenever I could by concealing rice for them. It was dangerous. Many times I witnessed the wrath of the Japanese soldiers when someone was caught. Father Douglas warned me time and time again to be careful or the sword would become a thorn in my life. Nevertheless, I admired the guerrillas and vowed to become one when I was old enough.

"Even at the age of ten the mental torture of picturing my beloved priest suffering for my people was almost unbearable. I became a man that day and vowed I would find the perpetrators who had taken away the echo of the padre's footsteps. My distress multiplied my hatred for the Japanese and overshadowed all the teachings my father had ever given me.

"After the war I inherited a small rice farm from an uncle in Baras and left Morong. This brought me closer to the grave of my father."

He tried to collect himself, the memory of the death of Father Douglas and his father as well as the hardships of the war overwhelming him momentarily. Then he continued, "I believe there will be great joy in the hearts of the Filipinos and much celebrating when the good news is heard throughout Laguna Province, but perhaps there may also be many discomforts and upheavals when they hear their martyr might still be unmarked. They will ask, 'How can this be? If it is so, then he must be a saint.' We shall see what comes of this miracle."

The Laguna grapevine had done its work. All week long there were Filipinos entering Pililia from every direction: some walking, biking, arriving by jeepney, crossing Laguna Lake. There was little left to sell in the market place except carabao. Relatives and friends moved in with relatives and friends. Pililia bustled.

Father Demato worried the church would not hold the multitudes on Sunday. He mused over the parable of the seven loaves and fish and wished he could create seven more churches.

Through the efforts of the Legion of Mary he was able to get loudspeakers installed outside the church. He asked Rafael, "Will you toll the bell every hour on Sunday and twice after sunset?"

"I will walk in my father's footsteps, and with the bell, call the shepherd back to the heart of Pililia and to his garden of roses."

Rafael tolled the bell for the eight o'clock Mass. When the echo carried off into the maze of hills, Father Demato blessed himself, went into the church, genuflected before the altar, ascended the altar, and then looked out over the congregation of humble, crammed and attentive worshipers in the crowded building. He was aware there was an unusual stillness for such a large audience.

When Father Demato finished the gospel and looked up to address the captivated assembly, he saw what he had always seen: people looking for another dream, another fulfillment, another quest for love. Now he was about to fulfill their dream. Father Demato spoke softly, as if he were about to caress a rose.

"'What is one finger when one gives his life? What is one hand when one sheds his life? What is one arm when one gives his life? What are a thousand thorns when one gives his life? What is a tear but a sign of love? If I must, I will shed my flesh and cover it with my grief. I tell you this: I will shed no tear because of the pain of it, but my heart will ever cry for the Bamboo Shepherd.' These are the words of Clastres Bulatao, a man we know so well, and still the leader of the seven remaining guerrillas who long ago asked us to be patient. Yes, it has been a long time for them to carry the burden of a covenant created among them, including Clastres, Laudez, Hilaria, Ramon, Raul, Fredrico, Alvita and the other one hundred and eighty-eight others who have been called to the Lord. Their sacrifice was beyond measure. Somewhere in the hills, hidden from our vision in obscurity but well known to us who remember, exists the greatest sacrifice a man can make for his fellow man. Today it is the will of these remaining guerrillas you see seated before you to make known the place where our martyr rests. (This brought a stirring in the pews.) This has not been an easy task, and only because there is another who has known where he sleeps is there concession in revealing the burial site. There has been much discomfort from this disclosure, but the result has given them the opportunity to cast off the yoke of the covenant loyally held within their hearts.

"Today we will begin the first part of that trail by describing the location of the remains of our beloved padre, who still reminds us to be like the rose. We have been searching for this answer for the better part of our lives, but now, as I stand here before you, my eyes climb to the slopes of Mapalug Mountain, the majestic Mapalug, a symbol of strength in our community."

Not a whisper was heard. The entire congregation was rigid with intensity, and then Father Demato softly spoke again.

"After many miles of constant struggle, the guerrillas carried our rose to a chamber above a water basin on the eastern slope of Mapalug Mountain. He is sealed in a catacomb above the water, and he awaits our deliverance."

Then, for the first time while attending any Mass, I watched a priest sit down in what seemed to be the middle of his sermon. However, Father Demato seemed to know exactly what he was doing.

His announcement brought a tremor of relief to those gathered there, especially to the seven former guerrillas. For them it was over. The personal ordeal of harboring the secret had now vacated their lives. Their heads bowed in unison. Then the hundreds of others parishioners, especially the elders and the survivors of the occupation, relaxing their passive and patient reserve, turned and embraced one another. Not even the Laniti could contain the well of water that had been concealed behind the masks of indifference. It poured upon the floor beneath their feet. The hidden pain that had been lodged in their hearts and souls for so long escaped into the winds of Pililia and up the great crest, drifting into the basin containing and shielding the promise that all would become as gentle as the rose. For this one blissful moment they were just that. The Bamboo Shepherd was coming home, and no one had to keep him buried in his heart, where all had individually and collectively protected him for years.

At the same time came the realization that they had forfeited the right to embrace something everlasting. Now they had to relinquish this attitude just as the mighty Mapalug had to give up its ghost. To release their hold on something intangible had also diminished their embrace on hope. What had been positive, firmly locked in their hearts, was now dissipating, escaping their dream of complete freedom and independence. The weight of the yoke was gone, and the joy of being able to see their long lost shepherd come home would have no bounds. A sacrifice had been made, and now came the weeping because of it. They were now patiently and courageously waiting for a new message from the Bamboo Shepherd that would rejuvenate their existence. Above and beyond their love was this, and wanted most of all.

Father Demato watched them closely and felt this was as expressive as his flock had ever been. The mask had been removed. He thought of Amanda Gonsalves, a keeper of roses who had vowed her rosebush would flower at the side of the concealed priest. It would be a long way to carry a rosebush, he thought, but then he reflected on the long trek by his companions, and he thought he would like to carry the rosebush up the mountain to the man who said, "Jose Demato, you are a flower in the firmament of God."

The good priest waited piously and patiently until there was a semblance of calm within the walls of his church. Then he continued.

"The good news of the risen Christ descended upon the apostles and the believers; similarly, the good news has fallen upon our ears. We must go to the mountain that shields our faithful servant. We shall loose the waters that surround our shepherd and we shall all herald him back to his pastures. In the days ahead let us gather the virtue of humility into our lives as he who humbled himself beneath the sword. Let us show his words did not fall upon deaf ears but rather, they penetrated into the depths of our hearts. We must be as gentle as the rose. You cannot let your sandals wallow in the dust of the road as the carabao does in the mud, but rise above the indignity of our existence, as he did when he faced the thorn of the sword. Within the week I will meet with the seven who carried the priest and the missing cassock through the hills, and we will decide just what kind of an expedition should be carried out. Let us pray."

Rafael and I went back to Mrs. Temporado's to escape the bedlam in the streets, but the words of Father Demato went up the old guerrilla trails, spreading like the four winds into every niche in Laguna de Bay.

The seven guerrillas waited for word of a meeting to discuss the future of Nikono and Alvarez. Most of the elders in Pililia were alive at the time of Father Douglas's abduction and were therefore familiar with the exploits of Nikono and the circumstances surrounding Alvarez participation in the torture.

The following week Nikono stood before the somber faces in the administration building and for the first time in his life was asked to swear on the Bible, a request he would have refused years ago. He understood the sincerity behind it even though he did not fully understand the strength of it, especially if someone were lying. How could a book make one speak the truth? Yet during the entire hearing he received the impression the elders seated in judgment knew who was and was not speaking the truth.

The tribunal began. The retired Japanese colonel flatly denied Alvarez had offered to participate in the interrogation for any reason whatsoever. At times Nikono detailed his own role in the episode, which Alvarez in turn verified, claiming the Japanese colonel was not actually present in the baptistery when the vicious beating took place. Nevertheless, neither this nor the testimony of Alvarez is what really saved Nikono from the persecution of the Filipino tribunal. It was the words of the only witness, a most silent one, Father Douglas, who had taught everyone the value of forgiveness. During the hearing Nikono heard numerous quotes that the elders attributed to Father Douglas, most of them in reference to the rose, a flower he had seen growing abundantly in the towns. He saw how much it meant in their lives, and by doing so he saw the meaning of it in his own daughter's life. It was the slain priest who actually exonerated his tormentor. Nikono was spared from repeating his narrative in its entirety, because the seven guerrillas testified to it throughout the three-hour tribunal. When it was over, the elders acquitted the two men (the tormenter and a man who had only carried a bucket of water).

Rafael turned to me and said, "The verdict seems to mean more to Alvarez than to the rice merchant. Maybe Nikono has yet to fully understand the attitudes of the Filipinos."

Once again Clastres was called upon to select prudently and discreetly the best to recover the body of Father Douglas. Of this group five were the original guerrillas; the others included one hundred ninety Filipinos, Rafael and Father Cannon.

Clastres commented, "It is a proper testimony to the memory of all the guerrillas living and dead." Then he outlined the plan, "We will ascend to the basin, recover the bamboo coffin and carry Father Douglas off the mountain to the church in Pililia, just as if the trek had never ended. Rafael, you will ring the bell."

"It will be the greatest honor ever bestowed upon me," he said, "and I will ring the bell so long and loud my father will hear it."

Within a week the throngs began to dissipate, returning to their towns and villages to prepare for what would probably be the biggest event in most of their lives, and mine.

I asked Clastres and Father Demato, "May I make the climb with the others?"

"We shall present your request before the panel of guerrillas and elders," they responded.

It was now the middle of May 1978 and the rains were ready to descend upon the hills and valleys above Pililia. When Rafael heard of my intentions, he was quick to advise me, "You are aware of the conditions that exist?"

I reminded him, "I had been here with the 43rd Reconnaissance Troop in 1945."

To this he only smiled and said, "You were not forty-five hundred feet up the slopes of Mapalug, especially in the month of July."

I understood his meaning and message, but worked hard to get into condition. Within a week my request was granted. I believe it was my determination to find the body of Father Douglas that convinced the elders. I was overjoyed with the opportunity.

They selected the northern slope to ascend Mapalug, which was the way Nikono had selected the first time he had taken his men off the mountain. They agreed all the guerrillas except Clastres and Alvita would make the trip. Father Cannon, the Columban Father in Morong, would go in place of Father Demato and perform the blessing of the coffin on the mountain. Rafael would ascend the pinnacle with his mother's rosebush lashed to his back. Laudez, still second in command of the aging guerrillas, would lead the entire excursion, one hundred ninety-eight climbers in all. Father Cannon was in his thirties, and I was the oldest at fifty-seven. We all knew who would have to be roped a good deal of the way up the mountain, and back down.

Nikono was asked to offer guidance through the swamp and the hills beyond to the base of the mountain. His limp and ailing back would not permit him to go any further.

During the interim I made a few visits by bicycle to see Mrs. Gonsalves. "Your rosebush is beginning to bloom again," I said.

"Rafael is going to take it on his back to my confessor," she said with pride in her voice.

With each passing day there was an increased fever in the streets. Father Demato kept a keen watch over his parishioners, noting relatives who had not been seen for years were coming to church. In the middle of July he called for another gathering of the panel, "I am concerned about the increasing number of people entering Pililia. I do not want my church in ruins, and it surely will be if the remains of Father Douglas were brought into the church. I suggest the use of the administration building."

The elders frowned on this. They did not want their building destroyed either. The discussion reached a stalemate until Clastres, always the arbitrator, recommended, "We will have volunteers rope off a good-sized circle near the dampa, construct a six-foot-high bier in the center of it, and place the coffin on it. In this way nothing will be destroyed, and no one would dare intrude upon the sanctity of the hallowed earth beneath the elevated martyr."

This proposal was accepted, and Raul and Ramon were elected to oversee the plan. It was Father Demato's hope the throngs would subside after a few days so the coffin could then be brought into the church.

In the third week of July it was clear the Laniti River was not the only stream running through the valleys and into the outskirts of Tanay and Pililia. A stream of walkers, bicycles and skiffs on Laguna Lake descended upon Pililia to pay tribute to Father Douglas. Many of them walked more than thirty miles and for three days and nights ate very little.

Throughout the commotion Nikono kept a low profile. He wrote to his wife and daughter telling them he would be home the first week in September, but he did not tell them what had detained him so long.

Luis could no longer maneuver his jeepney through the crowded streets and had to operate from the outskirts of Pililia, a mile from its center. The shore road was submerged in mud half the time, making walking difficult for me. There would be much more severe obstacles on the mountain, so I welcomed this chance to keep my legs in reasonable shape.

Mrs. Gonsalves informed Father Cannon he had been selected to make the climb up Mapalug and offer the blessing in the crypt. He was overjoyed by the news and immediately contacted Father Doyle of the Columban Fathers in Manila.

The Columban Order still considered itself the genuine representative of the missing missionary, because, after all, he was one of them; however, the Filipinos did not quite see it that way. This was one of the problems the guerrillas discussed on the hillside above Pililia in 1943 and ultimately was one of the main reasons why the covenant was undertaken. Clastres called a hasty council of the other six guerrillas, and they decided, as their leader, he should visit the Columban Order in Manila and present the sanctity of the covenant and the strict wishes of the original one hundred ninety-five guerrillas, or there would be no excursion to Mapalug.

The following day Clastres approached Father Doyle. Clastres informed him, "Father Demato had brought Father Douglas out of the peninsula and will serve as the main celebrant of the Mass said for the soul of Father Douglas. Father Doyle, you and the other priests will function as assistants."

Father Doyle reluctantly agreed, realizing it was not the time to test the legendary guerrilla who was about to conduct the second attempt to conquer the mighty Mapalug during the rainy season. Clastres politely but emphatically continued, "Father Douglas belongs to the people and no one will take him from us. We have protected him for thirty-five years and will continue to do so. Only Father Cannon will be permitted to participate in the procession from Baras to Pililia, that is, if he is in any condition to do so after his climb up and down the mountain. We carried our Bamboo Shepherd to the mountain, and we will bring him home."

Again Father Doyle did not object. He did not believe too many of the clergy were overly zealous about walking ten miles in the hot sun or pouring rain.

With all ceremonial rites and observances clearly understood, Clastres returned to Pililia, where the combined panel accepted the program. With the religious issue settled, Pililia gathered itself for the physical challenge.

On July 23, at the suggestion of Nikono, Ramon rounded up four pickaxes, two sticks of dynamite and a detonator. Nikono, ever the engineer, explained to Clastres, "If the remains of the priest are to be brought out of the mountain on July 27, the concealed vent of the basin will have to be released on July 26 at the very latest, provided the group has reached it by that time. I estimate it will take two hours for the basin to drain enough after the vent opening has been blasted in order to allow access to the chamber."

On July 24 the expedition to the crypt on Mapalug filed out of Pililia as thousands of solemn spectators blessed themselves, then looked to the domineering mountain that sheltered the legend of Laguna de Bay. There was a strange silence in Pililia; I felt it all around me. A glistening white cassock, which Luis had brought from the ancient church in Manila because Father Demato's cassocks were far too short, had been carefully folded in Laudez's pack. Father Doyle had blessed it with Holy Water before it left Manila.

The ten-mile walk to Baras was accomplished with a slow but steady pace and under a tropical sun, which I was just beginning to tolerate.

I concluded the Filipinos could walk forever; they seemed tireless. The column reached Baras, passing large groups who had come out of the Laniti Valley and the villages fringing the valley north of Mapalug. Tired and exhausted, the throngs slumped and rested by the side of the road. The image of anguish and love would remain always with me, an image no artist could ever capture.

The column did not stop in Baras but continued for two more miles. The old guerrillas were hardly winded, making me feel embarrassed over my own heavy breathing. They politely ignored my discomfort and went about preparing for a night's encampment. I was glad to put down my haversack with its canteen, food, poncho, flashlight, mosquito net and a pressed rose.

The following day Nikono met us at the edge of the swamp with twenty crafts. He had driven his company car from Pililia, accompanied by Clastres, then left the vehicle some distance from the swamp and walked the rest of the way. He and Clastres were going to guide the boats through the six miles of treacherous bog.

For a brief moment I saw a slight change in the features of the two men, once former adversaries, as they gazed in the direction of the great mountain dominating the entire landscape. No doubt they were remembering how their paths had crossed in the wilderness of hills. I thought of the man who had brought these two antagonists into an arena of reconciliation, now standing shoulder to shoulder, ready to send a contingent up a mountain that neither one would ever climb again.

The first launch pushed away from the shore with Rafael, Father Cannon, Nikono, six guerrillas and me. Clastres and Nikono stationed themselves in the bow directing the course. All the others were dispersed into the trailing crafts along with the supplies.

The convoy threaded its way through the maze of stumps, vines and floating debris brought in by the tributaries. The propeller of one launch became entangled in a mass of vines, rendering it worthless. It had to be towed the remaining distance, causing some delay.

There would be no ascent today because the six-mile trek through the lesser hills exhausted all but the younger Filipinos. Nikono would go back with the launches in the morning. The night descended with a blanket of darkness, and so did the swarms of mosquitoes.

We were up when the night's shadows were giving way to the first flushed fingers of morning. I took my first real look up the slope of the majestic monument that was harboring the hope of Laguna de Bay in its bosom. In the coolness of the morning we started the climb. Mist was still cradled in the glens between the hills.

Before the first step was taken Laudez turned and waved to Clastres, whom none of us would see again until we were off the mountain. I detected a solemn air about the one-armed guerrilla as he watched us get under way. Laudez did not look back, and I was sure he was uncomfortable with the thought that Clastres had brought the original band up the mountain and should be doing it again.

Laudez unfolded the maps, which Nikono had given him. From these he directed the ascent, although he did ask for some advice from the volunteers. Nikono's directions were remarkably accurate. Every overhang and ledge was pinpointed. It was easy to understand why the veteran soldier had been held in such esteem during the war.

The long line of Filipinos moved fairly rapidly, scrambling skyward without fear of discovery. They were hiding from no one this time.

The heat of the sun began to draw on me, and we had ascended only five hundred feet. Although this slope was by far the most accessible and least hazardous, it was still a test for a fifty-seven-year old.

The ropes had not been necessary at first, but then the incline became steeper and Laudez called a halt. We secured the ropes around our waists. If I slipped or fell, it was unlikely I could drag them off the mountain. Hilaria was anchored in the middle of the line, and the other former guerrillas were spaced intermittently. We succeeded in reaching the plateau below the last five hundred feet to the Kalinawan Caves, almost at the precise planned hour, when Laudez ordered another respite.

The sun was now beating upon our backs. Sweat was copiously flowing down our faces and beneath our shirts. I had wrapped a small towel around my head to avoid chasing a hat on the side of the mountain, and this too was soaking wet. Many of the others did not wear headgear, but they all had bandanas, which kept most of the stinging perspiration from getting in their eyes.

When dusk and the mists that came with it began to settle in, Laudez called a halt on the crest of a ridge overlooking a huge gully. This indentation had been noted on the maps provided by Nikono. My legs, like those of the others, were aching, and I feared cramp spasms. I welcomed the respite. In the fading light we huddled together above the hollow.

At dawn we braced ourselves for the day's endeavor to the gaping orifice above us. It was a grind, but the aged guerrillas were still like surefooted mountain goats. At one point they were taunting one another as to who would be the first one carried up the rocky slope by the others. Father Cannon seemed to be managing well. He maintained an exuberant attitude over the opportunity to lay his hand on a crude coffin in the vault of the mountain.

The former guerrillas were the first to enter the Kalinawan Caves. We followed. There was an awesome silence in the interior, broken now and then when the wind blew through the tunnels and corridors. Just inside the opening rested the rusted, blackened and once formidable weapons eroding in the hands of time. There was solitude in the gloom of the caves. The faint echoes denoted the desperation that had been born in this place. There were a few old artillery shell casings standing like sentinels against the inner wall where the winches for the cannons had been embedded in the solid rock. All other reminders of the disaster that had taken place here were gone, even the door. Only the cannons represented the strength, fortitude and discipline that had once existed within the walls of this embattled catacomb. Now, only the memories remained.

Laudez and Hilaria beckoned for silence, then poised in the center of the hollow. Hilaria cocked her head like the roosters in the villages, then signaled she could not hear the trickling of the water above the ceiling, which indicated the basin on the eastern slope should still be filled to capacity. Off to the northern interior, where Nikono's men had blasted a hole in the side of the mountain, there were other memories buried beneath the fragments of shale. The former guerrillas gathered at the spot where Garcia had fallen on the grenade, standing there without expression. I was sure they were praying. The flickering shadows caused by the swinging flashlights flashed across their grim and stoic features. Courteously, we waited until they ended their brief vigil. Then everyone undid their packs, ate cold food then fell asleep on the hard cave floor that was not meant for sleeping. I spread my poncho beneath me.

On the cool morning of July 27 I could see the faint scar on the slope that had been the path of the cannons' ascent. I thought it was just as well that Nikono did not see this reminder of his labor of love. His limp and ailing back were reminders enough.

We struck out across the ledge of the bare wall that partially encircled the southern and eastern slopes, bringing us to the trail the guerrillas took years ago. When we reached the eastern face where the wall disappeared into the mountain, Hilaria gazed up at the peak to get her bearings. The main body of Filipinos stretched out across the end of the ledge, moving as close as they could to an indentation on the mountain. I sensed what was about to occur, so I pleaded with Laudez for permission to take part in the next phase of the expedition. He consented. Then four volunteers carrying dynamite and wire, the former guerrillas, and I carefully slid down the shale and rock.

Forty feet down Hilaria halted the descent and stood in front of the barrier the guerrillas had made thirty-five years ago. They could hardly believe the dam was still as intact as the day they had molded it with their bare hands. A stick of dynamite was rammed into the side of the plugged gap and a wire attached to the detonator and fuse. Then we climbed back to the main group and took cover behind a ledge.

The explosion rent the clouds, putting the eagles to flight. The pent-up water spilled into the old dried-up gully and went cascading down the mountain. Fresh air blew into what was once a sealed bowl and found its way to a bamboo coffin resting in a chamber above it, awaiting a long overdue blessing.

The runoff finally ceased. We made our way up to the basin, taking an hour to do so. There was only room for ten on the precipice, so no one made a motion toward the opening but patiently waited for the original guerrillas to reach the ledge. This forced many of us to spread out and cling precariously to the side of Mapalug Mountain.

Perched on the threshold the guerrillas conferred, then stepped aside as Rafael unstrapped his battered rosebush, turned his pack upside down, and dumped a pile of dirt into the half-filled puddle to the front of the opening. He scraped up fragments of shale which he mixed with mud, then planted the bush in the center of the muddy mixture. Amanda Gonsalves's wish had been fulfilled, and the son of the bell ringer had seen to it, although we knew the sun would eventually drain all life from the plant, and the petals would wash down the gully, finding their way to the valley below.

We huddled on the threshold, waiting for Laudez to descend into the musty interior. He was lowered down the slight incline into the opening, where he signaled he could see all the way across the basin with his flashlight (a verification of Nikono's earlier prediction). Then he disappeared from view. We held our breath and waited.

Father Cannon fidgeted with his breviary and brushed the tattered fatigues he had worn throughout the climb. I was aware of his anxiety and nervousness through the composure he was trying to maintain.

Laudez, soaking wet, was hauled back out through the opening. No one uttered a word except Laudez, who merely said, "It is the same."

He had verified what only the original guerrillas had witnessed. Father Cannon thought he was referring to the presence and condition of the bamboo coffin; only Rafael, the original guerrillas and I fully understood the significance of his words.

Laudez motioned to the other guerrillas. One by one they slid into the dank hollow and out of sight. There was another ten-minute wait before they reappeared. Laudez motioned again, this time for me, Rafael and Father Cannon to enter the basin, instructing the priest to bring his breviary and leather case. I slid into the opening and was immediately immersed in water up to my chest but was able to distinguish the far side of the cavern in the dim light. I waded across behind Father Cannon and the others, carefully following the instructions of the guerrillas. In the semidarkness the only sounds were the heavy breathing and the swishing from our bodies as we made our way toward the upper chamber.

My pulse began to race as I drew closer, and I felt a tremble in my hand that held the flashlight. We then reached the elevation leading to the chamber and crawled up to the chamber. There in the murky light was the most beautiful but most crude coffin I had ever seen.

It rested on a bed of rock. The hand-hewn sides, poles and lashings were still intact. I moved closer for a better look, my light flickering along the sides of a bamboo creation that had not cracked or split through the years, although this closer inspection revealed stains from the salts and minerals from the cavern, which also preserved it. In the solitude of the chamber the placid expressions of the guerrillas portrayed their feelings.

They were ready to bring their shepherd home. Laudez asked Father Cannon to bless the coffin and the chamber sheltering it.

In the dismal but sacred room amidst the flickering light, Father Cannon placed one hand on the coffin, and then read by the light of my flashlight, bestowing a blessing on a martyr of the church. Then he took a bottle of Holy Water from his case, again laid one hand on the crude cover of the coffin, and with the other sprinkled the entire chamber. Then he stepped back as the seven guerrillas lifted the coffin off its bed of rock. Father Douglas was on his way home.

They wrapped their ponchos around the coffin, and then gently floated it across the pool of water for the second time in their lives. At the opening the coffin was pushed up and into the bright sunlight. The old refrain, "My Everlasting Rose," resonated down Mapalug and out over the valleys.

The descent began. The coffin had to be lowered, horizontally at all times. We managed to reach the caves before darkness set in. The former guerrillas maintained a close vigilance around the hallowed coffin at all times.

Once inside the caves Hilaria was quick to note she could hear running water through the channel above the ceiling. During the night we listened to a pounding storm crashing on the mountainsides and valley below. Amidst the thunder and lightning I thought of the terror rampant in these corridors during the final bombardment of Nikono's stronghold. A few yards away the silent muzzles attested to the truth: "might is seldom right." I could almost touch the terror experienced within these walls, just as I could almost touch the love within the bamboo coffin. We slept that night beside the hollow, listening to the rain rush through the gully.

It was dusk of the following day when we finished the descent. Father Cannon was as fatigued as I, and we both collapsed at the base. Rafael chided us about being out of condition. After a quick supper of cold soup and biscuits, I slept like a log, nothing able to awaken me through the night, not even the mosquitoes.

I awoke cold and shivering and was glad when we moved out before daybreak. When we reached the swamp Laudez and the other guerrillas looked pensively up at the pinnacle still overshadowing us. They realized they would never come this way again. They also knew the memories would never leave them.

The launches awaited us, one of them draped in black along the gunnels and across the bow. After the coffin was placed in the center of the craft and the guerrillas seated themselves around it, the convoy began the journey back through the swamp.

When we landed the coolness of the swamp left us, and I knew it would be a parching six miles of road and rice paddies back to Baras. The ponchos were removed from the coffin. Then we set out with our precious cargo, now carried by the volunteer Filipinos who had climbed the mountain.

As we approached Baras the solitary Filipino standing near a nipa hut or in a rice paddy increased to two, then four, their numbers greatly multiplying in the last two miles. When we reached the populated area of Baras, where we would spend the night, I saw the roses in their hands. This continued all the way to the town and through the crowded streets.

The walk from Baras to Pililia was an epic in itself, and one I will never forget. Thousands of Filipinos lined the shore road all the way to Pililia. For ten miles they deluged the bamboo coffin with roses. Father Douglas was coming home, buried beneath an avalanche of roses. It was a time of mourning, joy, reconciliation, prayer. They knelt and prayed along the way unmindful of the heat and dust kicked up by the plodding carabao and the thousands of bare feet.

A half-mile from the church in Pililia the procession halted. The crowd was immense. Somehow out of its depth appeared Clastres, Alvita, Mrs. Gonsalves and Father Demato, all of whom joined the procession. Laudez went to Clastres's side, opened his battered knapsack, reached in, and then pressed a withered and mildewed rose he had taken from the coffin into the hand of his leader and close friend. The seven guerrillas then carried the coffin to the forefront.

The moment the hands of the guerrillas touched the coffin, thousands of black headnets were donned. The men removed their hats when Amanda placed a beautiful bouquet of roses on the lid of the coffin. The entire multitude stood devoutly and reverently. There was not a tear to be seen.

Years ago, at one time or another, every one of the former guerrillas had handled the coffin during the overland trek. Now, once again, the legendary leader placed them around the coffin in such a way that six of them were handling the coffin simultaneously while the other led the procession. They rotated seven times within the half-mile stretch. Earlier a decision had been made that Clastres should lead the final rotation into the circle that surrounded the platform.

The road was now lined with ropes, and the volunteers lined the route to the crowded marketplace, protecting the path of the procession. The funeral dirge took a slow, deliberate tempo. Rafael left the formation, going ahead to be sure he could get through the doorway leading to the belfry loft. He would begin the tolling at three o'clock, exactly as his father had done when he tolled out the message that the guerrillas had brought the body of Father Douglas out of the peninsula.

There were forty thousand people in Pililia, an incredible sight. "My Everlasting Rose" filled the air amidst the tolling of the bell. Thus, on July 29, 1978, the guerrillas of Laguna de Bay brought Father Douglas home to his parish, St. Mary Magdalene's. It had taken them thirty-five years to return to the origin of the legend: the old Spanish church in Pililia, St. Mary Magdalene's.

There was new blood on the already stained hemp that was sending the metal tongue into the sides of the bell. It was as red as the crimson roses bedecking the bamboo coffin. However, Rafael did not heed the flow as it ran from his palms and down the length of his arms, dripping to the floor that had felt the touch of it before. He rang the bell furiously. In the marketplace, in the hills and rice paddies, along the rivers and roads, every head bowed. For the first time in thirty-five years a tear ran down the cheek of Hilaria and splattered the dust at the foot of the bamboo coffin. Their shepherd was back in his garden of roses.

The coffin was placed on the bier and the volunteers guarded it constantly. Not one spectator entered the circle or even made the attempt. The respect was uncanny and bewildering. They milled around the enclosure for most of the following week. I had no idea where the majority of them ate or slept.

I managed to get to Mass that Sunday and was fortunate enough to be able to stand in the side aisle. When it ended I went out the side door to observe the bamboo wreath. It had been untouched. In the middle of the week I returned to find it in the same condition. Both times the wreath was hidden beneath a cloak of crimson roses.

Father Demato was bracing himself for the second time. He was carefully analyzing the energy in the streets, knowing full well his next announcement would practically shake the bell out of its tower. He and the other guerrillas held another meeting to decide when to present the reason for the covenant to the parishioners. They decided to have a custom-made glass case built with a hinged cover full of one-inch holes and a brass lock. On the front would be a hand- carved bamboo wreath embossed with roses. A solid coffin of bamboo was to be constructed in case the crude one should deteriorate. It was also decided Father Demato would inform Father Doyle that his presence was requested for the special event that was going to take place on the second Sunday in August.

The glass case arrived and was placed to the right of the main altar. Immediately after it was positioned, Ramon built a ten-foot kneeler and placed it in front of the glass case. Father Demato waited until the middle of the week before he had the coffin removed from the bier and placed inside the glass case. Then he prepared the most delicate and somber choice of words he would ever utter. He prayed to the Holy Spirit and to the soul of Father Douglas for guidance and for the protection of his church.

Through the years there had been many Masses offered up for the soul of Father Douglas. They were solemn, never embellished or elaborate ceremonies, because the people were inclined to temper their lives with the belief that someday his body would be right where it was and they could perform a proper burial. They were unable to release the soul without the body, but now, in their eyes, the two were united. On August 15, the Feast of the Assumption, they would place his soul in the arms of the Blessed Virgin, and she would carry his soul through the winds and clouds to the paradise he had lived and died for. The parishioners knew they must let their martyr go, and there was sadness in the knowing. Meanwhile, those in Pililia were preparing another grave in the center of the cemetery beyond the one of Francisco Gonsalves. There, in the heart of the hallowed cemetery, all paths would lead to the man who had instilled within them a tolerance that surely had governed their actions.

Before the week was over Father Demato discovered he did not have to inform the parishioners he was going to make a special announcement on the Feast of the Assumption. The grapevine, as usual, was somehow ahead of his words. By mid afternoon the marketplace became crammed with bodies once again. They were going to be at the doorstep of the church long before the first peal of the bell.

Rafael, who was staying with me once again at Mrs. Temporado's, awakened me at three o'clock in the morning. He had advised me I would never get into the church Saturday night if I did not follow in his footsteps before dawn. In the early hour I soon saw how correct he was. We made our way as best we could through the other early risers who wanted to be in the first pews. Even in the shadows I sensed the somber determination in the squatters in front of the locked church, many of them either dozing or resting. Early as it was, I was amazed to see that every one of them clutched a rose. The coffin was going to be showered with love again.

My friend climbed to the belfry and I followed. We sat against the octagonal railing, dozing for nearly four hours. At seven o'clock he grasped the rope, winced, and then pulled on it, sending the first peal into the breeze of Laguna Lake. Today, the bell would toll gently and deliberately into the ears of all who cared to listen. The already blistered hands of the son of Francisco Gonsalves bled once more until the gloves he was wearing were as red as the roses that were greeting the mystical morning of the Feast of the Assumption.

The first gong was more angelic than any other Rafael had ever tolled, but in the tower after the second gong, the vibration forced me to flee to the room at the bottom of the stairs. There I waited while Father Demato, Father Doyle, Father Cannon and six other priests from the diocese of Manila walked with the seven legendary guerrillas between the two lines of rope that led to the church. Then they made their way down the center aisle leading to the altar; simultaneously, Rafael silenced the bell. Thereafter, Rafael and I entered through the side door and sat with the former guerrillas while the parishioners filled the church. At precisely eight o'clock Father Demato, followed closely by Father Doyle and the other priests, opened the glass case and blessed the bamboo coffin with Holy Water. Father Demato then returned to the altar and began the Mass.

The church was quiet and filled with expectation as Father Demato

spoke, "My friends in Christ, today we offer this Mass for the repose of
the soul of one we have come to call the Bamboo Shepherd. There are
many of you who sat in these very same pews and heard him speak of
humility, understanding, the love we should have for one another, and the
love he had for you. He told us we were roses in a garden of thorns, but
if we struggled for the faith our Divine Savior presented to us through his
crucifixion, we would grow in the shadow of the cross, shielded by the
strength of it. 'We must be as soft as the rose,' he had said, as he wiped
the tears from our eyes.

"Thirty-five years ago our beloved priest was put to the sword and he
suffered in silence and loneliness. We could not reach out to him as he
had reached out to us, but we suffered every moment of that terrible time.
For many years we buried him in our hearts, disciplining ourselves with
his words.

"On the day of his sacrifice, our own dedicated companions rescued
his tormented body from his torturers and brought him into the hills,
where they established a covenant that many of you have never completely understood.

"As I stand before you here today you will understand the final reason
why this covenant was made and why the guerrillas had steadfastly never
been shaken from it. They did not do it for themselves, but for him,
Father Douglas, and for each and every one of you.

"What I am about to do has been done before. Do not be alarmed.
Clastres, Laudez, Ramon, Fredrico, Raul, Alvita, Hilaria and I are living
witnesses of what inspired the reason for the covenant."

The parishioners began to stir in their seats. I sensed a quiver of
apprehension penetrate the stoic attitude of the listeners.

"Therefore, I ask you in the name of God, in the sacrifice of the
Divine Son, Jesus Christ, and in the name of our Blessed Virgin Mary, to
kneel before this bamboo shrine and be witnesses to the phenomenon
that inspired their death-defying covenant."

The guerrillas maintained their composure, although they realized
anything could happen in the next few moments. Grasping the container
of Holy Water, Father Demato left the pulpit, strode over to the side of
the glass enclosure, gazed into the faces of the disciples of Pililia, and said
the words that would ring in their ears for the rest of their lives.

"Our Bamboo Shepherd is incorruptible."

Then, amidst a frightened gasp from the kneeling, he reached inside the glass case, loosened the bamboo lashing that girthed the coffin, and gently raised the cover.

Father Demato gazed upon the peaceful features he had last seen on a rainy hilltop overlooking Pililia. The unemotional became emotional and the frightened gasp became a loud sigh as the timid and the sturdy blessed themselves over and over again amidst the tears and fainting. The priests could not believe their eyes, staring, as their lips created prayer after prayer. I stood up, hardly realizing I had done so, and looked upon the face of the man I had come to search for. There he was, lying under a cassock of white in a bamboo coffin, hands folded. There was no trace of any marks upon him. The unsteady flames of the vigil lights cast shadows upon the glass, causing a glow to intermittently sweep across the face of the man long at peace.

Hilaria and Alvita moved to the side of Mrs. Gonsalves, who had been sitting directly behind the guerrillas. The three of them wept with unabashed emotion. The tears of Mrs. Gonsalves spilled from her cheeks and brought new life to the two bouquets of roses she had been holding to her breast.

In the streets people scrambled about once they heard what had occurred, running and shouting to one another with the good news. Most of those outside had never seen Father Douglas, some a few times in their childhood, but all were well aware of what he had meant in the lives of their relatives, elders and, above all, the guerrillas. This respect was part of their lives as well.

Inside the church it became relatively calm. The seven guerrillas, accompanied by Mrs. Gonsalves, knelt before the coffin. Mrs. Gonsalves was the only person permitted to approach the coffin and place a bouquet within it. She clung to her other bouquet as if it were the last one on earth.

Rafael and I knelt before the coffin after his mother made her way back to the pew. The tossing of roses commenced once again; they were all thrown at the foot of the coffin so as not to block the view of the thousands who would follow.

Eventually, all the stained glass windows had to be opened to let the accumulating heat and the scent of roses escape. Rafael escaped through the side door. At the first gong of the bell Mrs. Gonsalves raised her head slightly and looked up at the cross. I moved beside her.

In her quiet, easy way, her voice barely a whisper and without turning her head, she said, "I saw the calluses on his hands."

Father Demato knew it would take two weeks before the majority of believers, nonbelievers and curious would have satisfied their curiosity about the phenomenon of Pililia. As they shuffled and straggled into the town he welcomed them patiently and tirelessly on the steps of the old church, beckoning them into the hallowed chamber. The guerrillas returned to their seclusion, and Mrs. Gonsalves and thousands of others placed roses on the grave of Francisco Gonsalves. Within the church volunteers had to constantly remove the pile of roses, as it was making a huge crimson stain on the floor. These tokens of affection were leaving a mark that generations of visitors would recognize.

Throughout this chronicle of religious significance, Nikono had remained relatively secluded, observing from a distance and intently studying the sincerity of what was taking place. Little escaped his eyesight or insight. From the moment he had left the base of Mapalug Mountain in 1945, the words uttered by the guerrillas in the mists began to challenge the doubts he had developed. He had lived to witness forty thousand Filipinos hailing a crude coffin on the bier, and now they and ten thousand more were claiming a miracle had occurred in Pililia.

Father Douglas, during the suffering at the hands of the Japanese, had displayed a devotion to a cause Nikono had not understood. The nagging bewilderment that had tormented Nikono since then began to subside as he again observed the same devotion, the same earnestness and belief in the people Father Douglas had died for. The Filipino reserve, which was usually held in abeyance, relaxed. Their devotion to Father Douglas was displayed for the entire world to see. Nikono suddenly understood the wisdom in the decision Clastres had made to secrete the body of the priest. He had no doubt his Japanese superiors would not have permitted the Filipinos access to a coffin they were claiming held the body of an unmarked man whom he had witnessed otherwise during the interrogation. The demonstrations, unlike the peace that was presently occurring, would have been disastrous. Clastres had saved more than the body of a priest—he saved Pililia from annihilation.

The bell was tolling, and Nikono began to recognize the dedication in the simple task of ringing it. Every rhythm, whether in cadence or not, was becoming a message understood by Nikono. He was beginning to realize devotion to the Bamboo Shepherd was more important than rebuilding the dilapidated bridge between Pililia and Tanay. The bell continued to toll, and it seemed to demand he make one more important decision. Should he listen to the bell? Was it calling him to be a witness again? Was it calling him to look upon the face of a man whose dedication had discomforted him for countless nights? Was the condition of the priest accurate, as the Filipinos were declaring, or was it all a hoax?

Nikono paid a visit to Mrs. Temperado and requested to speak to me. We met the following day on the outskirts of the rice market where he expressed his feelings.

"We are both foreigners in Pililia, drawn back to the old scenes when we were much younger," began Nikono. "It is ironic that we should both have returned for a reunion of the past at the same time."

I knew he was deceiving himself. "I know why I have returned to Pililia, Nikono, and my quest has been fulfilled. Have you satisfied your quest?" He did not reply and I pressed him further. "One does not return to a scene when the threat of death is prevalent, such as in your case. Your timing could not have been better though; the pardoning attitude fostered by the event at hand, which you seem to be avoiding, has prevented this from happening."

"Is it true what I hear that there are no marks on the priest?" asked Nikono.

I responded, "You are similar to one of Christ's apostles, Thomas, who would not believe until he felt the imprinted marks on the body of Christ. You, Nikono, will not believe there are no marks on the body of Father Douglas until you see with your own eyes. Unlike you and Thomas, these faithful parishioners would have had the same conviction whether the coffin had been opened or not. You would have seen this for your himself if you had attempted to understand them instead of just buying rice from them."

"It seems the conviction of the Filipinos concerning the death of Father Douglas is stronger than the conviction to hold me responsible," muttered Nikono.

"You should have felt privileged to have witnessed the executed before his death. Now you have another opportunity to feel that privilege by witnessing him after death. It seems to me you are searching for the same thing as these fifty thousand people. The only difference is that Father Douglas showed them how to go about it. They had his words, the words from a man who refused to answer you for fear of retaliation on the people he had adopted as his own. Father Douglas had a greater and purer conception of love, and he shared it willingly and freely with all he came in contact, whereas others have a conception of love that is self-centered, never to be freed."

I watched Nikono as I said, "others." I sensed he understood I was referring to him and his own concept of love. I continued, "Reparation and reconciliation can bury the sword in the past and eliminate the sleepless nights, as well as opening the gates to heaven. In the end, Nikono, you have to go beyond yourself, then search for the future as the Filipinos are now doing."

He listened to some extent and replied, "I am afraid I am still much like your doubting Thomas."

I smiled and said, "Go with the people who are entering the church, and when you get to the bamboo coffin you will meet St. Thomas." I was sure if he listened closely to the bell on a Sunday morning, he would get the real message, the one that had called him all the way from Kyushu.

The next morning Mrs. Temporado approached me and said, "Nikono was seen placing a rose on the grave of Francisco Gonsalves, but he did not enter the church."

"The grapevine never dies in Pililia," I replied.

Meanwhile, Father Demato, the seven guerrillas and the elders of Pililia and Paete held another meeting to consider permitting cameras and television crews into the church. Father Demato, usually reserved, spoke sternly, "I oppose the intrusion into my church and the sanctity of a man I already consider a saint."

The others all nodded in agreement, although they all knew modern trends with all their trappings could never desecrate the interior of St. Mary Magdalene's. However, a moratorium of one year was put into effect, banning all cameras, television and electronic equipment. The volunteers who went up the mountain organized a twenty-four-hour watch.

Every window and door was locked securely one hour after dusk, when the bell pealed into the shadows of Pililia as the scent of roses descended upon the silence within St. Mary Magdalene's.

From the glorious morning of August 15, the legend of Laguna de Bay was heard all over the world as countless thousands of all nationalities came and knelt at the side of the Bamboo Shepherd. Many times I followed the procession of believers and nonbelievers to the side of the coffin, always struck with amazement at the sight before me. Father Douglas was an everlasting rose that, like his words, would never fade away.

All through the drama unfolding in this obscure town, the church never intervened against the will or the wishes of Pililia. Father Douglas was a Columban Father first, but he belonged to the Filipinos last. They had preserved his memory as well as his body and retained all that he had bequeathed to them, mainly his example and above all his love. To take him out of the garden would be a sacrilege in their eyes and a deprivation from which they would never fully recover.

Father Doyle, always with the knowledge of Father Demato, brought so many priests and missionary pilgrimages to Pililia (which kept a smile on the face of Luis), that the padre of St. Mary Magdalene's began to wonder who was carrying on the priestly duties in Manila. Father Doyle caught up with me one day and said, "I still cannot get over the fact that you climbed the rugged Mapalug to help bring back the hope of Pililia, if not the world."

I grinned and said, "I cannot believe it sometimes myself Father."

He shook his head, put his arm around my shoulder and thanked me for the effort I had contributed in bringing the Bamboo Shepherd home.

I now understood why the Filipinos had fabricated their explanation during the investigation in 1948 about the location of Father Douglas. They simply were not sure where his body was. By implementing the fabrication they put an end to the question at the time, although they yearned for the answer themselves. They had safeguarded a viable memory—a living memory—that would survive long after many of the facts were forgotten.

It was an intangible vigil of hope that had brought the covenant into their lives. It bound them together in an aggressive and apathetic world, one that neither invaded nor neglected them. Their shepherd had united them in the covenant; they knew if an occasion arose, his words would unite them again.

A few days later I saw Nikono busily conducting transactions in the marketplace, which was slowly returning to its original intent. The trappings of the funeral procession had been removed and the vendors were back to doing business. The residents and venders were constantly referring to the event, and Nikono could not escape overhearing them. I noticed Nikono walked with less than his former enthusiasm. He wore the same sunglasses and hat and still kept his beard carefully trimmed, but he could not disguise the effect the thousands of strangers entering the church were having on him.

My thoughts of home were beginning to beset me, and the colored leaves of New England were beckoning me in my dreams. I could hear the whispering whir of the winds by the brook in Maine. Visions of autumn and the call of the whippoorwill from deep in the woods began to overtake the presence of the heat and rain in Pililia. I found myself getting restless. I offset the yearning temporarily by catching the jeepney to Morong. The curtains that once sheltered the curious when I first arrived here were now replaced with open doors and open hearts. I was still careful not to slight anyone during my visits. A wave of the hand was considered an extreme greeting; thankfully, I was now receiving many of them.

I visited with Mrs. Gonsalves, whose hip was improving little by little. Although she realized it would never fully mend, her spirits never weakened, and she was as good-natured as ever. I did not mention the roses I had found at the foot of my bed at Mrs. Temporado's. I would have only embarrassed her. Mrs. Gonsalves had her own way of expressing her feelings, and without saying a word.

"Mrs. Gonsalves," I said, "my thoughts are turning homeward." She quietly walked out the front door and looked silently up the street at the old Spanish church. I read her thoughts.

"Father O'Reilly or the 43rd Recon?" I asked.

"Both," she replied wistfully.

"And Father Douglas?"

"My Francisco was honored to ring the bell for him."

She could not have put it more simply. I thought it was the greatest tribute I would ever hear. As she stood before her crimson roses I thought, "She is the living rose of Laguna de Bay."

Just before I left her it was her turn to read my thoughts. She startled me with her words.

"I will pray for Nikono Yashima." That Sunday evening she led the Morong Legion of Mary in prayer.

She must have had a way with the Lord. In the middle of the third week in September, when the line entering the church was but a handful, Nikono purchased his last shipment of rice. At the end of the day, when the last sound of the bell echoed out into the Laniti Valley, he met me in the shadows of Mrs. Temperado's porch. His expression seldom changed, but this time there was haste about him. He made no attempt to hide it.

Nikono said, "I heard you are preparing to return home. I, too, am making the same preparations. I am not certain why, but before you leave, will you accompany me into the church?"

I immediately held out my hand and he extended his, and there made my own covenant with a former Japanese soldier. "I would be honored," I replied. "I will meet you on the steps of the church tomorrow, just before Father Demato tolls the bell at twilight." Then he smiled, which was equal to a hand wave by the Filipinos.

That night a fierce storm lashed Mrs. Temperado's house, but the pounding of it could not equal the pounding of my pulse. I had a very restless night and thought of entering the church tomorrow. I knew the rustling of beads would be like thunder in the ears of Nikono Yashima.

The next day I watched the sun on its course from the moment it came over the peak of the majestic Mapalug, as it dazzled the moisture from the heavy rain, to its descent beyond the Laguna waters. It would be the longest day of my life in Pililia. When the shadows of the church began to stretch across the steps, I left Mrs. Temperado's and walked to the church. The shadow of the church stretched up the street that led to where there were now thirty-five hand-carved roses on the grave of Francisco Gonsalves.

I knew just when Father Demato would leave the bench, bless the bamboo wreath, and enter through the side door that led to the belfry. He was sitting on the bench saying the rosary when I approached the church. Nikono was standing at the bottom of the steps, and even though Father

Demato could not see him, he knew he was there. The usually stoic faces
of the worshipers showed surprise when they saw Nikono standing on the
steps of St. Mary Magdalene's. When I met him on the steps he was
aware of the curious, and it brought him a great deal of nervousness. I rescued him from his predicament by ushering him into the vestibule. For
the second time in his life he entered a Catholic Church—the first time
being July 24, 1943, when Father Douglas was taken to Santiago
Apostol's in Paete.

It was as silent as a tomb within the archaic structure. Two huge vigil
lights, one on each side of the inner doors, threw their shadows at the feet
of Nikono. Several women were saying the Stations of the Cross. Streaks
of sunlight splintered through the stained-glass windows behind the altar.
The altar lights glowed, and the rows of smaller vigil lights encased in
round glass holders danced wildly as the puffs of wind flickered the
flames feeding on the wicks.

We stood at the end of the center aisle. I politely waited until he was
ready to take the first step into the past. He glanced at me questioningly
and I whispered, "I have come to St. Mary Magdalene's prepared." I then
handed him a copy of the "Our Father" and said, "Read it to yourself at
the kneeler." Then to ease some of the tension I smiled and said, "Follow
me and you will be following the wishes of the Lord." Nodding, he
acknowledged my request, and then we both stepped forward into the
past and toward the outstretched arms of the man who was calling upon
the world to take him down from the cross.

We walked shoulder to shoulder down the center aisle toward the
altar, passing those kneeling in the shadows of the church. It must have
been a long walk for Nikono.

Halfway to the altar he hesitated, head cocked as he heard the
rustling beads shatter the quiet—a rustling he had heard many times
above the sounds of war, a haunting rustling he could never silence. He
looked in the direction of the bamboo coffin as if he knew where the
sound was coming from. Then he removed his dark glasses, and I could
sense the uncertainty and struggle he was enduring.

For one brief moment the seasoned soldier was caught between the
old entrenched attitudes in which he had disciplined his commitments
and the old entrenched beliefs in which the faithful disciplined their

attitudes. He dangled, like a bead on a rosary, separated yet together, joined by simple links that kept the prayers alive. He was suspended in midair like those who had lost their footing on the apron of the Mapalug.

I did the only thing I could think of at the moment. I placed my hand on the shoulder of the man whose expertise had once terrorized Laguna de Bay. It was enough to keep him from abandoning his decision and forsaking our own personal covenant. We continued the walk through the shuffling and breathing that fractured the silence in St. Mary Magdalene's until there was nothing between us and the bamboo coffin but the kneeler.

For the first time in his life Nikono knelt in a position of prayer and gazed upon the face of a man whose labor of love had conquered his own. He knelt for a long time, never taking his eyes off this vision of peace. I thought he would never read the "Our Father," but eventually, when the spell had been overcome, he shook his head, took out the reading, and read the words of Holy Scripture to himself. When he was through he took another long look at the man whose discipline had survived the threat of the sword. He bowed his head, and I knew his moment of reconciliation had come. Nikono Yashima had come home. Father Douglas, martyr of Pililia, had saved another soul without saying a word.

Shoulder to shoulder, Nikono limping beside me, we left the dancing shadows of the vigil lights with the peace he had been searching for. He had put the sword to rest, burying it in a garden of roses. When we stepped out into the moment between dusk and dark, the call of the bell reverberated up the slopes of Mapalug Mountain, and the one-time soldier paused to listen to it. Father Demato knew when to call the lost sheep home to pasture.

Shortly afterward, with the last sound of the bell fading into the shadows, Alvarez placed his knees on the kneeler before the martyr of Laguna de Bay. There, amidst the dancing flames of the candles, he removed the sword of anger that had been imbedded in his heart for thirty-five years by saying a prayer for Nikono. The silent speaker of roses resting before him had, once again, placed another flowering rose in the garden with God.

In the few days I had remaining I visited the homes of each of the former guerrillas. Hilaria, as usual, was at the door before I went up the steps. Clastres and Laudez, along with Fredrico and Ramon, came to bid me good-bye. We conversed for some time. Every time Father Douglas's name was mentioned they immediately blessed themselves. I could visualize the rush of memories that must have returned to them. I felt as privileged as any man could be to have known them.

As the rains began to abate I put my legs and the bicycle to the test again and paid my last visit to Morong. I rode by the river and passed the women attending to their never-ending task. The clothes they were pounding were sparkling white, as white as the cassock of a saint. Approaching the main street I saw Raul and Alvita. I stopped to thank them for accepting this outsider into their home, which had been the stepping-stone past the reserved ways of their fellow neighbors. After informing them I would be leaving soon, Alvita stated, almost demanded, "You come back to Morong, you promise to stay with us." I replied, "I would not think of staying anywhere else." We shook hands and said our good-byes.

The scent of roses beckoned me on. As I approached the Gonsalves' home, I knew the grapevine, as usual, found its way to Rafael before I did, as he was standing at the door grinning and waiting for me. He had sold his rice farm and moved back to Morong, where he could attend to the needs of his mother and to her rosebushes. We had a simple meal together and talked for a while. I knew it would be hard to leave them and especially to say good-bye.

"Whitey," Rafael said, "You must come back and visit us again, no saying good-bye."

I replied, "Only if you come to visit me in America, especially in Maine in the autumn when it is cooler and the landscape is crimson, orange and yellow; the coolness will surprise you and the color will astound you."

"I would like very much to visit America and to see my friend Whitey. Then it will not be so hard for you to leave."

Mrs. Gonsalves, with tears in her eyes, placed a crimson rose in my hand and said, "You write me and I have my Rafael write you, then we still be close, as close as I am to my Francisco."

We said our farewells outside next to the rose bush, the scent of which will forever linger within my senses. I turned my bicycle around and began to pedal away. I then turned and waved good-bye, assured the distance would mask the tears in my own eyes.

The following Sunday I attended my last Mass at St. Mary Magdalene's, which was crowded as ever, back to front, wall to wall. Afterward, Father Demato walked with me back to Mrs. Temperado's, something he had never done before.

"The kneeler," began Father Demato, "will remain forever because the pilgrimages will be forever. A miniature white fence will be erected around the symbolic bamboo wreath for those who do not understand the sacredness of the tender gesture of these people.

"You should know Nikono has asked to embrace the Catholic Church and abide by its faith. The Japanese veteran has returned to Kyushu for his wife and daughter. They will return with him to witness Nikono being received into the church. The guerrillas have all agreed to sponsor him.

"Also, before Nikono left for Japan he declared Pililia and Tanay should never be separated from each other; upon his return, he is going to pay the cost and supervise the construction of a new bridge over the Laniti."

"Nikono is making reparation by using the method he knows best," I replied.

I took my last bicycle ride out of Pililia, pedaling as far as I could beyond Baras to the edge of the Black Swamp. I stopped to gaze up at the mists curling and twisting toward the crest of the great Mapalug. Somehow it looked lonely and lost in the cumulus clouds, even with the eagles perched on the ledge of the Kalinawan Caves surveying their domain. The sun, long since gone over the summit, blazed upon the western slope. The carabaos behind me sought the comfort of the mud holes, closing their eyes to the glare.

I turned away from this monarch of a mountain and never looked back. It was dusk when I returned to Pililia. I rode past Mrs. Temperado's house on my way to one last visit to the grave of Francisco Gonsalves. I could only stand there shaking my head at the enormous pile of roses that smothered the site. The thirty-five hand-carved roses, glimmering in the fading light, were reflections of the courage that one individual could muster for many. Francisco was a representative of those who sought the simple, basic right of freedom and the right to exercise it.

I was going to have to turn my back on many things and many friends here in the Philippines. When I rode back down the road I could not turn away from the appealing stare of a bata waving to me from the roadside. I rode up to him, ruffled his hair and handed him a piece of candy. I could see the mud ooze from between the toes of a child who would someday be tall enough to pull on a rope—a bata who would someday ascend a belfry and ring out the call of freedom.

In the middle of the week I said good-bye to Mrs. Temporado and made my last visit to St. Mary Magdalene's. I prayed for the soul of Pililia and the soul of the shepherd who would never leave his flock again. After one last look upon the face of the Bamboo Shepherd, I knew Father Francis Vernon Douglas was walking somewhere in the garden with God. I went back up the aisle with the words of Clastres Bulatao ringing in my ears.

"What is one finger when one gives his life? What is one hand when one sheds his life? What is one arm when one gives his life? What are a thousand thorns when one gives his life? What is a tear but a sign of love? If I must, I will shed my flesh and cover it with my grief. I tell you this: I will shed no tear because of the pain of it, but my heart will ever cry for the Bamboo Shepherd."

I went through the church doors into Pililia. There at my feet on the threshold of the church was a bouquet of roses. Like the legendary one-armed guerrilla of Laguna de Bay, I took one and hid it in the palm of my hand. I would forever hold on to the symbol of the Bamboo Shepherd, the everlasting rose in a garden of roses.

Father Francis Vernon Douglas

EPILOGUE

If you go to Luzon you will hear the bamboo. It sways gently, touched by the tepid breeze. If you let it, it will lull you to sleep. When you walk the dusty or muddy road to St. Mary Magdalene's in Pililia, you will come upon a bamboo wreath laden with roses by the side of the church. In Paete you will find a crude piece of bamboo in the dusty road beneath the cross of St. Santiago Apostol's Church.

On July 27 thousands of Filipinos gather throughout the day, standing silently for three hours, each hour representing one day of the torture of Father Douglas. There will be the rustling of beads, the only sound breaking the sorrow of Laguna de Bay. You will hear the bells of Pililia and Paete begin their tolling at exactly three o'clock in the afternoon, then again on the hours of four and five. At the half hour after dusk on the third day, July 29, there is but one gong in Pililia; as it resounds in the hills, a single hand-carved bamboo rose, painted crimson, is placed on the cross over the grave of Francisco Gonsalves, a man who died with a rope in his hands and the ring of freedom in his soul. After that one final toll, as the echoes of it die in the hills, the thousands of sentinels look east and northeast and sing the chorus to the song "My Everlasting Rose." When the sound of their voices has drifted away, fleeing across Laguna de Bay and the surrounding hills, the women remove their black headnets. And that night the great Laniti carries their tears into the waters of Laguna de Bay.

The Bamboo Shepherd is dwelling in their hearts, and the silence of the land becomes deafening.

Kevin "Whitey" Corbett was born in Roxbury, Massachusetts, and grew up in Arlington, Massachusetts, where he graduated with the Class of 1940. In 53 years of marriage to his lovely wife, Patricia (Mead) Corbett, they raised five sons and four daughters. They lived in Arlington and Billerica, Massachusetts; Sarasota, Florida; and Henniker and Concord, New Hampshire, where he died on October 16, 2002.

During World War II Kevin took basic training at Fort McLellan, Alabama. He entered the Pacific Theater as a member of the U.S. Army 43rd Cavalry Reconnaissance Troop (known as RECON) of the 43rd "Winged Victory" Division. His tour of duty, which lasted over three years, brought him through Guadalcanal, the Solomons, New Guinea, and the Philippines. He received the Bronze Star and the Combat Infantry Badge for his service.

After the war he worked for the U.S. Postal Service for 28 years. He wrote numerous poems and songs, several of which were published in the *43d Bulletin.* In addition to *The Bamboo Shepherd,* he wrote *The Parade,* an account of his three-year tour of duty with RECON.